FAIRLY STRANGE

For Meg –
Keep it strange!
Smattox

SUSIE MATTOX

This book is a work of fiction. Names, characters, places, and incidents either are products of the author's imagination or are used ficticiously. Any resemblance to actual events or locales or persons, living or dead, is entirely coincidental.

Cover and interior design: Andrew Earley
Editing: Teresa Kennedy, Village Green Press LLC

ISBN 978-1697166866

CHAPTER 1

The first time I died was all my fault. I'd been a brat. Relentless. Spoiled. But the second time? Not so much.

Contemplating the error of my ways, I sketched angels in a cemetery at twilight and breathed in magnolias sweet as sin. Some called me rotten – to the core. Maybe I was, to have such awful things happen to me. The headache stabbed behind my eyes and I fought the voice. The one that said I was stupid, worthless, evil.

Yeah, I was wrong. Would give anything to redo that night. My headache whined to let it go. The deed was done, my scars hidden beneath a blue, tie-dyed scarf and layers of sarcasm.

I wasn't stupid. I knew the scars ran deeper than any jerk of a ninth grader could see. But what was a girl to do? Marinate in my own pity party until I was pruny? I'd rather gut it out, rub some dirt on it, put on my big girl panties and act like it didn't faze me. Just a girl sitting in a Confederate cemetery drawing vicious angels because I'm so freaking normal. Yeah. That's me. Normal.

Among the rusted cannons and sprawling live oaks, a marker rested in front of me. An angel hovered over it, her sharp-edged wings protecting her little plot of grass. Or, rather, Elijah Pickens' plot of grass. He was six years old when he died, which sucked big time in anybody's book.

Somebody must have loved him, though. A low edging of bricks lined his small grave. A whole regiment of angels, all shapes and sizes, guarded the tiny wall, followed by a platoon of Easter bunnies, then two garden gnomes. I tried to ignore the candy wrappers and empty water bottle as I hatched charcoal pencil into my angel's wings.

Stupid tourists.

The angel I'd drawn wasn't as angelic as Elijah's. She was at war, her legs braced for battle, her sword stabbing some invisible foe. Those are the worst; the ones you never see coming. She was the fifth angel I'd drawn that day, my sketchbook full of them. All dark. Avenging. Deadly.

Sitting cross-legged on a stone bench, a line of pines shielded me from the narrow snake of Hamilton Bay Lane which led to the Hamilton Bay Country Club. Another stretch of pines blocked the eighteenth fairway. Don't ask me why they thought it was a good idea to put a golf course next to a Confederate cemetery. But sketching here seemed to corral the headaches. Didn't get rid of them, necessarily, but kept them from crippling me. They'd plagued me ever since my death. The first one.

Beyond the two hundred and forty-two dead Confederate soldiers marked with white wooden crosses, a live oak stood guard, bearded with Spanish moss. I read somewhere that Spanish moss, though pretty and delicate, is really a parasite. So, it wasn't so much an old man's beard the breeze teased into a gentle snore. It was more like an old man's beard that'd come alive and turned on him. It looked innocent, harmless, but was actually feeding on him, eating him alive.

Nature's pretty brutal that way; everything feeding off of something else, the same way the worms fed off those soldiers underground. Maybe that's why I liked the cemetery. I knew better than most it can be a real struggle just to stay alive.

I worked to match my breathing with the rhythm of the breeze easing through the moss. Counting one. Counting two.

A violent splash of orange sunset bruised the sky purple before settling into a dreamy pearl gray. The scent of magnolia and jasmine gave heft to the air as the shadows crept long behind the tombstones. The breeze coaxed strands of my hair, duller than red Alabama mud, from my ponytail into my eyes. I brushed them aside. My hand cramped and I stopped and dug the heel of it into my right eye. I fought the nausea, the stinging tears. I paused at the rustling of leaves and glanced up.

A young man stood at Hiram Walker's marker, his long, dark fingers resting on the stone. He seemed a bit older than me. And considerably taller. But solemn, with eyes more white than dark and a scar that ran underneath his lower lashes. He wore loose trousers, wrinkled like linen. His shirt hung nearly to his knees. His feet were bare.

My heart raced. Was it the surprise of his appearance? Being watched when I wanted to hide? Or his fixed gaze that held the intensity of a freight train bearing down? He was dark and gray. Soot and ash. I imagined his skin, rough beneath my fingertips.

"I been waiting for you," he said.

"Oh, yeah?" My pencil stuttered over the page. "I don't think so. I'm Cat Turner. New in town. Nobody's waiting for me."

He fell silent.

I hatched a cross pattern into my angel's wings, darker, fiercer, the tips spiky enough to impale heads. Hadn't I learned my lesson? *Do not engage. Ignore. Keep your head down.* Eventually, they'd move on.

"Your head," he said, "it pains you? Queenie showed me a remedy. You soak your feet in hot water."

Well, heck, that wasn't weird advice coming from a total stranger.

I hatched and scratched onto the page and said, "How long you been watching me?"

"Not long." He eased around the front of the tombstone and stopped at the foot of the next marker. I uncrossed my legs and lowered my green Converse sneakers to the ground.

"Did you need something?" I perched on the edge of the bench. "Because my mama's expecting me back at the hotel."

He scratched his elbow and glanced over his shoulder. "The hospital?"

"Ho-*tel*," I said. "The Fairly Grand?" Wait. I eyed his pajama-like clothes, his bare feet. "Are you looking for the hospital?"

"No," he turned back to me, "just wanting to leave." He eased forward, barely stirring the leaves that curled like dead beetles over the sandy ground. I jumped off the bench. Beneath the darkening sky, one tree blurred into another. A few stars already winked down at us. The paper crackled in my fist.

"Can I see what you're drawing?" He got as far as Elijah's angel and reached toward me.

Not a chance. I knew better than to show my sketches to anyone. A lesson painfully learned. My mouth ran dry. My head pounded. I clutched my sketch pad and tried to still my trembling hand.

"You're working something fierce," he said. "I bet you're skilled."

Well, I was no Picasso.

Before I guessed what he was up to, he hovered over me. I stumbled backward, nearly dropping my sketches. He studied the marble angel, then my paper. Crickets thrummed in the weeds. A firefly flickered above the stones.

"They don't favor much, do they?" he said.

"No." I backed away and hugged the pad to my chest, gripping my pencil like a dagger.

He frowned and scratched the back of his wrist.

I didn't owe him any explanation, but offered one anyway. "Sometimes what I see in front of me and what comes out on paper don't exactly match."

"Perhaps yours is closer to the truth."

"The truth about what?"

"Angels."

Was he making fun of me? "I've got to go." I sidled toward the road. "You gonna be okay, waiting for somebody?"

"I need your help," he said.

I backed away. "I can't help you, chief. I'm new here. I don't know anybody."

"I've got to go home."

"Well, I don't have a car. Or money." I continued to put distance between us. "Maybe I could call somebody for you."

"Call?" He tilted his head.

"Family? Friends? I don't have a cell phone, either, but I can call from the hotel. Give me a name. Here, I'll write it down." I was close enough to the road to stop and flip open my pad. He stopped beside my vacated bench.

"Culver," he said.

"Culver?"

"Culver Calhoun Washington."

"That's who you want me to call?" I scribbled the name and said, "You got a number?" My foot crunched gravel. Somewhere in the distance, an engine rumbled to life. "What do you want me to say?"

When he didn't answer, I glanced up to see the edges of him shiver, not quite holding their shape.

"I didn't want to go to war," he said. "I hope that doesn't make me a coward."

"Well, no," I said. "I mean, who wants to go to war? Are you talking about Afghanistan? You look awfully young to be a vet."

"Horace made me go," he said. "Cannons thundering so's you couldn't hear over the roar. The air was alive with lead. Bullets ripping saplings in half. Balls screaming a hair from my head." He hesitated and closed his eyes. "Bodies sinking legless, headless into the earth. Mud holes red with blood. Hogs gnawing on the scattered dead."

Wow, post-traumatic stress disorder?

"Flames," he opened his eyes and stared toward Mobile Bay, "lit the night like the seventh level of hell."

"Dante's *Inferno*," I said. "You've read it?"

He stared at me. "Mister Josiah used to preach on it something powerful."

"I had a teacher like that at my school," I said. "Scared the daylights out of me."

His gaze drifted to the relic of a cannon resting in the scrubby grass, moving toward it as if he was reliving the firefight over again. "The woods lit my face aflame. And lit Horace's eyes like a demon come to life. The grin he give me was fearsome."

My own nightmare flared to mind. The cross ablaze in my front yard, Easter lilies scorched at the foot of it, flames leaping toward the porch and the moonless sky. Mama's cries. Daddy's cursing. The terror as I searched for my golden retriever through the flames.

I didn't want to remember. Hadn't thought of that night in weeks. Hadn't Mama and I uprooted ourselves and traveled hundreds of miles south not to be reminded? But now, as the boy relived his war, the image of that fire seared my brain. The vandalism didn't drive Daddy away. It was simply one more horror in a series of catastrophes orchestrated to humiliate me.

A screech of tires in the distance snapped me back to the present. I shook off the burning cross, scorched flesh. "Horace was your army buddy?"

His expression lit up. "We grew up together. I worked for him, but we were more like brothers." He faltered. "Until the war."

"What war did you say you were in?"

He picked at his elbow. "It snatches something from you, war does. Draws terrible things from deep inside."

"We've all got our cross to bear, I suppose." And I wanted to kick myself. Kill the image. Bury it so deep it'd never see the light of day. Didn't Mama say we couldn't change the past? We had to move forward, which is exactly what I intended to do. "I've got to go," I said.

"I need to leave this place."

I sighed. "Sorry, chief. Even if I had a car, I just turned fifteen. Not old enough to drive. And even if I were, I've only been here a few weeks, so I don't know my way around."

He surveyed the cemetery as if seeing it for the first time. He settled his solemn gaze on me.

"Best I can do is call your buddy when I get back to the hotel," I said. I shoved the cross, the flames, my ex-best friend's smirk deep into my gut, as the boy stood, transfixed in front of me. I adjusted my scarf and stepped through the pines to cross the road and leave him behind.

"Someone's coming," he said, and I turned back to him. An engine rumbled behind me, followed by a shout of laughter. The boy's big hands blurred into his sleeves, then disappeared, a trick of the dying light.

I ignored the growing rumble, the high-pitched whine of shifting gears, as I searched the shadows for the boy's outline. Air whooshed behind me and I turned too late. Metal flashed and the golf cart slammed into me.

There was a scream, mine, I think, as the cart lifted me off the ground. Gravity slammed my head into asphalt and I stared at the sky and struggled to focus on the one bright star above me. Maybe it was Venus. Or Mars. Paper fluttered to the ground like wounded birds and I attempted to shut out pain so bad I thought I might be sick. And then the air exploded around me.

Someone cursed. Someone made a phone call. Footsteps crunched through gravel toward me, brown docksiders loose around tanned feet. They paused before stomping away and cursing some more.

I stared at the stars as the road melted warm against my back and pain seared my elbow. I guess hiding was out of the question now. I closed my eyes.

Taunts and accusations. Betrayal and pain. An endless cycle, apparently. Flames scorched my elbow, sticky with blood. Flames leapt at my chest, stealing my breath. Memories engulfed me, threatening to snuff me out. I rolled my head and found the strange boy hovering beside the bench, staring at me. He shimmered like a thousand stars before fading away.

CHAPTER 2

My legs dangled off the white slab of an examination table, crackling the paper beneath me. The triage was usually reserved for more critically injured patients, but the examining rooms were full and we'd already been waiting for what seemed like hours. It smelled of antiseptic and somebody's dinner of Kung Pao chicken.

Monitors beeped. Nurses padded in and out in their orthopedic shoes. Operators paged doctors overhead.

The room held five other beds, each partitioned off by curtains the nurses scraped back and forth as patients came and went.

A woman with a spike of blonde hair and deep black roots slumped in a corner. A small girl sucked her thumb and wrapped herself around the woman's leg. A man rustled behind a curtain, calling for someone to fetch him food. I sat closest to the door, near the wall of glass separating us from the hallway.

Mama and Sheriff Stone Hamilton stood near the window, their voices raised in agitation. The man behind the curtain called for food.

Really, weren't most hospitals pretty much the same? Bright lights, noise, blood, sickness, death.

I didn't remember the last emergency room I was in. But I remembered the stay afterward. The stares. The faces shying away. The shock of it. Mama crying and Daddy sitting in the corner of my hospital room, staring blankly at the muted television on the wall.

This accident was a bit of a blur, too. I remember lying on the

ground, gravel digging into my shoulder blades, my sketches fluttering around me. I remember much cursing in the dark. I thought there
was whimpering. I think it was me. I wish I didn't remember that. I
was pretty sure I begged someone, anyone, to call 911. Someone called
his mother instead.

The doctor stitched the gash beneath my chin and it stung as
the shot of lidocaine wore off. I fingered the stubby black thread and
wondered how bad it would scar. As if I didn't have enough of those
already.

While Mama and the sheriff discussed the accident, we waited for the x-ray of my elbow, the one with a bloody hole in it, and the
results of the CAT scan of my head, which throbbed like I'd been hit
by a semi-truck and not some souped-up golf cart.

The doctor said I probably wouldn't have sustained any inju-
ries by the average cart. They couldn't travel faster than fifteen or so
miles per hour. But the cart that hit me had been going at least thirty.
He reckoned it must've been due to the special oversized tires.

I touched my tongue to the cut inside my cheek and tasted
blood and grit. I wiped it with the edge of my scarf. The paramedics attempted to cut the cotton free, but I freaked out so totally they
agreed to leave it on if I would loosen it so they could check for inju-
ries. It dangled from my neck, ragged and stiff with dried blood.

On the ride to the hospital, I begged the paramedics to go
back. I didn't have my sketchbook. And I had to have my sketchbook.
These weren't just any drawings. People tended to react badly to these
drawings. And I'd already suffered a nasty taste of what could happen
if my sketches fell into the wrong hands. The paramedics refused. I
couldn't make them understand.

Through the wall of glass, I saw the two boys who'd run me
over leaning against the corridor wall. According to the sheriff, the
dark-haired pretty boy decked out in a polo shirt and plaid shorts was
Bobby. The scruffy blonde in raggedy basketball shorts and a tattered
Bob Marley tee was Tate Channing.

Bobby was the driver, and the mother he called did not arrive
at the scene of the accident or the hospital. She did call the sheriff,
however, who transported the boys in the back of his patrol car. I almost felt sorry for them. Almost.

A nurse with a brown ponytail bounced past them in green
scrubs. They flashed a number of fingers, a handful from Bobby, a
hand and thumb from Tate. A few seconds later, a tiny brunette with
dimples swaggered past them and received a seven from Bobby and
an eight from Tate. Next, a tall blonde with long legs and a cascade of

curls received two tens, as well as much elbowing, ribbing, and high fiving after she disappeared from view.

"What do you mean, you can't do anything?" Mama's voice was loud enough to quiet the man calling for food behind the curtain. "Not even a ticket?"

"Ma'am," the sheriff scratched the back of his blonde buzz cut with a freckled hand, "we don't issue tickets for pedestrian accidents."

"Excuse me?" Mama moved to my side and I grabbed her arm in warning. She pulled away.

"You're new here, aren't you, ma'am?" the sheriff said. "From Georgia?"

"Shelby, yes. Outside Atlanta."

"Been in town a few weeks, right?"

"I'm the new manager at the Fairly Grand Hotel."

"Assistant manager, I heard."

Mama's green eyes narrowed, the skin beneath them puffy. As angry as she was, she still managed to appear fatigued. "Yes," she said, "assistant manager."

"Funny how that came about," the sheriff said. "Thought Andrew Hamilton had the job. Well, never mind. It'll get worked out."

"Excuse me?"

He heaved a sigh and scratched his chin. "Well, ma'am," he drawled, "in the state of Alabama, the law used to be that an officer had to witness a pedestrian accident to write a ticket."

"But he admitted he hit her."

"Yes, ma'am." The sheriff swiveled toward the boys wrestling in the hallway, banging off the walls. He frowned and turned back. "But by law, he could've hit your daughter in a car going a hundred miles an hour and killed her and still not gotten a ticket. It's really up to the discretion of the officer on duty."

"That's the stupidest thing I've ever heard," Mama said. "My daughter has a hole in her arm. She's covered in scrapes and bruises. She's traumatized."

"I'm not that traumatized," I said.

She gave me a look that shut me up.

"Mrs. Turner," the sheriff tucked the pad of paper he had yet to write anything on into his khaki uniform pocket, "it was a golf cart. Your daughter appears okay to me."

"Okay? Okay?" Mama gestured at me. "She has stitches in her chin, her arm's probably broken, and she may have a concussion."

"You need to calm yourself, ma'am."

"While those, those..."

We turned to find Tate pushing Bobby in a wheelchair. He shoved him so hard Bobby ricocheted off the opposite wall and into the path of a wiry woman in a white lab coat with a stethoscope slung around her neck. She shook a finger at them and they meekly abandoned the wheelchair and eased it back against the wall. The woman disappeared from view. Bobby gave her a zero and Tate gave her a one, no, he raised another finger, a two. They doubled over, laughing.

"They're good kids," Sheriff Hamilton said and hitched up his khaki slacks. "I know their mamas and daddies. They're good people. They're just a little bored since school let out. Once I get 'em home, I'm sure their parents will set 'em straight."

"Set them straight?" Mama said. She ran fingers under her bangs and through her hair. She was missing one of her favorite pearl earrings. "What does that mean?"

"It means they'll get a good talking to."

"A good talking to?"

"Ma'am, it was just a golf cart."

"You keep saying that like it was a tricycle. We've been in this emergency room for over two hours. I don't think my insurance has even kicked in yet. How am I going to pay for this?"

"Yes, ma'am," he nodded, "I'm awfully sorry for your trouble. Maybe if your daughter could be more careful in the future, you might avoid these situations. Stepping out in the middle of the road at night, she's bound to get hurt."

"I wasn't in the middle of the road," I said. "I was –"

"It was dark," he interrupted. "You've got nothing white or reflective on. It's a wonder you weren't hit by a car."

"I was on the side of the road," I said, "and it wasn't that dark. There was another boy there. He could tell you."

Nurse Avery, who helped stitch my chin, entered with a smile and a tiny paper cup of water. Thin and fresh faced, she scooted around the sheriff and stopped beside me. "Here's some pain medicine for that elbow, sweetie." She laid two tiny blue tablets in my palm and handed me the water.

"Oh, Sheriff," she turned, "Bobby says, could you please hurry? His daddy's going to be awful sore if he misses dinner."

Mama growled close to my ear. I stared at the pills in my palm.

The sheriff strolled over to the door and stuck his head out. "Pipe down," he said to the boys. "I'm not finished yet."

The nurse leaned toward Mama, giving us a whiff of Juicy Fruit gum. "I swear," she said, "Bobby's daddy and the sheriff don't look anything alike. One's as dark as the other is blonde. You'd never know they were brothers."

"Brothers?" Mama pushed her wilting bangs off her forehead. I thought she might cry. Or hit somebody. I pocketed the tablets and tossed back the water.

"Can we go, Mama?" I said. "I'm beat. I've got to find my sketch pad and then I just want to crash."

The sheriff returned and hitched up his pants.

"Your nephew?" Mama said. Her eyes shimmered. "That boy's your nephew?"

The nurse winced and slinked toward the door. "I'll see what's keeping those x-rays," she said and edged into the hallway. When she passed the boys, she got a five from Tate and a two from Bobby.

Idiots.

"That has nothing to do with how I do my job," the sheriff was saying. He hitched up his pants and I wished to high heaven he wore a belt. "The law's the law and I treat everybody the same."

"Right," Mama said. "Are we done here? Because I need to get Cat home."

"Well, yeah," he said, "I guess."

"Mama," I said, "I have to search for my drawings."

"Not now, honey."

"Yes, Mama." I grabbed her arm. "The paramedics didn't find my sketchbook, so it must still be there. I've got to go back and get it."

"Cat, sweetie," she pulled her arm out of my grasp, staring at the boys outside the window, "we are not going back to the cemetery tonight. It's too late and too dark. Tomorrow will be soon enough."

"Mama," the paper rustled beneath me as I scooted to launch myself off the bed, "I need it now!" I snagged the cream silk of her sleeve and jerked her around to face me. "You do remember the last time my sketches went missing, don't you?"

Her gaze finally left the boys to note my flushed face, my grip on her arm, the blood dried and crusted where my knuckles scraped pavement.

Facing the sheriff, she said, "Cat and I need a little privacy, please."

He glanced between us. "Yeah, sure. You be careful, now, Miss Turner. We don't want to hear about any more accidents."

"Sheriff," Mama's gaze locked with mine, "hadn't you best get those boys home for their supper?"

A doctor burst through the door, his white coat flapping behind him. He presented the x-rays with a flourish. "Results are back."

"Good," Mama said, "we're ready to go."

The sheriff moved toward us, thumbs hooked in his pants. There was a weighty silence as we stared at him.

"What?" he said.

The doctor coughed into his fist. "HIPAA laws, Stone. Unless Mrs. Turner wants to waive her rights."

"Mrs. Turner would appreciate some privacy," Mama said and turned her back on the sheriff. He frowned but had little choice but to mosey toward the door.

The doctor whipped the x-ray toward the track of fluorescent lighting. "Good news," he said, "nothing broken. And the CAT scan was normal, so she probably has only a mild concussion."

"Thank heavens."

"She'll need to rest, though. No texting."

No problem, I thought, thanks to those jerks back in Shelby. No phone.

"No computer, either."

No problem there. After what I'd been through, I couldn't stand to use one.

"And no physical exertion for at least the next week."

A trifecta. Working out had never been my friend.

"I'll want her to wear a sling for her arm," he said. "At least a week or so, to be safe."

A phone rang shrilly. The sheriff pulled his cell phone from his pocket and turned his back on us. "Stone, here. What's so dang urgent?" He turned back and fixed his gaze on Mama. "The Fairly Grand," he said, "on fire?"

Mama's mouth fell open and she sagged against the bed.

"I'll be right there," he said. And before she could ask, he banged out the door.

CHAPTER 3

I awoke the next morning to hammering outside my window. Mama and I were given a suite in the oldest part of the hotel, on the third floor above the main lodge. It was the last wing left to be renovated. The carpet unraveled along the edges and the peach-striped wallpaper peeled at the seams, but we had a balcony with a nice view overlooking the narrow strip of beach and Mobile Bay.

By the time we returned from the hospital, the fire was extinguished. But not before it destroyed the bicycle rental hut along the beach. Mama spent all night talking to the fire chief, reassuring the panicking guests, organizing the maintenance crew, and ordering a new thatch roof to be shipped overnight from San Diego. The maintenance crew wasted no time rebuilding the frame beside the investigation site, so they were nearly finished by the time the guests were even out of bed.

Mama also ordered me to stay in my room and rest, but I couldn't relax until I found my drawings. And fast.

I stared around my room in disgust. Clothes spilled out of the suitcase I tossed onto a luggage stand when we first arrived. Mama said I needed to unpack and settle in. But it didn't feel right, yet. Not without my dog, Ruby. I had gotten as far as storing my underwear in the armoire, but mostly to hide the makeup Mama hated for me to wear.

In Mama's room, face creams, lotions, and perfume bottles lined her bathroom sink. Color-coordinated tan and cream blouses, navy and black suits hung in her closet. Yawn-worthy pumps lined the floor.

I encouraged her to branch out and add one of my scarves for color, but she said it wasn't her job to stand out. It was her job to blend in. And I said if she blended in, then how would guests and staff find her so she could help solve their problems? She simply stomped over to the mirror and stuck some boring pearls through her pierced ears.

Personally, I believe the whole blending-in thing was left over from her housekeeping job at the Shelby Motorcourt. She'd been hired as housekeeping manager after she lost her job with the Atlanta mayor's office. To say it was a step down was a major understatement. She worked longer hours for a fraction of the pay, which I wasn't supposed to know. Given her lack of hotel experience, I still didn't understand how she got the job at the Fairly Grand.

After my accident back in Shelby, when Daddy lost his job and everything fell apart, she decided we needed a fresh start. So, she interviewed to be housekeeping manager at the Fairly Grand and was hired as assistant manager of the whole shebang. Nana and I never got an explanation as to exactly how it happened.

It wasn't that Mama wasn't plenty smart. She helped the mayor of Atlanta run the city for five years. But she knew diddly about running a hotel as fancy as the Fairly Grand.

The walls of our rooms were devoid of any artwork and I wondered if the manager, Ed Winer, didn't count on us being there long enough to waste it on us. I propped a picture of Ruby on my desk. But on the bad days it hurt too much to miss her, so sometimes I flipped it face down.

I also brought a picture of my ex-best friend, Mary Grace Chappell, with our faces painted like tigers at the school fair. But because she hadn't spoken to me in three months, I kept it stuffed in the bottom of my suitcase. And dang, if the cheap metal frame she gave me didn't stab my finger each time I rummaged for something. Why did I keep the stupid thing, anyway?

I hid it beneath the turquoise leopard scarf she gave me right after my accident. It was real silk and she'd used her babysitting money to purchase it. She said the leopard print would help me get back to my Cat-like self, which sounded cool at the time. But after she quit speaking to me, the scarf seemed kind of lame. And even though we were apparently no longer friends, and I refused to wear it, it was still one of my favorites. Which kinda made me hate my wussy self.

Favoring my arm, I dressed as quickly and painlessly as possible, even though I could barely lift it over my head. The idea of my sketchbook falling into someone else's hands spurred me on. I wound a green scarf with gold glints around my neck, eased my arm into the canvas sling, and left the room.

The Fairly Grand was built overlooking Mobile Bay in the early 1800s. Having survived two hundred years of war, fires, hurricanes, and floods, she wore her trauma well. I skipped down the staircase in the center of the lobby to the first floor. The circular room radiated outward from the brick fireplace that soared past the second and third floor balconies toward massive beams crisscrossing the ceiling.

Original oak paneling covered the walls. Oriental rugs splashed red onto hardwood floors beneath rose velvet sofas and gold-striped chairs. Glass cases embedded in the walls displayed antique Southern curios. Floral china, silver spittoons, steel whiskey flasks, and silver mint julep cups.

One showcased authentic Civil War weaponry, including a bayonet, a naval cutlass with a brass handguard and a wicked, curved blade, a .32 caliber Smith & Wesson, and a Bowie knife with a handle carved out of deer antlers. There were a few rifles and short blades I couldn't remember much about, except they appeared old and rusted. The day before, I'd stopped to study a surgeon's kit. The scalpel handle was carved from bone and I refused to speculate on the purpose of the surgeon's hatchet.

I hit the bottom of the stairs as Mr. and Mrs. Ira Fischer exited the Baytowne Grill, the smell of bacon wafting after them. With no time to hide, I had no choice but to stand my ground.

"Catalina, dear," the elderly Mrs. Fischer approached me. "How are you feeling this morning?"

"Fine," I lied.

Irene and Ira Fischer were ensconced at the hotel when Mama and I arrived. One thing I'd learned in the last three weeks was that sometimes it was better to avoid them, if possible. They had frequented the place since they were newlyweds in the 1950s, and I'd already heard more stories than I could recall.

At eighty-something, Irene Fischer carried herself with the gliding grace of an aging film star with a bob of silver hair and long, fake eyelashes curling toward two perfect, black-penciled brows. Her skin stretched taut over high cheekbones, her nose long and narrow, lips thin and painted carmine.

Encircling her skeletal fingers, a chunk of ruby overlapped a band of diamonds next to a cluster of emeralds, alongside a blue topaz. Barely an inch taller than me, she was known to defy her orthopedist with three-inch stiletto heels.

Not much taller than his wife, Ira Fischer sported seersucker suits in the summer, and according to the hotel staff, a Mediterranean tan year-round. Bald and well-oiled, he wore a single diamond stud in his left ear, which his wife pierced at some wild Mardi Gras celebration in the eighties. He smelled of maple syrup.

"No dizziness?" Mrs. Fischer said. She grasped my chin in her long fingers and tilted it to study beneath it. "You gave us quite a scare, Catalina. It appears that might scar."

I winced and pulled away. "It's only a few stitches."

"Even so," she tapped a metallic silver nail against my chin, "vitamin E."

"Excuse me?"

"For the scarring. You're much too pretty to mar your lovely face."

"It's already marred," I said. "It's covered in freckles."

"Darling," she said, "they're the best part of you. I can't imagine why you try so hard to hide them. You're much too pretty for makeup. I'm surprised your mother allows it."

"She doesn't. Much."

"Oh, dear. A bit of a rebel, are we?"

"Girls younger than me have been wearing makeup for years," I said.

"Leave her alone, Mrs. Fischer," Mr. Fischer said and plucked a knife from the pocket of his blue seersucker blazer and cleaned under his nails. "She's fine as she is."

"Exactly what I was saying, dear." She spread her palms wide. "It's practically a sin to cover such a face."

"Mrs. Fischer," he concentrated on his nails, "you wouldn't know a sin if it bit you on your lovely derriere."

"Oh, Mr. Fischer." She shoved him playfully, stumbling him backward and he nearly nicked his thumb. She grabbed his arm; he winked at her and resumed his manicure.

"I've got to go," I said. I scooted past them and made it all the way to the front desk.

"Cat," Mama emerged from the hallway leading to the managers' offices between the front desk and the concierge. "You're supposed to be resting."

I kept going and called over my shoulder, "I'm fine. Just going to find my sketchbook."

"Catalina Angelica Turner," Mama said. "You stop right there."

With a groan and a roll of my eyes, I stopped and turned. Irene Fischer stood by the stairs, dabbing at her husband's lapel and studying us. I had a few seconds at best.

Mama propped her hands on her hips. Her rumpled silk blouse had already untucked itself from her skirt. A chunk of hair escaped its bun and curled at the base of her neck.

I stomped back to her. "Why'd you start wearing your hair like that?" I said. "It looks awful."

"Thanks, kiddo." She tucked a strand behind her ear. "I'm trying to appear older."

"Why do you need to look older?"

"Why do you?" I opened my mouth and she sighed and raised a hand to deflect my retort. She lowered her voice. "I want them to think I'm competent."

I gripped her shoulder and stared her in the eye. "Mama," I said, "you are competent."

"Cat, you know I'm in over my head," she said. "Besides the fire last night, nobody can get the Wilkersons' room keys to work, the pool keeps running out of towels, the spa's overbooked, and Finnegan is freaking out over the new baby ducklings waddling throughout the property and into his crew's equipment. Marci, the new maid, didn't show for work again and Ed Winer's breathing down my neck. And that's just this morning."

The night before, when Mama and I had arrived back at the hotel from the emergency room, Mr. Ed had been waiting for us in the lobby in a wrinkled shirt and skewed tie. His shirt was soaked through and his slick black hair was even slicker and winging out over his ears.

We'd managed to avoid him last night as Mama hustled me into the elevator and off to bed. But he was already waiting for us this morning, not looking much better. Mama left me in front of the concierge desk to follow Mr. Ed into his office. The front desk clerk, blonde, willowy Giselle from Sweden, left her post long enough to stroll over to investigate my stitched chin.

Benito from Malta, sporting a sliver of a mustache so neat it appeared to be penciled on, had gone off in a stream of Italian, pointing and gesturing at the ceiling. I caught the words 'idiot' and 'imbecile' but wasn't sure if he was talking about me or the boys who hit me.

Mr. Ed's voice rose so loud we heard most of the conversation through the closed door.

"While your daughter was getting herself run over," he said, "the roof of the bicycle hut caught fire and burned to the ground!"

Mama murmured something I couldn't make out.

"The fire department put it out," he said. "Fortunately, the bikes were already moved. But it looks and smells like an unholy mess. We had to evacuate the entire west wing."

Mama's voice rose. I sidled closer to the door.

"Most guests were just coming in from dinner," he said. "Only a few were on the beach when it happened. Some of the old timers had to be dragged out of bed to stand around in their pajamas until we got it under control."

"I'll check on them," Mama said.

"You better believe you will. And don't go promising free wine and fruit baskets like you did with that Jorgenson debacle. You figure out how to smooth things over without costing me an arm and a leg."

"Do we know how the fire started?"

"The fire department's investigating. But if I find out those slacker twins were smoking, I'm going to fire their butts from here to kingdom come. And if you ever leave this hotel again without making sure there's coverage, I'll send you hightailing it back to Atlanta, missy."

"I didn't leave without coverage," Mama said. "I put Giselle in charge, and apparently you were here as well."

"Giselle? Giselle doesn't know squat about running a hotel and I'm starting to think you don't either!"

"My child was rushed to the emergency room in an ambulance," Mama said. "She was run over."

"By a freaking golf cart!"

"I didn't know that at the time. I heard she was injured. I had to check on her."

"I could hire twenty people this minute with no kids who could do your job without the unnecessary distractions."

"My daughter is not a distraction," Mama said. "And you knew I was a mother when you hired me."

"I didn't have much choice in the matter, did I? At any rate," his voice lowered and I strained to hear, "I thought you were a professional and could handle the demands of the job."

"I am and I can. But I cannot ignore my child when she's hurt. And I certainly couldn't predict a fire would break out in the two hours I was gone."

"You better get your priorities straight, Ms. Turner," he said, "before you land out on your ear. Dismissed."

The door opened and I scurried back to the concierge's desk as Mama appeared. Her cheeks were pink, her eyes bright. Her smile trembled, and she took a deep breath and tucked her hair behind her ear.

"You'll be okay, Cat?" She ran a hand over the top of my head and along my cheek. "I have to check on the bicycle hut."

"I want to see," I said.

Mr. Ed stuck his head into the hallway and said, "No, ma'am. We can't afford a bunch of kids traipsing through the investigation site. It's been hard enough keeping the guests away. I had to pay Bachus overtime to do nothing but stand around and shoo people away."

"We may need to set up another location to rent bikes in the meantime," Mama said.

"Then get on it," Ed Winer barked. "You're way behind on this one, Eva. For three weeks I've covered for you, but if the Algenons arrive unexpectedly, well..." He dismissed her with a flick of his wrist, disappeared into his office, and slammed the door.

"Mama," I squeezed her shoulder bringing us both back to the present, "take a deep breath. You're fine."

"Well, you're not. Look at your arm. You could've been hospitalized. And how could we afford that? And what about your father? What if he appears?"

"He's not going to appear," I said. "Stop expecting trouble."

"I know. I know." She tucked the stray curl behind her ear again. "Do you think it was a mistake to come? I didn't think so before. But with last night's fire and your accident, it feels, I don't know, like we're running away."

"Well, we didn't exactly have a choice, did we? You needed a better job. And I needed..." I had no idea what I needed.

"I feel so selfish," she said. "Taking you away from Ruby. She always makes everything better, doesn't she?"

"I don't want to talk about it."

"We'll get her here as soon as we can," she said. "Even board her at the kennel if we have to."

"Gee," I said, weighing the options, "running free on Nana's farm or cooped up in a pen. Which would be better for Ruby?"

"Cat, I was just trying to –"

"What? Make me feel better about leaving my dog behind?"

"It's not forever."

"It sure feels like it."

"I told you I'm working on it."

"Never mind. I've got to go."

"Where?"

"To look for my drawings."

"I don't want you going back to the cemetery."

"Mama," I gritted my teeth, "you know why I need to find them."

"Cat, this is a new place. A fresh start."

"Yeah?" I said. "Well, let's keep it that way."

Mama blew her bangs out of her eyes. "Okay. I'm with you. But can you please be careful?"

"Sure." I waved over my shoulder. I was nearly out the door when she caught me again.

"Before you go, can you run this out to the twins?" It was a cheap, cardboard-backed appointment book. "It's temporary until we get the computer running again."

I heaved a sigh and took the book from her. "Sure," I said. The bicycle hut was in the opposite direction I needed to go, but at least I'd get to see it. I pushed my way into the bright sunshine and trotted around the hotel to the beach and the new bicycle hut, reeking of scorched pine.

CHAPTER 4

By the time I reached the Hasher twins, the new bicycle hut frame was finished. The stench of burned thatch mingled with the smell of freshly-cut lumber and coconut oil from sunbathers on the beach. The morning sun blazed onto the blue plastic tarp the maintenance crew constructed over the new frame.

Wearing a cheesy Hawaiian shirt, Corbin Hasher leaned against the wooden frame and picked at his cuticles with a cocktail straw. I distinguished him from his brother by his scruffy ponytail and patch of blonde chin fuzz. Cody leaned over the rental counter in a matching shirt, texting furiously on his cell phone, wavy blonde hair tucked behind his ears and curling against his square jaw.

"Hey guys." I strolled over. "Heard you had some excitement last night."

Corbin grunted and Cody glanced from his phone. "You too," he said and nodded at my sling. "Heard you got yourself run over by a golf cart. Wicked."

"Yeah. Whatever. Here, Mom sent this for you." I handed the ledger over the counter. He ignored the book so I dropped it onto the rough surface. "So, what happened?"

Cody glanced at his brother, then resumed texting, his thumbs moving faster than I could follow. Corbin studied a piece of torn cuticle.

"You guys weren't smoking, were you?" I said. "If you were, I won't tell."

"Do we look like camel crushers?" Corbin said. His eyes glittered green before he focused on his nails. It was true. With the lean, tanned bodies of surfers, they definitely did not appear to be smokers.

"So, you were just messing around, then?"

"Look, Nancy Drew," Corbin stopped picking his nails, "we already got the third degree from big man fire chief and Ed-The-Brain-Dead Winer. We don't need you interrogating us, too."

"Ease up, bro," Cody said without pausing.

"I'm not interrogating you," I said. "But my mom's in real trouble about it and I'm trying to help her find out what happened."

"We didn't do anything," Corbin said and turned his back on me to stare out at the bay. He chewed on his thumb. I noticed the pile of ashes beyond him in the sand.

The staff occasionally burned bonfires on the beach, but always controlled, and always in a designated fire pit. This fire had been built in the sand and suspiciously close to the hut.

"But you were here when it happened," I said.

Cody shrugged and stretched to his full height. "we were getting ready to knock off, you know, riding the last bikes into the shed. The sun had set. We were on the verge of clocking out."

"What about the bonfire?" I nodded toward the pile of ashes. "was it lit yet? It's awfully close to the hut."

Cody turned to study it. "No," he said. "It was definitely not burning."

"Maybe it hadn't been put out completely," I said. "the wind caught a stray spark and poof!" I threw my hands in the air.

Cody consulted his brother. Corbin shrugged. Cody turned back to me. "It was dead cold," he said. He resumed his texting.

"But how do you know?"

He slammed his phone onto the counter and cocked his head. "Because I put it out myself."

"So, it was your fire."

"Dead cold, I tell you."

"What if it wasn't?"

Corbin pulled away from his post and strolled toward me. He lowered his voice. "That fire was put out two days before the hut even lit up. It had nothing to do with it."

"Yeah?"

"It was getting dark last night," he said. "We were moving bikes. We'd nearly finished. I think we were both on our last one."

"Except for the two-seater," Cody said.

"Yeah," Corbin agreed. "I was coming back for the two-seater when the roof of the hut exploded."

"Exploded." I crossed my arms.

"In one poof, like you said. It wasn't a slow burn. It wasn't a spark. It was an explosion. All at once. Lit against the sky just past sunset."

Sun going down. Golf cart around a curve.

"You're lucky you guys didn't get hurt," I said. The brothers exchanged glances. I studied the west wing of the hotel and the balconies overlooking the lawn. My room was near the end. "You reckon somebody could've thrown a cigarette from up there, or maybe a firecracker?"

Corbin scratched the fuzz on his chin. "A cigarette wouldn't carry that far. It would've landed in the bushes below. But a firecracker?" He shrugged.

"A firecracker would've made a pop," Cody said. "A loud one, and so would any other fireworks. There was no popping sound. Everything was fine one minute and then whoosh, in flames the next." He resumed texting.

I propped my hands on my hips. "Well, what do you think happened?"

Corbin frowned at his brother, whose texting bordered on manic. "Spontaneous combustion?" he said.

Cody stopped and glanced at me. "Maybe it was Red Maggie."

"Don't be stupid," his brother said. "She's never even been seen outside her room."

I'd heard of Red Maggie. Of course I had. The first week Mama and I arrived, Mrs. Fischer told me the story of the ghost haunting Suite 242.

Margaret Althea Hutchins, aka Maggie Hutchins, was a cigarette girl and sometime singer at the posh Hotel Regale in Mobile, across the bay. In the summer of 1944, when the Fairly Grand was converted into a maritime training camp, she met an army officer in training.

Young Harry Winston escorted Maggie about town. One thing led to another, and while Maggie was seeing visions of diamond solitaires, newly-commissioned Officer Winston was seeing another woman.

Maggie caught him red-handed, so to speak, in Suite 242, which had been converted into an officers' lounge. She lifted his service revolver from the desk, shot Harry and his consort, then shot herself through the head.

There was so much blood, the story goes, it seeped beneath

the door and out into the hallway, hence the name, Red Maggie. I laughed at Mrs. Fischer when she first told me the story, but it didn't seem so funny now.

"Have either of you ever seen Red Maggie?" I said. "And why would she want to destroy the bicycle hut?"

"Maybe she didn't appreciate the view from her room." Corbin crossed his arms and nodded at the second floor behind me. "That's it, right there."

The room he indicated was just beneath our suite. I half expected to see a woman staring out from behind the sliding glass door. There was no woman, but I shivered anyway.

I faced the twins and said, "I don't believe in ghosts."

Corbin shrugged.

Cody straightened and pocketed his phone. "Let's blow this joint," he said. "I need a soda."

They strolled, shoulder to shoulder, toward the pool. When they were out of sight, I let the sun warm my face as I squinted at the bright blue awning against a cottony sky. Two accidents. At twilight. Within a mile of each other. The thought of the cemetery reminded me I needed to retrieve my drawings pronto, before something worse happened.

CHAPTER 5

As soon as I left the Hasher twins, Mama caught me rounding the hotel toward the parking lot. "I need your help," she said. Two maids had called in sick and, as usual, the hotel was short-staffed. I ground my teeth. Apparently, my convalescence was over. And my drawings would have to wait.

With my one good arm, I ran fresh towels from the laundry room to the pool, and a bin of wet towels back to the laundry room. I replenished freshly-baked cookies for afternoon tea, tidied the croquet lawn, and as the sun sank into the bay, gathered abandoned toys and towels from the beach. I was in a near frenzy to get to the cemetery.

I knew we were in a new place. And people didn't know my past. And more than one person at the hotel felt the need to remind me more accidents happen at dawn and dusk than any other time of day. Yeah, yeah, yeah.

It's not as if I wanted to go back. But it was the last place I'd seen my book. And if experience taught me anything, it would be better if my drawings didn't fall into the wrong hands. Or any hands.

Mama insisted on having dinner in the restaurant, probably because she felt guilty about the accident, and making me work with a hurt arm, and we'd hardly seen each other since we moved to Fairly. During dinner, her cell phone never stopped buzzing. And her pager went off a kazillion times. By the end of my hamburger and fries, a mammoth headache pulsed behind my eyes. And my arm throbbed.

The doctor had prescribed painkillers, but something else I'd learned in the past year was I'd rather suffer the pain than have the room spinning out of control.

By the time I arrived at the cemetery, the sky had bled from pink to purple and the shadows stretched deeper, darker, more menacing than the day before.

I stopped at the site of the accident. No evidence suggested I'd been there. No smear of blood. No patch of torn fabric. No charcoal pencil. No sketchbook.

I backtracked to Elijah's headstone and its protective angel and the bench facing it. It made no sense the book could've landed so far away, but I dropped to my knees anyway and searched the ground.

The air weighed as heavy as a wet quilt. A rivulet of sweat ran from my ear along my neck and I dabbed at it with the cotton fringe of my scarf. I considered untying it and letting it hang free. What did I care what strangers thought of me?

But then, strangers became friends. At least, I hoped some would. And even best friends would betray you over the littlest thing. On my knees, I tugged on the scarf, angry at my slavery to vanity, and stopped. The grass rustled behind me.

I whirled around, but the tombstones stood silent among the faded plastic flowers, and unyielding pines, and old rusted cannons posted as watchmen at the four corners. A speck of white caught my eye. I stood and stalked over to it and plucked it from the base of Mary Pickens' headstone.

Mary Pickens died on her birthday, May 2, 1907, at the age of 41. Not a fun birthday for Mary. A devoted wife and mother, she departed the earth with dignity and grace. Or so her tombstone read.

I struggled to straighten the wad of paper against my thigh with my good hand. It was one of my earlier attempts at the angel I'd been sketching. But I hadn't crumpled it and tossed it away.

First of all, I didn't litter. Especially not in a cemetery. Secondly, I no longer tore sketches out of my sketchbook, even bad ones. It was infinitely safer keeping them together in my possession, safer even than tossing them in the trash.

A sigh over my shoulder whirled me around. The same boy stood in the middle of the tombstones, not seven rows away. I recrumpled the paper in my fist and said, "You again."

"Find what you's looking for?" He rested a palm on Marley Watkins' headstone, a simple little thing worn down by the elements. One bare foot scratched the other.

"I'm looking for my sketchbook," I said, "the one I had last night. Black? Fake leather?"

"The angel book."

"Have you seen it?"

His gaze swept the tombstones and landed on the stone bench where he'd watched me for who knows how long. "You took it when you left."

"Yes, I had it when I got hit by the golf cart."

He stared at me.

"You did see me get run over, didn't you?"

He scraped his thumbnail along his chin.

"You heard me scream? Tires squealing? Boys cussing?"

His gaze dropped to the sling. "You were wounded."

"Yes." I raised my arm in acknowledgement. "It's not broken. But there's a hole."

"Does it pain you?" He stepped closer.

I dug my toes into my Chuck Taylors and fought the urge to run. "What are you doing back here, anyway? You enjoy hanging out in cemeteries?" I guess he could've asked me the same thing.

"I'm waiting," he said, "to go home." He stared toward the hotel and scratched his ear.

"Waiting for a ride? For somebody at the hotel?"

He turned back to me and said nothing.

"Forget it," I said. "It's none of my business." I held out the ball of paper. "You see any more of these around? Any of my sketches torn out of my book?"

"No."

"Okay. I'm going to keep looking." I eased away from him, keeping a safe distance and avoided stepping on the graves. His gaze was steady as he followed my progress.

When he was between the road and me, I experienced a moment of panic. Was darkness falling quicker than the night before? I jumped at the caw of a crow perched on a power line, blacker than the sky behind it. I crushed the wad of paper.

"Guess it's not here," I said. "You didn't take it, did you?"

His expression remained blank. "No," he said, "I didn't."

I studied the road, then the spot where I was hit by the golf cart. Everything went flying. The driver called his mother, babbling like an idiot. His mother must've called the sheriff because he arrived and called the ambulance.

Maybe the sketchbook got put into the ambulance without the paramedics noticing. Or maybe the sheriff took it. To use as evidence against me. Evidence of what? I hadn't done anything wrong. Not yet.

But, then, that never stopped the accusations from flying before.

I pressed my fist with the crumpled paper against the dull throb in my temple. This was a new place. Different people. A fresh start. No reason things wouldn't work out just fine this time. No reason for anybody to imagine I was some freak of nature who couldn't get along...

"Uh, miss –"

"Aaaaah!" I turned to find his cold breath on me. I stumbled to a safe distance, my head and heart pounding.

"Didn't mean to scare you, miss," the boy said, "but I need your help."

I pressed my fist to my heart and breathed deeply, counting one, counting two. "I can't help you," I said. "Remember? New here? Don't know anybody?" Which was a lie. I now knew the sheriff.

"I got to get home."

"And yet, you keep showing up here. Maybe you could walk to the hotel and call a cab. Or the country club. It's a little closer."

"I'm stuck." He scratched one foot with the other.

"No money, huh? I'm sure somebody would loan you some." I patted my pocket with my good hand. "I've got nothing on me or I'd help you out. Maybe somebody could give you a ride wherever you need to go."

"I can't leave."

"I don't understand."

"Those angels you draw."

I crushed the ball of paper.

"You talk to them?" he said.

"What? Are you crazy? What makes you think I talk to them? Did somebody tell you that? Is this a joke?" Panic rose like vomit in my throat.

"I just thought," he scratched his arm through his faded sleeve, the same sleeve he was wearing yesterday, the same loose pants, the same bare feet, the same ashen skin, "since you talk to me," he said, "maybe you talk to them. And if you talk to them, maybe you could tell them to come and get me, 'cause I'm ready to go."

"Okay." I eased away from him. "You're talking crazy." I glanced to the road and back. "Did you wander away from a hospital, or some kind of home? Some place where they take care of people who are...well, never mind. You've got people searching for you, I bet."

I was nearly to the road when I realized this was exactly how it happened the night before. Before I got hit, before he disappeared. "I'm going to call the sheriff," I said. "He'll know what to do. You stay right there."

"It won't do no good," he said. "You're the only one who can help me."

"Oh, yeah?" This would've been an awesome time to possess a cell phone. As far as I knew, I was the only fifteen-year-old who didn't have one. And if it wasn't for those fools back in Shelby, I wouldn't be standing helpless in front of some crazy person. "What's so special about me," I said, "that I get to be the only one who can help?"

He scratched his hollowed cheek below his scar. He blinked long, curling lashes and whispered, "Because, you're the only one who can see me."

CHAPTER 6

I stood at the entrance to the bar and stared at the back of Wet Willie's stubbled gray head. His shirt was a crisp white against dark skin as he dried a beer glass and watched the baseball game on a television hanging from the corner of the ceiling. Willie loved baseball.

Head bartender for forty years, he knew everything about the Fairly Grand. And every face. He'd know who was hanging out at the cemetery. But before I asked him, a flash of red clawed at me and I yelped as the skeletal hand morphed into the bejeweled diva.

"Mrs. Fletcher, I mean Fischer," I pressed my scarf to my throat, "you scared me."

She polished a shiny red apple on her green chiffon sleeve and handed it to me. "I thought you might be hungry, dear, and they looked so pretty."

"I'm fine."

"You seem jumpy, Catalina." She peered at me. "Are you okay?"

"Yes." I sucked in air, counting one, counting two, and my heart slowed its galloping.

"Your arm's not bothering you, then?" She nodded at the sling.

"No. I mean it aches, but it's fine. Where's Mr. Fischer?" I searched the lobby in hopes he might take his wife off my hands.

"We enjoyed dinner and now he's resting in the room," she said. "My hip gets stiff if I sit too long. I'd rather be up and about. Hadn't you?"

I opened my mouth.

"Yes, of course you had," she said. "So much youthful ener-gy. Don't ever take it for granted, Catalina. No, I imagine you won't. How's your mother doing? The hotel seems awfully quiet after yester-day's excitement."

"Yes, ma'am. She's fine, ma'am."

"I saw the repairs on the bicycle shack. The awful blue tarp simply does not lend any sense of elegance, does it? It's a shame, real-ly. In my many years of coming here, I've never seen anything like it."

"No, ma'am."

"But your mother, dear, handled it fine, no matter what the sheriff or Ed Winer says. She was absolutely right not to panic. There's not one thing to be gained by worrying the guests."

My head ached. "Mrs. Fischer," I pressed fingertips to my temple, "I need to catch up with Wet Willie. Can we talk later?"

"Of course, dear." She pressed her carmine lips together. "William is a fine conversationalist. One of many reasons he's been here so long. A wealth of information, that man."

"That's what I thought."

"Mr. Fischer and I have conversed with him for hours over drinks. He enjoys his bourbon, too, you know."

"I didn't know."

"You're right, I probably shouldn't be telling you such things. You should have no knowledge of the evil drink, Catalina, at least until you're good and married. Liquor never touched my lips until I married Mr. Fischer, which is the proper way to be introduced to it, dear."

I pointed at Willie's back. "If you don't mind, I'm going to go and say hello before he goes off duty."

"Of course, dear. Take him an apple."

I took the apple and scooted past her into the bar. The lights were dimmed for the evening and chunky white candles flickered on the tables. I plopped onto one of the leather-capped stools and rested the apple on the bar.

The happy-hour crowd had moved on to dinner, leaving the clubby chairs empty around tables still sticky with spilled liquor. Laughter floated from the croquet lawn outside the bay window. The scent of freshly-sliced lemons and sweet cherries blended with the smell of stale beer.

"Hey, sister," Willie greeted me without turning. An outfield-er caught a fly ball and the game flickered to a commercial.

"How'd you know it was me?" I massaged my shoulder to ease the ache from the sling.

"'Cause you always smell like sunshine, sister." He turned and frowned. "What's with the apple?"

"Mrs. Fischer asked me to give it to you." I rolled it toward him.

"That woman." He shook his head. "Always trying to feed somebody."

"Hey, Willie," the apple rocked on its side, "you're familiar with pretty much everybody around here, right? Even the teenagers?"

He plucked a wet glass from the rack by the sink and dried it as he waited.

"I saw this boy," I said, "older than me, seventeen or eighteen, maybe. He was in the cemetery right before my accident. And then again tonight."

"You don't need to be carousing around no cemetery taking up with no riff raff," Willie said. "Didn't your mama tell you not to go back there?" He banged the glass onto the counter and snatched another one and ran the cloth around inside it.

I leaned over the bar and found the bowl of cherries used for garnish. I found one without a stem and popped it in my mouth. Sweet and juicy. Willie frowned and moved the bowl out of my reach.

"He didn't appear to be riff raff," I said and plopped back onto the stool. "He was tall and African-American –"

"You sure don't need to be hanging out with no black fellas in the graveyard, neither." He banged the glass onto the counter and reached for another one. "Can't nothing but trouble come from that place."

"It's quiet there," I said. "I can actually think. But I wasn't hanging out with him. We were just talking."

He banged glass onto wood and glowered at me.

"Do you know the kid?" I said. "Tall, thin, with these big, round eyes? His hair's cropped short, short as yours, and he was wearing what appeared to be pajamas. And his feet were bare. Hey, you missed a spot." I pointed to the water droplets still on the last glass.

"I'm telling you, sister," he reached for another glass, "your mama ain't gonna cotton to you conversing with some boy out in the graveyard. After dark. By yourself. It ain't safe. You see what done happened to you." He nodded at my arm.

"That wasn't my fault," I said.

"Maybe not. Then again, maybe you were distracted by this here fella."

"I wasn't distracted," I said and reached for the apple and rolled it toward me and tried to ignore the sting of his words. "Anyway," I said, "he ran off after the accident. Or sort of disappeared." I frowned at the thought of how he seemed to fade away, same as the dying day.

"See there," Willie said and reached out to stop my rolling of the apple. "Obviously he can't be counted on to help a girl in trouble. Riff raff, I say. Good riddance."

He plucked the apple from my fingers and placed it out of reach.

"Maybe," I said. "Maybe he's a patient at the hospital. He talked about being in some war."

"More reason not to go near the place. Catch some disease or something."

"Maybe he has post-traumatic stress disorder."

"Maybe he's crazy."

"There was definitely something different about him."

Willie snorted. "Lordamercy, teenagers all imagine they're something special."

"He mentioned a fellow named Culver," I said. "Culver Calhoun. I wrote it on my sketchpad, which I can't find."

Willie ran the towel around the inside of the glass and stared at the ceiling. "That's an odd name," he said. "Only one Culver I ever heard of."

"He kept asking for help."

Willie's eyes narrowed and he stopped drying. "Washington," he said.

"Yeah," I said. "Culver Calhoun Washington. He wanted me to call someone to come get him."

"Sister," Willie's mouth tightened into a grim line and he rested his palms flat on the gleaming wood, "that would be some mean trick."

"Oh, yeah?"

"Yeah," he said. "'Cause Culver Washington's been dead nearly two hundred years."

CHAPTER 7

"First off," Willie continued, "your mama said don't go back to the cemetery and you should mind your mama." I opened my mouth to protest but he cut me off with a raised palm. "That boy is messing with you," he said. "He heard you're new in town and thought it'd be fun to play a trick on a newcomer. You can't be fooling around with nobody like that."

He took a glass and scooped ice into it.

"He didn't seem to be kidding," I said. "Or having any fun. He was acting weird and twitchy and scratchy."

"Probably got into a patch of poison ivy running around barefooted. Can't tell kids nothing nowadays. They think they know everything." He poured thick red syrup from a tall silver cylinder into the glass.

"And he talked funny."

Willie huffed and with a nozzle splashed Sprite onto the ice. "Like I said, he's messing with you. Probably had his buddies hiding in the bushes taking pictures on them cell phones."

"Well, that's not creepy," I said. "Who is this Culver Washington, anyway?"

"Ancient history and nobody for you to concern yourself with. We keep the past in the past. We got enough worries for today."

"Sometimes we learn from the past," I said. "So we don't repeat our mistakes."

He stirred the drink with a cocktail straw, speared a cherry with a pink plastic sword and slid the drink to me. "I done told you, there ain't no good reason for you to go back there. Can't nothing but trouble come of it."

"But I have to find my sketchbook and the cemetery's the last place I saw it." I sipped my Shirley Temple, more bubbly than sweet, exactly the way I liked it.

"I thought you said you already searched and it wasn't there."

"I did. And it wasn't. But one of my drawings was. Maybe he lied. Maybe he does have it."

"Forget about it," Willie said. "Get yourself another book. The bookstore in town sells all kinds."

"I've got to get this one back."

"What's so important about this one?" Willie crossed his arms. "You draw lots of pictures, sister. Draw yourself some more."

"You don't understand." I couldn't tell him the last time somebody dug my sketches out of the trash, lots of bad things happened. Nasty looks in the hallways. Whispers. Lies. And that was just the beginning. My breath caught in my throat. I scrubbed at the sting in my eye.

"If these pictures get out," I said, "if anybody sees –"

"Laws, sister," Willie interrupted, "what kind of pictures you drawing can't nobody see?"

"It's not like that," I said. Panic gripped my chest and squeezed. "They're not bad pictures, not dirty pictures. But people don't understand. They see them and think..."

It was my fault. It started after the awful night in Shelby. The ambulance screaming to the hospital. Waking up hooked to those machines. If I hadn't been so stupid. If I hadn't insisted on my own way, none of it would've happened. No scars. No headaches. No flashes of light. No brilliant white wings beating the air. No sketching. No trouble. No horrible fake website.

I'd still be in school. Still at home with Ruby. And Daddy. And Mary Grace. I fingered the soft cotton wrapping my throat. It was tightening, cutting into my skin.

I sucked in a deep breath and counted one, counted two. I struggled to calm myself. Counting one, counting –

"Sister?" Willie's expression told me something was horribly wrong. "Sister, you got to breathe."

I was trying. Truly, I was.

"It's just..." I choked. My scarf became a slithering snake, a green-threaded python squeezing my neck. I clawed at it. It tightened. "It's just bad things..." Willie was around the bar and beside me as I tilted backward, falling... "bad things happen." A flash of silver shimmered over my shoulder, a roar of wings muffled Willie's voice. I lay on the carpeted floor as Willie's long fingers plucked the scarf from my neck.

"No," I said, "don't." I fought to stop him, but then a rush of air flooded my lungs. I gulped at it, choked on it.

"Laws, sister," Willie rocked back on his heels beside me, palms pressed into his black pants, eyes wide.

I palmed my neck and closed my eyes against his shocked expression. "Please," I whispered, "don't tell anyone."

His voice was hushed. "No, sister," he said. "I won't tell nobody."

I fumbled for my scarf and pressed it against my mangled throat and counted one, counted two, counted three.

CHAPTER 8

Morning grumbled toward noon and into evening with a testy gray sky. The heat and humidity dragged my feet and melted my sassy orange bandana into a limp rag around my neck.

I tugged at it and glared at the bicycle wobbling beneath me, its dented fender scraping the front tire. Blast those twins. Of course they had to give the guests the best bikes. But did they have to give me the worst?

Ed's orders, they said.

I thought a ride around the grounds would lighten my mood. I was wrong. Sweat trickled along my jaw. My feet kept slipping off the pedals. My arm ached without the sling I'd left in my room. I already regretted the short ride to the clubhouse and back. I'd barely make it home before the bottom dropped out.

The sky glowed a lurid green between the gray mass of clouds and the darkening line of trees. I passed the cemetery and glanced over, wondering if there was any place within its borders my sketchbook might still be found. The strange boy stood among the tombstones, watching me.

"You have got to be kidding," I said, and almost kept going. But something snapped hard as a rubber band against my ribs and I veered toward him instead. At the edge of the grass, I dropped the bike and stalked toward him.

"Why did you tell me you were looking for Culver Washington?" I demanded. Thunder rumbled in the distance.

"What? I didn't." He stood beside the grave of Ward Bodie Buchanan, 1822-1868. The marker read, *A Gallant Soldier. An Honest man.* "You said, 'what do I call you?' And I told you."

"Do you think I'm an idiot?" I cried. "Did you imagine I wasn't going to find out he's been dead two hundred years? Why are you messing with me? Who put you up to this? Was it Bobby Hamilton?"

"Hamilton." He scratched the back of his wrist. "I helped Horace Hamilton with his affairs. Trimmed him. Dressed him. Shined his boots 'til I saw my face in 'em."

"Cut the crap." I was done being made a fool of. "Run along home and I won't have to call the sheriff to pick you up for, what, loitering? Harassment? Compulsive lying?"

His back stiffened. "I've never born false witness in my life. Mister Josiah –"

"Cut it out," I said. "It's not funny, so stop wasting your time. And mine. Leave. Vamoose." I flicked my fingers at him.

"I don't understand what vamoose is," he said. "But I tell you truly, I want to leave. But I can't."

"Right," I said. "Nobody to pick you up. For what, three days? Wait," I surveyed the area, "is this some crazy Civil War reenactment?" I'd heard about those. I peered around the tombstones, hoping desperately people wouldn't start popping out from behind the markers.

Maybe it was one of those awful punked TV shows. I hated those things. I'd already experienced enough humiliation for a lifetime, thank you very much. I squinted at him. "This isn't a skit for TV, is it?"

"What's teevee?" he said. Thunder rumbled overhead.

"Okay," I said. "You're not going to level with me. Fine. I've got better things to do than stand around with some loser who can't even admit when he's been caught." In two strides, I was halfway to the road.

"Wait."

I jumped to find him right behind me.

"Jeez," I said, "stop sneaking up on me."

"You're the only one who can see me," he said.

"Duh, I'm the only one here."

"No," he said, "in the last, what did you say? Two hundred years?" His lower lip quivered.

"Look, you won't give me a straight answer. Who dropped you off? Who put you up to this?"

"Two hundred years is a long time to be bound," he said.

"Okay. Bye, now."

"Why would I still be here, if I could leave?"

"I have no idea. What's keeping you?"

He scratched his elbow and stared in the direction of the hotel. "I ain't sure."

"Give me one good reason I shouldn't walk away and leave you here to rot."

He blinked his long, curling lashes. "Because you see things."

"What're you talking about?" Thunder rumbled and I glanced skyward.

"Silver flashes of light," he said. "And sometimes shadowy ones. You startle when they appear."

"How do you..." I hesitated, "what are they?"

"Angels, maybe," he said. "I ain't sure. But they don't scare me as much as the dark ones."

"You see them, too?"

He shrugged. "I get a glimpse. A spiked wing. The tip of a broadsword now and then."

"You are so totally messing with me."

"Are you dead?" he said.

I jumped back. "What? You mean spiritually?"

"No." He held out his palm. "Like me."

"Buddy," I raised a hand to block his craziness from reaching me. "I was kidding before about you being crazy, but you...you..." I was at a loss for words. I needed to get away.

"If you're not dead," he moved toward me, his bare feet brushing the leaves without stirring them, "how can you see them? How can you see me?"

This was not happening. "Who told you about me?" I said. "About my accident?"

"You mean the horseless carriage?"

"No. In Shelby. Before I got here." I clutched the bandana at my neck. Who in Fairly could possibly know? Mama would never tell. I hadn't talked to anybody outside the hotel and certainly not about that.

"You were struck by another strange carriage?"

"No. I have no idea who goaded you into this," I stabbed a finger at him, "but I am not going to discuss my past with you or anybody else. You think I'm going to make the same mistake again? I am not. So, go ahead and play your little mind games on somebody else. It's evil. Wicked. I can't imagine how you – you live with yourself."

The boy's voice was soft. "Stop."

"What?"

"Over your right shoulder. A dark one. Duck."

I dropped to a crouch as the air whooshed above me. A black-tipped blade flashed and was gone. Thunder rumbled so loud it shook the ground.

"What was that?" I peered from my crouch, my legs trembling so bad I wasn't sure I could stand.

He fixed his gaze on me. "I ain't lying," he said. "And I need your help."

CHAPTER 9

Of course he's a ghost. Because, what with my dying and being brought back to life and seeing angels and maybe demons and getting kicked out of school and having to move and leave my golden retriever behind, only to get run over by some dude in a golf cart apparently wasn't crazy enough.

Why is this happening to me, God? I glanced skyward. Gray clouds scuttled against the eerie green backdrop. One morphed into a race horse. I shook the image away. *Focus, Cat, focus.* Thunder rumbled on top of us. I struggled not to dwell on the strangeness of the sunset or the trees darkening around me.

"Okay," I said to Culver and scrubbed my eye. "I'll play along. What's your story? You were a soldier? You died and got stuck here? That sucks. Welcome to hell."

He blinked.

"Awkward kidding aside," I said, "how come you're stuck? And what makes you think I can fix it?"

"I ain't sure," he said. "But it might have something to do with Horace."

"Your master?"

"We was blood brothers."

"Right." I nodded. "Blood brothers." Because that was so common in the Old South.

"I failed him," Culver said. "I was supposed to take care of him. He wanted me to do something for him. Something to save his life. But I couldn't bring myself to do it."

"Uh, huh. So how do we find out if it's Horace keeping you here? Are there some kind of ghost experts we can consult?" The Hasher twins and their fascination with Red Maggie came to mind, but I dismissed the thought.

He scratched one foot over the other. "We had this old slave woman, Queenie, back on the farm."

"Of course you did." This had to be some reality show. I simply couldn't see the cameras.

"She practiced voodoo," he said. "Talked to the dead. Truth be told, there was some mighty strange doings in her cabin."

"Well, I have no idea where to find a voodoo priestess," I said. "Went to a museum once in New Orleans. Pretty lame. It probably wouldn't help. You happen to know Red Maggie?"

"Who?"

"Never mind. I don't suppose we could simply dig up your bones and salt them good like on TV?"

"This teevee," he said, "what is it?"

"It's a box. With moving pictures. Forget it. Anyway, so we figure out why you're still here and we fix it, right? Let's start with some details. You died in the war."

"Not exactly."

"What exactly? You were this Horace Hamilton's slave, valet, whatever?" Thunder rumbled and a streak of lightning flashed beyond the pines.

"I don't remember much before Horace and the big house at Oak Grove," he said. "I don't rightly know where I come from. Some say Georgia. Some say the Carolinas. I don't remember much. Mister Josiah, Horace's daddy, loved to tell me he bought me for nothing more than a red silk handkerchief. But I happen to know he bought me for a handkerchief plus his favorite saddle. He tried to give twenty dollars and the silk handkerchief, but the solicitor wasn't interested. What he was hankering for was Mister Josiah's finely buffed saddle, worn close as a glove.

"Mister Josiah said, 'No sir. Not gonna part with Bessie,' and he patted the saddle. 'I got her exactly the way I want her.' But Horace, barely seven at the time, tugged on his sleeve and said, 'Daddy, I want him.'

"I couldn't have been more'n five years old myself. I mostly remember what Horace told me. And he told me he wanted me something fierce. He was a pretty boy. Prettier than his sister Adeline, with hair that shone dark as the nighttime sky. And skin so pale you could nearly see clear through to his bones.

"His daddy said he wasn't trading his prized saddle for no scrawny young'un. He couldn't even speculate as to how I might develop. Or whether I had any smarts at all.

"Horace said, 'I'll teach him, daddy. I'll train him good. He's gonna make me a fine companion.'

"Mister Josiah said he ain't looking to buy no companion, especially not with his favorite saddle.

"Horace said, 'But Daddy, I need a boy. I'm by myself in that big ole house.'

"'You got your sister.'

"'She don't care nothing about man stuff.'

"'You ain't a man.'

"Horace puffed out his chest and said, 'I'm gonna be and I need somebody to help me.'

"'Thought you's gonna teach him,' Mister Josiah said. 'Which way's it gonna be? Who's gonna teach who?'

"'We gonna teach each other,' Horace said.

"Mister Josiah turned to me and said, 'What's your name?'

"I said, 'Everybody just calls me Boy.'

"'It's up to you,' he said.

"I pondered on it awhile. There was an old slave who died in the fields wherever I come from. He was kind to me. And there was the first president of the United States. Couldn't ask for a more important name than that. 'Culver,' I said. 'Culver Calhoun Washington.'

"'Well, that's a mouthful.' Mister Josiah laughed. 'An awful big name for a scrawny young rooster.'

"'I'll grow into it,' I said.

"The man never did say no to his first born, not so long as I lived. Which was okay by me. Somebody somewhere wanted me, and that weren't a bad thing. And I come to know how much Mister Josiah loved his old saddle 'cause he never let me hear the end of it. That's how I come to be at Oak Grove, in the house of the Hamiltons. I could've done worse. But Mister Josiah sure did rib me about his red silk handkerchief. Laws, sometimes I wish to high heaven he would've let it go.

"Horace and me growed up side by side. One time we's throwing corn cobs at the hogs and Horace fell into the pen and nearly got trampled to death. I jumped in and covered him, not thinking about myself atall. I couldn't bear to see Horace hurt. He dragged me, bloodied and bruised, to old Queenie, 'cause his daddy'd be awful sore if he'd known we'd been messing with his hogs. Give us both the switch. But, lordy, I was sorely pained and hollering. Horace kept covering my mouth and telling me to hush before his daddy got after us.

"Inside her cabin, Old Queenie laid hands on my back and it healed straight away, no salve, no nothing, like magic. I couldn't see it. But Horace did. He got this queer look in his eye and kept muttering something I couldn't understand. I kept asking, 'What, Horace? What you saying?'

"That's when he pressed his lips to my back. Careful at first, then all over. Fevered with the miracle of it, I reckon. I had no idea what to do. So, I sat there, hunched over the table, with Horace's cool lips pressed to the back of my neck.

Old Queenie watched with glittering eyes and a strange twist to her lips, sort of a smile, but not. I crossed my arms over my bare chest as Horace's lips crept to hover near my ear. Which I thought was mighty peculiar. But like I said, there was always talk of strange doings in Old Queenie's cabin.

"She said, 'Say, you two boys is practically brothers. You want to be blood brothers?' Her cackle set my skin to crawling. Horace broke off, lit with some unholy glow and she smiled at him. I never seen her smile before or hence. She grabbed his trembling jaw and smiled into his eyes, the same color as hers. And then she kissed his lips. Next thing I know, she drew a thin blade across our wrists, one white, one black. She commingled our blood and spouted some gibberish we couldn't understand.

"Then it was over. She pushed us out the door and slammed it. All I remember was her cackling as we stumbled off the porch, struggling to remember how in tarnation we got there. Horace kept saying, 'You're mine, now. Really mine and can't nobody separate us.' Which I thought was mighty queer 'cause everybody knew his daddy done bought me five years before.

"After that, the old butler, Folmar, learned me the ways of the valet. I cottoned to the word right off. I learned to shine Horace's boots 'til I saw my grin in 'em. I brought his morning hot chocolate while he was still abed, topped with a dollop of thick cream, the way he liked it.

"I sat with him through his lessons and helped him with the ciphering when he struggled. Master Duke didn't want no darkie in the classroom. But he wanted to keep his job. It got so he was harder on me than Horace and he'd rap my knuckles something fierce with his wicked stick even when I got the answer right.

"I weren't allowed to read, though. It was the law. And even Mister Josiah wouldn't break the law. Not for me. But I picked up words here and there without nobody knowing. Horace read to me from the Good Book. Or some books his daddy ordered from a place north of Atlanta. Tales of pirates and adventure on the high seas.

"That's what Mobile Bay was to me, as mysterious as the high seas. When I finally got to the hospital that used to be a fancy hotel, I'd lie on my pallet and try not to think on the awful, bloody war. The things we done and the things done to us. I'd gaze across the water and dream of what lay beyond.

"Maybe that's why I'm still here," he said. "I've done some terrible things. Seen worse things than I could've ever imagined. But I went along with everything Horace asked me to, except in the end."

A jagged streak of lightning chased the sky and I flinched. Thunder rumbled closer. Culver ignored it.

"When we started hearing rumors of war, it was all Horace talked about," he said. "He was barely four and ten."

The wind sent a shiver along my spine. My bandana had dried stiff around my neck. I glanced at the hotel, but Culver seemed oblivious to the approaching storm. Of course he did. He was dead.

"Horace's talk of war drove his daddy to drink and his mama from the dinner table in tears on more than one occasion. Nothing could muzzle him on the subject."

There was a flash to my left. Lightning, or an angel?

"When war finally broke out," Culver said, "Horace's daddy refused to let him sign up."

A crow landed on the power line above the trees. He ruffled his feathers in a fluff before settling into a sleek black comma against the troubled sky, head tilted as if judging Culver's story.

"But Horace had this way about him. He could talk roosters into laying eggs. When he got into his daddy's whiskey and Mister Josiah found out, Horace talked old Folmar into taking the blame. Horace weren't more than twelve at the time. Folmar confessed and got sent to the sweatbox for three days. It nearly killed him. Only reason Mister Josiah let him out early was 'cause he got tired of fetching his own brandy.

"Well, wasn't that convenient," I said sarcastically.

"That was just Horace's way. He was sweet to his sister, and laws, how he loved his old bluetick hound, Beaumont. But his daddy couldn't hold him off forever. On Horace's eighteenth birthday, they hosted a fancy ball at the big house to give him a send-off to war. I dressed him for the festivities, then snuck downstairs to peer through the windows in the dark. It was mighty fine to see them colors swirling around the ballroom to a lively tune."

"I've seen the movies," I said.

"Horace didn't care nothing for it, but lord, how I loved to watch them swirl through the new dance called the waltz. The preachers were fit to be tied. A boy's hand on a girl's waist with nothing but the silk of her dress separating his skin and hers? Who would've thought it? Horace appeared bored with the idea and the pretty girls. But he promised to teach me to dance.

Thunder clapped loud enough to shiver the tombstones. I glanced at the hotel, feeling as if I'd stepped into an episode of the *Twilight Zone*.

"I wasn't no more than sixteen when I followed Horace to war," Culver said. "Mister Josiah sent me along to tend to his first-born's needs and keep him from trouble. The night before we left, girls gave Horace their hair ribbons, strips of rainbow, and flowers he dried and pressed into a book he carried to keep his balances and figures to account to his daddy back home."

Book. My sketchbook. I'd been sidetracked again. Dang. I had to find it.

"I watched from the shadows," Culver said, "but Horace found me and pressed a ribbon into my hand, and then a wilting camellia. At dawn the next morning, we presented ourselves to the 32nd Regiment in Mobile for training. And lordy, what a ragtag bunch we was. By then, most soldiers couldn't afford matching uniforms. Some of 'em didn't even own a pair of shoes."

He frowned. "I know now, seeing war up close, there ain't nothing to compare to it. It'll kill your very soul. I've seen more heads and legs blown apart than I care to recall. I've seen docs and sometimes cooks saw off limbs eaten with gangrene. Stumbled over bloody buckets of arms and legs and hacked-off feet. And them not even men, most of 'em still boys, screaming for their mamas 'cause the laudanum done run out."

"Please," I flashed a palm, "you don't have to say more."

"But Horace and me," he said, "we got through it together. I didn't have no weapon, but I was there, doing his wash, tending him when he took sick." He scratched the top of his head.

"After we were run out of Stone River, Horace got himself into a bit of trouble. It wouldn't be proper to explain the nature of it to a young lady such as yourself."

I swiped hair out of my eyes.

"Truth be told," he said, "when Horace got into trouble, Captain turned on him. It hurt him bad. All he ever wanted was to defend his land and make his family proud. But when Captain picked a handful of men for a dangerous mission, our real troubles began."

He scrubbed his brow, paler than before. "The Union army was moving southward fast. Vicksburg had fallen. Old Farragut was tearing into Mobile Bay. But here at home, it was mostly covert, minor skirmishes. Yankees infiltrating and plundering, trouncing one farm after another, setting fire to everything along the way.

"A band of us, seven in all, was ordered to sneak up on the Yankees camped out at the Houston house, south of Tuscaloosa, and report back as to the count of soldiers and cannons and such. If we's to find ourselves in a position to provide a bit of devilment without getting caught, we's to do so. Turn horses loose. Set fire to tents. Steal muskets, rifles, whatever we could manage.

"For two days, we crept through woods and thickets, risking no campfires to draw attention to ourselves and eating nothing but hardtack or a bit of beef jerky nearly too tough to chew. And if we's lucky, a rotting apple or two along the way. I heard men was eating their own shoelaces elsewhere, so I didn't complain.

"Once we reached the Houston place, our bellies growled so loud I was afraid they'd give us away. I shouldn't have worried. By the time we arrived at the farm, them Yankees was whooping it up something big."

"That's how you died," I said, "in the raid?"

"No, miss." He scratched the back of his neck. "I didn't die at the hands of the enemy."

"Then who?" A car rumbled along the lane, heading toward the country club. I turned long enough to see it streak white through the trees. "Was it friendly fire?"

When he didn't answer, I turned back. Thunder rumbled overhead. Lightning streaked across hallowed ground. And Culver Washington had disappeared.

CHAPTER 10

I returned the rickety bike to the hotel as the storm unleashed its fury on the bay. I tossed and turned that night after retiring my sling permanently. I spent the next few days at the hotel, running errands for Mama, helping Portia from England with afternoon tea, folding towels at the spa, and staying out of Ed Winer's way.

It was Thursday before I could catch the shuttle into town, offering to pick up a prescription Mama took for panic attacks at the drugstore. She was running low on her medication, and given the stress she was under, couldn't afford to run out.

Her attacks were scary. She'd had the first one after my accident and thought she was having a heart attack. She struggled to breathe. Her hands went numb.

But the one after Daddy left, before she got fired, I'm glad I wasn't there for it. She passed out at work and hit her head on her desk. By the time Nana and I got to the hospital, her face was bruised and her right eye swollen shut.

I didn't want to blame Daddy. Even Nana said he couldn't have known his shenanigans would trigger more of them.

But I did blame him for getting her fired from the mayor's office. He'd started drinking again, like he did before I was born. It got so bad he lost his job at the trucking company he managed. He stole Mama's laptop from work and pawned it for liquor money, breaching the city's security. It was incredibly sad, but there was nothing to do but shake those memories loose and keep going.

When the shuttle dropped me off, I didn't go straight to the drugstore, but headed to the one place I could always find answers, no matter what the question.

Fairly Avenue, the main thoroughfare through town, dead-ended at Primrose Street, with a fat-columned, green-shuttered antebellum home at the end of the block. The town library.

I reached the building and pushed my way inside the front door, expecting to escape the stifling heat. But the air weighed as wet and heavy inside as out. The main floor smelled of floor wax and mildewed paper. Dust motes floated in a milky haze and patches of sunlight beamed from the upstairs windows. Inefficient air conditioning units grumbled and huffed cool air as loud as battered beasts from within its cavernous depths.

A grand staircase swept upward to the second floor. To the right of it, a girl perched on a stool behind an oak desk. Hunched over a book, a long braid of black hair streaked with lurid green hung over one shoulder. A gold stud pierced her nose.

Besides the juvenile delinquents who'd run me over, she was the first person my age I'd had contact with outside the hotel. It seemed like a good time to make new friends who were A, not trying to kill me, and B, actually not dead. I approached her with what I hoped was an engaging grin. "Whatcha reading?" I said. "Is it any good?"

She heaved a sigh, rolled her heavily-kohled eyes, and flipped the book cover for me to see. She stared past my shoulder as I read something about vampires, or zombies, or both.

"Cool," I said. She returned to reading. "Um," I interrupted again, "can you tell me where the history section is?" She heaved a heavier sigh and pointed a purple-polished pinkie toward the second floor.

I could've researched Culver on the library's computer. It had been long enough since my accident. Heck, I could've done it back at the hotel's business center. But I couldn't bring myself to do it. Not after everything that happened in Shelby and at school. It was silly. They couldn't touch me here. But it still scraped my insides raw. An invasion so deep I couldn't help but stuff it, bury it with everything else, just to keep my feet moving.

I climbed the stairs to find an air conditioning unit rattling so violently it threatened to dislodge itself from the window. I loved books better than computers, anyway. Perusing the shelves, I pulled a half dozen on history covering the Civil War and settled myself at a scarred oak table near the stairs. I lifted the first tome and flipped through it.

For well over an hour, I waded through battle after battle before I found anything about the Mobile Bay area. Another twenty minutes passed before I found a few paragraphs about the Fairly Grand.

The hotel was converted into a hospital for wounded Confederate soldiers in 1863, which explained Culver's confusion in our original meeting. Most of the soldiers who came through were survivors of the Battle of Vicksburg.

As I read, I dabbed at a trickle of sweat behind my ear. I'd left my hair loose and while I turned pages with one hand, I bunched a chunk of it in the other and waved the makeshift ponytail to create a breeze. It would've felt good, too, if I hadn't had to wrap a stupid scarf around my neck.

The fuchsia one was not my favorite. It was a lighter cotton, but a scratchy vein of silver ran through it. However, it did contrast nicely with my green Converse.

The front door opened and voices murmured below. I pulled a red book sporting a battle flag toward me and flipped through it. More of the same. Battles. Skirmishes. Confederate generals. Union soldiers. Conflicting reasons for the war.

Footsteps creaked on the stairs as I reached the photo section at the center of the book. Black and white faces stared at me from glossy pages.

Some soldiers stood in uniform, some in rags. Some wore boots, but many were barefoot. And then I found him, staring at me with those round, white eyes. Culver Calhoun Washington.

Was his name printed anywhere? I scoured the photo caption for confirmation.

"There you are." A hand clamped my shoulder and I slammed the book closed. My breath held. The silver tip of a sword flashed in the corner of my eye. I might've swayed in my seat.

"Whoa, little lady," the voice said. "Didn't mean to scare you."

I steadied myself with the table, found my breath, and turned to find a small plug of a woman at my side. She stood barely five feet tall, sturdy as an Easter Island statue in a purple pantsuit with a small American flag pinned to her lapel. Her hair swooped around her head in a tease of steel wool. A gash of bright red lips revealed tiny, terrier teeth.

She stuck out her hand. "Mayor Harrie Ann," she said.

I couldn't think of anything to do but take her hand and pretend not to wince as stubby fingers bit into mine and shot pain throughout my injured elbow and shoulder.

"Some call me Hurricane Harrie," she said, "but don't let that scare you. You can call me Harrie Ann." She released me and I curled my fingers into my palm and flexed feeling back into them.

"You're new in town, aren't you?" she said. "Saw you get off the shuttle down the street. I sure do like to get to know my people. You're from the hotel, eh?"

"Yes, ma'am."

"Tried to catch you, but blasted Billy Boudrow stopped me on the corner with some nonsense about bringing his mule to the Celebration of the Dead ceremony in August. You hear about our big shindig?"

I shook my head.

"It's similar to the Hispanic Day of the Dead."

I frowned.

She laughed. "It's not as morbid as it sounds. It's a celebration we borrowed from our south of the border friends to honor our heroes. You know, Fairly's founding father, our heritage, that sort of thing?"

"Maybe I heard something about it at the hotel."

"Good. Good. We can definitely use the publicity. We're going to block off Fairly Avenue. Give pony rides. Rent those bouncy balloon thingies kids love. Sell corn dogs and cotton candy and sugared skulls. And of course, our world famous frozen lemonade."

"Frozen what?"

"You haven't experienced one of those over at Rexall Drugs? Well, you have simply got to try one. World famous, I tell you."

As diminutive as she was, I still felt at a disadvantage.

"You're obviously not a tourist," she said, "so you must be Cat Turner, the new girl in town."

"Yes, ma'am." I was more than a little unnerved.

"Heard about you and your mama." Harrie Ann propped hands on her hips flashing a simple gold wedding band. "Heard about the trouble you had over there."

"The fire," I said.

"Well, yeah, but I was talking about your accident. Heard you got yourself run over by a golf cart." It sounded ridiculous the way she said it.

"Yeah," I said, "some idiot apparently wasn't looking where he was going."

"Bobby Hamilton, I believe."

"Yeah," I said, "the sheriff's nephew. Along with his lame cousin, Tate. They didn't even get into trouble."

"Hmmmm." She cocked her head. "So, how're you doing? Arm's out of the sling, I see. Heard you got stitches." The mayor certainly knew her gossip.

"The doctor said I only had to wear the sling for a week." I fingered my chin. "He said the stitches would dissolve eventually."

"Got run over by an F150 pickup truck myself last year," she said. "You believe that? Came away with barely a scratch. At my age. Go figure. You settling in, Cat? You and your mama?"

I nodded, but she didn't give me time to elaborate.

"Glad you found the library." She surveyed the shelves, the soaring ceiling. "It's my pride and joy. My husband's great-granddaddy built it back in 1892 after he founded the town. Of course, back then it was his town house. But I added the sculpture garden." She strolled to the window and stared at the bronze children and dogs frolicking on the lawn.

"Same artist is sculpting his statue for the celebration. It wasn't my idea. I thought it a bit much. My oldest boy, Bedford, talked me into it. I reckon it's a little vain, myself. But the old man was the reason Fairly became a town." She strolled back to me. "Glad to see you're interested in our history."

She spun the book around with a finger to read the title. "This one should have some history about the Fairly Grand in it."

"Yes, ma'am." I pulled the book to me and said, "I've got to go." I gathered the rest of the books sprawled on the table. "I've got to get Mama's prescription filled."

"The Rexall Drugstore," the mayor said. "I'll walk you over."

I hesitated with my arms full of books. "That's not necessary. I've got to reshelve these."

"Don't be silly," she said, "I'll help," and took the top three books. I shoved the book with Culver's picture into the wrong place so no one would check it out before I returned.

When the last book was shelved, the mayor said, "Let's go get you a lemonade."

"Really," I said, "it's not necessary."

"Of course it's necessary," she said. "Your first one ought to be Fairly's treat."

And I could think of nothing else to do but follow her through the musty haze, down the stairs, and back out into the simmering heat.

CHAPTER 11

As we strolled west along Fairly Avenue, the mayor kept up a running commentary. "We've got a few businesses the others revolve around. Merchant's Hardware, over there on the corner, has been there as long as I've been alive." She peered at me. "That'd be eighty-two years."

The hardware store sat low and flat, with a row of white rocking chairs lining the front. A green canvas awning shaded the sidewalk adorned with hanging baskets of purple petunias and pink impatiens.

"Some smart guy tried to get old H.M. to change its name to something catchier like, 'The Turn of the Screw' or some such nonsense, but he wouldn't go for it." We approached the traffic light and she gestured to our left. "The Pen and Page Bookstore's been around nearly fifty years and draws a good number of writers for readings and book signings. You probably won't see Stephen King there, but we had John Grisham once, and that little red-headed gal, Fannie Flagg."

I got a glimpse of it, two blocks behind the drugstore as we crossed the street. On the corner, yellow daylilies and orange zinnias spilled over brick sidewalks. More baskets of pink petunias dangled from wrought iron posts.

"The Burger Barn, the Pizza Emporium, and Bud's Bar are all stable businesses," she continued. "You've enjoyed a burger at the Burger Barn, right?"

I shook my head and dabbed at the sweat tickling my neck.

"Mama and I haven't gotten to town much."

"Mighty tasty," she said. "You've got to try one. The boutiques come and go," she said. "The Style Shop doesn't sell as many designer labels as it used to." She nodded at an elderly woman adjusting a mannequin in the store window. "Janelle's is now strictly old-lady leisure and travel wear. But then we've got a lot of elderly gals who visit us on a regular basis, what with the art festival in May." A bold, zebra-print scarf in the window of the Style Shop caught my eye.

"The wedding shop's down the street," she said. "Your mama's probably getting to know them real well. And Flo's Florist." We stopped in front of the drugstore's worn brick facade. A bumble bee buzzed a patch of yellow and orange Gerbera daisies at our feet.

"The Rexall here was the first business in town. Been here since 1872." I followed the tall, narrow building three stories up to the pale blue sky.

"It's coming back, the town." The mayor surveyed the main thoroughfare. "We've still got a reputation for being an artists' community, on account of the artist colony over on Vermilion Circle. For example, Jane Sanders is designing jewelry on Crimson Lake Lane. Oh, hey, Aletha."

A woman with a head of white, tightly-curled hair shuffled toward us in a tent of a dress, a white handbag slung over a trembling arm, her fluffy pink slippers slapping the pavement.

"Lordamercy, Harrie Ann," the woman wheezed, "I got to get my bursitis medicine. Shoulder's been hurting like the dickens."

"Sorry to hear it," the mayor said and patted the woman's stooped shoulder. "Give Hershel my love, will you?" The woman nodded, and with a wave, disappeared into the store.

"Artists by nature are restless and move around a lot," she continued. "It's blown glass today, ceramic snakes tomorrow. The trick is to keep it fresh. Make sure each time people come to Fairly, they see something they've never seen before."

I wondered how much a frozen lemonade could possibly be worth and glanced around for someone, anyone, to rescue me. I fanned myself with the hem of my scarf.

"Then, of course, there's our new Celebration of the Dead ceremony I mentioned earlier." Harrie Ann waved to an elderly man in overalls who dropped into one of the rocking chairs in front of the hardware store.

"With all the Hispanics immigrating to Alabama and new legislation coming out of Montgomery, we wanted to make sure our south of the border friends feel more welcome. The idea started in Central

America, I believe. Celebrating those who've gone before us. After the war, my husband's great-granddaddy, Horace Tidewater Hamilton, turned this muddy little one-lane outpost into a thriving town."

A squeak escaped before I could stifle it.

"You've heard of Horace?" Harrie Ann said. "Thanks to him, Fairly's one of the few small towns that prospered instead of being swallowed up by those thieving carpet baggers after the war. The Fairly Grand's certainly helped along the way."

"What can you tell me about Horace Hamilton?" I said.

She squinted along the avenue and I shifted my weight as the sun burned the top of my head.

"He was a good man," she said. "A real pioneer. And a Civil War hero. Only one to receive the Confederate Medal for Valor. My son, Bedford, has it displayed in his office." I stared longingly through the window into the cool, dark recesses of the drugstore, my need for information battling my desire for escape.

"I've been mayor thirty-five years," she said. "My husband, God rest his soul, was mayor before me. We've seen some lean times. But we've seen some incredible growth, too. Now's the time to enjoy the success we've achieved and pass our heritage along to the younger generation. Like you, Cat. You'll settle in here, won't you?"

"I hope so."

"Get to know your peers? Overlook their mistakes? We're all just trying to get along, aren't we? Compromise isn't such a dirty word."

"Yes, ma'am."

"Try not to make yourself a target, Cat. Teen years can be awfully tough. Wouldn't live those over again for all the gold in Billy Boudrow's teeth."

"Yes, ma'am."

"I believe you'll find if you give this town half a chance, it'll do you proud." She squinted at a man exiting the hardware store. "Here in Fairly," she said, "we believe in giving everybody a fair shake. We'll judge you on your own merits, not a bunch of hearsay. If you treat folks right, they'll respond in kind."

"Yes, ma'am." I swiped the sweat trickling near my ear.

"We're a small town, Cat. Everybody here tends to know everybody's business. That's a good thing if you're in a spot of trouble and need help. On the other hand, it's a bad thing if you're the one causing the trouble. Know what I mean, Cat?"

I had absolutely no idea what she meant. I said, "Of course."

"Sheriff Hamilton runs a tight ship. He doesn't allow much in the way of shenanigans. You fly right and don't cause any more trouble and he can be your best friend."

Wait. What were we talking about?

"He's the most laid back of all my boys and he's got a good heart. Takes his job mighty seriously. He truly wants to help the kids in this town stay on the straight and narrow. Know what I mean, Cat? You go to church?"

My head felt light on my shoulders. Did I really want to share my current boycott of God with a total stranger? I thought not.

"There's First Baptist," she said, "most of my family goes there. Then you've got the Methodists, not as strict, but still a fine congregation. Our Baptist-Methodist softball game in the spring raises money for the Children's Ranch outside of town. Baptists have won three years straight."

"Ma'am?" It was difficult following the conversation. What was it she said about Sheriff Hamilton being one of her boys? The basket of petunias swayed in front of me.

"There's the Catholic church over on Cerulean Circle," she said. "You aren't Catholic, are you, Cat? No, you didn't look it. And then there's the non-denominational church out on the bay. I'm not sure about a church that doesn't seem to commit to anything. But my grandson, Tate, sure loves it."

Whoa, whoa, whoa. My brain was sparking. Maybe from the sun burning a hole through the top of my head.

"You've met Tate, right?" she said. "He worries his uncles something awful. But I suppose it's the nature of sixteen-year-old boys. He's a good kid. Needs a fire lit under his behind as far as grades go. But still, dependable as a cocker spaniel."

Sheriff Hamilton. Tate. Bobby Hamilton. Harrie Ann.

"Well," she finally pushed the door open to the drugstore and a bell jingled, "let's go get you that lemonade."

I followed her inside, relieved at the break from the heat. We strolled past toothbrushes and toothpaste, bandages and antiseptic wash, pain relievers and antacids, toward the back of the store. It took me the entire length of the aisle to snap the pieces into place and realize I'd actually called the mayor's grandson an idiot.

CHAPTER 12

I shoveled in iced lemonade as I meandered along Carmine Street toward the bookstore. Mama's bottle of Zoloft rattled in the pocket of my jean shorts. I finally escaped the mayor when she stayed behind to talk to the pharmacist about recurring hip pain.

Tart and sweet, the lemonade dried the sweat above my lip, at least for the moment. I gobbled it too fast and pressed my tongue to the roof of my mouth to ease the brain freeze.

The scent of grilled burgers drifted toward me from across the street. The Burger Barn sat nestled between the Carmine Street Bakery and Acuppa Joe's coffee shop. Unbelievably, at a table in the middle of the courtyard sat the local miscreants, Bobby Hamilton and his cousin, Tate Channing, drinking their soy lattes or whatever, from insulated cups.

Bobby's golf cart was parked on the street, sideways, in a handicapped space. I backed into the shadows of the antique store. Bobby sat in pink shorts and popping a collar with his dark hair tucked behind his ears and brushing his shoulders. His big, fat docksiders sprawled into the chair at the next table. An elderly woman shuffled her way from the bakery and stopped at his outstretched legs. He refused to move, forcing her to circle around his table to reach the street.

Tate sat hunched in a tight tee screaming some obscene rock band, basketball shorts below his knees, black high tops with no laces, and a day's growth of blond fuzz on his ridiculously sculpted jaw. If

Bobby Hamilton looked like he'd just bounced off the tennis court, his cousin appeared to have just crawled out of the gutter after a three-day bender.

Bobby's cup was halfway to his lips when he noticed me. He lowered his drink to the table and said something to his cousin. Tate twisted in his seat to stare in my direction. I should've run, but I pressed deeper into the brick store behind me.

Bobby's nostrils flared as if he smelled rotten fish off the bay. He said something to Tate and took a swig from his cup. It triggered a heated exchange that ended in Tate laughing at his cousin and scratching his cheek with his middle finger.

Bobby's feet hit the patio brick. He scraped his chair back and snatched his cup off the table. Tate continued to laugh and for a second, I thought Bobby might toss his drink in his cousin's face. Instead he stalked to his golf cart, climbed aboard, puttered out of the parking space on regular, eighteen-inch tires.

I shoveled in lemonade as the golf cart disappeared from view, then glanced back at Tate. He hesitated for a second, then stood and strolled toward me. I nearly choked on my spoon.

As nervous as a squirrel caught in the middle of the road, I debated whether to stay or run. His grimace eased into a grin. But as he stepped off the curb, a black Camaro rumbled past, giving me enough time to turn and run to the drugstore.

I had no idea where to go. The mayor might still be inside and I didn't want to risk running into her again. The light turned red, so I flew across Fairly Avenue. Hitting the curb, I glanced back as Tate crossed after me. I panicked and hightailed it down the street, past the hardware store, a sliver of a hat shop, a record store, and ducked into the next doorway.

CHAPTER 13

I waited inside the doorway for my vision to adjust to the dimness. An antique chandelier fashioned from deer antlers flickered weak light overhead. A desk lamp glowed green at the far end of a long counter. The store smelled of musty, dry excavations and murky tombs. And maybe a little wet fur.

"Can't bring that in here," a voice said beyond the desk lamp.

I glanced at my cup of lemonade. "I'm nearly finished," I said.

"Take it out."

I stared out the window. Tate Channing strolled toward the store. I shrank from the door and pressed myself into a wall of shelves as he stopped outside the window. Then kept going.

A full-size skeleton grinned at me with knotty fingers propped in a wave. I stepped further into the store onto a ragged strip of faded rug and found myself surrounded by the oddest collection I'd ever seen.

Skulls lined the shelves next to the skeleton. Mink. Ostrich. Camel. Labeled by peeling strips of faded paper taped beneath them. A scratching sound came from the back of the store.

I passed a mounted assortment of bats from around the world. Fruit bats, brown bats, vampire bats. Next to the bats were shadow boxes displaying beetles, scorpions, butterflies.

Opposite the insects, a glass cabinet ran the length of the narrow space, showcasing spiders in blocks of resin and exotic beetles mounted in glass domes. A small basket held a collection of sharks' teeth beside a basket of polished stones.

Beneath the glass countertop, a dried rattlesnake curled along-side a fish skeleton. Scorpion paperweights were displayed beside malachite jewelry boxes, bear claws, and jawbones of different shapes and sizes. I licked the lemon stickiness from my lips and peered inside the case at a collection of bones. Penis bones. Mink, fox, coyote. I popped upright.

"What kind of store is this?" I said. "Is this stuff for real?"

"Of course it's real," the voice said. "Each item was legally obtained from around the world. And I've got a license from the Alabama Department of Environmental Conservation to sell them." The man drew a breath. "And I told you to take your drink outside."

I found him at the end of the counter in the far back corner, perched on a stool wearing dusty blue jeans, a faded heather tee, and a scowl dug deep into his broad forehead. His dark hair was thin and edged away from his forehead. I guessed him to be a little older than Mama. Something about the way he sat gave me the idea he could've just as easily been found on a stool on a dark, smoky stage picking at a guitar and singing the blues.

He wielded a long, silver pick in one hand and held a handful of packed dirt or stone in the other. Near him, a stuffed black bear towered on hind feet, paws outstretched. A Mets baseball cap perched between pointed ears. A carpeted staircase led to the second floor with a chain stretched across and a sign that said, *Keep Out.*

I strolled to the bear and ran a finger along a curved claw.

"Don't touch," the man said. "Can't you read? Danged kids."

A sign at the bear's feet, read, *Don't touch Brother Bear!*

"You'll get your sticky mitts all over everything."

"I'm sorry," I said and rubbed my fingertips together. "But they aren't that sticky."

"You can't go around touching everything in here," he said. "And you're always spilling stuff. You know how many times I've cleaned up after you kids?"

I studied my cup. There was barely any lemonade left, melted and sloshing around the bottom. Better to go ahead and get rid of it, and so I tipped it up.

"No!" the man shouted.

Startled, I lowered the cup. "I was just going to finish it so I wouldn't spill it."

"Out." He launched off his stool and stalked toward me, rock-ing Brother Bear on his feet.

I stumbled backward and tripped over a crease in the carpet.

He lunged and caught my cup and knocked it out of my grasp. I hit the wall hard, banging the back of my head before collapsing to the ground. A trio of mounted dragonflies tumbled like giant dominoes on top of me. One of the sharp corners dinged my temple before landing in my lap.

"Look what you've done!" he shouted.

The door opened and Tate Channing filled the doorway.

I groaned and touched the sting in my forehead. I studied the blood on my fingertips.

"Look at this mess," the man said. "You're going to pay for this."

"What's going on?" Tate said.

"Her!" The man stabbed a finger at me. "She spilled one of those stupid lemonades all over everything. I hate those things. I keep telling the druggist I'm going to burn his store to the ground if they don't stop making them. And now she's gone and knocked my prized dragonflies off the wall. They just arrived from Indonesia."

He snatched the one off my lap and held it close to his face. "And she got...blood on it!"

I grabbed the other two off the floor and scrambled to my feet.

"I'll clean them off," I said, and swiped at them ineffectively. On trembling legs, I eased the frames onto the counter and dabbed at the blood trickling into my brow.

"For crying out loud, she's bleeding, Bragg," Tate said. He moved closer to get a better view. "Can you get her a tissue or something?"

"A tissue?" Bragg said. "Do I look like I'm carrying a box of tissues? What about my floor? She spilled freaking lemonade all over the carpet." A small dark stain spread near the fallen cup. Tate laughed.

"That little spot?" he said. "I'll clean it, old man. But can you get her a Band-Aid or something?"

"Yeah," Bragg said, "because my pockets are full of Band-Aids. And don't you 'old man' me."

"Well, it was your frame that cut her. You're lucky she doesn't sue."

"I'm fine," I said and slid a palm along the counter to steady myself as the floor tipped away from me.

"She banged into it," Bragg said. "She's lucky I don't sue her."

"For what," Tate said, "clumsiness?"

"Really, I'm fine." I was a few feet from the door.

"This place is too small, anyway." Tate dropped to his knees and pulled a wadded paper napkin out of his pocket and dabbed at the stain. "You can barely turn around without knocking something off the wall."

"What'd you come in for, anyway?" Bragg said.

I staggered out the door, blinking in the bright sunshine. I stared at the name painted on the window. *Genesis.*

Head pounding, I dabbed at my forehead and hurried toward Fairly Avenue before the crazy store owner could chase me down and have me arrested.

"Genesis, my eye," I snorted. Not much appears to have evolved in that place.

CHAPTER 14

"Hey, you there!"

I turned to find Tate Channing jogging after me, a grin on his stupid mug. A man wearing thick, black-rimmed glasses jostled my elbow and disappeared into the record store with a brown paper bag from the Burger Barn.

My ears hummed. I rounded the corner of Fairly Avenue and ducked into the hardware store. A rush of cold air cooled my cheeks. I maneuvered around plastic lawn chairs and gas grills, galvanized buckets of tiny American flags, citronella candles, and stacks of plastic checkered tablecloths.

The sting of fertilizer mingled with onions from somebody's lunch and freshly-mixed paint. The lemonade soured in my belly and I rubbed it as I side-stepped two men; one with rolled-up shirtsleeves, the other in overalls.

A woman in a navy suit studied brooms hanging on the wall. I passed a table lined with cardboard boxes where a teenage girl dropped an armful of screwdrivers into one of them. Tate found me staring into a box of silver-plated screws.

But once he found me, he didn't appear to have any idea what to do with me. He grabbed a handful of lug nuts and rattled them like dice.

"So, you're okay?" he said.

"Fine," I said, though my head pounded. I moved to study a

galvanized bucket of brass doorknobs.

He sidled next to me and gave me a sideways glance. "You're still bleeding."

I touched the stinging in my forehead and studied my blood-ied finger.

"There's also a trickle there." He pointed at my cheek.

I swiped my thumb at it.

He winced. "You didn't actually get it. Here." He pulled an-other crumpled napkin from his pocket and handed it to me. I stared at the Burger Barn logo. I gave him a you've-got-to-be-kidding look.

He pulled back. "It's clean."

I dabbed at the blood.

"Appears it's already dried."

I crushed the napkin in my fist, my face flamed by this latest humiliation. "I've got to go," I said and brushed past him.

"Hey," he called after me, "I've got your book."

I turned. "What?"

"Your book." Tate rattled the lug nuts in his fist. "Of draw-ings. I found it after the ambulance left for the hospital. Those pictures are really something."

I stalked back to him. "What did you do with them? Did you tear them out? I found one crumpled in the cemetery."

"What? No. That wasn't me."

I glared at him and he stepped back.

"Who tore them out?" I curled my fingers.

He dropped the nuts into the box and stuffed his hands in his pockets. "It was just the one."

"Was it Bobby?"

He shrugged. "He was just fooling around. He didn't mean anything by it. I got the book from him. The rest are fine. Girl," he shook his head, "you have got some imagination."

"I want it back," I said, "now." The thought of Bobby Hamil-ton and his cousin rummaging through my sketchbook and laughing over my drawings sent a shiver to the base of my skull where it met the pounding already there.

"Well, sure," he said. "It's safe. At my house."

"Go get it," I said. "I'll wait."

"Whoa, where's the fire, princess?"

I glared at him, wishing I could burst him into flames. The tips of my ears burned.

"I can't," he said and plucked a screwdriver and tapped it on the side of the box. "I don't have a ride and I live on the other side of town."

"You're so fond of riding around in your cousin's stupid golf cart," I said, "get him to drive you over and back."

He kept tapping. "No can do. He's mad at me."

"Oh, yeah?"

The tapping stopped. "And he won't come back for me. He never does."

"Then I'll go get it," I said. "Tell me where you live and I'll walk."

"Walk?" He snorted and studied the flat head of the screwdriver.

"I want my sketchbook," I said, barely hanging onto my panic. "Now. Before you yahoos do anything else to it."

"I told you, it's safe."

"Excuse me if I don't believe you."

He started tapping again. "Why wouldn't you believe me?"

I raised my scarred elbow. "I just got this out of a sling, thanks to you."

"That wasn't my fault."

"Right. You were just along for the ride. Isn't that what you told the sheriff? Oh, I'm sorry, your uncle?"

"It was an accident. We didn't mean to hurt anybody."

A growl rumbled low in my throat. "Whatever. Why didn't you tell me you had my book before now? I've been searching everywhere for it."

"I haven't seen you until today."

"You knew who I was. Your uncle knew where I was staying."

"I've been busy. And I don't talk to my uncle. Well, much."

"Seriously?" My brows couldn't arch any higher.

"I'll bring it to the hotel."

"Today."

"Jeez, this afternoon."

"Before dark." I turned and his tapping stopped and I stalked out of the store, refusing to turn and see why.

CHAPTER 15

Pacing the lobby in front of the concierge's vacant desk, I was glad Gloria Jackson was nowhere in sight. I wrapped the ends of my scarf around my finger, turned, and let it uncurl. Wrapped, turned, and uncurled. Even the heavy scent of lilies from the towering arrangement on the entrance table couldn't calm my jitters.

As I paced, Mrs. Fischer descended the stairs, as regal as any star on the silver screen. I ducked into the gift shop and hid among the palm-splattered shirts. She stopped at Gloria's empty desk, surveyed the lobby, and moved on to the bar.

I headed for the front door leading to the valet parking to wait for Tate there. A covered walkway connected the hotel to the conference center and I stood in the shade. Gloria strode from the parking lot and I stepped aside to let her pass.

"Oh, Cat," she flipped her expensively-streaked hair off her shoulder, "I have a message for you. A Mr. Channing called." Her smile was smug.

Panic gripped hard.

"It's at my desk." She crooked a French-manicured finger at me and I followed. She leaned over her desk and rummaged through a pile of papers and reservation confirmations until she plucked a pink sticky note from the stack and handed it to me. It read, *Meet me at the Confederate cemetery at 5:30.*

"What time is it now?" I said.

She consulted her Cartier watch. "Five thirty-five." She smirked. "Thought the cemetery was off limits to you."

I stared at the note and pretended to ignore her arched brows. "Guess I don't have a choice. He has something of mine and I need it back." Dang stupid Tate Channing. The words blurred on the page. Why couldn't he do what he said he would? I glanced up and blinked. "Mama doesn't have to know, you know? She would only worry."

Gloria's smile was tight. "We'll see." She sank into the chair behind her desk with a flip of hair. "Run along now." She shooed me with a flutter of nails. "You're late as it is. And boyfriends don't appreciate waiting."

"He's not my boyfriend."

"Whatever." She rummaged through her papers, flicking her fingers at me. "Move along. Some of us have work to do."

Sucking air, I counted one, counted two, and let my breath out noisily as I left. At least Mrs. Fischer didn't treat me like some annoying kid.

Outside, a warm, blustery breeze whipped my ponytail against my cheek and jitterbugged the ends of my scarf around my shoulder. The sky was a yellowish gray with the threat of storms as I trotted along the driveway toward the guard shack.

"Where you headed, Cat Turner?" Pete Bachus, the security guard, stepped outside the guard shack.

"Country club," I lied. "On an errand."

"Storm's a brewing," he said. "Already crossing the Mississippi now. You can't get a ride?"

"I won't be long."

"You know," he said, "more people get struck by lightning in the summer than any other season."

"Yes, sir." I sped to a jog. The cemetery was in sight when the cramp in my side finally forced me to walk. By the time I reached it, my hair was more out of my ponytail than in, and my scarf was clammy with sweat. I swiped my upper lip with the back of my wrist as I left the road and stalked toward Elijah Pickens' remains.

Except for the wind bullying the trees and the scraping of leaves, the cemetery was quiet, with no sign of Tate.

"Hey!" I called to the rusting cannons. Had he left already? Or was he hiding? "What's the deal?" I said. "You were supposed to meet me at the hotel."

Pine needles crunched beneath my sneakers as I eased around the tombstones. "Tate Channing!" I yelled above the wind. "You here?" Thunder grumbled. "Of course you're not here," I said, "who's stupid enough to meet in a cemetery with a storm bearing down?"

Another rumble of thunder drew my attention skyward. A mass of angry clouds scuttled toward the hotel. This was ridiculous. Apparently, he'd come and gone, if he'd meant to meet me at all.

I turned. And screamed.

"You're late," he said. He leaned against Earl Pickens' marble marker next to Elijah's. My sketchbook was tucked between his folded arms and his tight black tee with the sleeves hacked off. His sculpted biceps indicated more than a passing fancy with the gym.

"Give me my book," I said, my fingers itching to tear it from his sweaty paws.

His finger was a windshield wiper swishing. "Uh, uh, uh. You didn't say please."

My voice growled in my throat. "Give...me...my...book."

"Easy, princess," he said, "I just wanted to talk a minute."

"I talk better with my book in my hands."

"See, now I think you'd grab it and run."

"You're holding my book hostage so I'll talk to you?"

"Hostage is an awfully strong word."

"A storm's coming," I said, "and I'd like not to be in it."

He shifted his weight. "A little scary, huh? Being in a grave-yard in the middle of a thunderstorm?"

"No," I said. "It's stupid."

"Anybody ever call you Little Miss Scaredy Cat?"

I rolled my eyes. "No, never." My fists clenched. "Now give me my book before I come over there and take it."

"Oooh," he said, "little kitty's got some claws."

"Give me my book!"

He was at least a head taller than me. So I glanced around for a weapon. A stick. Anything I could threaten him with.

"Teasing aside," he said, "why do you draw them? The angels, demons, whatever."

I swung back to him. "None of your business."

"Seriously."

My chest constricted. I knew how this went. Some idiot's curiosity. Me falling for it, trying to explain. Me getting laughed at. Ridiculed.

And yet.

He appeared so earnest. Sincere. And I desperately wanted someone to understand.

A chunk of hair blew into my eyes and I swiped it away. "They're in my head," I said. "I put them on paper. It's no big deal.

Now, give them to me."

He shifted his weight again. "What'd you mean in your head? You dream about them?"

How could I tell him about the headaches, the flashes of light, the humming in my ears, the brush of wings against my cheek? He'd think I was a freak, just like everybody else.

"It's a hobby," I said. "They don't mean anything."

He tapped the binding of the book against his thigh. "Now, I don't believe that's true."

"You think I'm lying?"

"I think they absolutely mean something."

"Why don't you tell her what we really think, cuz?" Bobby stepped from behind a tall pine, a smirk marring his pretty face as he chomped a wad of gum. He stalked toward us and the scent of mint drifted toward me.

He stopped, took the gum out of his mouth, and tossed it aside. It landed among the leaves and I wondered who would step on it and have to scrape it off their shoes. I turned to Tate without saying anything and let my expression say it for me. You set me up.

"Forget it, Bobby," Tate said and held the book out to me. I lunged for it, but Bobby was quicker. He laughed and twirled away from me.

I clenched and unclenched my fists. My throat was dry and I swallowed hard and struggled to count. Counting one...counting two...

"Give it to her, Bobby," Tate said.

"Oh, I'm gonna give it to her," he said. "Or, better yet, you tell her what we've been talking about, cuz."

I turned to Tate. "You've been talking about me?" I fingered my forehead where the cut was still raw.

"That's right," Bobby said. "A freak, and a klutz. No wonder somebody ran you over. Apparently, you can't keep from tripping over your own fat feet."

"Bobby," Tate warned.

"Tell her how we researched her on the internet," Bobby said. "Found her freak of a Facebook page."

"It's not mine," I said. "Somebody made it up. As a joke. They put my name on it and posted all kinds of crazy things about me."

Bobby nodded. "Quite enlightening."

"I begged Facebook to take it down."

"Not angels like we thought," Bobby said. "But demons. What kind of weirdo draws demons for fun? You a demon worshipper, Catfish?"

"Don't be idiotic," I said. "Give me my book."

"Naw." He opened the sketchbook and stared at a drawing. "I believe we'll take these to Uncle Stone. That'd be Sheriff Stone to you. He might find it interesting how you're always hanging out in the cemetery drawing satanic pictures."

"Is drawing pictures in a cemetery against the law here?" I said. "How open-minded of you."

"Hand it to her," Tate said.

"What's wrong with you?" Bobby turned on his cousin. "Earlier today, you were laughing about what a retard she is and now you're taking her side."

I glared at Tate.

"It wasn't like that," he said. "I wasn't laughing about the accident. Accidents." He said to Bobby, "and it's her property. Give it to her or I will."

"Can I help?"

Culver Washington stood among the tombstones beyond Whatley Hicks, who died in 1963 at the age of ninety-seven.

"What can you do?" I said.

He shrugged. "Something."

I turned to find Tate and Bobby staring at me.

"What the heck?" Bobby said. "Who you talking to, Catfish? You got some imaginary friends, here, too? Some little demon friends?"

"Leave her alone," Tate said, "and for the last time, give her book back."

Bobby glared at him and Tate lunged. Bobby barely sidestepped him.

"Fine," he said. "Take the stupid thing." He heaved the book at Tate, who caught it against his chest, pages fluttering. "But don't expect a ride from me. Find your own way home." And he took off running toward the country club.

"He called the hotel, didn't he?" I said. "This was his idea and you went along with it. What have I done to make him hate me so?"

Tate handed the book to me and I snatched it from him and hugged it. He stepped back and stuffed his hands in his pockets.

"He doesn't hate you. He's just sore because he got in trouble with his dad the night he hit you. He wasn't supposed to be driving the golf cart. And Uncle Robert didn't know he'd paid to have the tires changed. He was already grounded for," he hesitated and stared toward Culver, then shivered and turned back, "something else."

"You're saying he blames me for getting him in trouble?"

Tate winced. "Sometimes he has trouble admitting he's wrong about anything. He's a little hot-headed."

"And you go along with him."

"He's my cousin. He's been through a lot. You don't realize what it's like having a preacher for a dad. After his mom left, his dad's been really tough on him."

"Whatever." I turned to go. Culver stared at me, a palm resting on the headstone of old Hicks.

"I just wanted to ask you about the sketches," Tate said. "Why you draw them."

"Why do you care?" I whirled around. "So, you can make some more fun of me?"

He licked his lips and stared toward the eighteenth fairway. The wind shuddered through the pines. I shivered as it danced along my bare arms. Thunder rumbled close.

His voice dropped. "I had a cousin," he said, "who drew pictures like that."

"Then go ask him."

"Her." He scrubbed a thumb under his eye. "And I can't."

"Oh, yeah," I cocked my head, "and why not?"

His hand dropped to his side. "Because she's dead."

CHAPTER 16

Okay, I felt bad after Tate told me the story of his cousin Emmie, Bobby's older sister. It was beyond coincidental she'd suffered a near-death experience like me. Hers was a swimming accident. She only stopped breathing for fifteen or twenty seconds. And everything appeared fine until the headaches began.

Unlike me, she took her pain medicine. In fact, Tate said, she took a lot of it. And it helped, as did the sketching. She'd always been artistic, he said, working with wood, fabric, Twizzlers, whatever. But, she'd never drawn things before. Until the angels. Well, he said, it was hard to tell what they were. Could've been demons.

"And the weird thing is," Tate said, "she didn't have any idea why she was drawing them, either. She said she heard things."

"What things?"

He studied the great live oak. "I don't want to make her sound crazy or anything. She was awesome. Really grounded, you know?"

I resisted the desire to roll my eyes. Weren't we all? "But?" I said. "There's a but in there somewhere. What'd she hear?"

Something tickled my ear. A flutter of air brushed it, soft as the wings of a butterfly. Then I heard a sigh, and a whoosh of air so loud I dodged it. I caught the flash of silver before it disappeared behind me.

"Whispers," Tate said, "flutters, the rush of wings. What does that even mean?"

Honestly, I thought he was messing with me. I mean, what were the chances? Near-death experiences? Headaches? Angels? It was as if she and I crossed into some other realm. Like a curtain ripped open and we saw and heard things others couldn't.

What were the chances I'd land in the same town as another girl with the same curse? Tate was messing with me. Of course he was. Same as I thought Culver Washington was in the beginning, only, he wasn't.

But how could Tate Channing possibly know this about me? The website, yeah, I couldn't erase it. It was on the internet for everyone to see. But the accident? The visions?

I folded my arms to protect my sketchbook and pretended to appear as bored as possible. But my heart quickened and I concentrated on breathing to calm it.

"When she started hearing things," Tate said, "the family thought she might be, you know, she might've come, 'unglued' was the word Uncle Bedford used. But I didn't. She was always the same to me. Maybe she'd changed a little. She was so sharp and sarcastic. But funny. I mean, seriously funny. Then she withdrew into herself. I thought it was the headaches."

"They were probably pretty bad," I said.

His glance was sharp and I cursed myself for not keeping my mouth shut.

"She was seventeen. But cool, you know? She didn't hang out with just anybody, but she'd talk to me. I was barely thirteen at the time. But she never treated me like some dumb jock. When everybody wanted to shut me up, she cared about what I thought. She wasn't just humoring me, you know?"

I shrugged.

"You don't know the Hamiltons," he said. "Well, you've met Uncle Stone. And Uncle Bragg."

"The guy who owns Genesis is your uncle, too?"

"You might've realized they're not the easiest family to get along with. Besides Uncle Bragg, I never fit in." He squared his shoulders. "I'm not whining about it. It's the way it is. Emmie didn't fit in, either."

The ache was building in the base of my skull.

"I'm not sure why I'm telling you this." He scrubbed his cropped hair. "But when I saw those drawings, they just slammed me. Bobby won't talk about it. My friends all think I should be over it by now."

I glanced at Culver, who scratched the back of his hand and stared at me.

"I just thought you might understand," Tate said.

I didn't want to be talking to a stranger I had absolutely no reason to trust, but I couldn't help asking, "So, what happened to her?"

He squinted at the storm clouds darkening the sky. His lashes stuttered over green eyes flecked with brown, the color of the bay.

"The headaches got worse. The drawings got darker. Her parents took her to neurologists, psychologists, psychiatrists, I don't remember who all."

The wind streaked a chunk of hair against my cheek and I brushed it away.

"I guess she started thinking there was something wrong with her, too," he said, "not just physically, but mentally. And maybe it couldn't be fixed."

He strolled to Elijah's grave, squatted, and plucked a white plastic rabbit from the border to study it.

"She was already on the pain killers pretty heavy. Then one night," his voice dropped so low I was forced to step closer to hear, "she talked Bobby into smuggling some vodka from their parents' liquor cabinet. Mixed with the painkillers? She never woke up. Bobby blames himself."

"How awful," I said, then clamped my mouth shut. I could not afford to get involved. And Tate Channing could not be trusted.

He scrubbed his jaw. "Everybody said it was an accident. But I think she was in so much pain, she didn't want to go on."

"Why'd they insist it was an accident?"

"Some members of my family don't believe people who commit suicide go to heaven. But Emmeline Hamilton was the best person I've ever known. If she didn't go to heaven, who does?"

I caught Culver's eye. He eased closer.

Tate brushed a smudge of dirt off the rabbit, replaced it, and stood. "After she died, Bobby's family fell apart. He wasn't close to his sister. Maybe he was a little jealous of how much everybody loved her. But still, it was horrible for him."

I struggled to imagine Bobby Hamilton with an older sister. Dark. Pretty, like him.

"Aunt Dora started taking Xanax," Tate said. "Uncle Robert quit the insurance business to go into the ministry. Maybe he thought if he couldn't save Emmie, he might be able to help somebody else. Aunt Dora left and Uncle Robert withdrew into the church. And it's been Bobby and me ever since."

"With Uncle Sheriff looking out for you."

He shrugged. "He tries."

The wind whipped my hair and I pushed it back.

"But now you see how Bobby's had a pretty rough time of it."

"I see how he hates me and I haven't done anything to him. And after the stunt he pulled tonight, I wouldn't mind taking a big, fat stick and cracking him over the head with it."

Tate grunted. "Me too, sometimes."

The wind swayed the trees and tossed my hair. I swiped it back.

"I better go," I said. "The storm's nearly on us."

"Yeah." Tate eyed the dark sky. "Guess I'll see you around." His gaze dropped to my sketchbook. "You might want to keep a closer eye on that," he said and turned and trotted after his cousin toward the clubhouse.

The idea of Emmie and Bobby swirled in my head. Accidents and blinding headaches and jealousy and suicide. I wanted to shake the images loose, but they kept grabbing hold. The restaurant and Mama screaming for a doctor and Daddy hollering and cursing and the light fixture, one of those Tiffany knockoffs, swinging overhead as I stared up from the floor.

Me gasping for breath. The room going dim. Mary Grace smirking in the school bathroom. Our last conversation, stares in the hallway, those awful images on Facebook. Mr. Stubbs' lifeless body on my front porch.

I gasped and stared at Culver, now bathed in a shimmer of silver light. I counted one, counted two, counted three, and worked to steady the vision of him that kept sparking around the edges.

I sucked in a deep breath, and another, until I could speak. "What do you think?" I asked. "Was he telling the truth? Or making a fool of me?"

Culver gazed at the line of trees blocking Tate and his cousin from view. "I didn't live on this earth more than seven and ten years," he said. "Though the Hamilton family took me in and was good to me, so's I couldn't complain much, I've had plenty long to reflect." He met my eyes. "And this is what I feel. Sometimes, when we're so close to those we care for most, we can't always see the truth of things."

And then, with a flash of lightning, Culver was gone.

I hesitated for barely a second, before hurrying home, hugging my sketches tight.

CHAPTER 17

The tree limb that toppled Bobby Hamilton and gave him a ghastly black eye reportedly came out of nowhere. According to him, he was jogging to the clubhouse after leaving the cemetery when the limb flew through the air, smacking him to the ground.

It was off a sycamore tree, snapped clean and thick as a baseball bat. Beneath the black eye, Bobby's cheek swelled into a misshapen lump. The doctor said he was lucky he didn't sustain a concussion. More than one person mentioned the fact that there were no sycamore trees along the road to the clubhouse.

"Well," Sheriff Stone said, scratching his head, "those hurricane-force winds tossed all manner of debris around last evening. Could've come from anywhere."

Later, I heard from one of the hotel maids, Bobby tried to blame me for the accident. But seeing how I was with Tate at the time, Sheriff Stone shut him down real quick.

"Son, you can't go around accusing people," he said. "That's slander, unless you got proof."

"I'll get proof," Bobby said. "I'll prove Cat Turner's a witch and up to no good."

The storm did not leave the bay cool and refreshed, but rather a few degrees shy of sweltering bath water. More than once, I cursed and tugged at the purple scarf encircling my neck. It might've started out a kickass plaid, but was now soaked with sweat.

I cursed my vanity. I cursed myself for letting some kids' re-action to my scars drive me to mummify myself in cotton and silk and chiffon. I cursed the friends who weren't real friends after all. I cursed myself for not being able to let it go and move on.

Little did I know I'd left the hotel in another crisis, albeit a small-er one than the bicycle hut burning to the ground. The storm didn't just take out Bobby Hamilton and create oven-roasting conditions. It also flooded the basement of the Fairly Grand, with a foot or so of water seeping into a storage room that was once the manager's office.

Mama arranged for a company to pump out the water and recruited whatever staff she could spare from housekeeping to rescue hotel records, bills, old photographs, and memorabilia. They spent the night and most of the following morning moving anything sal-vageable into the hallway and wine cellar next door until the room could dry out.

When I offered to help, Mama brushed me aside.

So I borrowed a bicycle from the bicycle hut while the twins argued over whether a guest in Room 242 actually saw Red Maggie. As I pedaled out of the hotel parking lot toward town, I wondered if Red Maggie would appear to me as Culver did. Maybe they'd get together and exchange notes. I shook my head and swerved hard into the grass to miss an oncoming Lexus. I had to stop thinking crazy thoughts before I started believing them.

Mel's Quick Stop was about a half a mile from the hotel. Mel didn't carry much more than the hotel gift shop, but it felt good to have the breeze in my hair and the sun on my shoulders.

Along the bay, stuccoed mansions sprawled behind massive iron gates and manicured lawns. In between, pockets of woods shel-tered tidy bungalows among the palm fronds. The noon sun glared, pinkening my shoulders and the tip of my freckled nose.

I heard the peal of church bells before I saw the white cross rise from the steepled roof of a small clapboard building tucked among the resort homes overlooking the bay. Until the bells sounded, I'd forgotten it was Sunday.

I stopped my bike shy of the gravel driveway and braced it be-tween my knees as the congregation spilled onto the scrub grass lawn. A young, sandy-haired man stood at the door in a loose Hawaiian shirt and khakis, shaking hands and greeting people. The congregation emerged into the sunlight, blinking and shading their eyes. Women gathered in small groups in breezy sundresses and sandals as children squealed and shrieked through the grass in t-shirts and shorts.

Most Sundays back in Shelby, we attended the neighborhood

church. Shelby United Methodist was as simple as the church in front of me. The floors were hardwood and the pews even harder. But the people were friendly. And the minister's wife served Dr. Pepper and macaroon cookies during Sunday school.

After my accident, Daddy stopped going. After I got kicked out of Holy Mercy, I didn't feel much like going, either. And Mama didn't have the heart to make me.

Suddenly, Tate Channing filled the doorway in khaki shorts and leather Chuck Taylors. He was as tall as the preacher and broader through the shoulders. He pumped the man's hand a few times, then trotted down the steps, and onto the gravel drive.

A squeal separated itself from a pack of kids and a chubby little girl rushed at him, red hair in corkscrew pigtails bouncing as she ran. He caught her hands and swung her in the air and around in a circle until he was staggering. He set her on the ground and she showed him the gap where her front tooth had been. He high-fived her and sent her running, screaming, back to a small woman with a baby riding her hip. He continued his stroll along the drive.

My foot fumbled for the bike pedal as his eye caught mine. He stopped and I hit the pedal hard, scratching through the gravel as I peeled out.

"Hey!" he called after me. "Cat, wait!"

I turned to find him running after me and felt stupid trying to outrace him. So I heaved a sigh, stopped, and waited for him to catch up. He circled in front of the handlebars, blocking my escape.

"Where you headed?" he said. "Town?"

"Mel's. That your church?"

"Yeah." He caught the eye of a dark girl about our age with long black hair. She waved. He lifted a hand in return. "That's India," he said. "You'd like her." He turned to me. "You don't go to church?"

I wanted to say it was none of his dang business if I went to church. Instead, I swiped the trickle of sweat along my cheek and said, "No."

"Just don't want to, or haven't found one yet?" People milled around the yard. I studied his profile, the square jaw, the jutting chin.

I couldn't figure him out. One minute, he appeared friendly. The next, he was calling me names behind my back. But then, why should I be surprised? It was pretty much what I'd come to expect in the past year.

"Why don't you go to church with your family?" I said.

His gaze fell on me. "How do you know I don't?"

"Mayor Hamilton told me. Your grandmother?"

"Hurricane Harrie?"

"You call her that?"

"Not to her face. But a lot of people do." A few cars rumbled along the driveway and turned toward town.

"So, what's so great about this rinky dink church, anyway?" I meant to offend, but he simply smiled.

"I guess it might appear rinky dink to you," he said. "Coming from hot shot Atlanta. You've seen First Baptist downtown? Big, fat columns, marble steps? Pretty impressive."

I wiped my sweating palms against my white shorts as I balanced the bike between my knees. "I'm not from Atlanta."

"First Baptist is Uncle Robert's church," he said. "It's got these stained-glass windows and red velvet cushions. They have this organ specially made by some artist in Oregon. Only ten of them in the entire world."

"So, why don't you go there?"

He shrugged and stamped his feet as if he was stomping out a fire. "You ever want to do something different just because it's different?"

I shrugged.

"The people here," he nodded toward the yard, cleared of all but a few groups of people, "they're genuine, you know?" He swung his head toward town. "They don't do stuff to impress people."

A black Buick whizzed by, followed by a puttering white Honda. An old station wagon with wooden side panels rumbled along the church driveway, the back seat full of kids. It eased onto the road and turned right.

"You want to come sometime?" he said. "There's a youth thing –"

"I don't think so," I cut him off. How could I tell him I might be, ever so slightly, still mad at God?

"Cool," he said. "I just thought with your drawing angels you might be interested."

"I've got to go." I fought to find the pedal without looking for it.

"Wait." He grabbed the handlebars. "I really want to talk about your drawings sometime."

"Really?" My face felt like the proverbial burning bush. "You want to make fun of me some more? Call me a freak and a retard and a devil worshipper? You want to get me into church to see if I'll bust out screaming or melt or something?"

"Whoa," he said, "you've been watching way too many horror movies. And I never called you those names."

"You laughed when your cousin did."

"Sometimes I'm laughing at Bobby," he said, "not with him. Sometimes he can't recognize the difference."

"You enjoy making fun of him, too?"

He sighed. "I try to be funny, you know, to lighten the mood. Everything gets so heavy sometimes. I just want everybody to chill."

"Sometimes things are heavy, you know?" My foot finally crunched the pedal. "Sometimes you get called names and people leave dead pets on your front porch and you get run out of your own school for no good reason."

He jerked away from me and his shocked expression stung tears in my eyes. With horror, I realized I was about to cry.

"Go," I said, "go chill with your demon-hunting cousin." I ground the bicycle into gear and pumped the pedals furiously, refusing to sit, eating gravel, and putting as much distance between us as possible.

I was stirred with fresh fury, knowing he would watch and judge me until I was out of sight.

CHAPTER 18

A few days passed before I saw Culver again. I purposefully stayed away. It's one thing to get flashes of angels and demons surrounding you. The flicker of light out of the corner of your eye, the quickening of blood in your veins, the smell of snow when it's ninety degrees outside. An iciness that numbs the fingers, a creak on the stairs when you're alone, a flutter against your cheek.

It's the quickening, turning, knowing that catches them off guard and arrests them long enough to get a glimpse, caught between this realm and theirs and then, poof! Gone. But Culver seemed to be neither angel nor demon, merely some poor sap caught between this world and the next. And I had no idea what to do with him.

I returned to the library to retrieve the book I'd left behind. But I couldn't find much more information than what Culver told me. Just enough to prove he existed and was indeed the slave of one Horace Tidewater Hamilton.

In the summer of 1863, there was a skirmish at the Houston plantation south of Tuscaloosa. Details were sketchy. Apparently, Culver was shot after stealing a musket and shooting his owner in an attempt to escape to join the Union army being routed. Horace Hamilton was the only soldier to survive and was awarded a medal for courage and valor.

I was willing to help an escaped slave find eternal freedom. Not so much an attempted murderer. I needed another opinion and returned to the hotel.

"Willie," I slid onto a bar stool in front of him, "tell me about Culver Washington."

"Sister, that story ain't fit for virgin ears."

Heat crept up my neck and into my cheeks. The Fischers sat at a table behind me, pretending to sip their drinks. But the way Irene Fischer leaned in, I knew she was listening. "I watch movies," I said. "I read books, too, you know?"

"I bet you do." He ran a cloth over the already polished bar.

"So, you can tell me the story without worrying about my delicate sensibilities."

"Sister, at the barest mention of impropriety, you done burned ten shades of red. Ain't no way. No, sir. No how. Your mama'd skin me alive."

"Willie." I grabbed his wrist. He glanced at my white hand against his dark one with raised brows.

"Please." I dug in my nails.

"Yes," Irene Fischer slid onto the bar stool next to me, her glass of sherry in hand, "do tell us the story, dear William. I'm sure you can make it PG-rated."

She patted my arm. "And Catalina dear, please remove your grip from poor William's wrist. He's not used to being treated so indelicately."

I snatched my hand away.

Mr. Fischer hopped onto the seat beside his wife with a martini and a handful of olives he popped into his mouth one at a time.

"Now, Miss Irene," Willie said, "you've known me long enough to know there ain't nothing delicate about me."

"You do mix a mean martini," she said. "But you're changing the subject. Please tell us about this Culver Washington. You've made him sound so intriguing."

"Oh, lordy." Willie rolled his eyes. "Can I freshen your drink?"

She took a sip. "You're stalling, William."

"There ain't nothing to tell." He scrubbed at an imaginary spot on the immaculate counter. "He wasn't exactly a boon to our race. He was a scoundrel and a scallywag. And I'd rather not get into the particulars."

"Oooh, but it's much too late, dear," she said. "We're all aflutter."

I didn't know if I was aflutter, but I definitely wanted to scream in frustration.

Willie heaved a sigh. "He was a slave." He pulled Mrs. Fischer's near empty glass away from her, plucked a bottle off the shelf behind him and poured amber liquid into it. "He belonged to Horace Hamilton, the founder of Fairly. You know, he got the name of the town from the hotel. It was here long before Horace ever thought of stirring a town from dust."

"How kind of him," Mrs. Fischer said.

Willie frowned. "Well, the War Between the States broke out and Horace T., not much older than you, sister," he glanced at me, "well, he signs up. Not many young men didn't. Horace is stationed with some regiment, I don't rightly remember which, and he takes Culver with him, since they'd been together since they were young'uns."

So far, so true.

Willie continued, "This Culver, he goes to war with Horace, doing his laundry, toting his stuff, taking care of him, right?"

Mrs. Fischer sipped her drink. Mr. Fischer pulled a silver bowl of nuts toward him and picked out the cashews.

"So, you realize all sorts of bad things happen during war, right?" He looked at me pointedly. "People getting killed. Houses being plundered and burned."

"We understand war, William," Mrs. Fischer said over her drink.

"Well, the soldiers out in the woods, or in camps, hire these washer women," he said, "laundresses, to travel with them and take care of their laundry, right? Some are wives of soldiers, some are widows, but most of them are without any menfolk 'cause they're off to war, too."

"Please continue," Mrs. Fischer said.

"Well," Willie scratched behind his ear, "Vicksburg was under siege and old Farragut was threatening to return to the bay. Reinforcements started working their way southward."

"What does this have to do with Culver?" I said.

Willie frowned at me. "These washer women are traveling with the soldiers and one of them is comely enough the men are vying for her affections. At some point, one evening when the wash was done and the women were taking their leave, Culver takes it upon himself to catch the young woman unawares. He drags her off into the woods and," he hesitated between Mrs. Fischer and me, "takes advantage of the situation."

"You're saying he raped her?" I said.

"It was virtually unheard of among slaves," Willie said. "If they raped a white woman they'd get strung up, no questions asked. But Horace wanted Culver to have a fair trial. So they took him to

Judge Houston's plantation. He didn't realize Union soldiers were already there. In the melee, Culver saw his chance for escape. He shot Horace and took off running. Horace survived and captured him."

"But Culver didn't have a gun, right?" I said. "They wouldn't issue guns to slaves, even in the war. So how did Horace get shot?"

Willie frowned at me. "Do you want to tell the story?"

"I'm simply asking." I folded my hands on the bar and waited.

"Apparently, he stole a gun during his escape and shot his owner. Horace returned fire and they both landed at the hospital at the Fairly Grand."

I tapped my finger against the back of my hand. Something wasn't right.

"Justly, Culver died of his wounds," he said. "Horace recovered and won some medal of honor and went on to found the town of Fairly. End of story."

Irene Fischer raised her drink and said, "That is quite a story, William." She sipped her sherry and eyed him over the rim, making me wonder what in the heck I'd gotten myself into.

CHAPTER 19

"You were supposed to help me," Culver said as I arrived at the cemetery.

"Listen," I said, "I may see glimpses of angels, but it's not like I can talk to them. It's not as if I can enlist their help. What am I supposed to do? You haven't even told me the whole story. I've read the history books and I've heard what others have to say. And it isn't pretty."

Culver stared past me and scratched his elbow.

"History says you did some bad things," I said. "Maybe that's why you're still here. I don't blame you for trying to escape, anyone would, but maybe you should make amends for the awful things you've done."

He shook his head and scrubbed the top of it.

"You shot Horace," I said. "But there's also the rape of some laundress at the campsite."

"Lucie." Culver frowned.

"They were taking you to Judge Houston for a trial to sort it out. That's when the shooting started."

"They weren't taking me to Judge Houston," he said. "And I didn't, would never hurt Lucie. She was sweet. Real good to me. We talked about music and dancing. She loved the waltz, same as me. Promised to teach me sometime. She was one of those folks who didn't care about the color of your skin."

"Culver," I said, "the history books –"

Culver shook his head hard. "I don't know what they say," he said. "I only know the truth. Horace and me completed our training and headed toward Tennessee. Like a pack mule, I toted his belongings twenty, thirty miles a day, and when we made camp, I polished his effects and laundered his uniforms. That's how I met Lucie. She belonged to one of the washer women who traveled with us from Mobile. A niece, maybe. She come out to meet us north of Tuscaloosa and worked alongside her aunt to help her family.

"Lucie was a hard worker. She could boil the vermin off a shirt faster than jack rabbit. And she was a sight, stirring a tub of wash, with red hair bright as a flame escaping about her sweet face. Many a soldier kept a bold eye on her."

I propped my hands on my hips and shifted my weight.

"Horace took along his old fiddle and sawed away in camp. Least, before he lost it in a card game. Cribbage, I reckon. I told him not to do it. But Horace got this way about him when his dander's up. It just made him more determined.

"I still remember that music, so high and sweet it liked to make me bawl. And the dance, the waltz, Horace called it, I was desperate to learn my way around it. That's what Lucie was telling me that night. She'd teach me to waltz. And Horace didn't cotton to that.

"He didn't appreciate Lucie and me conversing in such a familiar way. 'We got a reputation to uphold,' he said to me. 'We're from a fine family. Rich in money and heritage and the laundress you're conversing with is white trash. Best you keep your distance when you're working.'

'We were just friends,' I said. "She's sweet, and funny as a hoot in a holler. And pretty enough to sit for a portrait.'

'They're poor dirt farmers,' Horace said. 'Don't have more'n a pot to piss in.'

'Why you getting sore?' I said. 'She ain't hurting nobody.'

'Hurting nobody?' He showed me his wrist. 'See this cuff? This dirty, dingy cuff? You washed this yesterday. It's an embarrassment. She's taking your mind off your work.'

'I'm sorry, Horace. Let me rewash it. I'll have it sparkling, good as new.'

'Never mind.' He brushed me aside. 'I don't have time. You best keep your mind on your business and leave that girl alone.'

'But she's promised to teach me the waltz.'

'I done told you I'd teach you the waltz.' He grabbed my bare arm where I'd rolled up my sleeves. It sent sparks clear to my elbow. 'But right now,' he said, 'we're at war.' His voice was soft, as soft as his thumb rubbing the inside of my arm.

'But Horace,' I said, 'Lucie is a girl. And boys waltz with girls.'

Horace dropped his hand. 'I said I'd teach you the waltz, not dance it with you.' His eyes took on a hardness I ain't never seen before. His smile was so tight his lips thinned out. Maybe the war was getting to him.

'I know what Lucie's doing,' Horace said. 'She's wanting to turn you against me. To sweet talk you into escaping up north while nobody's looking. But you and me is blood brothers. You can't leave me.'

'Horace, I wouldn't –'

"Don't you worry,' he said. 'I'll take care of Miss Lucie.'

'Horace, you don't have to…Lucie and me is simply whiling away the time as we's working. She don't mean nothing by it. We don't mean nothing.'

'We'll see,' Horace said, and stalked away.

"It was twilight when Lucie leaned into me, laughing at Crawford and Sutton scrabbling in the dirt over a poker game. I tried not to laugh. Truly I did. But she smelled sweet as fresh strawberries and her eyes crinkled when she laughed and there'd been little enough to laugh about during the war. I caught Horace's eye through the fire. He was sore something awful and he give me a hard look before stomping off toward the woods.

"After supper, the soldiers eased off to a game of cards by the fire or reading or writing letters in their tents. Horace came to us, Lucie and me, working side by side over the boiling pots.

"She was showing me the blisters on her palm, laughing as I tickled a finger over it. He asked her to take a stroll with him along the edge of the woods. Said he'd show her the sweetest blackberry patch she ever did see. She said she had to finish her work.

" 'Culver'll do it,' he said. 'He's fast as lightning. When was the last time you had fresh blackberries?'

"She admitted it'd been before the war and her mama served 'em with fresh cream. Lucie promised to bring me back the fattest, juiciest berries, a whole apron full of 'em. I wanted to say I thought it might still be a little cool for blackberries. But I held my tongue.

"As they headed toward the woods with nothing but the moonlight leading the way, Lucie give me a grin and a quick wave over her shoulder.

"They didn't come stumbling back until after everybody bedded down. Miss Lucie's aunt had long finished her wash and had been stomping the ground between tents for some time. Miss Lucie lagged some ways behind Horace. And she wasn't smiling no more. Her dress was torn about the shoulder, her apron stained, and her lip bloodied.

"I said to Horace, 'Lucie appears hurt.'

"'She ain't hurt,' he said. 'I simply explained it ain't nothing and nobody ever gonna come between you and me.'

"'Horace, what did you do?'

"'We enjoyed ourselves a little talk and ate blackberries' he said. 'That on her lip is blackberry juice. She's right as rain.'

"'What about her apron?' I said. 'The stains. Why didn't she bring no berries back?' But Horace hauled off to his tent and left me with an uneasy settling in my belly as her aunt escorted her out of camp.

"The next morning, an unholy ruckus erupted from the captain's tent as a posse of fellas on horseback guarded the outside of it and one fella stalked inside.

"The matter was resolved after much wrangling. Horace was forced to turn over the bulk of his allowance to Lucie's daddy. But it didn't help Lucie none. Any decent chance in society was most likely ruined. The best she could hope for was to live life as a spinster, shamed to her core, or disappear to travel among relatives.

"Horace was relieved to get out from under that situation, though he took to lamenting his lack of coin. I never saw Lucie again, but we heard later of her demise.

"What?" I cried. "Demise?"

"Horace didn't understand. His daddy raised him to take over the farm one day, take charge of things. He just went too far."

I pressed a hand to my belly to still the queasiness there and swallowed hard.

"You're upset," he said, "but Horace was sorry. He made amends."

"He gave her father money because he was forced to," I said. "To buy her silence. You already admitted it wouldn't make up for her loss of reputation. Her life was destroyed."

Culver turned from me. "I'm to blame," he said. "I let him go. I should've stopped him."

"Were you his conscience, too?"

"It was my job to take care of him."

"Was it your job to keep him from raping a woman? Or worse?"

"Mister Josiah trusted me."

I threw my hands in the air. "I don't think I can help you if you can't admit the truth."

"Oh, Miss Cat," Culver said, "that's the way it was." He scratched behind his ear. "The Hamiltons were better than most."

"Right." My sarcasm could've sliced aluminum.

He peered at me. "We can't go back and change the past, Miss Cat. Best to move forward."

"Yep." I moved away from him before his optimism could infect me. "That's what I keep hearing. But if we can't change the past, then what are we doing here, you and me?"

The graveyard fell silent except for the crickets. I studied Elijah's angel.

"If we can't change history," I said finally, "maybe we can correct it. If you're telling the truth, then there's a story being told that's a lie."

"I don't want to hurt Horace and his family," Culver said. "I wouldn't harm them for the world."

"Do you want to leave, or don't you?"

"Horace and me are blood brothers," he said. "Queenie said so. I won't destroy Horace's reputation to save my name."

"Your name?" I stepped closer. "You think this is about your reputation? Do you see him stuck here? I can assure you, he's moved on. And you need to do the same. Why do you keep defending him? He's done horrible things."

"He suffered for his failings," Culver said. "When the orders came for us to join the scouting party, I understood. The South was hurting for warm bodies. They couldn't afford to get rid of Horace, no matter what he'd done. And he weren't the only soldier in the war to take advantage of a situation. But still, they could kill two birds with one stone by dispatching him on a mission he had little chance of surviving. And that's what they did. And me along with him."

CHAPTER 20

Before Culver could finish his story, a black Mercedes thundered past us toward the country club. `Culver shimmered and faded into the pearly twilight. I left not knowing what to think. The story he told, and the history books, and Willie's story were all at odds. I wasn't sure who to believe. Worse, it was impossible to challenge the facts without letting on I was seeing ghosts.

I wanted to forget Culver Calhoun Washington. Really, I did. I wanted to meet some girls my age and go shopping or maybe get my nails done or go to the movies. I wanted to forget my past, and Culver's past, and enjoy the summer making friends and settling into a new home.

But who in the world was going to be my friend as long as I was plagued with ghosts? Angels and demons were bad enough, but dead people? I saw the movie. It didn't end well.

To get rid of Culver, I had to find out why he was still here. And to do that, I needed to discover the true story. And only one other place might have some pieces to the puzzle.

The next morning, I took the shuttle into town and crossed Fairly Avenue at the light and passed the drugstore heading toward the bookstore. Staring back the way I came, I nearly ran into the back of Sheriff Stone Hamilton, huddled with his nephew Bobby in the middle of the sidewalk. I beat a hasty retreat and pressed myself into the prickly brick wall of the pharmacy and peeked around the corner.

A tall, steel-haired woman approached, a satchel slung over an arm, fingers flecked with dried paint. She frowned down her long nose at me before pushing the door open and disappearing inside. I eased away from the wall to peer around the corner. Sheriff Hamilton squeezed Bobby's shoulder.

"Now, listen, boy," he surveyed the street, "don't do anything stupid."

"What about Cat Turner?" Bobby said. "She's weirder than a one-eyed monkey."

I bristled.

The sheriff snorted. "Don't worry about her. Spending her days moping around the cemetery might be creepy, but it's not illegal."

"I showed you the website," Bobby said. "I'm telling you, she's into some kind of freaky hoodoo voodoo."

"I'll check into it," his uncle said. "You steer clear of her. You can't afford to get mixed up in her brand of craziness."

Craziness? I squinted at the two of them and envisioned a baby grand piano falling from the second floor of the antique store onto their thick, fat heads. Behind me, a Coca-Cola truck rumbled along the street and stopped in front of the drugstore. Smoke billowed from the exhaust and engulfed me, forcing me to hold my breath to keep from coughing. Covering my mouth, I edged closer to the antique store.

"What about Tate?" Bobby said. "I've seen him talking to her. At Genesis. And church. He even took her side at the cemetery."

"Leave it to me," the sheriff said. "If there's so much as a smudge of dirt on Cat Turner, I'll find it."

"And then Tate, with his precious bleeding heart, won't go near her," Bobby said.

"You just stay out of trouble."

There was a crash behind me and a case of soft drink bottles lay shattered in the middle of the street. Cars honked and the delivery man stood over the mess and cursed. I ducked into the darkened doorway of the antique store.

By the time I'd gathered enough courage to peek around the doorway, Bobby's golf cart rumbled along the street and the sheriff was nowhere in sight.

"Whatcha doing?"

I jumped, banging my head on the door frame. Turning, I glared at Tate Channing hovering over me with his stupid grin.

"Nothing," I said, and rubbed my temple.

"Spying?" he suggested.

"Of course not." At least my head wasn't bleeding this time. "Not that it's any of your business, but I was on my way to the bookstore."

"Doing your summer reading already?" He sneered as if that were a bad thing.

"Doing research."

"Oh, yeah? On what?"

"Nothing you'd care about."

"Try me."

I huffed. "Why are you following me around?"

"As if. What's with the scarves? You're always wearing one, even when it's blazing hot."

I fingered the fringed pink and white gingham. It gave off a little aw-shucks, square-dance vibe. But it was softer and lighter than most. And infinitely more cheerful than I felt.

"I'm doing research on," I tried to conjure something that wasn't a total lie, "on the cemetery by the golf course."

"The Confederate cemetery?" he said. "That's why you spend so much time out there? Research?"

"Sure," I said, "let's go with that."

"That's kind of creepy."

I gritted my teeth. "I like the headstones," I said. "The carvings."

"The angels."

"Yeah."

"You couldn't find angels to draw somewhere else? Maybe church?"

What was with him and church? "The cemetery's quieter," I said.

He laughed. "That's for dang sure."

I made a face and he laughed and rocked on his heels. His laugh was deep and rumbly.

"There's a book on Fairly that just came out," he said. "A picture book. For decoration? My mom bought one."

"A coffee table book?"

"I guess."

I bit my lip. "I'm looking for more than pictures," I said. "I'm searching for information about a slave buried there during the Civil War. Culver Washington."

"Not that old story."

"You know it?"

"Everybody in Fairly knows it. Question is, how do you know it?"

"I, uh, Wet Willie told me. At the hotel."

"Willie," he snorted. "He never liked talking about it."

"So, what do you know?"

He scratched the back of his head. "He was a slave belonging to my great-great-great- grandfather, Horace. My family's not proud of it, but there's nothing we can do about it now. Horace carried him off to war with him. Culver raped some woman and shot Horace to escape. Horace returned fire and Culver died before he could be hung. Something along those lines. But you probably won't find his grave in that cemetery."

"Why not?"

"Slaves weren't generally buried with white people," he said. "And Culver wasn't exactly an exemplary fella."

"Because he was a slave?"

"Because he was a rapist."

"Accused rapist."

He stared at me. "You got any reason to believe he wasn't?"

Evidence appeared to be piling against Culver.

"Listen," Tate said, "Horace went on to win some medal for bravery. The war ended. He returned to Oak Grove and built the town."

"You sound like your grandmother."

He shrugged. "It's what the big celebration in August is about. Horace and the founding of Fairly a hundred and fifty years ago. Honoring our heroes. The town's going crazy with it."

He glanced toward the hardware store. "Uncle Bragg could tell you more about it, though. He's the expert on digging up history. You should talk to him."

"I'd rather go to the bookstore," I said.

"You scared?"

I tilted my head and squinted at him. "Let's say I don't think there's a mutual appreciation there."

"Ha," he said, "you're scared. Bragg's all bark and no bite."

"Unlike your Uncle Sheriff."

"Aw, Stone's a teddy bear compared to Uncle Bedford. You met him yet?"

"Is there anybody in this town you're not related to?"

"Nathan Bedford Forrest Hamilton. Uncle Bedford."

"You've got to be kidding."

"Nope. All my uncles were named for Civil War heroes."

"How many are there?"

"Braxton Bragg, Stonewall Jackson, aka Uncle Stone, Robert Edward Lee, that's Bobby's daddy. Even my mother was named for a

Confederate spy, Belle Boyd Hamilton Channing."

"That's insane."

"Yeah. I was spared, thanks to good ole Dad. Even Harrie Ann couldn't talk him into it. Obviously, it was long before they started yanking down Confederate statues."

An uncomfortable silence settled between us as traffic moseyed by. Little old ladies tottered past, protecting their pharmacy prescriptions. Some kid on the corner howled as his frozen lemonade splattered the pavement.

"I've got to go," I said.

"Hey, let's grab a burger." He nodded toward the street. "You tried the Burger Barn yet?"

"It's ten-thirty."

"Yeah," he said. "I'm starving."

I studied the area. There was no good reason I should spend another minute with Tate Hot Shot Channing. His uncle and cousin were in cahoots to brand me as some criminal. His Uncle Bragg couldn't stand the sight of me. And so far, he hadn't exactly been trustworthy.

"Come on," he said, "it's not going to kill you. You made any other friends, yet?"

I lifted my chin defensively. "Some."

"I mean outside the housekeeping crew at the hotel."

Was he spying on me, too?

"Come on." He grabbed the fringe of my scarf and tugged me toward the street.

"Hey," I slapped his hand and he laughed and let go.

And rather than stand stranded in the middle of the street, I followed him to the courtyard and the notorious Burger Barn.

CHAPTER 21

"You want to dig up some dirt?" Tate said. "Uncle Bragg's the man for the job. Best archaeologist in the South." He bit into a hamburger the size of a Frisbee.

"Don't be stupid," I said, "it's not that kind of digging." I stabbed at the frozen lemonade I'd bought to avoid the sight of him chomping meat and bread.

"Doesn't matter." He swiped his mouth with a napkin and slurped his cola. "I'm telling you, the man is an expert at finding things." I jabbed at my lemonade and squinted against the searing glare of sun.

"Why would he help me?" I spooned the slush into my mouth. He nearly halved his burger with one bite. He chewed. And chewed. And slurped his drink.

"Because it's what he does." He popped a French fry in his mouth.

"So," I sought to change the subject, "you and your cousin spend the summer riding around in your fancy golf cart terrorizing the good people of Fairly, huh?"

"I have a job." He popped in another fry. "I work construction for my dad. We're currently on hiatus. Some environmental nut jobs are protesting the loss of the habitat of the red-winged beetle, or blue-billed warble, or some such nonsense. We can't go back to work until it gets resolved." He swiped at a blob of ketchup in the corner of his mouth.

"You don't think beetle and bird habitats should be protected?"

"I don't think they should cost a man his livelihood."

"What about Bobby?" I said. "Does he work?"

"He's got some modeling gigs."

I snorted lemonade out my nose and pressed the back of my hand to it, mortified.

"Seriously," he said. "The black eye he got? He had to cancel a job at the boat show over in Mobile. He was so mad he slammed his cell phone against his golf cart and destroyed it. He had an even bigger job in Atlanta a month ago. With Polo. His dad made him cancel it when he lost his BMW."

"He had a BMW?" Of course he did.

"His mom bought it for him. Probably to compensate for leaving the family."

I wiped the back of my hand on my shorts. "So, how'd he lose it? The car?"

"I'd rather not say." Tate snatched a couple of paper napkins from the metal container in the center of the table and leaned back in his seat. "It was something even Uncle Stone couldn't get him out of." He wiped his palms.

I fiddled with my spoon. "I can't imagine owning a BMW at sixteen."

"Me, either." He wadded the napkins into a ball. "Give me a classic any day. I'm about to be the proud owner of one sixty-seven Mustang convertible." He tossed the wad at a nearby trash can. It rimmed and dropped in. His smile was smug.

"So a relic, then."

He flexed his shoulders. "She could use a little work. But man, is she a sweet ride. Spinach green with cream leather seats."

"Mmmmm." I hoped he could tell how totally unimpressed I was.

"I'm serious," he said. "She's a beauty. Big Al called as soon as she arrived on his lot. Allen, his son, and I played football together. I've been working for V ever since."

"V?" I said. "You named your car a letter?"

"That's right, baby. Short for Vesper. You know, Bond girl? Every job, every birthday check, every Christmas, every penny goes into the pot."

"She must be pretty pricey," I said, "if she's a *classic*."

He frowned. "Like I said, she needs a lot of work. Dad said he'd help me get her in shape. Two hundred and twenty-three dollars and fifty-nine cents to go. By the end of summer, she'll be mine, free and clear."

I couldn't imagine owning a car in any foreseeable future. We had to sell Mama's used Volvo to have enough money to make the move.

"Until then," he said, "I take all the odd jobs I can. The little girl you saw me with at church? I babysit her sometimes."

"You're kidding," I said. "I never heard of a guy babysitting."

"Don't be sexist. I'll do whatever it takes to get my car. I'd sell my own blood if I could. Besides, Gracie's a sweet kid. I take her to the park and the beach. I read *Jurassic Park* to her. She loves the dinosaurs and the blood and gore. It drives her mom insane."

"I don't have a car," I said, "but I do have a dog I had to leave behind."

"Oh, yeah?" Tate said. "What kind?"

And I told him all about Ruby and how much I missed her, and then felt totally stupid about revealing anything even slightly personal to someone I didn't trust.

Across the street, a woman stepped outside the designer boutique with a hat box in one hand and a shopping bag in the other. She tottered on four-inch heels in white capris and a tight white tee, flashing blood red nails. Her pale blonde hair was slicked back in a high ponytail, the tips of it brushing her shoulders. She tilted her face slightly toward the sun and pushed black Jackie O sunglasses along her nose. She looked vaguely familiar.

Tate's plate was empty except for two fries and he slurped his way to the bottom of his soda. In a flash of white, Miss Fancy Pants strode toward us. I spooned my melted lemonade into my mouth and the spoon stuck there as she stopped at our table.

She smiled at Tate and said, "Hey, sweetie. I didn't realize you were in town."

My mouth dropped open, but the spoon stuck to my tongue as Tate leaned back in his chair and wiped his hands on his shorts. "Hey, Mom," he said.

I might've fallen out of my chair if the arms hadn't held me in. Tate stared at me and made a funny movement with his brows until I realized the spoon was still in my mouth. I yanked it out and it clattered to the table.

"Who's your friend, sweetie?" Tate's mom arched perfectly plucked brows at me.

"This is Cat," he said. "Cat Turner. She's new in town. Her mom's the new manager at the Fairly Grand."

"Oh?" Belle Channing tilted her head like an exotic bird studying a dull, gray worm. "I've heard of her. But I haven't seen her around town."

"She doesn't leave the hotel much," I said.

"The Garden Club's always looking for new members." Mrs. Channing's smile brightened. "I'm the secretary. I'd be glad to put in a good word for her. We love new people coming into Fairly, don't we, Tate?"

Tate peeled the plastic lid off his drink and shook crushed ice into his mouth. With both of us watching, he stopped, finished crunching, and said, "Yeah. Sure, we do."

It was as if my brain dropped through a black hole. I had no idea what to say. Mama at a garden club? She couldn't keep a cactus alive. "She's uh, busy," I said, "you know, with all the stuff going on at the hotel."

Mrs. Channing's smile froze.

"You know," I said, "the fire, and the, uh..." I glanced at Tate. His grin was huge as he chomped ice with his big, white teeth. "She's busy," I said finally. "Uber busy."

"Of course," Mrs. Channing said, "we're all busy. Maybe once she's more settled."

"Yes!" I snatched at the lifeline and nearly knocked over my half empty cup. "I'm sure she'd love to join. Later. When she's less busy. I mean, you know, settled."

Tate's mom frowned and said, "Then I look forward to meeting her." She laid the most beautifully manicured hand I'd ever seen on her son's shoulder. "Tate, honey, you'll be home for dinner, won't you?"

"I don't know, Mom," he glanced from her hand to her face, "will you?"

"Well, sweetie, it's Thursday." She studied her diamond-studded Rolex. "You know I've got a six o'clock with my trainer. Won't be done in time for dinner. But you and your daddy go ahead and eat without me. There's pizza in the freezer."

"Don't worry, Mom," Tate said. "We know the drill."

"You're the sweetest one." She bent to plant a kiss on his head and he tilted out of reach. She pulled away with a pout.

"Okay, Mom," he said, smiling at me. "Buh-bye, now." Her wounded gaze fell on me. I smiled sheepishly.

She dropped her hand to grip her purchases. "Nice to meet you, Cat," she said, pivoted on her heels, and strode toward a black Lexus.

"You, too," I called after her.

Tate's smile didn't fade until she'd flung the car door open, tossed her packages into the passenger seat, climbed in, and roared away. He leaned forward in his chair, eyed my abandoned lemonade, and said, "Now, where were we?"

CHAPTER 22

I pushed the door open and Tate and I stepped inside the cool, dark store. As I adjusted to the dim light, I wondered if Bragg Hamilton intentionally kept his store dark so he could size up his customers before their eyes adjusted.

We found him in the far corner on his stool, running what appeared to be a dry round brush in and around the bleached eye sockets of a long, narrow skull.

I strolled past the bits of rocks and carcasses and bones. "What's that?" I said staring at the skull in his hand.

He didn't bother looking up. "What do you think?"

"What would anyone do with that?" Tate said.

Brother Bear sported a fishing hat with lures dangling from the brim, which was funny, if a little cliché. Tate strolled over to him to study the lures.

Bragg glanced at me. "What do you want?" He continued brushing, dusting, as he turned the skull over and over.

"Got anything from the Civil War?" I pressed fingertips onto the glass counter and he snorted at my electric blue nail polish.

"What do you want with Civil War memorabilia?" he said. "You don't appear to be much of a history buff to me."

"Summer project," I said and surveyed the store. Nick, the human skeleton, sat in a chair behind the register with his legs crossed. A new display of black and orange striped beetles hung on the wall behind him.

"Hey." Bragg brought my attention back to him. "I don't have time for foolishness. Now run along and steal a car or whatever you kids do for fun these days."

"You got anything from the Fairly Grand when it was turned into a Confederate hospital?" I said.

He stopped polishing. "What do you know about that?"

I trailed my fingers along the counter and stooped to study a collection of old coins. "Any of these Confederate?"

"Get your grimy fingers off the glass." He jumped off his stool. "I got to clean that case every time you kids run your sticky hands all over it."

"You actually get a lot of kids in here?" I said. "Most of this stuff is pretty pricey." I plucked a twenty-five-dollar chunk of pink quartz out of a wicker basket.

"So?" He tapped the wooden brush on the glass. "It's all authentic."

"Uh, huh." I eyed the saber-toothed tiger skull.

"You don't believe me?" The tapping got faster and I thought he might crack the glass.

"Vampire bats," I said, "really?"

He stopped tapping, but the sound continued to bore into my skull. "Somebody had to dig this stuff up, dry it out, stuff it, mount it, whatever. It's a legitimate business."

"Okay. Ever think of putting some of your stuff in the Fairly Grand?"

"Why would I do that?"

"There's this artist, they've got his paintings plastered throughout the lobby. And this other artist makes pictures out of teeny, tiny pieces of bark. There's a display of Civil War weaponry. Maybe they could display your fish fossils."

He studied the skull in his hands and said, "I stay away from that place."

"What's wrong with the Fairly Grand?"

"I don't want to talk about it."

"Well, do you have any Civil War stuff or not?"

"No."

"You sure?" I glanced around. "You got a lot of history here."

"I said no!"

My head snapped back. "What's wrong with Confederate stuff?" I said.

"You might've noticed with all the Confederate flag burning going on and statues being toppled," he said, "it's not exactly popular right now."

Tate strolled back to the glass case and leaned a hip against it. "She's just looking for some information about the old cemetery out by the hotel."

"I said no. I meant no." Bragg banged the skull onto the counter and picked up a femur. It might've come from a dog, or maybe a wolf. Patches of gray feasted on the bleached white bone.

"But you know everything there is to know about this town," Tate said. "All the history."

"That doesn't make me the damn town historian." Bragg glared at him. "Y'all run along and shoplift something. Or better yet, harass Harrie Ann. She'll give you a job. Heard they're already stringing lights along Fairly Avenue for the big celebration. Planting marigolds. Putting flyers in store windows. Make yourselves useful."

"This is important," I said.

He leveled his gaze on me. "What's so dang important about the cemetery? There's nothing but dead people rotting there."

I raised a finger to tell him. But, how to explain that as long as a ghost was haunting the cemetery, and I was the only person in a hundred years to see him and therefore the only one who might figure out how to get rid of him, Mama and I would never have any peace and I would never have any friends? I curled my finger and dropped my hand.

Tate grunted. "She's looking for information about the slave Culver somebody, who shot Great-Great-Great-Granddaddy back in the 1800s."

Bragg gripped the bone, his knuckles whitening. "You don't want to be mucking around in that business." He followed our gaze to the raised weapon in his fist. He lowered it. He breathed deeply and tapped the bone against his thigh. "Best to research somebody else. Old Chess Jamison was quite a character. He fought in the Civil War, too. Survived only to get himself shot on a Mississippi riverboat, cheating at cards. And then there's Bones Malloy, who blew up the Luna Belle. Research them."

"Tell me about Culver Calhoun Washington," I said, "what really happened to him."

Bragg stopped tapping.

Tate glanced between his uncle and me.

Bragg lowered his voice. "What are you really looking for?"

The blood pounded in my ears and my fingertips tingled with a charge of electricity in the air. "Like Tate said. Culver Washington."

"You said Calhoun," Bragg accused. "Nobody knew his full name. You're making it up." His grip was so tight on the bone I thought it might snap.

"Why would I?"

"Where'd you get it, then?"

"From a book."

"No," he said, "you didn't. It might've said Culver, or Culver C., but nobody knew what the C stood for. Slaves didn't usually have more than a first name back then. They sure didn't have middle names. Story goes that Old Josiah favored him so much he let him take the full name he wanted. I've done my research, too, and there's absolutely no record of anybody knowing his middle name, except maybe Horace and he apparently took it to his grave. So, my question to you is," he stepped toward me with the bone quivering in his fist, "who are you, and what are you doing in Fairly?"

"Uncle Bragg," Tate laughed uneasily, eyeing the threatening bone. "She's just a fourteen-year-old girl."

"Fifteen." My toes dug into the thin carpet.

"She moved from Atlanta." Tate glanced between us.

"Actually, a small town outside Atlanta. A wee, small town." I indicated with my forefinger and thumb just how small.

"Her mom's the new manager at the Fairly Grand."

Bragg Hamilton stopped and the bone clattered onto the glass counter alongside the skull. His hand trembled as he swiped his stubbled chin. He turned, walking his fingers along the glass as he moved behind the counter.

"You best forget about Culver Washington," he said massaging the back of his neck. "No sense stirring up more trouble. We've got this dang celebration gearing up, and there'll be enough history bandied about to satisfy your juvenile curiosity."

"I can't forget Culver," I said.

"And why not?"

"There's some stuff I can't explain."

He glared at me. "Why should I care?"

"Mama and I are trying to fit in here," I said. "She's struggling to keep her job."

He rested his fingertips on the counter. "Well, dragging up some dead forgotten slave isn't going to help."

"What are you afraid of?" I said.

Tate snorted. "Uncle Bragg? Afraid? He's hacked his way through the jungles of Africa. He's been trained with the Contras. He's –"

"You don't know what you're doing," Bragg interrupted. "Leave it be."

"And I'm telling you I can't," I said. "If you know something, you've got to help me."

"The hell I do. You have no idea what you're getting into. The best I can do is warn you to leave it alone. You think losing a job is the worst thing to happen to you and your mama? You don't know Bedford

Hamilton. Now, Tate, take your little girlfriend and get out of here. I've got work to do."

Tate grabbed my arm, "Cat, come on," he said, and dragged me toward the door.

It jingled open and I heard Bragg swear and thunder up the stairs as we stepped into the sweltering heat.

CHAPTER 23

"What was that about?" Tate turned to me outside the store.

"What?" I headed toward Fairly Avenue to wait for the shuttle back to the hotel.

He grabbed my arm and stopped me. A woman sidled past us in yoga pants, her hair in a messy bun, chopsticks poking out of it. Her flip flops slapped pavement as she continued on her way.

"What exactly is it you're investigating?" he said. "And why?"

"I told you." I pulled my arm out of his grip and continued walking.

He kept in step. "No," he said. "You told me you were doing research. But this seems personal."

I shrugged. We reached the corner and I turned toward the toy store.

"I can't help you if you don't tell me what you're doing," he said.

"I don't need your help. I'll figure it out myself."

"Really?" He stopped in front of the hardware store. "Because it's my family's story. Seems like we'd be the ones with the answers."

I stopped and turned. "Seems like it. But apparently you aren't. You didn't even know Culver's full name." And I immediately cursed myself for bringing it up again.

"Yeah," he said. "How'd you know that? If it's not in the history books and Uncle Bragg didn't even know?"

"Forget it," I said. "Forget you were ever involved."

He cocked his head. "Why are you so determined to do this by yourself?"

A man in red suspenders rocked in front of the store with a woman beside him, her ankles swollen and overflowing her orthopedic shoes.

"Because," I said, "I've learned you can't count on people. Even your best friend. Or family. They'll turn on you in a heartbeat. Or leave you high and dry. So, I'll do it myself and you don't need to worry about it."

"You're dragging my family into it."

A trio of girls in raggedy blue jean shorts and tank tops approached, all various shades of blonde, hair swishing against tanned shoulders.

"Hey, Tater," the tiniest one said. She was barely a wisp of a gypsy, as if she subsisted on carrot sticks and good wishes. Her hair fell past her shoulders in a curtain of white lightning. "You going to the pool party tonight?"

"Summer," he said, "you know I don't go to that church anymore."

"You can come if you want," the tallest blonde said. She could've just stepped off a European tennis court, or maybe the cover of German *Vogue*.

"Thanks, Katy. This is Cat." Tate nudged his chin in my direction. "She's new in town. Can she come?"

The three girls exchanged looks before presenting matching fake smiles. But it was the girl in the middle who spoke.

Of course she can come," she said with a tilt of her head and a swish of tawny hair. "Would you be bringing her as a date?" Her grin dimpled her cheek, then disappeared. Something about her reminded me of Lizzie Lee at school. It was more than the blonde hair. And it stung.

"Claire," Tate said, "you know I don't have time to date."

"Right." She ran fingers through her hair, rattling the cuff of friendship bracelets encircling her delicate wrist. "Football, huh?"

"My one true love. Well, that and my Mustang. Besides, Cat's barely out of junior high." He turned to me. "I guess I could give you a ride. Want to go to a pool party?"

I gritted my teeth at his patronizing grin. I hadn't been in a pool since my accident in Shelby. I couldn't imagine going now. "I have to work," I said.

"Sorry, girls," he said. "Cat's a little shy. And apparently allergic to church and church-related activities."

"That's what we heard," Claire said.

"Maybe next time," he said. "But thanks for asking."

The leader of the blonde squad gave me a quick, tight smile and headed into the hardware store with her posse trailing.

I turned on him. "Allergic to church?"

"You're not going to make new friends, Catniss, if you don't accept their invitations."

"You didn't accept their invitation."

"I'm not trying to make new friends. I know everybody already. You, on the other hand, could use a few."

"Yeah, you can never have too many insincere friends."

He feigned shock. "I'm sincere."

"I don't know what you are. Yet."

He waved away my cynicism. "Back to Culver. What do you need to know about him and why?"

"How he died."

"I told you. He was shot attempting to escape."

"I don't think so."

"And why not? What could you possibly have heard otherwise? And why does it matter anyway?"

I stared through the store window. Claire, Katy, and Summer were trying out mini motorized fans, blowing their sun-bleached hair, giggling and stumbling into each other. I turned back to Tate, who waited expectantly. There was no way I'd risk telling him the truth.

"Wasn't your uncle's reaction to Culver a little over the top?" I said. "Didn't he appear he had something to hide?"

"Of course he has something to hide," Tate said. "He left his last archaeological dig in disgrace. He drinks too much and he ignores the rest of the family. He's always been secretive."

I shook my head. "No, it's something else. Something specific. About Culver and your family. What did he say, 'you think losing a job's the worst thing that could happen to you?' And then he said something about your Uncle Bedford."

"Well, Bragg might be crazy," Tate said. "But there's one thing he'd know the truth about."

"What's that?"

"Uncle Bedford is one mean son of a bitch."

CHAPTER 24

Why have I always been cursed with such bad timing? Sunday, I was in town sucking on frozen lemonade (who knew those things could be so addictive?), heading toward the strip of park along the bay, searching for a shady spot to sketch. I wanted to be as far from Culver and his sordid story as possible.

Two blocks from the First Baptist Church, the bells chimed the noon hour. By the time I crossed in front of it, the doors opened and the Hamilton clan spilled out onto the steps. A minute earlier and I would've passed by and never looked back. A few minutes later and I would've been swallowed in the crowd, hidden from Bobby Hamilton. As it was, I landed right smack on the sidewalk at the bottom of the marble steps.

At the top of the stairs, Mayor Hamilton stood in black lace and pearls, shaking the hand of a hefty balding man in a black robe. A taller man with peppered gray hair hovered at her elbow, wearing a Hugo Boss suit and a ferocious scowl.

Tate's mother tottered down the steps in blue silk and Prada stilettos beside a tall, sandy-haired man, an older version of Tate. But it was Tate who called out to me. He pushed past his grandmother to descend the stairs and halt on the step above me, hands shoved into his pressed khakis, rocking back on his heels. He wore a navy blazer and red striped tie.

"Whatcha doing?" he said.

"Look at you," I said, "all fancy." Flustered and fluttery, I licked the stickiness from my lips and glanced around at the silk dresses and pearls and tailored suits. I shuffled my black high tops and said, "I thought you didn't go to this church."

"I don't." His mother stopped a few feet away, her head cocked toward her husband's low voice, but her eyes were on me. "There was some dedication thing for the Celebration of the Dead ceremony in August." He grimaced. "Mom made me come." Stuart Channing moved to shake hands with a man in a tan suit and his wife sidled toward us.

"Hello." Belle Channing slid her perfect red nails into the crook of Tate's arm. "Cat, wasn't it?"

"It still is," Tate said, his smile forced.

"Of course." She laughed and dug her nails deeper into his arm. Her smile appeared as brightly forced as his. "Do you go to church, Cat?" she said. "My brother, Robert's the minister here. You'd like his sermons."

"No," Tate said, "you wouldn't."

"Tate, please," his mother tugged on his arm, "there's nothing wrong with your uncle's sermons."

"Nothing a good nap wouldn't fix."

"There's no reason to judge by one –"

"No use recruiting her, Aunt Belle." Bobby Hamilton sauntered down the stairs in a black suit. With his hair slicked back with fistfuls of hair gel and his black eye unsuccessfully covered with makeup, he looked like a juvie gangster. "Cat doesn't do church."

Belle Channing turned a troubled frown on me. "Well, what do you do on Sundays?"

My sketchbook twitched in one hand, my cup of melting lemonade in the other.

"Mom," Tate said, "it's none of our business." He pulled his arm out of her grasp.

"Yeah," Bobby straightened his black tie with a tilt of his head. "What do you do while the rest of us are in church, Cat? Been hanging around any cemeteries lately?" Everyone's gaze dropped to the paper cup in my hand, and I glanced around, desperate for a place to toss it as if it was the perfect representation of my utter sinfulness.

"I go to church," I said, and licked the sin from my lips.

Bobby folded his arms. "Oh yeah?"

Tate laughed. "Can we please stop interrogating her?"

"Cat Turner," Harrie Ann called as she eased down the steps sideways, one at a time, "how lovely to see you. How's your mama?"

She stopped with a little huff of breath beside Bobby.

"She's fine." The crowd dispersed around us, and the Hamiltons gathered to face me. And I was on the bottom looking up.

"Tell them why you don't go to church, Cat," Bobby said.

"It's not a crime to not go to church," Tate said. "She can do what she wants."

"Sure she can, honey," his mother said. "Why don't you go to church, Cat? Haven't you found one you like?"

"She hasn't exactly been looking," Bobby said.

"How do you know?" Tate stared at him. "Are you stalking her?"

"Why are you always taking her side?" Bobby hissed.

Tate laughed. "I'm not taking anybody's side. I just don't get what the big deal is."

"Well of course it's a big deal," Belle Channing said.

"Church is just a place," Tate said. "You can believe in God without believing in some manmade institution."

"Watch what you're blaspheming there, boy," the scowling man left the minister and stomped down the steps to close the gap between us. His navy striped suit was perfectly tailored to his broad shoulders. Fat chunks of gold winked from starched French cuffs. Tate's father followed him.

"It's not blasphemy, Uncle Bedford," Tate said, "if you don't want to go to church."

"Read your Bible, son," Bedford Hamilton said.

"I do read it, Uncle," Tate said. He jerked away from his mother's tightening grip. "Do you read yours? Because I'm pretty sure it also talks about not leaving widows and orphans destitute. And abandoning your own kin."

"Tate, enough," Stuart Channing said, and I wondered if anyone would notice if I simply slipped away.

"What about Jane Sanders?" Tate lifted his chin.

Bedford snorted. "She's not a widow."

"She might as well be. You bullied her husband into a heart attack and now she can't pay his medical bills, much less his legal ones."

"Tate!" his father thundered. "Enough."

Heads swiveled toward us.

Through a tight smile and clenched teeth, Harrie Ann said, "Can we please not air our dirty laundry on the steps of God's house?" She waved and nodded to a stooped, white-haired man clomping a walker along the sidewalk.

"It's not dirty laundry," Bedford said. "It's business."

"I'm sorry, Grandmother," Tate said. He mussed his hair.

"It's all her fault," Bobby stabbed a finger at me. "She causes trouble everywhere she goes."

"Me?" I squeaked. "What did I do?"

Bobby pushed Tate aside to tower over me. "Who knows what kind of evil you've brought here."

"Wh...what?"

"Bobby," Tate's voice was low, "have you lost your freaking mind?"

Bobby shrugged him off. "Tell them why you don't go to church, Cat."

"Bobby, enough," Harrie Ann said.

My face flamed a thousand shades of hell. Blood pounded in my wrists. My scarf tightened and sweat popped out above my brow. Soon it would trickle down my cheek, my neck, taking, I imagined, my exquisitely applied makeup with it. Freckles would pop out all over. I clutched my sketchpad as if it could somehow protect me.

"Tell them, Cat," Bobby said. "Tell them why trouble and chaos follow you everywhere you go." He fingered his bruised eye.

"I have no idea what you're talking about." I sounded breathless. My scarf squeezed the oxygen from me.

"Because," Bobby leaned his nose into mine, his hot breath reeking of mint and burped Dr. Pepper, "you worship demons. And their master."

Belle Channing glanced around in confusion. "Satan?" she guessed.

"Bobby," Harrie Ann said.

Bobby pulled back with a smug curl of his lip. "And I have proof."

CHAPTER 25

By the time I reached the hotel, Mama had already heard about my run-in with the Hamiltons. Gloria, who was off duty and sometimes at the Baptist Church spying on her ex-husband and his new wife, over-heard the Parkers, a couple who ran the Out of Time antique store, gossiping about some poor girl the Hamilton family took to task for skipping out on church. They accused the girl of being a Wiccan or a Satanist or something. I suspect Gloria relayed the information to Mama with relish.

By the time I stalked my way through the hotel lobby, Mama was waiting for me in front of Gloria's empty desk. I stormed past her. "Cat, honey, wait," she called and jogged to catch me. She grabbed my arm. "Cat, sweetie, are you okay?"

I spun around. "Okay? Do I look okay?"

"Well, no, honey. You look upset."

"Upset," I ground through my teeth, "doesn't begin to cover it." A woman waiting in front of the gift shop in a broad black hat and slinky palazzo pants stared at us.

Mama lowered her voice. "Tell me what happened."

"I don't want to talk about it." Two boys in swimsuits and flap-ping beach shirts trotted through the lobby, staring at us, goggle-eyed.

"Not here." Mama squeezed my arm. Her nails were ragged. When did she start biting them? "Let's go in the bar," she said. "It's quiet there."

"I'm not talking about it."

Her fingers pinched my skin. "Catalina Angelica Turner."

"Stop calling me that!" I yelled. "It's Cat! Just Cat!"

Ed Winer's slick black head popped out of his office. His eyes narrowed as he honed in on us.

"Get in here," Mama hissed and dragged me into the bar.

"Oh, Mr. Winer," Giselle distracted him before he reached the check-in counter, "can I get your opinion on this?" The door to the bar swung shut.

"Sit down," Mama ordered. "Willie, two colas, please. Make mine diet." She pushed me into a leather chair at one of the round tables. The Fischers burst through the door from the patio. Mrs. Fischer was arguing the validity of global warming. Mr. Fischer was picking at a tooth with what appeared to be a tiny plastic saber.

More bad timing.

"Why, Catalina," Mrs. Fischer strolled over to us, "are you okay? You appear pale, dear. And on the verge of tears."

"She's fine," Mama snapped. She sank into the chair opposite me and pressed her fingertips to her brow. "I'm sorry," she said. "I didn't mean to snap. I have no idea how she is. She won't say."

"I did say." My eyes burned as my mascara flaked into them and blurred my vision. "I'm fine. Now can I leave?"

Willie brought our drinks and Mrs. Fischer ordered a Manhattan, Mr. Fischer, a Scotch and water. I groaned inwardly as they slid into the vacant seats at our table. Willie returned to the bar without a word. I scrubbed my right eye, praying for Mama, Mrs. Fischer, and Mr. Fischer to magically disappear.

"Tell me what happened," Mama said.

"You've obviously heard already. So just let me go to my room and forget the whole thing."

"Who was it?" she said. "Who can I call to give a piece of my mind?"

"I don't think you can afford to lose any more," I said.

She was not amused. "This is not the time to be funny, missy. I will not tolerate this happening again. I waited way too long to step in the last time. It was so ludicrous, so absurd, I thought it would simply go away. But not again." She took a long swig of her diet soda.

I stared at mine and watched the ice melt.

"Is there anything I can do?" Mrs. Fischer injected into the silence. She glanced between us. "I hate to see two of my favorite people so obviously upset."

"That's sweet," Mama said, her focus on me, "but this is something Cat and I have to work out. Who is it, Cat?" she said. "Who's causing you this pain?"

I stared at her and gripped the edge of the table. My voice was glacial. "You cannot help me."

She flung herself backward, indignant righteousness leaking out of her like a punctured balloon.

"That was always your mistake," I said, "you never could." I probably couldn't have wounded her more if I'd slapped her.

Willie approached with the Fischers' drinks and Ed Winer burst through the door.

"Eva," he barked, "I need to speak with you." He jerked his head toward the lobby.

"I'm in the middle of something," she said and smoothed her hair behind her ear. It was the first time I'd seen it out of its bun in days. "I'll be there in a minute."

He glared at her. "Excuse me?"

"I'm talking to my daughter." Mama stared straight at me. "We're in a bit of a crisis. I'll be there when I'm finished."

"Is she, is she bleeding?" Ed Winer stuttered. "Is she incapacitated in some way?"

Mama gripped the arms of her chair and faced him ever so slowly. "I'd rather not do this in front of guests," she said, "but I am not on the clock. It's my day off. The first one I've had in the four weeks I've been here. And I've been putting out fires and dodging bullets until exactly ten minutes ago when my daughter fled from town. I'm going to finish this conversation and make sure she's all right and then I'll meet you in your office. Okay?"

He glared at her until I wanted to scream at him myself. "You're always on the clock, Ms. Turner," he said finally. "You'd better get used to it." He whirled around and stalked back to his office.

"Cat," Mama said.

"Go." I waved her away. "Just go."

"I'm not leaving," she said, "until I know what happened and who to call."

There was no way I could relive the embarrassment of the last hour even for her. My lips remained in a mutinous line.

"Why don't you go, Eva?" Mrs. Fischer said and twirled the stem of the cherry in her drink. "Ira and I will keep Catalina company until you return. We'll be okay, won't we, dear?"

I blinked at her and wondered what fresh hell I was going to be subjected to.

"I'll be back," Mama said and pushed herself away from the table.

"Right. Sure. Great," I muttered under my breath and watched her leave me for, like, the gazillionth time. I couldn't stand her helplessness, anyway. And it made me want to pound Bobby Hamilton into a bloody pulp.

CHAPTER 26

Mama refused to let me leave the hotel for the next few days, which was fine by me. I'd endured as much of the Hamiltons as I could stand. I watched reruns of Supernatural. I helped housekeeping replace bath towels and set out miniature bottles of shampoo and lotion. I served afternoon tea.

Mr. Ed thought Portia Farringer from England would be at least a little experienced at tea serving. But she served guests orange pekoe when they requested chamomile. She picked at her nails when they asked for butter for scones. And she let the cookies run out every single day.

I enjoyed serving afternoon tea, with its steaming teapots and rich, cinnamon smells. But after three days, I'd had as much of the hotel as I could stand, too.

I hadn't given much thought to Culver since Tate and I argued. And what little thought I'd afforded him was mainly spent questioning my sanity and whether I'd imagined the whole thing.

In the meantime, Mama took matters into her own hands. The day after the church incident, while I was folding towels in the laundry, Mama left the hotel for the first time since our emergency room visit.

She attempted to address the mayor first, but Harrie Ann was out. Fortunately for everyone involved, Bedford Hamilton was also unavailable, as he was out of town on business. And so, in her own mind, she did the next best thing.

I have it on good authority that she marched into Genesis and said to Bragg Hamilton in a voice cold enough to freeze molten lava, "I want to know exactly what you were doing attacking my daughter outside of church."

He glanced up from the book he was reading on the lost art and treasures of European Jews during the Holocaust. Marking his place with a forefinger, he squinted from his stool. "Who's your daughter?"

"Catalina Turner," she said and marched further into the store, tripping over a wrinkle in the carpet. She caught herself with a palm slammed onto the glass counter. That's when she noticed the display of penis bones mere inches from her fingertips. She snatched her hand away and massaged it as she stared with distaste at the stuffed bats on the wall, the dead chipmunk perched on a tree limb, Brother Bear's beekeeper hat and veil.

"I don't know any girl named Turner," Bragg said and resumed his reading.

"Mr. Hamilton," she stopped in front of him. He sighed and gave her his full attention. "I will have my say and you will listen." He tilted his head with more patience than he was usually willing to muster.

He would later describe her as a petite little thing in a prissy pencil skirt, a simple white shirt with French cuffs, and sensible pumps. Her hair was a shade more auburn than her daughter's, with bangs fringing green eyes that hissed sparks.

Her hair was pulled into an unattractive bun, but wisps curled and stuck to her flushed cheeks. He wasn't sure if he'd ever seen a more flustered, harassed, or cuter woman in his life.

He placed the book on the counter. "Who are you?"

"Eva Turner." She huffed her bangs out of her eyes and propped a hand on her hip. "I work at the Fairly Grand."

Something in his brain clicked. "The new manager."

"About Cat."

"I don't know a Cat," he said. "I mean, I know a cat. I know lots of cats. I just don't know a girl named Cat."

Mama was not amused. "She's been here several times," she said. "She cut her head on one of your," she swept the store with disgust, "your things." She peered closely at the shadow box to her right, a display of colorful dragonflies. Was there a smudge of blood still on the glass?

"Oh, her," Bragg said.

He stood and leaned a hip against the counter and folded his arms. Eva Turner might be the cutest thing to grace his store, but he wasn't too keen on her looking like she'd stepped in cow dung.

"Well, she's definitely got your sense of grace," he said, "I'll give you that."

Mama's eyes widened and for a second, Bragg regretted her wounded look. But then her lips hardened and she said, "I don't know where you get off accusing my daughter of all sorts of evil things."

"And I don't know what the hell you're talking about," he shot back pleasantly enough.

"I'm talking about you and your family accosting my daughter outside of church yesterday and spreading nasty rumors about her."

"I don't go to church," Bragg said.

"She's a kid," Mama's voice grew louder, "who's had a rough time of it. Something you and your ivy-league family wouldn't understand. And she comes here desperate to make new friends and fit in. And you people want to drag her back down, spreading vicious lies."

"I don't go to church," Bragg said, enjoying the way the color flamed into her cheeks as her eyes flashed emerald bits of hardness.

"And your nephew," she stabbed a finger at him, "keeps acting nice to her while making fun of her behind her back. The other one, Bobby, ran her over in his stupid golf cart and she had to have stitches and she just got her arm out of the sling last week. She's working to get back on her feet, and I can't look out for her because Ed Winer's breathing down my neck begging for a chance to fire me and then there was the fire and the flood at the hotel and I'm doing the best I can. But since the accident I can't protect her." She threw her arms wide. "And she won't talk to me and she's wearing those crazy scarves, and the headaches and those drawings and Jimbo's gone and I'm trying to do everything and I'm, I'm at my wit's end!"

The air in the store had grown stifling. Bragg thought he heard a hiccup. And then she fell silent, a palm pressed to her forehead, her eyes misting.

"I don't mean to be rude," he said softly, "but exactly what are we talking about? Who's Jimbo?"

Mama blinked rapidly. What in the world was she doing? Had she lost her mind?

Bragg reached out. "Look, whatever happened at church," he said, "I wasn't there. I stopped going to that church years ago. So did Tate. What exactly was said?"

Mama's hand dropped to her mouth. "You really don't know what I'm talking about?"

He shook his head.

"Oh. My. Lord."

"It's okay." He straightened from the counter. "Let me get you something to drink." He ducked behind it. "Something stiff. Like in the movies. There's," he dropped to his haunches, "vodka, scotch, bourbon." He peered over the counter at her. "You probably need something strong."

She reached out to him. "I'm sorry." Tears spilled over, sparkling her eyes, darkening her lashes. "I'm so sorry. I don't know what I'm doing."

He stood and she stumbled backward over the same wrinkle in the carpet and righted herself.

"Eva," Bragg said.

"I'm so sorry. Please don't tell Ed Winer I was here. I need this job. Please."

"Eva. Stop."

She stumbled out the door and stopped briefly outside, a hand to her stomach, before hurrying out of sight. By the time Bragg reached the door and snatched it open, she was gone.

CHAPTER 27

Some old blue hair from First Baptist sniffed, "Why, Eva Turner better take herself back to Atlanta if she imagines to take on the Hamilton clan. Bragg Hamilton's an odd enough fellow, but the rest of the Hamiltons are good people. There wouldn't be a Fairly without them."

Another said, "Sheriff Hamilton does a serviceable job. There's practically no crime to speak of besides the fire at the hotel. And Harrie Ann, who can even remember a mayor before her, including her husband? And you couldn't ask for a finer preacher than Robert Hamilton."

Still another chimed in, "If anyone has a problem fitting in this town, it's Eva Turner and her strange daughter. I've heard rumors about devil worship and animal sacrifices. It's enough to give me the willies." Another said she heard I wore scarves to hide some tattoo of the beast.

On a balmy summer evening, no Fairly eatery exuded as much charm as the Pizza Emporium. To celebrate Mama's thirty-ninth birthday, we sat on the upper deck outside where a huge, ancient oak sprouted through the wooden plank floor, its limbs creating a canopy above us. White twinkling lights draped the deck railing, as delicate as fairy garland. Fat white candles flickered on pub tables on the upper deck, and picnic tables on the lower.

The pizza was exotic, with strange pairings of shrimp and bacon, artichokes and grilled salmon, chicken and pesto. I chose the mac and cheese pizza and sank my teeth into a thick, sweet crust drenched in melted mozzarella and cheddar cheese, loaded with creamy macaroni and roasted garlic.

Mama nibbled around the edges of a slice and sipped her white wine and kept glancing at the door to Genesis.

"I should go back and apologize," she said.

"You already apologized." I bit through a string of gooey cheese.

"I mean seriously."

"You were serious." I plopped my half-eaten slice onto my plate. "Uber serious." I sipped my cola. "Now can we please forget it?"

"I don't want him to think badly of me," Mama said. "I mean, the hotel. My position as manager. He could send a lot of business our way. And the mayor," she pressed fingertips to her temple, "what must she think?"

I slurped my drink. "He probably didn't tell her," I said. "I don't imagine they talk much."

Her tired face lit up. "You think?"

I shrugged.

"Oh, I'd feel so much better if I knew. Maybe I should go ask him."

"Can we please stop talking about the Hamiltons for one night?" I said.

"Well, sure." She peered over her wine glass. "You haven't had trouble with Bobby since then, have you?"

"What? No. He's a moron."

"Cat."

"Well."

"Well, a negative attitude won't win you many friends." She set her glass on the table and stared at Genesis. Bragg Hamilton's shadow moved in the window.

"Nothing's going to win me any friends if he keeps going around blabbing about..." and I stopped.

"About what?" Her attention popped back to me.

"Nothing." I raised my slice of pizza and crammed half of it into my mouth.

Mama lowered her voice and leaned over the table. "He hasn't said anything since Sunday, has he? We've nipped it in the bud, right?"

I glanced around to see if anyone was listening. The three girls Tate and I met outside the hardware store were sitting at a picnic table on the lower deck. The blonde squad. They laughed as the waitress handed them their check. I swallowed hard and turned my back on them. "Sure we did."

Mama pointed at the corner of her mouth. "Got a little cheese right –"

"Whatever." I swiped it away.

She frowned. "Well, if it isn't Bobby Hamilton," she said, "then what? You know, honey, you've been more than a little moody these days. Are the headaches back?"

"They never leave." I crushed my napkin in my fist.

"Your arm," she nodded at it. "How's it doing?"

"Fine."

She sighed. "Cat, I can't help you if you won't talk to me."

"You can't help me at all."

She huffed back into her chair. A movement caught my eye. Bragg Hamilton was locking the front door to Genesis. He glanced our way, hunched his shoulders and hurried along the sidewalk, before disappearing around the corner.

"What about Dad?" I said to her. "Do you ever hear anything about him? Does he have any idea where we are?"

"Cat, honey."

"Just saying."

"What?" she said. "What are you saying? You think I wanted it to end this way?"

I fiddled with the crust of my pizza.

"He left us, Cat."

I shifted in my seat and tore off a chunk of crust and stuffed it in my mouth.

"You think I didn't try to get us help?" She swiped her bangs out of her eyes. Her pained expression made me wish I hadn't mentioned it. Almost.

"Where is he?" I said. "Do you think?"

She stared past me, her lips set in a grim line. "He stole my laptop and pawned it to drink himself into a stupor. He crashed your school wasted."

"He wanted to help me."

"He got me fired from my job with the mayor."

"I remember. You don't have to say it." I breathed deeply at the pain crushing my chest.

"I loved my job," she said. "I was good at my job."

"You're good at this job."

Her gaze fell on me. "I suck at this job."

"Mama."

"I do. I don't have any idea what I'm doing."

"Not true. You're doing what you always do. Working to make people happy."

She shook her head and sipped her wine.

"But don't you miss him?" I said. "Don't you feel there's a hole deep in your heart since he left?"

"Hey," she said brightly, "thanks for my book." She tapped a fingernail on the photographic book of Fairly Tate had recommended. "It should help me with my job. And thanks for my earrings." She flicked the turquoise drops already dangling from her ears.

"You needed more color," I said.

She sighed and rested a palm on the book. "Yes, I definitely do."

"Hey, Kit." I jumped to find Claire, Katy, and Sunshine, I mean Summer, at my shoulder.

"It's Cat," I said.

"Right." Claire smirked. "Cat."

"This is my mom, Eva." I indicated Mama and magically their smirks melted into lovely, innocent smiles.

"Hello, Mrs. Turner," they said.

"Hello." Mama smiled and reached for the stem of her glass and toyed with it.

"They're friends of Tate's," I said.

"Tate?"

I gritted my teeth. "Channing."

"Right, right."

"Sorry we missed you at the pool party," Claire said. "Wow, that's a cool scarf, can I..." she reached for it and I jerked backward and knocked my drink into my pizza. It flooded my plate and dripped off the table onto my lap. I jumped up and bumped the table, and Mama grabbed her teetering wine glass in the nick of time.

"Wow," Claire said. "I didn't mean –"

"No, it's fine," I said. "I'm stupid, clumsy."

"I'll get the waitress."

"No, really. I'm fine." I swiped at the dark stain spreading across the front of my white jean skirt.

"Well, okay, then," Claire said. "Guess we'll be going."

"Okay," I said. "Great. Good to see you." I dabbed at my lap as my face burned.

They snickered as they scampered down the steps, and once they hit the street busted into full blown laughter.

"Cat," Mama said.

"Forget it." I waved her away without looking up. A waitress brought a dry rag and wiped off my chair, the table, and removed my soaked plate of pizza.

"Take mine." Mama shoved it toward me.

"I'm not hungry anymore," I said.

"Cat, honey."

"Mama, please, forget it." I stared into the purple crepe myrtles lining the deck with their lovely, twinkling lights, and blinked furiously at how another dinner was ruined by the colossally clumsy, terminally awkward, Catalina Angelica Turner.

CHAPTER 28

The sun was high in the afternoon sky as I wandered along the sidewalk winding its way through the hotel grounds toward the bay. I passed two leggy girls in bikinis and sunglasses, their hair wrapped in messy buns, texting without ever looking up. A boy on a bicycle two sizes too small, with his knees to his chest, wove his way around them.

A man with clipped gray hair in expensive sunglasses and a pale green Izod sat alone at a poolside table for four. A young man strolled along the beach in black pants and a black hoodie. He couldn't be more out of place if he wore a mask.

I turned from the splashing and shrieking of children at water's edge to find Bobby Hamilton in my path.

"What are you doing here?" I said. "Spying?"

He hooked his thumbs in his white shorts, a melon sweater tied around his pink polo shirt. "I don't have to spy," he said. "I come and go as I please."

"How'd you get past Pete Bachus at the guard shack? He's got a pretty sharp eye."

"He goes to church with my family. Known him for years. We chatted." He rummaged in his pocket and pulled out a stick of gum. He unwrapped it and popped it in his mouth. Tate told me it was expensive, teeth-whitening gum for his modeling career.

I clenched my teeth and struggled not to be too disappointed in Pete Bachus' lack of judgment. I thought he had better taste. And sense. "So, what do you want?" I said.

"To hang out. With friends. That a crime?" He crumpled the silver wrapper and tossed it in the bushes. It disappeared among the leaves.

"Guess not. I'll leave you to it, then." I moved past him.

"You know, Catfish, everybody's laughing at you behind your back, right?"

I pivoted. "I don't really know anybody here," I said. "So exactly who would that be?"

"Your mother, storming into town, attacking Uncle Bragg?" He chomped his gum. "It's all over town. You're not the only one looking like a fool."

My insides burned at the thought of it, but I said, "So she's a mama bear, so what? Bragg didn't appear too upset."

"Bragg's a freak. Like you. And her."

I wanted to smack him, but fluttered my lashes instead. "Your insults are rather unimaginative, Bobby Hamilton," I said, "as if I hadn't been called names before. But just because you say it, doesn't make it true."

"Oh, I bet you've been called worse." He moved closer, his jaw working hard enough to smell the mint. "I'm fully aware of the trouble you caused at your fancy Christian school."

Blood throbbed in my veins, pulsed in my fingertips. "I didn't cause any trouble and it apparently wasn't that Christian. Anything else you want to discuss, or do I have to listen to this tiresome drivel all over again? If I recall, you said something about having some proof to show everybody. Well, do you?"

"Oh, I've shown it. Everybody who needs to know knows."

I rolled my eyes. "Whatever. I've got to go. Oh, and by the way," I hesitated, "no real guy wears a sweater like that. Apparently you've been drooling over too many Polo ads."

"I came from a photo shoot, you little witch," he said. "They made me wear it."

"Right."

"Bobby!"

Tate jogged along the sidewalk toward us. "Uncle Stone sent me to find you. Dinner's at the country club. Seven sharp."

"How'd your uncle know he was here?" I said.

Tate ignored me. "Dude," he said. "You look like a tool. Your mama been shopping for you again?"

Bobby turned on his cousin. "Shut up, jerkweed. You know where I've been."

"Right. Modeling." Tate wiggled his hips and struck a pose with a grip on his chin staring into space.

"Hey, you're good," I said. "You should give it a go." He broke the pose, laughed, and knuckled me.

Still chuckling, he shook his head at Bobby. "The crap they make you wear."

"Listen, douche," Bobby shoved Tate's chest, "I was in the middle of telling Little Miss Catfish I know all about her getting kicked out of school."

"That again?" Tate grinned. "What'd she do? Get caught making out with a tenth grader? Way to go." He punched my shoulder, rocking me sideways. I fought to stay on my feet. "Smoke a little weed outside the restroom?"

"No." I rubbed my shoulder.

"She's a freaking demon worshiper," Bobby said and stabbed a finger at me. "She sacrificed a cat. She's got blood on her hands."

Tate stopped laughing. I studied the pale blue sky streaked with orange and wondered when this would ever end.

And then Tate burst out laughing.

"What's so funny?" Bobby said. His lips flattened white. "I'm telling you, she's a freaking Satanist. She's into it, man. Those pictures we couldn't make out on her Facebook page? Burning crosses? Animal sacrifices? All part of it. That's why they kicked her out of school."

Tate fell into his cousin laughing so hard he knocked Bobby's sweater off his shoulders and it slithered to the ground. Bobby shrugged him off.

"Go ahead," he said and shoved Tate. "Act a fool."

Tate stopped laughing and swiped at his eyes. "Calling a fourteen-year-old girl a demon worshiper seems pretty foolish to me," he said.

"I'm fifteen," I said.

Tate ignored me. "Anybody could've faked the web page."

"I got proof she's fascinated by demons," Bobby said. "Can't get enough of them."

"Where'd you get proof?"

Bobby snatched his sweater off the ground. When he straightened, his lips were a mutinous line.

Tate glanced from me to him. "Seriously, man," he said, "how'd you find this out? You know somebody at her school?"

"I know somebody who knows somebody."

"Oh, you 'know somebody who knows somebody'," Tate said. "Sounds real legit."

"My school records were sealed," I said.

Bobby turned on me. "So, you're admitting it's true."

"Of course it's not true."

"That's not why you got kicked out?"

"I'm not a demon worshiper," I said. "That's beyond crazy."

"How do you explain the pictures?"

"What pictures?" Tate said.

"The ones she drew," Bobby leaned into my face, "of demons."

"They're angels," I said.

Tate's voice lowered, "We've already gone over this. Emmie drew pictures like that and she wasn't worshipping demons."

"Do not even think about comparing this freak to my sister," Bobby said. "Or I might hurl all over your stupid high tops." He turned to me. "The pictures from your school sure as heck look like demons."

"How would you know?" I said. "The school destroyed them."

"Apparently not."

"How do you know this?" Tate said. "Did you drive to Atlanta?"

"Of course not."

"The school's not in Atlanta," I said. "I'm from Shelby."

"Uncle Robert took you?" Tate said. "No, he'd never leave the church that long. Uncle Stone? He went to Atlanta?"

Bobby's chin lifted. "He called. They sent him stuff. Pictures. Apparently, there were some unexplained incidences involving missing animals."

Poor Mr. Stubbs. I thought I might be sick.

"It was classified," I repeated stupidly, and stared at the sweater Bobby strangled in his fists. "They destroyed the pictures."

"Don't worry about it," Tate said. "It's bullshit."

"Don't worry about it?" I said. "I've been fighting these lies for a year."

For a second, I stood back in the hallway of Holy Mercy with Mary Grace and Lizzie Lee blocking my locker. Mary Grace, my ex-best friend covered her mouth and whispered something to Lizzie. Their giggling followed me long after I slinked along the hall.

Brant Rogers made a cross with his fingers as I passed, as if to ward off a vampire. The words *demon slut* were bored into my notebook so deeply it imprinted each page to the last. Mr. Stubbs' poor, lifeless body lay on my porch, my blue chiffon scarf dangling from his neck.

My eyes stung and I blinked quickly. A dark shadow flashed behind Bobby's head. I ground my teeth. Not here. Not now.

"I said don't worry," Tate repeated. "Bobby's not going to tell anybody, are you?"

"Well," Bobby said.

"Well, what?" Tate's broad shoulders blocked all but the top of his cousin's head.

"I already told some people."

"You what?"

I pivoted and strode, eyes stinging, blinking, a flash of silver to my left, another to my right. I tugged on the scarf choking me.

"Cat," Tate called, "wait."

And then I ran, arms and legs flailing. I caught my toe on the sidewalk and stumbled, windmilling my arms to keep my balance. Ed Winer staggered out of my way and glared as he stumbled off the sidewalk. I ran faster and faster, the fringe of my scarf fluttering behind me. I didn't slow until the pain in my side squeezed the last breath from me as I hit the doors to the lobby and banged inside.

CHAPTER 29

"I been waiting for you," Culver said.

"I've been busy." I plucked at my rainbow-striped scarf. "The Fourth of July's this week and the hotel's booked solid. Guests have been checking in all week. You can hardly turn around without tripping over somebody."

"Day after day," he said, "soon as the sun sinks into the bay I watch. And wait. But you don't come."

"I'm sorry." The sting of guilt made me less than charitable. "I've been running myself ragged helping out at the hotel."

"Miss Cat," he said, "I got to get free of this place. I got to leave this infernal itching and lonesomeness behind. And I'm much afeard you're gonna disappear for good and I won't have nobody to help me for the next two hundred years."

"Calm down," I said. "Don't get your jammies in a wad."

He frowned.

"I'm doing the best I can," I said. "I happen to be plagued with people who want to destroy me."

"Miss Cat, each time you leave, I got no idea if you're ever coming back."

"I get it. But it doesn't help to hear it constantly. There's a lot of stuff going on out there you don't have a clue about. And I'm struggling to deal with it. And I'm trying to help you. And nobody's cooperating."

He strolled away. "You got to give people what they want," he said.

"Yeah? And what's that?"

"Old Queenie says you catch more flies with honey."

"You want to lecture me on how to treat people?" I said. "I've been nice. I've been polite."

"Miss Cat, you're getting mighty sore."

"Sore?" I said. "No, not sore. Frustrated. Like you. I want you gone as much as you do. Okay, I didn't mean it that way. You're frustrated and the hotel's being attacked and bad things are happening and you want to move on. Like I want to move on. We want the same thing, right? I mean, you're a cool guy, well, ghost. But this isn't your place. And it doesn't appear to be mine, either. But I'm stuck, too. So, we've got to make the best of it. There's nothing else we can do. Except maybe avoid the Hamiltons."

He stared at me and scratched his elbow.

"How'd you work for them, anyway?" I said. I pushed my heavy, sweat-soaked hair off my shoulder. "I'm not sure I wouldn't have run away."

"Big Ned ran away once," he said, "and they sliced him above both heels so he couldn't run no more. Lazy Luther didn't even run away. He simply took himself to visit his wife on a neighboring farm. The overseer Black Jake put his eye out with a cattle prod."

"Okay," I stopped him. "It was horrific. I get it. But there are no more slaves. Everybody's free."

"Except me."

Crickets thrummed and the first fireflies of the evening sparked. Lightning streaked across the sky in the distance, but there was no thunder. Nana called it heat lightning.

"You never told me what happened at the Houston house," I said. "History says you were being taken to the judge because you raped Lucie. You claim it was some sort of mission."

He scrubbed his hair and said, "We reached the house about twilight and it was a sight. Half of us kept watch from the woods while the rest crept forward to observe the shenanigans. It didn't look like no army camp, I can tell you. A whole hog roasted over a pit on the front lawn. The smell of it got my jaws to watering and Horace swiped the back of his hand over his mouth, his eyes full of fire and flaming hog. We hadn't eat meat since we joined up.

"Sutton crept forward while Horace and I eyed the yard. Cooper, quiet as a redskin, skirted around to the back of the house, keeping to the shadows. The revelry didn't subside until after midnight. When Cooper finally returned, he hauled a shirttail full of bones picked nearly clean. We set on 'em savage as a pack of wild dogs. To his credit, Horace shared with me what little victuals he could grab.

"Cooper said the bluebellies destroyed everything inside the house. Bayonets stabbed furniture. Family pictures was used for target practice. Animals were butchered, bloodhounds shot on the back lawn, mules and goats shot in the fields.

"Soldiers drunk on who knows what paraded in Mrs. Houston's petticoats and ruffled bonnets. Busted perfume bottles mixed with the stench of dead and rotting animals. Food lay strewn over tables. Spoiled peaches and apples was smashed against walls. The reek of death and destruction was stifling.

"'What do we do?' Sutton said.

"'Burn it to the ground,' Cooper said. 'I'd rather the house be destroyed than desecrated by those Yankee heathens.'

"'What about the Houstons?' Crawford said. 'It's their house.'

"Cooper fixed him with a glare that would've twisted steel. 'The Yanks said they were gonna torch it anyway,' he said. 'In two days hence, I heard 'em plotting in the old woman's parlor while soldiers used her bone china for target practice.'

"So, it was agreed," Culver said. "We'd torch the place before sunup and flush those Yanks out. Hovater and Sutton would release the remaining livestock. Crawford and I was to sneak onto the front porch and set it ablaze. Cooper would send fire along the climbing roses to the back balconies. Horace was to cover the road and pick off soldiers as they escaped.

"It wasn't what the Captain commanded. But what could I say? I can hardly bear to recall it. The fire, the screams of the men. The ones we knew. And the ones we didn't.

"When the last candle was snuffed and watchmen settled with rifles over their shoulders, a full moon peeked from behind a cloud. The front porch windows were open so the curtains weren't hard to light. Once the flames leapt the walls, all hell broke loose. Men come running from every direction, half-naked, barefoot, weapons drawn.

"Cooper was shot off the back balcony, but not before he threw a Ketchum grenade through a window and the room exploded into a fireball. Crawford was shot in the back on the front porch. I jumped the porch railing and felt a sting in my back sharp as a rattlesnake strike that tumbled me to the ground.

"I lay staring at the stars before coming to my senses. Rolling to my feet, I hightailed it to Horace. He stood frozen at the edge of the woods, his face lit by the flames licking the sides of the house. Horses thundered past us, shouts rang out through the yard, wood crackled, and Horace stood there, pistol limp at his side. I hollered, but couldn't manage to snatch him out of his trance.

"Shots whizzed past our ears. The heat from the house was an inferno and still I couldn't do nothing but throw myself against Horace as bullets rained upon us. I felt another sting in my side and pulled back a bloody palm in the moonlight.

"'Horace,' I said, 'we got to get out of here.' But he'd dropped his gun, lost it in the bushes. I had nothing but the knife Captain give me to protect Horace with.

"There was a strangling sound behind me. A Union feller. He couldn't have been more than ten and six. He raised his gun to Horace. With no time to think, I slashed my knife across his thigh and he staggered to the ground and onto his back. The wound didn't appear too bad. But when I reached him, he lay dead, eyes and mouth frozen in surprise.

"Horace managed to find his gun and was up and running. Shots rang out and I feared he'd been killed. When I finally found him, he'd tripped over a log, and shot himself clear through the foot.

"Horace and I was the only ones to come out alive, far as we knew. We wandered the woods for days, bleeding, starving, half out of our minds. We finally staggered to a dusty road and joined some gray-coated stragglers and wagons loaded with the wounded who'd escaped Vicksburg. They were headed to a hotel-turned-hospital down in the bay."

"The Fairly Grand," I said.

Culver fell silent.

"That is definitely a different story than Horace's," I said.

"It's the truth."

"It's still your word against, well, everybody else's." I strolled away and studied Elijah's angel, her sweet face, her sheltering wings. "We need an eyewitness account. Somebody who was there." I shook my head in frustration. "But everybody's dead and gone."

"Doc would tell the truth. If he was here."

"Doc?"

"Doc Perkins. The surgeon in these parts. Delivered all the Hamilton babies, even Horace. He was at the hospital when we arrived. Tended my wounds. Dug the ball of lead out of my side."

"I've never heard of him," I said. "He wasn't in the books."

"He's over yonder." Culver tilted his chin.

Easing around the tombstones, I found the doctor and stared at the modest headstone. Doctor Latimore Perkins. Beloved father and physician. Born 1811, died 1901.

"What am I supposed to find out about this doctor?"

"He kept records." Culver scratched his collar bone. "Of everything. He would've kept records of all the soldiers. Even me. That's the kind of man he was. Like Lucie, he didn't care about the dark of my skin. Or the fact I was a bought man. He treated me same as he treated everybody else." He bent and plucked a long, green weed from the doctor's headstone.

"He asked me about Lucie." He stared at the blade. "I acted like I had no idea what he was talking about. That was my shame. I should've said something. When Doc Perkins told me some poor white girl washed up on the shore, I knew. I knew in my gut it was Lucie. I simply couldn't figure out how she got to us. Or how she came to such an awful end."

"So, this doctor," I stared at the grave, "he knew about Lucie. He knew about the raid. But how are we going to prove it?"

"Don't suppose I know." Culver tossed the weed aside and scrubbed the back of his head. "He hauled this book around everywhere, like Horace. Leather bound. But fatter, thicker. He was always scribbling."

I shook my head. "Something's been bothering me," I said. "If you never left the hotel and died there, why are you here at the cemetery? Why aren't you haunting the hotel?"

"Haunting." He frowned. "That word don't sit well with me."

I spread my hands wide. "Gracing me with your presence?"

"I don't recall my last moments of breath," he said. "I remember floating above my body, and the blind beggar beside me hollering. And then I was here. Doc Perkins stood under the big oak there, beside a freshly-dug plot, hat in hand. And I'd see him there now and again after that. And then one day, he didn't come no more. Some folks came and stood around this marker here. More folks than I could count on two hands, dressed in black. Then others through the years. Doc Perkins was a good man."

"Listen," I said, "I'll see if I can find out something about this Latimore Perkins. But you've got to understand something. I have a lot going on. Mama's struggling at the hotel. Bobby Hamilton's skulking around spying on me, digging up dirty laundry so he can run me out of town."

"Dirty laundry?"

"Never mind. I'm just saying I can't promise anything. I'm new here, and no matter what Mayor Hamilton says, these people have not been tremendously welcoming."

"If you don't help me," he said, "I'll be bound here forever. It's up to you, Cat Turner."

"Listen, chief, if I get run out of town, I'm not going to be helping anybody. Did I mention Bobby Hamilton's got me in his crosshairs?"

"Time's running out," Culver said, "before they celebrate, what was it called?"

"Celebration of the Dead," I said. "If they stick Horace's statue in the middle of town, nobody's going to give two cents what he did or didn't do before he became a hero."

"I don't want his memory sullied," Culver said. "He may've froze and shot himself in the foot, but he did the best he could."

"Why do you keep making excuses for him?" I said. "He was evil."

"He wasn't evil, Miss Cat. He weren't never evil. He maybe got scared sometimes."

"Why do you insist on believing things that couldn't possibly be true? He raped a woman. No, a girl. He may've even killed her."

"You ever care for somebody who says they care for you?"

"Yeah?"

"They say they love you, then do something bad to you?"

The last time I saw Daddy, I caught him rummaging through my chest of drawers, looking for money. He kicked Ruby into a wall over a shattered bottle of cabernet. Mama said he left because he was so mortified about his drinking and losing his job, he couldn't face us. He couldn't help me with my problems at school and blamed himself for the whole thing. So he left and never came back. Never even called. And then there was Mary Grace.

"Well, nobody falsely accused me of rape," I said.

"He didn't mean it," Culver said. "He would've taken it back for anything."

"How can you believe that? There's absolutely no evidence to suggest he cared for you at all."

"Because," Culver said, "if I thought he cared so little for me he'd send me aswinging with no remorse, then I'd have to believe I weren't nothing more than a slave to him. Not a blood brother. Not even a friend. Just flesh bought and paid for with his daddy's handkerchief. And I can't abide it, Miss Cat. Whatever else I got to live and die with, I simply can't stomach that."

I sighed and turned away. It's not that I didn't understand. It's not that I didn't feel the same about Mary Grace. It's just…I scrubbed my face and turned back to him. "Here's my problem," I said. "If you're not angry at Horace because he framed you for rape and bound you for hundreds of years, I'm not sure exposing him is going to gain your release. How are you going to move on?"

He strolled toward the Walker monument, his thumb rubbing his lower lip. "The Good Book says the truth will set you free." His gaze met mine. "And I got to believe, whatever else, the Good Book don't lie."

I stared at the live oak, its branches sprawling protectively over its sacred plot.

"I'm sorry it's depending on you, Cat Turner," Culver said. "But you're all I've got. And I ain't waiting another score of years 'cause you've had a hard life and think you can't do no more. I want you to go in peace. Truly I do. But I will leave this place and you're gonna help me." He lowered his head, his gaze steady on mine. "Or I'm afraid you're gonna wish you had."

CHAPTER 30

Nothing like a nice threat to end your day. I trudged along the narrow, tree-lined road back to the hotel and struggled to understand. If there was somebody, one person who could free me from the prison of my past, I'd beg them to do it, wouldn't I? One person who could see me. Hear me. Not just keep walking past while it ate away my insides. I would cling to them, wouldn't I? I'd grab hold of that person with the panic of a drowning girl and hold on for all I was worth. For all eternity. I'd be foolish not to.

But there was no savior for me. No help on the horizon. There was nothing but one foot in front of the other, day after day, until it was so far behind me I couldn't remember it.

Culver was completely at the mercy of my whims. And if I didn't come through, he'd eke out his days, alone and itching infernally. If I couldn't help, he'd be stuck until the next slightly psychotic supernatural-seeking sap came along. Which might take fifty years. Or fifty thousand.

What's it like to be somebody's savior, you might ask. Well, it's dang depressing. You want to help, but you're scared, paralyzed by the fear that if you ask questions, 'kick up a ruckus' as Nana would say, somebody might kick around your past. And there was plenty in my past I'd just as soon not revisit.

Maybe if I was stealthy enough, nobody would notice. Though Bobby Hamilton already appeared to be hellbent on destroying me.

But Bobby wasn't really the problem.

The truth was, after eight years of Christian schooling, and fourteen years of good, solid churching, I wanted nothing more than to take a red-hot flatiron to Mary Grace Chappell's naturally curly hair until smoke rose and her curls burned off one by one and her head lay bare and the stench filled the room.

I wanted to smash the bottles of makeup she caked on every day, thinking she appeared so much more mature than me. I wanted to give her the name of a good plastic surgeon to fix the crook in her nose.

That's if I were really being honest.

The last time she spoke to me was at school in the girls' bathroom while the rest of our class dozed in math. She told Mrs. Farnsworth she was sick and needed my help to hold her head out of the toilet.

Instead, she sat on the counter, nose to the mirror, her Ugg boots straddling the sink. Like me, Mary Grace wasn't allowed to wear makeup so she swiped some from her mother's dresser and applied it at school.

"What'd they call you into the office for, anyway?" she said as she painted a thick line of kohl around her puppy brown eyes.

"It was those drawings," I said. "The ones Mr. Wallace turned in to the headmaster."

"That old fart." Mary Grace dabbed at the corner of her eye which left a smear, as crooked as a crayon out of control. "Damn." She wet her fingertip and dabbed at it, then dried it with her thumb. "So, what was it this time?" She drew the line heavier, "those crazy-ass demons?"

"You shouldn't cuss," I said.

She shrugged. "My parents say worse. I heard old man Wallace say 'shit' yesterday getting into his car. So," she stroked the other eye with the brush, "if it wasn't those," she peered at me through the mirror, "freaking demons."

"Angels," I said.

She held the brush aloft. "I told you to stop. You can't draw that stuff. Not at this school."

"They're angels," I said. "You know how many times angels are mentioned in the Bible?"

"No. But I bet you do."

"It's a lot."

"Not like that. Nobody thinks angels look like, like monsters. They've got furry white wings and a halo. They sit on clouds strumming guitars singing "Kum Ba Yah"."

"That's stupid," I said. "Nobody believes that."

She shrugged and peered into the mirror and stroked the silky brush along the curve of her eye. "This school does. Draw them that way and nobody freaks out."

"It's not how I see them." The bathroom tile was cold against my shoulder.

"You don't see them at all," she said. "You make them up, like everybody else. And why do you have to make them so evil-looking, so dark and deadly so nobody can tell them from the demons? Make 'em soft and pretty, same as everybody else."

"But that's how they really look."

"Stop it." The brush slipped and slid over her cheek. "See what you made me do?" She snatched a paper towel from the dispenser, wet it, and dabbed it with the antibacterial soap strong enough to peel off layers of skin. She scrubbed her cheek.

As the last trace of eyeliner disappeared she sighed. "Stop being so weird. We've been here since kindergarten. You know what they're like. Why do we have to sneak off to the bathroom to put on makeup? They're hopelessly out of touch. Archaic." She shrugged and leaned into the mirror. "Just play the game."

I blinked at her. "The game?"

"Don't be naïve." She fingered the red rash across her cheek. "You don't see angels. Or if you do, keep it to yourself. Stop being so weird."

"You said that already."

"Brant Hollings said he was thinking of asking you to the homecoming dance." Her gaze flickered to mine in the mirror. "You don't want to scare him off, do you?"

I shrugged.

"Just make sure you wear a scarf."

I fingered the rainbow cotton encircling my neck. "Brant Hollings flipped us off the other day and you called him a troll."

"But a popular troll." She grinned at the mirror and rubbed a spot of lipstick off her front tooth.

"You used to care about more than makeup and dating the most popular guy," I said. "You used to care about me."

Her eyes narrowed. "Is this about me making cheerleader and you not?"

"Of course not." I twiddled with the hem of my scarf. "I've been to all your games. I even sat there while you blew me off for your cheerleader buddies. Even the ones you used to talk about behind their backs."

She snorted as the door whooshed open and Lizzie Lee stalked in.

"M.G." Lizzie strolled over and fist bumped Mary Grace.

"When did you become M.G.?" I said.

Lizzie's blue gaze widened as she swung to me. She sized me up and down. "Nice scarf," she said and turned back to Mary Grace, who bit her lip and slid her feet off the counter to make room for Lizzie at the sink.

While Lizzie primped her long, blonde hair in the mirror and dabbed a fingertip at the corner of her red-painted lips, my best friend grabbed the edges of the counter, her boots swinging, and cocked her head at me.

"I don't know," she said, "I guess it's the accident. Because before that, I swear you were never this strange."

CHAPTER 31

I was halfway to the hotel when I heard the sirens. I crossed the main road and passed the guard shack as two sheriff's cars roared past me, lights flashing, sirens wailing. I broke into a run. By the time I reached the front door, the sheriff's cars were parked.

"What's going on?" I asked Sammie the valet as I yanked the door open.

He raised his hands and shrugged.

The lobby was quiet. Too quiet. Giselle and Benito huddled with Gloria behind the front desk. Mama stood talking to the sheriff, her back to me. Willie hovered in the doorway of the bar, running a towel around and around a beer glass, wide-eyed.

"Willie," I ran to him, "what's going on?" And then I followed his gaze to the lobby where shattered glass covered everything.

Time slowed. The sheriff, Mama, and deputies moved in slow motion. I fought my way along the corridor toward the fireplace in the center of the room. My gaze slid to the rose velvet sofa. A bayonet protruded from the center of it.

And then everything sped up.

"Hey. You there. Back up, missy." Sheriff Hamilton strode toward me.

I stepped back and my foot crunched glass.

"Edwards!" The sheriff snapped his fingers at one of the deputies talking to Rosalie by the stairs. She wrapped an arm around Martina, one of the maids from Venezuela. Martina clutched her broom to her chest. Rosalie's lips moved, but no words came out. Maybe she was praying. Or cursing.

A musket jutted from the carpet at her feet and I couldn't for the life of me imagine how it got there.

"Secure this here perimeter," the sheriff ordered.

Deputy Edwards glanced at me, frozen in my tracks, and back to the sheriff.

The sheriff strode to me. "Where have you been, Miss Turner?" He stopped and hitched up his pants and for a second, I thought he might spit, like he was in some old western.

I eyed the knives and guns and glass littering the room. A knife as long as my forearm bullseyed an oil painting above the fireplace. A sword protruded from the center of the coffee table, as inextricable as Excalibur. Two rifles appeared to have blasted holes in the wall, one near the bar about a foot from Willie's head, and one near the doorway heading into the restaurant. A musket skewered a cushioned ottoman like a giant toothpick in an olive.

"Hey," the sheriff snapped his fingers in front of me. I blinked at him. "I asked you a question."

Mama appeared at my side. "You can't believe Cat had anything to do with this."

"Ms. Turner," Sheriff Hamilton flashed a palm. "You don't want to be interfering with an official investigation."

"I don't even understand what this is," I said and backed away crunching more glass.

"Stop moving!" he shouted. Conversations around us halted.

"What happened?" I said.

The ransacked Houston house Culver described flashed to mind. Slashed furniture. Shattered china. Culver Washington with a knife in his hand. Horace frozen on the road with his gun at his side. Flames lapping at the front porch. Screaming. Yelling, Horses thundering along the road as shots rang out and the upstairs exploded.

"Are you on drugs?" the sheriff said. He snapped his fingers again.

"Sheriff." Mama frowned.

"Listen, lady," he turned on her. "We've got the most bizarre case of anything I've ever seen right here in this dang lobby. You want to pussyfoot around? Because I don't have the time. Somebody could've been killed here. Look at this unholy mess." His hand swept the area.

I crunched my way through glass to the empty display case.

"It's vandals," Mama said. "Nothing more than some kids playing a prank." She ran a hand under her bangs and blew out a heavy sigh.

"You sure about that?" the sheriff said.

I stared at the empty case. Deadly shards of glass stabbed from its frame. An explosion. A force of nature so violent it blasted weapons in every direction.

I turned to stare at the musket buried in the stairs. No simple prank, that. Practically an act of God.

"Cat Turner." My attention was brought around to the sheriff who appeared to be about to implode.

"Where have you been?" he demanded.

The lie slid smoothly from my lips. "On the golf course."

"Sheriff Hamilton," Mama said, "Cat had nothing to do with this."

"Lady," Sheriff Hamilton propped his hands on his hips, his fingertips inches from his holstered gun, "you've experienced two bizarre phenomena at this here hotel since you arrived. First the fire. And now this. We never had a problem at the Fairly Grand until you two appeared barely a month ago."

"Except for Red Maggie's very public murder-suicide," I said.

He stabbed a finger at me. "Watch it, missy. That was way before my time."

"Okay." Mama huffed her bangs off her forehead and flung an arm toward the stairs. "How could Cat have possibly accomplished this?"

The deputy finished with Rosalie and Martina and they scurried to the front desk to huddle with Giselle and Benito.

"Maybe she had help," the sheriff said.

"Who?" Mama glanced around. "She doesn't know anybody here."

I couldn't resist. "I know your nephew, Bobby," I said to the sheriff. "Maybe I'm in cahoots with him. He's been seen skulking around the hotel."

The sheriff glared at me. "Maybe it's them Chicanos," he nodded his head toward Rosalie and Martina. "Maybe they're pissed about all the illegal alien legislation being passed in Montgomery."

"That's ridiculous," Mama said. "Rosalie is from Guatemala and Martina is from Venezuela. And you can clearly see they're terrified."

"Well, what's your idea?"

"Locals," she said. "Cat's right. Bobby Hamilton knows his way around here pretty well. He's been seen at the pool. And the beach."

"Now you hold on a dadgum minute," Sheriff Hamilton said. "You got no proof he's done anything but hang out with friends."

"And you have no proof my daughter's involved."

"I was on the golf course," I repeated.

"Oh, you golf, do you?" the sheriff said.

"I was sketching."

Mama frowned at me before turning back to him. "Why don't you go, maybe dust for fingerprints or something? I assume you know how."

"Mama," I cautioned.

She smoothed her bangs with her trembling fingers. "The Fourth of July's in two days. And I've got this mess to clean up. I'll be in my office if you need me." She turned and stomped a few steps and then whirled around. Her shoulders lifted with a tired sigh.

"I'm sorry, Sheriff. Once you've finished your investigation, please stop by the restaurant for free coffee for you and your deputies. I'll make sure they have a fresh pot waiting for you." And she marched through the lobby and disappeared into her office.

While the sheriff and his deputies milled around the debris, I simply wanted to go to my room and call Nana and have her hold the phone to Ruby's ear so she could hear my voice and know I hadn't forgotten her. The deputies blocked the stairs, so I headed toward the elevator. That's where Mrs. Fischer found me.

"Catalina, dear, are you okay?" Mr. Fischer joined us, rubbing his bald head.

"I'm fine," I said, though I truly felt like hurling.

"Dear, you don't look fine. What in the world happened?"

"I'm not sure." I stole a glance past her toward the sheriff. "I heard the sirens, saw the sheriff's cars, came running, and found this. I mean, how could anything…look at this room. How could anyone do this?"

Mr. Fischer scratched behind an ear and poked a wing-tipped toe at a shard of glass embedded in the carpet.

My head pounded, my elbow throbbed, and I simply wanted to suck down the pain medicine the doctor prescribed and wake up in my bed on Ivy Lane with Ruby curled beside me.

Mrs. Fischer was talking, "…nothing a good root beer float wouldn't fix. Are you game, dear?"

I couldn't imagine anything I'd less rather do than make conversation with the Fischers over root beer floats. But her expression suggested resistance would be futile. And it might help Mama if I kept at least two of her guests out of her hair.

I heaved a sigh.

"Lovely," Mrs. Fischer said. I followed them into the bar while the outside lights twinkled on and the deputies crunched through broken glass behind us.

The bar lights were dimmed and candles flickered on the tables. The three tables at the back of the room were filled with guests, drinking and murmuring about the sheriff's proceedings.

Wet Willie set my float in front of me, followed by the Fischers' drinks. "So," I swirled the bubbling root beer around my mound of ice cream, "what do you think happened?" Willie scowled and returned to the bar where a line of orthodontists sat drinking beer and watching baseball.

Mrs. Fischer eyed her husband over her glass of wine. He shrugged and gulped his Gibson martini. Her attention returned to me. "What do you suspect caused it, dear?"

"How should I know? Mama and I just got here."

"Hmmm."

"You believe the sheriff?" I said. "That it's somehow our fault?"

"Don't be silly, dear. How in the world could you or Eva accomplish this disaster? And Pete Bachus already confirmed you were coming from the direction of the cemetery as the sheriff arrived."

"I told you not to go back there," Willie said from behind the bar.

I turned from him and said, "So what could've done it?"

"Interesting," Irene Fischer said, "you said *what*, not *who*."

"You've already said no person could physically cause it."

Mrs. Fischer sipped her wine, then set the glass on the table. "I've been coming here for fifty years," she said, "and I've never seen anything like it. Even Red Maggie's sightings have been rather benign. A glimpse here or there, a flicker of lights, a flutter of a figure at the window. Certainly nothing so violent as shattered glass and flying weapons."

"Poltergeist," Mr. Fischer said. He plucked the cocktail onion out of his drink and popped it in his mouth.

I stared at him.

"Not necessarily," his wife said.

"Physical movement of objects." He sucked the juice off his thumb. "Violent nature."

"Ghosts can be violent."

"We already said it wasn't Red Maggie," he said.

"We don't know for sure." His wife raised her glass. "Something could've triggered her. She did die violently."

"By her own hand."

My spoon clattered to the table. "How do you two know so much about ghosts?"

Irene Fischer leaned into the table, "Why, dear," she said, "didn't you know? We're ghost hunters."

CHAPTER 32

I nearly snorted root beer out my nose and pressed the back of my hand to it to hold it in. "You're kidding."

"Amateurs, really," Mr. Fischer said.

His wife turned her long, fake eyelashes on him. "We've been doing it for forty years," she said. "Which hardly makes us amateurs." She turned to me. "What Ira means is, we don't have an official degree or professional license."

"I thought you were retired school teachers."

"Oh, dear, how sweet," she said. "But no, I'm afraid we're not much good with children. Oh, we like you well enough." She patted my hand. "But then you're more of a young lady, aren't you?"

I couldn't think what to say.

"Ira and I actually operate several businesses," she said, "under the umbrella of I to I Enterprises. Get it? Ira and Irene? I to I? We thought we were being clever."

"Yes," I said, "that is clever." I studied my melting ice cream.

"Would you like another one, dear?"

Mr. Fischer finished his martini. He scraped his chair back and headed to the bar.

"No, thank you," I said.

Willie slushed ice in a shaker behind me and refilled Mr. Fischer's glass.

"How do you even get to be ghost hunters?" I said. "I mean,

I've heard of TV shows, and I enjoy *Supernatural* as much as anybody. But does anyone take that stuff seriously?" My head throbbed as if someone was pounding my eyeballs out with a hammer.

"I can assure you, Catalina," she said, "Mr. Fischer and I studied with the best minds in the business. Psychologists, psychiatrists, anthropologists, physicists."

I sat back, stunned.

"What was the doctor's name at the University of Virginia?" she asked her husband as he returned to the table.

"Gardner," Mr. Fischer dropped into his chair, "Frank Gardner."

"Right," Mrs. Fischer said. "We've attended every workshop he's sponsored. Survival of consciousness after bodily death, near-death experiences, apparitional experiences."

Mr. Fischer sipped his drink.

"However," Mrs. Fischer scrunched her nose, "working with psychics and mediums is entirely too annoying. They're too noisy, always yammering on about the voices they're hearing. They've ruined any stakeout we've ever been on."

Mr. Fischer nodded emphatically.

"So," I said, "you've seen a ghost?"

The husband and wife exchanged glances.

"You've seen Red Maggie?" I said. "Here in the hotel?"

Mrs. Fischer toyed with the stem of her glass, her silver nails flashing in the candlelight. "Well, no, not actually."

"In fifty years of coming here, you've never seen her? Not once?"

She leaned toward me, excited. "At the Hotel Del Coronado outside San Diego, we once witnessed a small antique clock slide off the bedside table and hit the floor. It was quite thrilling." Her husband nodded in agreement.

"That's it?" I said. I couldn't mask my disappointment. I picked up my spoon and swirled it around my melted ice cream.

"Well, dear," she said, "it's not as if they come right out and talk to you. You might get a blinking light bulb, or cold spots, or footsteps on the stairs. But to actually see and speak to a ghost?" She turned to her husband. "See?" she said. "Those psychics have done more harm than good. And television. Everybody imagines this job is so easy, so glamorous."

Her husband reached over and squeezed her wrist. "Darling," he said, "you're so brave to try to educate."

"So," I said, "in your many years of ghost hunting, you've never seen or heard as much as a peep, whimper, or held a conversation with a ghost?"

"Plenty of other people have," she said. "There are stories throughout history. Take the Civil War, for instance. Books have been written about all sorts of phenomena – premonitions, sightings of dead soldiers."

Her husband nodded and said, "There're more haunted houses in Vicksburg, Mississippi, than any other city in the South."

"Why, south of Tuscaloosa there's a house," Mrs. Fischer said, "the Houston house I believe. It was nearly burned to the ground but rebuilt. Every July they hear footsteps running up and down the stairs, glass breaking, and horses thundering over the lawn. Sometimes, you can even smell smoke though nothing's burning."

My spoon clattered to the table. The heat drained from my face. The room dipped and swayed as I clutched the edge of the table and stared at my melted ice cream. Willie was at my side.

"Laws, sister," he said. "You can't let the Fischers fill your head with this ghost nonsense."

"William." Mrs. Fischer reared back.

"I'm sorry, ma'am," he said. "You're some of my favorite guests. But this child's been through enough. She don't need to be worrying about no ghosts, nor poltergeists, nor any other such thing." I said to him, "But you've seen Red Maggie, haven't you?"

"Laws, sister, I don't want to talk about it. Enough's been said already."

I couldn't explain why the subject affected me so. I'd already heard it from Culver. But then my ears buzzed. A faint sound at first, a bee at the far end of a tunnel. But then it grew louder. My ears filled with an angry swarm as my vision clouded.

"Goodness." Mrs. Fischer's face swam close to mine. "Is there something you want to tell us, dear? Something about this accident? You look like you've seen a ghost. Doesn't she look pale, Ira?"

"She does appear peaked," he agreed.

Then I felt a horrible thump and everything went black.

I opened my eyes as coolness washed over my forehead like a welcome breeze.

"Told you." Willie's lined face came into view and then receded. "She's frailer than she lets on."

"My stars." Irene Fischer knelt beside me, pressing a hand to her heart. "You gave us quite a scare, Catalina."

I lay on the carpeted floor in the middle of the bar, next to the table where I'd been sitting. "What happened?" I blinked at the three of them hovering over me. "Why am I on the floor? Did you drug me?" I turned my head and the wet cloth fell to the carpet.

"Of course not, dear," Mrs. Fischer said. "We wouldn't dream, why…you fell right out of your chair."

I sat up. The room tipped and swayed. I groaned and palmed my forehead.

"Easy does it, sister," Willie said. "You should've gone straight your room. What're we gonna tell your mama?"

"Perhaps it's best, William," Irene said, "if we don't mention this to Eva. She has a lot on her plate as it is."

Willie rubbed the back of his neck. "Well somebody's got to get this young'un upstairs and I can't leave the bar."

"I'll take her," Irene said. "I'm such a ninny. I should've known she's still recovering from her accident."

"It hasn't been too long since she was in the ER," Mr. Fischer said.

"Of course," his wife agreed as he helped her to her feet. "I can't imagine what I was thinking."

"I'm right here," I said. "Stop talking about me like I'm not."

"You shouldn't be filling her head with that ghost nonsense," Willie said. "You're gonna give her nightmares."

"Oh, dear," Mrs. Fischer said, "I'd hate to imagine it. Catalina's such a level-headed young lady."

"Stop." I struggled to my feet and swayed. Mr. Fischer grabbed my injured elbow and I winced.

"I'm a big girl," I said. "A little ghost story doesn't scare me."

"William's right," Mrs. Fischer said. "I shouldn't be speaking of such things in your condition."

"I'm fine." I staggered toward the chair.

"Let's get you to your room," Mrs. Fischer said. "I don't want Eva mad at me."

Willie plucked the wet towel from the floor and slapped it against his thigh. I didn't like his expression when we left him. It was the haunted look of a man very much afraid.

CHAPTER 33

Of course, the local television crew caught wind of the incident. In a town of 8,500 residents, this was big news. They appeared in the lobby with their reporter's big flip of blonde hair and their bright cameras.

Mama refused to speak to them, and forbade the staff to engage with them as well. A cousin of Rosalie's, in maintenance, agreed to speak on camera, but he knew nothing except what he'd been told. He did not return to work at the Fairly Grand.

Fortunately, Mr. Ed was in New Orleans overseeing one of the Algenons' other hotels. When the news reached him later that night, he sent a terse message saying he would take care of things when he returned the next day. Mama read the text with her mouth set in a grim line.

It took three men from maintenance, with the help of deputies, to remove the weapons from the furniture. The sheriff dusted them for fingerprints and turned them over to be bagged and tagged. Guests were detoured through the bar area and around the outside of the hotel. By midnight, the rest of the debris was cleared.

Avoiding the deputies hauling out evidence to deliver to the county crime lab, Mrs. Fischer escorted me through the lobby. I hesitated at the sight of the empty display cases. It was Culver's handiwork. I was sure of it. And I couldn't stand by and watch him destroy my mother and our new home. I headed straight to her office and stopped outside the door.

"Catalina," Mrs. Fischer paused behind me, "perhaps now's not the time."

"It'll barely take a minute." I pushed the door open to find Mama with her elbows propped on a mahogany desk, her head in her hands. The surface was littered with stacks of paper, fabric swatches, rolls of white satin ribbon, a flip-over desk calendar bulging with notes and reminders. And prescription bottles.

"Mama?"

She scrubbed her brow before glancing up. Her eyes were bright, but dry.

"I have an idea." I stepped inside as Mrs. Fischer hovered in the doorway.

Mama slumped in her chair.

"You know Bragg's store, Genesis, right?"

"Please, Cat," she said, "not now. I can't deal with one more problem."

"I know, I know. But, I think he can help. He has these cool fish fossils. You might've seen them when you were there yelling at him. From some dig in Montana."

"Cat, seriously, honey, I can't even think about that right now. I've got this mess to fix. The Fourth is two days away. One of our biggest weekends."

"That's what I'm talking about," I said. "The hole left by the explosion. The display cases. Bragg's got artifacts and antiques and fossils you could fill them with."

"All I remember are crazy stuffed bats and," Mama wrinkled her nose, "penis bones."

"Well, yeah." I wanted to laugh at the expression on her face. "But he's got these retro displays, too. Framed butterflies and beetles. You know, Mama, Civil War memorabilia is not exactly politically correct these days. And it wouldn't hurt the hotel to go in a different direction. At least for a while."

"Cat, honey," she gripped the arms of her chair, "there is no way I can call him after the spectacle I made of myself in his store."

My head pounded and I wanted to fall into bed, but I persisted, "I'll call him."

"I can't ask you to do that."

"You're not asking. I'm offering. It'll be one less thing for you to worry about."

She stared at me, blinking rapidly, before lowering her head. She swiped at her cheeks with the back of her hand. I was already fumbling on her desk for the phone book when she nodded okay.

"Catalina," Mrs. Fischer said, "let's use Gloria's desk and give your mother some space."

I found Bragg in the phone book under Hamilton, B. After I punched in his number, for a horrifying moment I thought I called Bedford Hamilton by mistake. But Bragg's voice on his answering machine simply said, "Speak."

I left a garbled message explaining at least some of the situation and what we needed. I waited a good thirty minutes without hearing back from him before I finally headed to my room.

The next morning, I came downstairs to find three fish fossils of various sizes in one display case, along with a bear and fox skull. The other case displayed exotic butterflies from around the world.

Apparently, they arrived after I left, delivered by Bragg himself. Mama was on the phone when he unloaded them, but she sent him a thank you note offering a complimentary dinner at the hotel restaurant to which he didn't respond.

By the end of the day, an upholsterer repaired the chairs and sofas, an expert carpenter fixed the antique tables, and a glass cutter arrived to repair the glass cases. By the Fourth of July, new carpet on the stairs was installed, cushions were patched, the glass cases were redesigned and everyone breathed easier.

Unfortunately, two orthodontists and a family of five checked out, as well as a couple on their honeymoon and two elderly sisters. A high school reunion and a women's book club cancelled their reservations for the following week.

The story occupied the front page of the *Fairly Standard* with absurd hints and innuendos that made me want to storm their ridiculously small and incompetent office. But I realized it took a lot of energy to stay so angry. And anyway, we were overwhelmed at the hotel.

By the end of all the investigating and fingerprinting and photographing and conjecturing, Sheriff Hamilton didn't have a single lead to pursue.

Mama seriously considered closing the hotel until the perpetrators were caught. But Mr. Ed swaggered in, saying there was no way in 'h, e, double l' he was going to shut down the hotel at the height of summer. Since no weapons were actually missing, he concluded it was some kids' prank. And as soon as he found out who the punks were, he was going to kick their butts from here to kingdom come.

"Where were you when this was going down?" he asked Mama.

"Inspecting the garden for the Bachman wedding," she said. "Someone trampled the lilies and Finnegan and I were debating whether we could replace them in time. I told the sheriff this. Benito and Giselle were at the front desk and didn't see or hear anything until the glass exploded."

"And caused a musket to bury itself around a corner and into the bottom of the stairs?"

Mama combed her fingers through her hair. "I can't explain it. It doesn't make sense. Benito and Giselle said they left the desk immediately when they heard glass shattering and by then it was over. All the weapons dispersed. At the same time."

"A gang of hoodlums?"

"Nobody saw anyone come in or out. It's a miracle there were no guests in the lobby. Who knows what might've happened?"

"I know what would've happened," he said. "We'd be in the middle of one big, fat lawsuit, that's what would've happened." He surveyed the lobby. "This is a bleeping disaster. Did you ramp up security? Do it now." He raised his voice, "I want everybody to keep their eyes and ears open."

Gloria glanced from her desk and Giselle and Benito exchanged looks. Ed Winer stormed off to his office and slammed the door. I followed Mama to hers.

"Cat." She rubbed the furrows in her forehead. "Can you run to town and get a refill on my prescription before the pharmacy closes? I can't afford to experience a panic attack right now."

I was concerned I'd just fetched her prescription not too long ago and frowned at the puffiness beneath her eyes. I said, "Sure, Mama."

"Take the shuttle," she said and handed me the empty prescription bottle and several bills. "It'll be faster. And Cat," I turned back to her, "let's not mention this disaster in town, okay? We're getting enough bad press as it is."

"Who am I going to talk to, Mama?" I left the hotel tugging at the rumpled scarf around my neck.

CHAPTER 34

I caught the pharmacist minutes before the store closed for the evening and tucked Mama's pills into my shorts pocket. On my way back to the shuttle, I decided to make a detour to Genesis, where a soft light glowed.

"How's your mother?" Bragg said without looking up from the skull he polished. It was smaller than a human skull, and pointed. A wolf, maybe. Or a fox. "The last time I saw her she was," he paused and gazed at the ceiling as if the right word could be found there, "upset."

"Last night's accident didn't help," I said. "Did you see the lobby?"

"It was mostly cleaned up by the time I got there." He turned the skull over in his hands. "I waited to talk to her, but she was on the phone to Taiwan."

He waited to talk to her? My eyes narrowed. I tapped my lower lip. Was it possible I had something that might entice Bragg Hamilton to help? I trailed my fingertips along the glass counter. "She absolutely appreciated your coming to her rescue."

He glanced up. "She did?"

"Yep." I stopped a few feet shy of him. "She was especially impressed with your fish fossils. She wants to hear more about your excavation." I marveled at my newfound ability to lie.

"Really?" His face lit for a second and then fell. He buried his chin in his chest. "Tell her..." he scrubbed a spot on the skull..."never mind."

I moved closer. "You should meet her for a drink. Maybe at the hotel. Maybe dinner. Tell her the story. Check out how they're hanging in the lobby."

He stopped polishing and peered at me. "What's your angle, kiddo?"

"Angle?" I shrugged innocently. "I don't have an angle."

"Everybody's got an angle. What's the interest suddenly in getting my stuff sold?"

I surveyed the bats and beetles, the empty space where the butterflies had been, the safari hat perched on Brother Bear's head.

"I just thought you might enjoy sitting and talking to her when she's not actually yelling at you. Sometimes she can be quite nice."

He thumbed the eye socket of the animal skull.

"And she could really use a friend," I said softly, pitifully, with big kitten eyes as best I could manage.

"You're playing me."

I pulled back. "As if."

He raised the skull and rubbed a smudge off its brow. "Why would she talk to me?" he said. "She hates my entire family. And not, I might add, without reason."

"She doesn't actually know your family," I said. "Okay, she knows the sheriff. But this is your chance to present a different side of the Hamiltons. A kinder, gentler side."

He burst out laughing, stood, and placed the skull on the counter. "You're good, kiddo," he said. "I've got to give you credit. You bat those big gray eyes at Tate and that boy will be lapping out of your palm happy as a rescued puppy."

I snorted and stepped back. "Don't be ridiculous. "We're not, I mean, we're not even, like, friends. We're like, enemies who, maybe, sometimes talk to each other. Sometimes sort of friends. But mostly, you know, not."

"Uh, huh. Why are you here, Cat Turner? I don't believe it's because your mother needs a friend."

I ran fingers through my hair. My head was beginning to buzz. The pain would come, and swiftly. I didn't have much time.

"I need the truth about Culver Washington."

"I knew it!" He slammed the glass with his palm, rattling the skull.

"It is about Mama," I said. "She's going to lose her job. We're going to get kicked out of the Fairly Grand and there won't be any salvaging her career after that. There won't be any place for us to go. This is our last chance. Don't you understand? And Culver Washington is hellbent on destroying our lives."

"Whoa." He flashed a palm.

"I'm telling you." I slapped the glass next to him. "He's going to destroy the hotel. He caused the fire, he destroyed the lobby, he caused Bobby's accident. Maybe even mine."

"Hey, hey." He grabbed my wrist. "What the hell are you talking about? Culver's been dead two hundred years." He dropped my wrist and backed away, putting the counter between us.

"He's still here," I said. "And I think you know why."

CHAPTER 35

Speak of the devil.

The bell jingled and Tate Channing strode toward us. He grinned and spread his hands wide. "You started the party without me? Truly, I'm hurt."

"Knock it off, Romeo," Bragg said. "Little Miss Cat here was on her way out. Maybe you could escort her."

I crossed my arms. "I'm not going anywhere until I get what I came for."

"Oooooh," Tate said. "That sounds ominous. What'd I interrupt? Some secret pow wow? You're finally taking over the town, Uncle?"

Bragg glared at him. "Don't you have someplace to be?"

"Mom sent me to ask you to dinner." Tate plucked a couple of twenty-five-dollar quartzes from the basket on the counter and rattled them in his fist. "Some big shindig at the country club."

"Not a chance," Bragg said.

"Didn't think so." Tate studied the rocks. "Want to go for pizza?"

"Not tonight." Bragg glanced at me. "But Miss Cat, here, sure looks hungry. Why don't you take her?"

"Stop trying to get rid of me," I said, grateful for the dim lighting so Tate couldn't see my face flame hot enough to roast marshmallows.

Tate cracked the rocks together and Bragg winced. "Son," he held out his palm, "you couldn't afford them."

His nephew moved out of reach. "So whatcha talking about?" The rocks grated together. So did my teeth.

"Nothing, Nosy Nellie," Bragg said. "It's just Kitten here, has quite an overactive imagination. Now take her and go. What's the matter with you? You got eyes, don't you?"

Tate perused me up and down, then dismissed me with two words. "Jail bait."

I wanted to crack the rocks upside his head. Instead, I stuck out my chin. "Why don't you leave? This isn't any of your business."

"I know more about this business," he swaggered toward me, "than Bragg does."

"All right, that's it," Bragg said. "Everybody out. I don't have time for this foolishness. I have a date at Bud's Bar with Jack Daniels. And I'm late."

"I'm not leaving until you give me what I want," I said.

"And what's that?"

"The truth. You know it. I know it. I just need proof."

"You couldn't get your grubby little hands on it," Bragg said, "for all the money in Singapore."

"So, it does exist."

"Not in your world."

"What is it?" I grabbed his arm. "A black leather book?"

He shook me off and glanced at Tate, who stood in the middle of the store with his fist in mid-jiggle.

Bragg sighed and rubbed the back of his neck. He circled the counter and pulled a bottle from the shelf beneath the register. His date with Jack would start now. He banged a short crystal glass onto the counter and poured a hefty amount of amber liquid into it. He tossed half of it back and refilled the glass. His voice was raspy.

"Old Horace's ledger." He tossed back more liquor and swiped his mouth with the back of his wrist. "Some deathbed confession recorded in the back of it witnessed and signed by the family doctor, Latimore Perkins."

My stomach lurched and I pressed into the glass case. I was expecting Latimore Perkins' records, but Horace's ledger? Jackpot. "Where's it now?"

Tate emerged from his trance. "I remember," he said. He locked eyes with his uncle's. "You found it. At the hotel."

"Sam Perkins found it." Bragg studied his glass. "A buddy of mine. Manager of the hotel at the time. Some great-great-grandson or nephew of Dr. Perkins." He swirled the liquid around the glass and took a big gulp. "Hurricane Ivan flooded the basement of the hotel. Sam had no idea what to do with it. I'd taken a furlough from my dig and he brought it to me to authenticate it."

Tate's eyes widened. "You brought it to Dad. I was there."

Bragg waved him away. "You were a kid, barely five years old."

"I remember Dad's expression when you told him," Tate said. "I remember him going out that night and getting so wasted he barely staggered his way back home. The only time I've ever seen him drink. Ever."

"False courage," Bragg muttered into his glass.

"It threatened to destroy the family's reputation," Tate said. "Our legacy. He wanted to get Mom out from under the fallout. And she was going too, until Granddaddy got sick."

"We were stupid," Bragg said. "We took the ledger to Bedford. The lawyer." His laugh was harsh. "He swore he'd ruin us if we breathed a word of it."

"What could he do?" I said.

Tate and Bragg looked at me like I'd sprouted a horn from the top of my head.

"Shut down my dig, for starters, Bragg said." He nodded at Tate. "Worse for Stuart."

"But, but," I sputtered, "he's your brother. I mean, you didn't believe him, did you?"

Bragg's laugh was more of a bark. He swallowed the rest of his drink. "Brothers," he said. "Those are the people he loves to screw most. Damn Venezuelan government." He stared out the window at the darkening sky.

The store morphed from gloomy to macabre. Stuffed rabbits and foxes and ferrets grinned maniacally, baring teeth sharp enough to eviscerate a jugular.

"You're not talking about your last dig," Tate said, "before you opened Genesis." Bragg tilted the bottle and studied the label.

"You're not saying Uncle Bedford had a hand in that, are you?" Bragg stared at his empty glass. Tate said, "I thought you quit because of the curse."

I glanced from one to the other. "What curse?"

Bragg snorted. "It sounded better than your brother paying off the Venezuelan government so you'd be forced to return home 'cause your daddy was eaten up with cancer."

"Holy commoly," Tate said.

"You kids do what you want," Bragg said. "I need another

drink. And better company." He turned to his nephew. "Lock up, will you?"

"Sure." Tate said. I stared between the two of them, dumbstruck. for once.

"Oh, kids," the door jingled open and Bragg pivoted halfway through it, "remember, I warned you." He eased into the night, muttering, "I do want you to remember that."

CHAPTER 36

Tate and I were entombed in silence.

Latimore Perkins' record was on thing. But Horace's confession? That was so much better.

"Where would he keep it?" I said.

"You're not thinking what I'm very much afraid you're thinking?"

"Do you imagine your Uncle Bedford would simply hand it over? That he would even acknowledge it exists?"

"No."

"Then, where would he stash it?"

"You're out of your mind. He'd shred you into bright, bloody ribbons. You think Bobby's done damage to your reputation? Bedford accused a man of cheating him in a real estate deal. The man denied it. Bedford dogged him relentlessly, hit him with one lawsuit after another until they finally found the man swinging from the rafters of his summer home on Ono Island. He was a millionaire. Employed his own fancy lawyers. He was an elder in the church. You think you're going to go against Bedford Hamilton? Lamb to the slaughter doesn't even begin to describe it."

"What part of 'I don't have a choice' don't you understand?"

He deflected me with a flick of his wrist. "I don't understand what this has to do with you or your mother, but it would be better for you to move away. Get your mother and go. Hell, I wish I could leave. I've thought of it a million times. Boarding school. The army. Anything. Just get out of here and away from my family." He tossed the rocks into the basket. "They're so dang suffocating. I've lived under the shadow of Bedford Hamilton my whole life. My dad's a good man. Can you imagine what it's like to have your parent cower in fear of another man?"

"Yeah. My mom. Ed Winer."

"Oh yeah?" He scruffed his hair. "No offense, but Ed Winer's a teddy bear compared to Uncle Bedford. And my mother, she's so, so freakin' enamored with him she treats him like he's a god. Nobody in this family makes a move without Nathan Bedford Forrest Hamilton's say so."

"I couldn't live like that."

His hand dropped. "You'd rather be dead?"

He didn't mean it, but I gave it the weight it deserved. "Yes," I said finally. "I'd rather be dead."

"Bullshit."

"It's simply another form of slavery," I said. "Like Culver. He exchanged serving white people for being bound by a lie. He's not any freer now that he's dead."

"What are you talking about?"

"You and your family think you're free, but you're actually bound by the same awful lie. And you're letting one man control you. One. Man."

Tate snorted and shook his head. "You've seen the man, right? Are you listening to anything I'm saying, or Bragg's said, or anybody else has said about him? You and your mother wouldn't even register as a speed bump for him."

I thought of the man on the stairs of the church staring down his nose at me. The haughty lift of his chin. The cruel line of his lips. The dark, calculating eyes. It was the same expression I'd seen in the narrow blue gaze of Lizzie Lee. The self-righteous pout of Mary Grace's mother. The taunts of Bobby Hamilton. The hard, crushing heel of Ed Winer.

"He's a lawyer, right?" I said. "Got some fancy office a block from the library? It's got to be there."

"What are you talking about?"

"The ledger."

He shook his head. "No way."

"Tomorrow's the fourth. Y'all have some big family thing planned, right?"

"So?"

"Your Uncle Bedford will probably be there. At the country club. Fireworks and such?"

"I guess."

"And his office will be empty, at least for a while."

"Yeah?"

"I'll pay you to get me in," I said.

"You're out of your mind."

"The balance of your car. Two hundred and twenty-three dollars and fifty-nine cents."

"How do you have that kind of money?"

"It's a deal?"

"I could make that by the end of summer."

"You can make it tomorrow night. Your car. Free and clear. No more working. No more waiting."

"His apartment's connected to his office. You'd never have a chance."

"Dinner. Fireworks. Schmoozing at the country club? He should be gone for quite a while."

Tate crossed his arms mutinously.

"Last chance." I headed toward the door, more determined than I'd ever been in my life.

"You are certifiable."

I whirled on him. "I'm going to get in there with or without your help. It'd be easier with you. We'd both win."

"Not if we're both dead."

I shrugged. "Living in fear is no way to live."

He sighed and stared at the ceiling.

"Think about it," I said. "Let me know." I tugged the door open, jingling the bell.

"All right," he said.

I turned. "You're in?"

He ruffled his hair and let an expletive fly. "Yeah." He nodded. "Let me work out some details."

"Great." I hesitated on the sidewalk outside the store, bathed in the sweet scent of jasmine and cool, milky twilight before the door slammed and I headed for home.

CHAPTER 37

Culver was waiting for me when I arrived, breathless, at the cemetery the next day.

"Okay," I said, "you can stop your little manifestations." I pressed the stitch in my side. "I've found help. A Hamilton, no less. That's got to count for something, right?"

"The fair-haired one," he said. "The one who gave your book back."

"He wasn't thrilled."

"You promised him something he wanted."

"Yep. Cold, hard cash."

Culver scratched his ear.

"So, you're happy, right?" I said. "He's going to lead me to Horace's confession."

"Horace's confession? I thought you were searching for Doc Perkins' records."

"Well, yeah," I said, "but Horace's own words hold so much more sway, don't you think? What? Why are you staring at me like that?"

"The ceremony's not far off," he said. "We're running out of time."

"Fine. Great. Sure. Heap on the pressure." I tugged on my scarf against the stifling heat. "So, let's finish this thing. Tell me exactly how you died."

He strolled to Elijah's angel and ran his fingertips over the curve of her wing. "I don't remember exactly. I get to a certain point and I can't go no further."

"Tell me as far as you remember," I said. "Maybe it'll jog the rest."

He traced the wing to the angel's back, along her slender neck. "Once we arrived at the hospital," he said, "Horace and me got separated. They didn't allow coloreds inside. It was days before I saw him again. I was in and out of my mind. Doc Perkins spared me some laudanum, despite the other doctors' protests. 'Don't waste it on the darkies,' they said.

"By the time Horace hobbled out to converse with me, I was on the mend, lying on a pallet on the front lawn.

"'Culver,' he stood next to me on his crutches, 'they done give me a medal.' He showed me the silver piece attached to a flat, red ribbon. 'They haven't give a medal to nobody on our side,' he said, 'but lookie here.'

"I'm sorry to say, I was too worn out to care too powerful much. 'What'd they give you a medal for?' I struggled to sit, but was too tuckered out.

"'Outstanding bravery,' he said. 'Apparently, we done a better job rooting out the enemy than we thought.'

"'But Horace,' I said, and here's where the laudanum must've kicked in, 'cause I never would've said this without the devil prompting me, 'but Horace,' I said, 'you just stood there. Crawford set the house ablaze and Coop's the one who exploded the upstairs. And Hovater let the horses loose. They lost their lives. After I unfroze you, you ran off and shot yourself in the foot.'

"This look come over him like it did when we's arguing about Lucie. Hard. Cold.

"'That ain't the way I remember it,' he said, 'and that ain't the way I told it.'

"But Horace.

"'Don't you 'but me', Culver Washington.'

"The fellow beside me stirred. He'd been moaning something awful, his head wrapped in a dirty cloth soaked through with blood so he couldn't see nothing. It was twilight and the air was heavy sweet with jasmine. And magnolia. Same as tonight." He scanned the horizon. "The sky was the same as this, too. Pinks and purples, bleeding to gray."

The drunken flight of a firefly flashed on, flashed off, as it made its way over the stone bench.

"It seemed sinful to have so much beauty and gore in the same place. Buckets of bloody stumps. Feet and arms and hands."

I sucked in the image. "But not you."

"I was lucky. The bullet to my back weren't more than a scrape. The lead in my side, Doc Perkins dug out and said it'd heal fine. I'd be able to resume my duties for Horace soon as I recovered."

"How wonderful," I said sarcastically. "So, obviously, not life threatening."

"I'm ashamed to say after Horace ran off I gave a thought to turning myself over to the enemy in hopes I could gain my freedom up north. Horace was right, Lucie give me the idea. I'd heard of a few fellows doing it.

"As much as Horace and me was blood brothers, when he run off, I couldn't imagine what might become of me. But then, I didn't know what but things might be worse for me up yonder."

"Horace left you to die," I said. "You should've run for your life."

He fixed his gaze on me. "There ain't no honor in running, Miss Cat."

"Where's the honor in being owned by another human?" I said. "Where's the honor in Horace abandoning you?"

He shrugged. "I was powerful proud of the work I done. Proud that Mister Josiah trusted me to take care of his firstborn. And I wouldn't fail him for nothing."

I shook my head, folded my arms, and watched the firefly blink its way to Elijah's angel to hover near Culver's shoulder.

He continued. "So, there I was, stars starting to peek out, as Horace hobbled closer. 'You remember that sorry business we run into northways?' he said.

"I had to concentrate hard to cut through the laudanum. 'You mean Lucie?'

"He clamped a hand over my mouth and lowered his voice. 'Men come searching for the fellow,' he said. 'Pinkerton men.'

"I struggled to work my mouth and he removed his hand.

"'I thought they's working for Lincoln,' I said.

"'Apparently, Lucie had some rich aunt in Boston who hired 'em.'

"'So?'

"'They questioned me,' he said. 'I told 'em she wasn't nothing but white trash, hardly worth the trouble. Even so, I didn't suspect anybody in our outfit had done her any harm."

"'But you paid money –'

"He slapped me, hard. Full across the face." Culver fingered the scar beneath his eye. "It stung like the dickens. Blood trickled along my cheek. And I admit, as much as me and Horace was blood brothers, it didn't sit right with me. I'd already taken a bullet for him. And killed a boy."

"That's what I've been saying," I said. "You deserved better."

"Then Horace leaned in close and said, 'I done told them you did it. It was you who took the girl.'

"'But if they think I done it,' Culver said, 'they'll hang me for sure.'

"'I won't let 'em, Horace said, 'I'll tell him I'll mete out my own punishment. You belong to me. Trust me.'

"'But Horace,' his hand was on my arm, gripping and releasing, gripping and releasing.

"'I'll give you a scant whipping,' he said, 'nothing much hurtful. More for show. You'll do this for me, won't you, Culver?' he said, "A brother would do it for another brother.'"

The firefly blinked its way to the next marker, then the next.

"I been serving Horace my whole life," Culver said. "Sacrificed my life for him. But if I lied about hurting Lucie, I wasn't sure he'd be able to keep them other white boys from swinging me from a tree. I should've stopped him in the beginning, so it was my burden to bear. Mister Josiah trusted me to take care of his boy. But Miss Cat, I couldn't lie such as that. The Commandment says, don't bear false witness and I couldn't disappoint the good Lord. I told Horace so. Besides, Lucie wouldn't lie about such a thing.'

"'Haven't you heard?' he said. 'They found her body floating in the bay yesterday. One wrong step off the dock.' He shrugged. 'Who else gonna speak on your behalf?'

"'The men in the company,' I struggled onto one elbow, 'the ones we left behind. They'll speak the truth.'

'Dead or scattered with the wind. Everybody wants to go home and tend their wounds. Nobody cares about some darkie.' He shoved me backward.

'But we're blood brothers.' I stared into his cold eyes. 'You know I ain't never touched a woman thataway. I ain't never even danced with one.'

'You don't do what I say,' he said, 'they'll string you up before there's an investigation.'

'But Horace,' I said, 'ain't I been good to you? Ain't I been a faithful servant?'

'Yes, Culver Calhoun Washington. Yes, you have. And I need you to do this last thing for me. No complaining. It ain't becoming. I said I'd protect you.'

'But branded a liar and a reprobate? I couldn't bear it,' I said. 'I ain't got much, but I got my name.'

'Name?' he snorted. 'Calhoun was the name of a broken-down darkie who died on his knees picking cotton. The rest you concocted yourself and my daddy let you. Your name is going to be forgotten the minute you're gone. I know what you and Lucie were hatching. You were gonna leave me and head up north. But you belong to me, Culver Washington. And nobody leaves me 'less I say so.'

"The laudanum held a firm grip on me by then and I couldn't make sense of what he was saying. I would've never hurt Horace for nothing. 'I can't do it, Horace,' I said. 'I just can't. It wouldn't be right. It wouldn't be Christian.' And that's all I remember." He swiped his brow.

"Think, Culver," I said. "You and Horace were arguing. The man next to you was moaning. Did you get a pain in your side? Your chest?"

He shook his head and pressed fingertips to his lips.

"Culver, this might be the key to releasing you. Did your wound start bleeding again? You bled out?"

He curled his fingers into a fist. "Blood," he said. "On the blanket."

"Horace struck you," I said. "Hard enough for a concussion? Reopening your wounds?"

"Wool," he said, "gray wool clamoring over my face. I tried to escape out from beneath it. I was desperate to snatch a quick, hot breath. The air burned hotter. I struggled and the fella next to me hollered. 'Horace,' I said, but you could scarcely hear me, 'what are you doing?' My body twitched and stuttered. I grabbed for his wrists. But he was strong.

"'Horace.' My head felt strange. Loose on my shoulders. I couldn't tell which way was up or down. I struggled to suck in breath, but it came so fast. Galloping like a horse gone wild. I couldn't stop it. I fought the grayness, the swirling in my head. The pain, sharp as a hammer pounding against it. I don't remember how long I struggled. But then my body stilled. I lost control. I floated upward and stared at the top of Horace's head. He slid the blanket off me.

"'Oh, Culver,' he cried, 'what did you make me do?'

"The fellow beside me hollered for help. But there were lots of soldiers crazy out of their heads, moaning and yammering. And no one came.

"Horace hovered over me, eyes wide. He throwed himself

against me, akeening and carrying on. Still nobody came. Finally, he straightened away and wiped his cheeks. Then he done something queer. He kissed me full on the lips, same as Queenie done all those years ago. Then he folded the blanket neat and tidy again, and placed it beneath my head.

"He hobbled away with the medal pinned to his chest. And the poor sot beside me kept yelling bloody murder."

I drew a ragged breath. "You were murdered by Horace Hamilton," I said, "the founder of Fairly freakin' Alabama?"

"He didn't mean it. He was...he panicked. He'd always been able to talk anybody into anything. And wouldn't have hurt me for nothing. We was blood brothers. He wouldn't...he couldn't...he just didn't know what else to do when I told him no."

I staggered from the cemetery, seeing red under the weight of more than I could bear. The red ribbon of stolen valor. Vivid flames of a burning cross. Violent blood pouring from blasted bodies. Red wine dripping from a shattered bottle as Ruby cowered beneath my father's brown boot, bleeding. The blood of war and betrayed souls begging for mercy. And justice.

Blood flowed thick as a river, into my eyes, my ears. I tasted the metal of it. A river of murdered cats, and bleeding pups, and mutilated bodies. Bloody freaking war. Betrayal. I was filled to the brim with it. I arrived at the guard shack with no idea how I got there. And still, a red hot, bloody anger boiled within me and spilled over to soak the ground.

CHAPTER 38

I pushed my way into the hotel lobby. An eerie calm permeated the corridor. Gloria's desk was empty. Benito glanced up from the front desk and frowned. I stuck my head in the bar, but it was empty. Wet Willie's towel lay crumpled on the dark wood.

A voice whispered in my ear, "Have you heard?"

I yelped and whirled around. Mrs. Fischer's veined hand moved to her throat. "Catalina," she said, "you nearly scared the wits from me."

"I'm sorry." And then I shook my head at the absurdity of it, since she snuck up on me. "Have you seen Mama?"

Her lips pursed and she said, "You really should do something about that secret of yours before he collapses the hotel around our ears."

"What? Where's Mama?"

"The wine cellar, dear."

"What's she..." I took off running toward the stairs leading to the basement. I descended the winding stone steps two at a time. Rosalie and Carla huddled in the stairwell with Carla pressing a towel to Rosalie's arm. I thought I heard crying. I definitely saw blood. I burst through the cellar door and stumbled to a halt.

Blood splashed the walls. It ran in rivulets along the dank plaster. It dripped from the ceiling. It pooled on the stone floor. My belly heaved and I braced myself, prepared to find severed bodies.

Piles of hacked-off limbs.

Mama stood in the center of the room, a palm pressed to her forehead, her mouth open in shock, staring at the bottles of wine stored in their latticed notches in the wall. Willie stood apart, a hand clasping a grizzled chin, eyes wide and unbelieving.

I searched the dark corners for a dead body, a massacred army. "What happened?"

No one turned. I'm not sure they heard me.

"Great merciful God." Willie lowered his trembling hand. "Ain't seen nothing compare to this in all my born days."

"I don't even," Mama said and fell silent. She turned in a circle, trancelike until her shocked gaze stumbled over me. "Cat."

Willie turned, too.

I stumbled forward and the crunch of broken glass stopped me. I stared at the dark green bottle, broken off at the neck, still dripping wine.

And then I noticed the next bottle and the next. With the same white label, the grove of trees overlooking the sea. Echo Bay. The Durbin wedding. The shipment of red wine. Broken bottles littered the floor.

I side-stepped to a stretch of wall between wine racks and stared at the burgundy dripping there. I touched a thumb to it, sniffed, and then touched it to my tongue. Heavy and oaken, same as the inside of a barrel.

Wine drenched the walls, not blood. And then I caught something in the wall and moved toward it. A cork was embedded in the plaster. I struggled to pull it out.

"Cat," Mama said. I turned as she swayed on her feet.

"Take her upstairs, Willie," I said, "before she keels over."

"But sister," he said, "somebody's got to clean up this mess."

"Get Rosalie." I yanked on the cork from the wall. It wouldn't budge.

"She won't come back," he said. "She was here sweeping the floor when the ruckus started. She's got nicks and cuts covering her arms. She got a gash the length of my thumb. It's gonna be all Miss Eva can do to keep her quiet. Rosalie says the place is cursed."

Maybe it was. "Take Mama and Rosalie and send somebody else," I said. "Martina, Carla." I snapped my fingers. "The new girl, Pilar. She seems sturdy enough."

Willie moved closer to Mama and took her arm. "Come on, Miss Eva." She stiffened away from him and I knew she was about to lose it.

"Rosalie," Mama said. Her eyes wandered around the room.

"What about her, Mama?"

"Come on, Miss Eva." Willie tugged on her elbow. "We best get you out of here."

"She could've been killed." Her gaze met mine across the room.

"Willie," I said, "get her upstairs and Rosalie bandaged. And get on the phone and order more wine."

"Miss Cat, Rosalie needs a doctor."

I chewed on a thumb. We could not afford the sheriff finding out about this. "Isn't her cousin a retired nurse? Take her to her cousin. She might need stitches."

"Miss Cat?"

I didn't even know what I was saying. I was on autopilot. "Just do it," I said, "and get a cleaning crew down here. And for heaven's sake, don't let the restaurant staff find out. They can't keep a dang secret."

"Yes'm." Willie guided Mama to the door.

I stared at the walls for a few seconds and then plucked glass and broken wine bottles from the ground, two and three and four at a time. My hands trembled as I lined them against the wall. Each one of them with their corks blown and empty as hollowed gourds. All with the label Echo Bay. Not another bottle was touched.

I moved quickly, jumping at the slightest sound. There were still shelves and shelves of bottles. Who knew if Culver was finished with his shenanigans? I definitely didn't want to be another victim of exploding glass.

I cleared most of the bottles by the time Martina, Carla, and Pilar arrived with their cleaning supplies.

"Just an accident," I said as they peeked into the room. "No big deal." They eased forward.

"La misericordia," Martina said and set her bucket of soapy water on the ground. "What a mess."

"Yes, ma'am," I said. "It sure is. Those," I pointed at the broken bottles I'd already stacked, "go in the trash." Pilar moved toward the wall and snapped open a green industrial-sized garbage bag and dropped bottles into it. They pinged and smashed against each other.

I left, hesitating in the hallway at the sound of scratching. I crossed to the door of the storage room that had flooded. Was it the same one where Sam Perkins found Horace's ledger? Maybe there was more evidence inside. I tried the tarnished brass knob. Locked.

I found Irene Fischer in the bar, sipping a glass of sherry. "How do you know it's Culver?" I said, falling into the chair opposite her. My sweaty legs stuck to the leather.

She blinked at me. "What's a culver?"

"My ghost. Culver Washington."

"Oh." She leaned back and sipped her drink and eyed me over the rim. "The rapist slave."

"He didn't rape anybody," I snapped and pressed the heel of my hand to my temple. "I'm sorry. I'm tired."

"And a little frightened, I imagine."

I blinked at her. She continued to sip her drink and study me. Eddie took over for Willie behind the bar. He flicked a glance at me, shoved his rolled sleeves further up his forearms, and turned to watch baseball.

"Why is Culver doing this?" I leaned toward Mrs. Fischer. "I've been nothing but nice to him."

She sighed. "The personalities and manifestations of ghosts are as varied as the individuals they used to be." She set her glass on the table and ran her thumb and forefinger along the stem. "Generally, they linger because of some unfinished business. Something left undone. Perhaps a wrong needing to be righted."

I tried to ignore the tingle at the base of my skull.

"This ghost," Mrs. Fischer said, "this Culver. He has some connection to the hotel?"

"He was a patient here during the Civil War, when they turned it into a hospital. He may've died here. Out on the lawn."

She nodded. "The place of one's death has a particularly strong hold on the individual."

"Then why don't I see him at the hotel instead of the cemetery?"

She sipped her drink. "Perhaps he's buried there."

"There's more."

She clasped her hands and leaned in.

I lowered my voice, "The stories are wrong. He may have been murdered."

"Then his spirit must be quite strong."

"Strong enough to cause weapons to break glass? To fly off the wall and embed themselves in furniture? Strong enough to blow the corks off of eighty-four bottles of wine and pierce a stone wall?"

Someone hit a home run and the baseball game roared above us.

Mrs. Fischer's pale blue eyes glittered. She laid a hand on mine. "Maybe," she said, "violent enough to murder."

CHAPTER 39

Mama took her medication and calmed down in her office before she even considered resuming her duties. The Durbin wine was reordered. The wine cellar was scrubbed clean. And I couldn't stop thinking about the storage room across from it.

Mama said it was the hotel manager's office before they built the new wing. Maybe Bedford Hamilton didn't have the only proof of Culver's innocence. And I would've loved not to risk becoming a criminal and cross paths with him again. If there was any information about the hotel's past, or any proof of Culver's innocence, it should be there. I found Mama leaving the spa, crossing beneath the live oaks next to the pond and asked for the key.

"I don't have a key," she said. Her bun had been retightened, and her makeup refreshed, but her shoulders slumped. "Ed Winer's the only one who does. He locked it after we cleaned up after the flood. And he won't be back in town until the Durbin wedding."

"Great."

"Why do you want in there?" she said. "After today's wine cellar disaster, we can't afford any more trouble."

"I won't cause any trouble. I'm simply looking for information about the hotel during the Civil War. Did you know it was converted into a hospital?"

"I did." She blew her bangs out of her eyes. "How did you?"

"I'm working on a research project." I studied the sun sparkling off the water. A white-tufted duck sunned along the bank. The reeds beside him trembled and I caught a glimpse of a mama duck and the fuzzy head of a duckling.

"You've just enrolled in a new school," she said. "You won't start classes for weeks. How do you already have a research project?"

"I want to impress my teachers," I said. "Just ask Mr. Ed for the key."

"I can't," she said.

"And why not?" I swiped the sweat-plastered hair off my forehead.

Mama fingered her sleek bun. "Because I don't want to attract any more of his attention," she said.

I would've traded every scarf in my closet for one cool breeze. But the air around us was dead. Not much moved except the crickets in the tall grass and a grasshopper that launched from the sidewalk onto an orange tiger lily.

"You're the manager," I said. "How do you not have access to the entire hotel?"

"It's just a storage room. And Ed Winer wants it locked."

"Why wouldn't he trust you with a key to a storage room?"

"Apparently, because I'm always screwing up." She dropped her hand. "And he's always cleaning up my messes."

"No," I said, "he's not. He says he is, but by the time he gets around to doing something, you've already done it and he takes credit for it. Why do you let him do that?"

"You don't understand, Cat." Her gaze rested on the fountain of water, sparkling in the sunshine.

"You're right," I said. "I don't understand why you let him push you around. You stood up to Daddy. You stood up to my dumb headmaster. You even held your ground with Atlanta's mayor."

"This is different."

"How?"

"You don't know how I got this job."

"You interviewed for it. He hired you. What's to know?"

"I was interviewing for another position. It was a fluke."

"What difference does it make now? You're the manager."

"I'm a disaster!" She threw up her hands and stalked away.

I followed her. "You're not a disaster. Stop being so dramatic. You're the only person keeping this hotel afloat."

She shoved her hands into her armpits and turned away.

"What are you not telling me?"

The mama duck and her seven babies waddled to the edge of

the pond and splashed into it. Mama's chin dropped. Her expression drew me closer.

"Mama," I said, "what did you do?" My heart pounded. The ducks paddled behind their mother.

She glanced at me, tears glistening in her eyes. Her lower lip trembled and she bit hard on it. She blinked rapidly and whispered, "I threatened Mr. Ed."

If she hadn't looked so distraught, I might've laughed out loud. "Threatened him," I said, "with what?"

She was barely taller than me without her heels and didn't appear strong enough to fight off a starving kitten. "It's so sordid." She pressed a palm to her forehead. "I'm so ashamed."

"Did he make a pass at you? Did he attack you?"

"No." She shook her head hard and waved her hand. "And lower your voice." She moved toward the pond, startling the mama duck who paddled toward the reeds.

"Tell me." I dogged her.

She waited for an elderly couple to shuffle by. "You shouldn't be hearing this, Cat. You're too young for such things."

"Oh, for crying out loud. I'm fifteen."

"Practically a baby."

"That's what Tate keeps saying. And I hate it."

Her look was sharp.

"Never mind," I said. "Just tell me before I scream."

"Now who's being dramatic?"

"Quit stalling and spit it out."

She paused as if to launch into one of her lectures about how she was the parent and I was the child. Instead, she heaved a sigh and ran a finger over the brown fuzzy top of a cattail.

"I got here early that day. Remember?"

I shook my head.

"I left at dawn from Nana's, too nervous to sleep. Maybe you weren't up yet. I arrived about eight. My appointment wasn't until nine."

I huffed and rolled my hand to keep her going.

"I decided to tour the hotel. Get an idea of the layout. It was bigger than I expected and spread out with the different wings."

I swiped the hair brushing my cheek.

"I toured the main building, the lodge, strolling the halls, getting an idea of what the housekeeping staff looked like, what kind of equipment they used, how fast they cleaned, that sort of thing."

"Spying on the staff. Got it. Then what?"

She drew her shoulders back. "I wasn't spying."

"Whatever. Keep going."

She brushed the furred cone and I bit back a scream. "Mother!"

Her head snapped around. "Sorry. I've spent the last three months trying to wipe it from my memory. Some things you simply can't unsee."

"Okay." I calmed myself. Counting one. Counting two. "Confessing will make you feel better. You can't keep these secrets locked inside. It's how you get trapped. You've got to bring them into the light. Then they have no power over you."

She blinked at me.

"Seriously," I said. "Finish the story."

She gave a little terrier shake of her head. "I passed a room with a housekeeping cart parked outside the door. Spray cleaner, rolls of toilet tissue, bottles of shampoo, were scattered as if there'd been an accident. The door was ajar." She crushed the cone and stared into the bubbling fountain.

I envisioned her at the door, a palm pressed against it as she eased it open.

Her eyes shut and her fingers curled into fists. "I shouldn't have gone in. It was none of my business. I can't imagine what possessed me."

"Mama. What happened?"

"It was Mr. Ed," she said opening her eyes. "He was in the room."

"Cleaning it?" I said stupidly.

She shook her head. "No."

And then my stomach did a funny flip and I didn't want to hear the rest.

"He was with Rosalie," she said and moved closer to the water. "He stood behind her, his hands on her, his eyes closed. But hers were dark and open wide and she stared at me through the mirror. And I thought, why doesn't she move?"

"She was frozen," I said.

Mama nodded.

"What did you do? What did you say?"

Mama shook her head. "It was stupid. I said, 'I'm here for the housekeeping job.' And Mr. Ed stumbled back like he'd been shot. Rosalie stared at me through the mirror and though I was shaking, she calmly buttoned her uniform and said, 'I'm afraid the position has been filled'. Mr. Ed jerked his head toward her.

I was so shocked I couldn't think. I've heard of this happening, but I've never actually witnessed it. So I said, like an idiot, 'but

I've come all this way. I got here early'.

"Mr. Ed straightened his tie. And when he opened his mouth
to speak, Rosalie said, cool as you please, 'There is still the assistant
hotel manager position, no?' She glanced at Mr. Ed and then back to
me. 'Perhaps you would accept it, instead?'"

The breath I'd been holding hissed out of me and I said, "So, it
was Rosalie who threatened him."

Mama turned and frowned. "I don't know. It's a bit of a blur.
Mr. Ed said, 'Wait a cotton-picking minute'. And Rosalie pushed past
him to get to her cart and Mr. Ed said, 'I've already got somebody in
mind for that position. Besides, I don't know anything about her.' Rosalie plucked a feather duster from the cart and a roll of toilet tissue,
and said, 'but now she knows mucho about you'.

"She disappeared into the bathroom and Mr. Ed stood staring
after her as if he'd been struck by a Mack truck. Then he squinted at
me and said, 'You better be good'."

Mama left me by the pond, feeling like I needed another shower. The mama duck climbed the bank and waited while her babies, one
by one, struggled out of the water and onto shore. The last one made
an attempt, then another, and still another. I wondered at what point
it might give up and the mama duck might come back for it.

But she didn't. She simply waited. And finally, the duckling
made the leap. Immediately, the mama duck pivoted and the seven
ducklings scurried after her into the protection of the azaleas.

Tomorrow was the Fourth of July. I could've cancelled, but I
was running out of ideas. It would be Tate and me at his uncle's office
at night. Alone.

A shiver slithered through me. It was the danger of the mission. Of course it was. Not breaking and entering, exactly. Tate would
find a way. It had absolutely nothing to do with his broad shoulders,
chiseled jaw, or goofy grin.

I shook myself. He was just some dumb jock. Doing a job because I was paying him. Remember that, Cat, I scolded myself. Don't
ever forget he is not a friend. He is not to be trusted. He simply wants
his money. And I just wanted him to deliver.

CHAPTER 40

How pissed was I when Tate left me stranded at the Hamilton Building on the Fourth of July? Pretty dang pissed and I wished cussing about it would've made me feel better.

I was lucky Mama didn't notice I was gone. Of course she didn't. She was knee deep into trouble shooting at the hotel. The staff marched a parade around the property, then fired the hotel cannon. A barbecue buffet was served on the lawn. Fireworks exploded over the bay. I couldn't complain. She'd given me a heads up.

"Cat, I've got a lot going on, sweetie. Can you hang out with some friends and I'll meet you later?"

"Yeah, Mama, I'll hang with some friends. I've got lots of friends in Fairly freaking Bama."

And now, the one person, the only person I really knew and yet couldn't count on, never appeared. So, I missed dinner. Missed most of the fireworks hanging out in the shadows of the Hamilton Building. I heard the popping sounds, blasts and explosions, screams and squeals of children and stepped out long enough to see a burst of red and blue splattering the sky.

I cursed Mary Grace again and Lizzie Lee and everybody else involved in having my cell phone taken away. The obscene calls. The ugly texts. *Why don't you just kill yourself, already,* one said, *and all this will end.*

It was the final straw for Mama. She took my phone to the

police. They didn't take it seriously. They didn't take the website seriously. Kids' pranks, they said. Did it matter that the police chief was David Allen Lee, Lizzie Lee's grandfather?

I scrubbed my brow. Did it matter now? Would I ever get over it? Are people the same no matter where you are? I could hear Grandma Turner shouting in my ear, "Where's your faith, girl?"

My faith, Grandma? It's in the toilet, I wanted to scream back.

"I'd like to take those fucksters out and roll 'em in cow manure," Nana said, between puffs on her thin cigar, "so their outsides could match their insides…full of crap."

"Mother," Mama scolded. With a flick of ashes, Nana gave her a look that said, if you'd done your job as a mother, Eva, and not been so wrapped up in your high and mighty job with the mayor's office, your girl might not be in this unholy mess.

Or maybe it was just me. Wishing somebody, anybody, would've stood up for me. Hating myself at the same time 'cause I should've been strong enough to stand up for myself.

Would you get a backbone, you little wuss? I scolded. Grow it, steal it, forge it, whatever it takes, but you are sitting here, cowering in the shadows of this building waiting for a guy who's never going to show.

Finally, when the last boom sounded, and the last sputtering, sparkling, glittering light faded, I was left with nothing but silence and acrid smoke and a bitter, bitter taste in my mouth. Cat Turner. On the outside again. Fighting to earn my way back in.

And just as always, I had no choice but to move on.

Rosalie hadn't appeared for work in three days, but Mama refused to fire her. She couldn't afford to when Rosalie might go to the newspaper. Or the sheriff. She sent Carla to check on her and she and I covered for both of them until Carla reported back that Rosalie would not return until the evil spirits were exorcised. Mama made Carla temporary head of housekeeping.

I made the beds. I vacuumed. I served afternoon tea. The big buzz was a minor actress checked into the hotel to scout out the area for a potential site for a television series about vampires in the bayou. Which was pretty funny, considering. But I had bigger things on my mind than some wannabe actress and whether or not she approved of the Fairly Grand.

Mama, however, was totally wigged out, seeing it as the perfect opportunity for some positive publicity for a change. She sent fruit baskets and bottles of champagne and practically posted a bellman at the woman's door to assist her with any needs.

Raquel Vega exited her room in heavy sunglasses and a baseball cap, flipping her long brunette ponytail over her shoulder. I thought if she wanted to remain incognito, she might do a better job of it without trying so hard. When I served her tea, I treated her the same as everybody else. But the other guests fawned over her and she held court in the corner, regaling them with stories of Brad Pitt and George Clooney and how they were so old and if only she could be cast with younger men, blah, blah, blah. I turned away from the image of her and burned my thumb on the scalding tea pot.

"Hey." Tate grinned in front of me.

"Shut up." I sucked my blistered thumb. "You're just here to get a glimpse of Raquel Vega. I mean, what kind of idiotic name is that?"

"You think Rhonda Bloomenfeld has a better ring?" he said.

I wanted to smack the grin off his face.

"You were supposed to help me get into your uncle's office," I said. "On the fourth? Exploding fireworks? Distracted uncle?"

"I couldn't get away from my family," he said. "My mother dogged me the entire night."

"I waited for you. At his office. For hours."

He laughed.

I glared at him.

He stopped laughing. "Sorry," he said.

"Sorry? You couldn't call to say you weren't coming?"

"You don't have a cell phone. Which is, by the way, sort of ridiculous."

"It's a long story," I said. "You could've called the hotel. You've done that before. I know you know the number."

"But you were already in town."

"Where I had to watch the fireworks alone. Waiting for you."

"I said I'm sorry. Anyway, Uncle Bedford's office is too risky. There's got to be some evidence still in this hotel that can help us." He rubbed his palms together and surveyed the lobby.

"She's not here," I said. "She left first thing this morning to scout sites in Mobile."

He indicated the tea pot in my hand. "You going to have to do that all day?"

"I'm covering for Portia, who was supposed to return twenty minutes ago. Here she comes now."

Portia sauntered toward us, her wide hips swinging in her black gabardine pants. She brushed her bangs out of her eyes and gave Tate a sly smile.

He grinned back.

I rolled my eyes. "Come on, genius," I said and dragged him away. Portia smirked as she watched us leave.

"There's a room opposite the wine cellar that used to be the manager's office," I said. "I think that's where Sam Perkins found Horace's ledger." I led him past the soaring fireplace. He stopped to peer out the wall of windows. "What's going on out there?"

Mama stood at the edge of the pier with the wedding planner, the florist, the bride, the bride's mother and father, the groom and the catering manager.

"Durbin wedding," I said, and kept moving toward the stairs.

"Today?"

"Next Saturday, at twilight."

"They're already working on it?"

"They've been working on it for months." I pushed the door to the stairwell open and he followed me into the darkness. "It's the biggest wedding of the year."

I fumbled for the light switch. Weak fluorescent light lit the stairs. "W.E. Cummings' fourth. Marcy Durbin's first. You've heard of Durbin Lumber?"

"Of course. My dad's in construction."

"They've been working on this wedding for two years. They nearly cancelled after the weapons fiasco." I wondered what would've happened if they knew about the wine. "Mama assured them there would be no problems. I don't have to tell you, after all the trouble we've had, this one's got to go off without a hitch."

We reached the heavy oak door.

"Any reason it wouldn't?" Tate peered at me. I ignored him and tried the doorknob, knowing it wouldn't budge.

"Know how to pick a lock?" I said.

"I'm going to pretend you didn't ask me that."

I jiggled the doorknob. "Any ideas?"

"Who's got a key?"

"Ed Winer. But he left yesterday for Baton Rouge."

"That's it?"

I stooped to peer into the rusted keyhole, closing one eye. There was nothing but darkness. "Maybe Rosalie. But she's so rattled by the wine explosion –"

"Whoa," Tate interrupted. "Another explosion? How many

accidents have there been?"

I headed back up the stairs. He grabbed my arm and spun me around. "Listen," he said, "if I'm going to help you, you've got to level with me. Exactly what's going on here? Are we in danger?"

"Calm down."

"I'm calm." He dropped his hand and waited. The pale light cast shadows onto his face. I descended the few steps to stand eye to eye with him. "You're not going to believe it," I said, "and even if you do, you're not going to like it. You're going to say I'm crazy. And I've already been there, done that."

I stared at the wine cellar door and closed my eyes against the memory of blood red walls.

"You draw angels," he said. "I've heard it. So what?"

"Not just that."

"Okay, demons, too. You're a little quirky. Got kicked out of church school. Wear crazy-ass scarves. So what? Everybody's got their thing. You're taking this way too seriously."

"No." I opened my eyes and tried to concentrate to stop the feeling that my scarf was tightening around my neck. "I don't just draw angels." I curled my fingers into fists to keep from tearing at the scarf. "I see them, too."

He blinked at me.

This was it. Do or die. The last chance for me in this town. There was no other way.

"You mean, like, in your dreams?"

"And at dawn. And twilight. Sometimes when the light's sketchy I get a flash of wings. I hear a fluttering, then a roar, like birds filling the sky. I get a glimpse of their perfectly-formed lips, more beautiful and terrifying than anything you can imagine."

The air around us stilled. The light flickered overhead. The small space grew heavy and unbreathable. The wall tilted and I flattened a palm against it.

"Demons, too," I said. "Not so often, but enough to know they're there. You can't imagine the," I hesitated, "the darkness, coldness." I swam hard, struggling to surface, frog paddling my way up for air. I shivered, and thought Tate did too.

Our breath was ragged in the heavy silence. It had to be said. I couldn't hold it back any longer. If I tried, it would explode out of me, splattering blood and guts against the walls as surely as Culver popped the corks on those bottles and spewed wine against stone.

"Apparently," I said after a long stretch of silence, "I also see ghosts."

CHAPTER 41

Tate and I sat at a wrought iron table on the patio overlooking the pool. He leaned back in his chair, a bare ankle resting over his knee.

Johan from Columbia took our order, grinning and fluttering his thick lashes at me. My cheeks burned as surely as the sun scorched the tip of my nose.

Tate watched us with an expression I couldn't read. Disgust? Annoyance? Jealousy? I slammed the door on that thought.

We sipped our sodas and soaked in the smell of burgers grilling, pineapple and coconut grinding in the blender, a whiff of suntan lotion as guests drifted by. Kids squealed and splashed down the water slide as we sat, fascinated by everything around us and avoiding what was right before us.

"Well?" Tate said finally. He leaned in and sipped his cola from a plastic straw.

"Well, what?" Johan passed our table. He winked over a tray of strawberry daiquiris and I glanced away, wondering what in the world had gotten into him.

"Well," Tate said. "So, you see angels, which we kinda already knew. And now, ghosts. Which we didn't." He leaned back, dragging his drink with him, staring at me.

I sighed as the ice in my drink melted and I wanted to press the glass to my burning cheeks. "So now you know."

"Now I know." He licked his lower lip and studied me. For

once, he seemed to be choosing his words carefully. "Have you always seen ghosts?" he said. "Like the kid in the movie?"

"This is my first."

His lips pressed together. They were nice lips. He said nothing.

"You think I'm a freak," I said. "I see angels. Demons. Now, ghosts. I draw crazy pictures."

"And wear crazy-ass scarves, don't forget that."

I frowned. I wanted him to contradict me with 'No, Cat, you're not crazy. You're perfectly sane. And you're super cute.' What was I thinking?

"So," he said, after a slurp that nearly drained his glass, "you moved to Fairly and you're seeing a ghost for the first time. Maybe it's the trauma of the move? Maybe you're not seeing a ghost at all. Maybe it's, I don't know, your way of dealing with so many changes, leaving Ruby behind."

I wished he hadn't mentioned Ruby, and at the same time wanted to hug him because he remembered her name.

"How could I have come up with Culver's name?" I said. "And a perfect description of him?"

He shrugged and plucked the paper wrapper from his straw and played with it. "You read about him somewhere. And the picture's blurry. You could be describing any slave."

"Because they all look alike? Is that what you're saying?"

"I didn't say that." He folded the strip into an accordion. He smoothed it into a flat line.

"What about the accidents at the hotel?"

"Bad luck. Bad timing. Bad things happen all the time."

"But every time I see him?"

"Then stop seeing him."

"So, you do believe he's real?"

He glanced over his shoulder. A leggy teenager in a rainbow-striped bikini smiled at him over her French fries. He smiled back. I wanted to kick him under the table. Instead, I jolted it with my foot and brought his attention around.

"I'd have to see it to believe it," he said and I gritted my teeth. "But that's not to say I don't believe you believe it."

"In my own crazy made-up fantasy world?"

"Cat," he tilted his head at me, "you're young –"

"Don't say it," I interrupted. "Don't even. You're a whole whopping year older than me."

"Year and a half."

"I just turned fifteen."

"Oh, yeah? When was your birthday?"

"May fourth."

He thought about it. "Taurus, huh? The bull. Well, that explains it."

"Explains what?"

"Nothing. Forget it."

Johan brought fresh drinks.

"Thanks, dude." Tate said to him.

Johan turned to me. "Anything else I can get you, Miss Cat?"

I shook my head. His attention jangled my nerves. Tate grinned between us. But one look at my face made him choke back his laughter. Johan gave a slight bow and left.

"So," Tate sipped his drink, "you believe Culver's causing the problems at the hotel."

"Bayonets embedded in the stairs? Who else could've done that? Wine corks jammed so deep in stone walls they had to be dug out?"

He shrugged.

"And I'm not the only one. Mrs. Fischer thinks –"

"Whoa," he said. "Who's Mrs. Fischer?"

"A guest. She and her husband are these amateur ghost hunters."

"What!" Cola spewed from his mouth and he swiped it with the back of his hand.

I wiped the spray of droplets off my arm with a paper napkin.

"They've been coming here for years. And Willie confirms it. Well, the story about Red Maggie. He didn't know much about Culver. Except what he'd heard."

"Red Maggie," Tate said. "We grew up hearing those stories. Bart Walker snuck into her room once. I forget the room number. He attempted to talk to her. It used to be this big dare at school, but nobody I know has ever seen her. Hey," he said, "maybe we should have a séance in the hotel lobby."

"I don't need to conjure Culver," I said. "He's there each time I look for him."

"What about Red Maggie?"

"We definitely can't afford another ghost in the mix."

"Maybe they could duke it out."

I glared at him.

"So, no séance," he said. "What do you propose we do? What does he want?"

"He wants to leave. To go to his eternal resting place, wherever that is."

"And we're supposed to accomplish this how?"

"Mrs. Fischer says ghosts tend to linger over unfinished business or if they died under violent circumstances. I think Culver's still here for both of those reasons."

"And we're supposed to..."

"Right the wrong," I said. "Bring the injustice to light."

"Which involves what, exactly? What's the big injustice keeping him here?"

I stirred the straw in my drink. "Apparently," I said, "he was unfairly accused of rape."

Tate's brows arched.

I sipped my cola and said, "And then he was murdered."

CHAPTER 42

"So," Tate said, "if he was murdered, I guess we'd need to get some proof of it, right?"

"Right."

"Does he know who murdered him?"

"Yes."

"Great."

"But he won't admit it."

"Why not?"

"He thought he was a friend. I guess he still does."

"So, who's this friend?"

I sipped my drink.

"Well?"

"You're not going to like it."

"Why would I care?"

"It's Horace Hamilton."

He huffed back in his chair. "No way. Wait. Owners and slaves weren't friends."

I shrugged. "Culver's convinced they were blood brothers based on some ceremony this voodoo queen conducted when they were kids. They were practically the same age. They grew up together."

"Horace Hamilton. My great-great-great-grandfather. Who's being honored at the Celebration of the Dead ceremony next month."

"Yep."

"Horace Hamilton murdered his slave."

"And raped a woman."

His face darkened. "You can't go around saying that."

"I'm not saying it. Culver's saying it."

"You don't even know if he's telling the truth."

"Why would he lie?"

"Because he's an evil spirit?" He shook his head. "I can't believe I just said that. I can't believe we're talking about freaking ghosts."

"Listen," I leaned toward him, "I'd like nothing better than to get rid of him. He's not exactly making my life easy."

"I want to talk to him," Tate said. "Maybe I can talk some sense into him."

"Be my guest," I spread my palms wide, "but I don't think he'll appear."

He stared at me and said, "He was there when Bobby and I met you in the cemetery and gave your drawings back."

"Yes."

"Right before Bobby's accident."

"Yes."

"Did he do it? Did he attack Bobby?"

I shrugged and felt a twinge of guilt at my own thoughts about his cousin. "Maybe."

"Did you tell him to?"

"Of course not. Do you imagine I have my own personal ghost to command? Calm down." Several heads swiveled in our direction.

He lowered his voice. "This entire time you knew this and you're just now telling me?"

I cocked my head. "Don't pretend you would've believed me. I know exactly how crazy this sounds."

"Let's go talk to him," he said. "I have a few things to say."

"You can't go over there all steamed. You might make things worse."

"Worse? I doubt it."

"If he hurt Bobby, he might hurt you, too."

Tate puffed out his chest. "I'm not scared of some loser ghost. I can take care of myself."

"I want to go on record saying this is probably not a good idea."

"Oh yeah?" he said. "Well, maybe it's time for Culver Freakin' Washington to learn who has the real cojones in this family."

"Please." I rolled my eyes and gave him an exasperated look. "Just don't piss him off."

"We'll see."

CHAPTER 43

Tate and I arrived at the cemetery. Though it was nearing twilight, it was still muggy and hot and the mosquitoes were thick. I shooed them away from my face.

We called for Culver. We searched behind tombstones. Tate climbed onto the stone bench. He yelled. He taunted. He threatened.

Culver didn't appear.

"I told you, you're going to provoke him," I said.

The phone in his hand buzzed. He consulted it. "I've got to go," he said. "Mom's at the country club and I'm late for dinner." He stuffed it in his pocket. "Do this again, later? I'm not done with ghost man Culver Washington."

"Sure," I said, "later."

He trotted along the lane toward the clubhouse until the line of trees blocked him from view.

"He's a queer one," a voice said close to my ear.

I jumped and turned.

"Why wouldn't you appear?" I said. "He made a fool of himself trying to draw you out."

"Yes," Culver said, "he did appear foolish." He strolled away from me. "After our last talk, I've been thinking about the raid on the Houston house."

"Did you think of something that might help you? A clue?"

He scratched his elbow. "Ever since I saw you last, I keep

thinking about the animals." He stared after Tate. "Dogs and cats slaughtered for no good reason."

I thought of Mr. Stubbs' fluffy gray body lying on my front porch and shuddered.

"No reason to kill them," Culver said, "except pure meanness. Or sport."

I shut my eyes against the image of Mr. Stubbs' lifeless body with my scarf, the pale blue chiffon, wrapped around his neck.

"I mean, there were plenty of men killed, too," he said. "And that's awful. But those poor dumb animals. The lambs huddled next to their mamas. Goats still tied to the fence. Hound dogs and one little yappy thing on the lawn, bellies ripped open."

My stomach lurched as I thought of Mr. Stubbs. Hanging by my scarf, a cloud of perfection turned murder weapon. And Ruby howling to wake the dead.

"Stop," I said.

"I can't, Miss Cat." He stared at me with his big round eyes. "I've been here all this time thinking such things. Wasn't it enough for boys to be murdering other boys? Brothers. Fathers. Sons. Why did they have to kill the poor animals, too?"

I dug the heel of my hand into my heart as the air whooshed out of me. I sucked it back in. "I can't bear it," I said.

He nodded. "It's a harsh world to be sure. I bet you never did nothing bad in your whole life."

"Shut up," I whispered. "Just stop."

Mr. Stubbs. Named for his sad, singed whiskers. Survived a house fire. But couldn't survive me. Tears stung my eyes. I bit my lip and counted one. Counted two.

"You talk about your dog," Culver said. "I could tell right off you're an animal lover. Horace was, too. How he doted on his ole bluetick hound, Beau."

"I don't want to talk about it." I counted one. Counted two. Forced myself to breathe. I stumbled away. "I don't want to hear any more about Horace. He raped a woman, and framed you for it."

"Wasn't too fond of cats," Culver said. "But he wouldn't hurt one for nothing."

"Do you understand anything I've said?" I whirled on him.

Culver blinked at my fury.

"He murdered you."

"It was an accident."

"It wasn't an accident and you know it. It was murder, pure and simple. He tied the scarf around your neck, slung it over a tree.

And though your little body struggled and kicked and clawed, the idiot said it was some big joke. He didn't even try to untie you until your body went limp."

Culver stared at me.

I stalked back to him.

"He said he didn't mean it. He said he was just fooling around, wanting to scare me, but he waited too late!" I screamed at him. "He waited until Mr. Stubbs was dead before he cut him loose." Spit flew from my lip and landed on Culver's shoulder. He stared at me.

"What are you saying?" His voice was a quiet wall against my rage. "Horace never strung me up."

I clasped my brow, clammy with sweat, and struggled to catch my breath. I fought for control. Stupid Brant Hollings. Oh, how I hated what those boys did. I struggled to get a grip. "Horace murdered you," I said as Culver's body swayed in front of me. "The sooner you come to grips with it, the sooner you'll go home."

"You said Mr. Stubbs," Culver said softly. "Who's he?"

"Did I?" My thoughts stumbled backward. My head was stuffed with cotton. Culver's voice was muffled in my ears.

"Who's Mr. Stubbs?"

"Nothing. Nobody." I stumbled to Elijah's angel and grabbed hold of the edge of her wing. I cried out as it sliced my palm.

"You've hurt yourself." Culver stepped toward me as blood dripped onto the marble. I squeezed my fingers into a fist, as blood dripped onto the angel's heel where she knelt. Big, fat splotches. The blood of the innocent against cold, dead skin. Not skin. Marble. And I wasn't so innocent.

"Mr. Stubbs," Culver persisted, "was a friend?"

"I'm not going to talk about it," I said. Hadn't talked about it. Not with a friend I no longer had. Or my father who was no longer there. Or the cold, clinical psychiatrist. Or the pale, thin preacher with his steepled fingertips. Or my sad, struggling mother.

"You told me," Culver said, "I need to talk about my feelings, about the pain so I can let go. So I can be free. What about you, Miss Cat? What do you need to be free of?"

"That's bullcrap," I said. "I can't believe I was so stupid to say that. There's no getting free."

I wanted to be free. I wanted to rip the memories from me. Tear them into teeny, tiny pieces and shower the pond with them. Watch them sink into the deep, dark depths where the weight of water would bear them down. Where they couldn't reach me ever again.

I stared at the puddle of blood on the angel's foot. My blood.

My heart throbbed in my palm. I pressed my wrist to my waist and staggered from the cemetery toward the hotel.

CHAPTER 43

Frank Petty, the weekend guard, stopped me at the gate with a message from Mama. I hid my fist behind my back as he informed me she was at the hotel spa. The power in the building shut off for no apparent reason. And dinner awaited me in the restaurant.

Of course I blamed Culver for the outage. But that was fast work, even for him.

I headed straight to the lobby bathroom and washed my palm. It stung. But it was a clean slice and I refused to be a baby about it. I wrapped my hand in toilet tissue until I couldn't see blood and headed to the restaurant.

A waitress from Sioux City, Iowa, bagged a grilled cheese sandwich and chips for me and I took my dinner and sat on the lawn overlooking the bay. I forced the sandwich down despite the unreasonable panic fluttering in my chest. The sun sank into the water and splashed it as bloody as my hand.

On the beach, a mother collected her things as a baby boy squalled red-faced at her feet. She dropped a yellow plastic shovel into a blue sand bucket and both of them into her beach bag. She plucked a red towel from the ground, shook the sand from it, and folded it over her arm. She propped the boy on her hip and slung the bag over her shoulder and stumbled, sunburned and glassy-eyed, through the sand toward the hotel. For some, life remained ordinary.

I brushed the crumbs from my bare legs and wiped my buttery

fingers on the seat of my cutoff shorts as I strolled after the woman toward the spa between the Magnolia and Azalea Buildings to check on Mama.

The night was warm, and there was no breeze to flutter the beards of Spanish moss. Water gurgled from the fountains. A frog croaked, long and deep, and then splashed into the pond. I stopped as something crunched underfoot. An aluminum foil gum wrapper. Finnegan would have a fit, as he prided himself on a pristine landscape. I plucked it from the ground and dropped it into the trashcan beside the brick path curving toward the spa.

I had nearly circled the pond when a violent twittering erupted from the live oak sprawling above it. Something had upset the birds. Sometimes it was rowdy kids chasing the ducks, or even throwing things at them.

But as I drew closer and edged toward the pond, a horrible squawking competed with the birds. Even with the twinkling lights blinking on in the twilight, I couldn't find the source of panic. As I reached the reeds, the ground squished beneath my foot.

At the edge of the water the mama duck flapped frantically surrounded by what? For a few seconds I stared at the ground, not comprehending what was at my feet. Carnage. Baby ducklings.

Images flashed through my mind. The bicycle hut burning. Weapon displays exploding. Wine bottles shattering. The baby ducks...I couldn't even finish the thought.

I stood paralyzed for I don't know how long, and then did the only thing I could think of. I raced upstairs and grabbed an empty shoebox from my closet, grabbed a washcloth from the sink, and raced down the stairs and out the back door.

A few guests milled around the grounds, but most were out to dinner. I didn't stop to assess the situation. I simply dropped to my knees and with the white cloth scooped up baby ducklings, or what was left of them. Even as the twilight faded to dark, the birds in the trees twittered furiously. The mother duck rushed out from the reeds a few times, but I ignored her. There was nothing I could do for her.

The azalea bushes behind me rustled and a light glinted off the leaves. I jerked around. Did a cat do this? The rustling stopped. With nothing but tiny lights twinkling in the trees, it was hard to tell if the bushes actually moved, or it was my imagination.

What was I thinking while I scooped fuzzy duckling parts? Well, besides the possibility of a cat attack, a hawk might've done it. They did have wicked talons. But I hadn't seen any hawks in the area.

Maybe one of the gardeners ran over them accidentally with the lawn mower. Or clipped the shrubbery too close to the nest, even though Finnegan reminded them daily of the ducklings' presence.

How was I going to explain this to Finnegan? He'd want to know where they'd gone. He didn't care for the bunnies plaguing the garden, they were a nuisance. But he loved the ducklings.

Or it could be any number of things. All accidents, of course. Because it would be unthinkable, beyond heinous, to imagine someone did it on purpose. I couldn't entertain the thought, so I continued to scoop pieces and deposit them in the box until the cloth was bloodied red and I cried so hard I could barely see.

Each time the thought crept in, *you know who did this*, I swiped it away. I couldn't bear it. I continued my grim reaping. By the time the last deposit was made in the cardboard box, the mama duck had disappeared.

Somewhere in the dark, I heard Mama calling my name. But my hands were sticky with blood and lord knows what else. My tears were salty on my tongue and the sting of bile rose in my throat.

Poor Mr. Stubbs, I kept thinking. Poor little ducklings. A flash of light whirled me around again. Mama's voice grew closer.

I slammed the lid on the box and kept to the shadows, searching for a place to hide the grisly collection until I figured out what to do with it. I found a spot on the backside of the convention center, out of sight of the guard shack.

On my knees, I ignored the sharp spikes of palm fronds stabbing my bare arms as I pushed the box against the wall. It would be impossible to explain a trip to the cemetery tonight. I'd have to sneak some tools from the gardener, anyway. I'd wait until dark tomorrow and give the poor things a proper burial. And when Culver showed his chicken-livered face, I'd light into him like nothing he'd ever seen.

I dried my cheeks against my shoulders, holding my bloodied hands away from my body. How I hated to be a part of this unholy mess. My body shivered in revolt. I crept around the corner of the building and thought the bottom branch of the magnolia tree trembled. I moved closer and smelled mint.

A crunch of gravel, a woman's voice, then laughter scurried me back to the shadows. A couple passed along the drive, the woman's arm draped around the man's neck.

A series of loud beeps drowned out their laughter and the lights of a white Mercedes flashed on. I waited until they climbed into the car and drove away before I slinked along the shadows back to the hotel.

I would later regret forgetting about the flash of light and the trembling of the lower limb of a magnolia tree on a windless summer evening.

CHAPTER 45

I stumbled through the next day with a gray cloud of dread hanging over my head. I wanted Culver to acknowledge what he'd done. He murdered those ducklings. And for what?

If the killing of Mr. Stubbs was pure evil, what did this make Culver? Whatever Brant and Eddie said, they killed him to get back at me. Scare me. Was Culver doing the same thing with the ducklings? Maybe he raped poor Lucie, after all.

I could've tossed the shoebox in the trash. But those poor babies deserved better. I could've buried them at the hotel. But it would've been impossible to find a spot not covered by security.

Besides, I wanted Culver to know. I wanted to see his expression when he confessed to his latest disaster. I wanted the blood of those babies to soak into the ground beneath his feet, where he walked every single day, day after day, for maybe two hundred more years. And to realize as bad as Horace was, he was just as evil.

And so, I waited until well after midnight, after Mama finally fell asleep, and her soft snores droned from the other room.

I eased out of bed and threw a denim jacket over my sleep shorts and tee. Daddy left the jacket behind when he abandoned us and I thought it still smelled of him. I had to roll the cuffs that hung well past my fingertips. I slipped into my black Converse and eased out the door.

The shoebox was where I'd hidden it and I had to backtrack

around the entire hotel and spa, past the rental cottages, to avoid being seen. I would have no coverage crossing the road, so I had to count on Pete to somehow get distracted to escape without notice.

I hesitated on the edge of the road as a silver Cadillac rumbled past me. I waited in the shadows until it paused at the guard shack. Then I sprinted across the road with the box tucked beneath my jacket. I reached the employee parking lot on the other side and hunkered to zigzag my way through the few Fords and Kias of those working the late shift.

From the cover of one car to another, I stayed low and moved quietly. I squatted beside a Honda Civic, the last car in the lot before I could make a break for the trees lining Hamilton Bay Lane. Gravel crunched behind me. I sucked in my breath and held it, clutching the shoebox and counted one, counted two.

For the first time since I hatched this crazy plan, I realized how bad it would look if I were caught sneaking out of the hotel with a box full of bloody chick heads and body parts on my way to the Confederate cemetery. It would be virtually impossible to explain my mission without appearing psycho. Or a devil worshiper.

I stayed frozen long enough for my legs to cramp. When I heard no other sounds, I peered over the hood of the car. Maybe it was a squirrel. Or one of the bunnies from the garden. Or the poor mama duck stalking me and her dead babies.

I waited a few more seconds before sprinting toward the shelter of trees. I borrowed a small shovel earlier in the day and left it propped against the backside of the sprawling live oak close to the golf course. It was far enough from where Culver usually appeared that I could bury the ducklings before I went after him. The moon was so bright I didn't need the small flashlight I'd pocketed.

I found the shovel where I left it. The ground was softer than I expected, and after a few initial whacks at roots and rocks, I made enough of a dent to begin a hole big enough for the box.

The air was warm and still, and after a few minutes I prickled with sweat. I slipped out of the jacket and dropped it beside me. I shivered at the exposure, but dug faster without it. And I wanted the ordeal over as soon as possible.

My right palm stung from the cut beneath my bandage and I stopped to study the blister forming at the base of my fingers. I shifted my grip, but by the time I was satisfied with the size of the hole, blisters bubbled both palms.

I dropped to my knees and eased the box into the ground. A light flashed. I caught a movement out of the corner of my eye. It was brief, but in the breezeless air, it was something. I peered into the darkness straining to see. The trees remained still and silent.

Maybe it was moonlight flashing off a falling acorn. Or a cat clicking over pavement. Or a squirrel snapping a twig.

Leaves rustled beyond the tombstones and I hugged the ground to blend into the shadows. A gray, bushy tail flicked into the moonlight and disappeared up a tree.

Of course I was jumpy. Of course I was paranoid. I was in enough trouble already and this would be impossible to explain. I stared at the hole and felt, oh how to explain it? Sorrow, as if something valuable and precious had been lost and I'd never get it back.

With no real idea what to do, I did what I thought I'd want someone to do if it were me in the box, and I murmured the only verses I remembered from my days at school. *"The Lord is my shepherd, I shall not want..."*

I hated my voice trembling in the stillness of the nearly full moon and so I continued silently, my lips moving. When I'd murmured everything I remembered, I shoved the dirt onto the box and packed it flat.

I rested on my knees, fingers splayed over the fresh grave, dirt embedded beneath my nails. There was nothing left to do. I'd come back for the shovel in the morning. It would be easier to explain.

I struggled to my feet and leaned the shovel against the tree. A twig snapped and my head popped around. A shadow streaked to my left. Culver stood beside Elijah's guardian angel, his pale clothes glowing in the moonlight.

Fresh fury boiled inside me.

CHAPTER 46

"Come to admire your handiwork?" I said. "Sorry to disappoint you." I swallowed the acid in my throat. "But I must admit, you and Horace now have something in common. You're both murderers."

"Why are you here?" he said.

"Why are you?"

He surveyed the moon-tipped landscape. "I felt a disturbance."

"A disturbance?" I stalked toward him. "I'll give you a disturbance." I punched him hard in the chest. It was like punching through cloth. More substantial than air, but yielding. And I staggered through it, a coldness washing over me. I stumbled away from him and rubbed my grimy palms over the chill prickling my arms.

"What were you doing there?" He tipped his chin at the freshly-churned dirt beneath the tree.

"You know what's there." I gritted my teeth. "Your latest handiwork. Fortunately, I found it before anyone else did, so, you lose. But gee, thanks for playing."

"What is it? I couldn't tell."

"Too bad, chief. I'm done playing, exposing my little secrets so you can use them against me. Simply crawl back into whatever hole you crawled out of and we'll call it quits. How 'bout that?"

"You're mad."

"You think? You killed those ducklings. Ripped them to shreds. You set the bicycle hut on fire. You discharged those weapons in the lobby. You exploded forty-two cases of wine. You attacked Bobby Hamilton with a stick, and probably flooded the basement of the hotel." My elbow twinged. "You may have even caused my accident."

He thumbed his scar. "You wanted to hurt the Hamilton boy," he said. "You said you wanted to hit him over the head. It's what you wanted."

"Are you crazy? I don't want to go around hurting people."

"Don't you?"

I huffed and ran a hand through my sweat-soaked hair. "I mean, I may have said it out of anger, but I'd never..." I shook my head and tried again. "A lot of bad things happened to me this past year. But Mama and I are starting over. I'd never cause trouble. I'd never do anything to hurt anybody."

"Threats can bring out the worst in people," he said. "Horace –"

"I don't want to hear anything else about Horace Hamilton. I'm sick to death of the name Hamilton. And you've already admitted you've done horrible things."

"I said I'd do what I needed to loose myself from this earth. I don't understand how these things, the fire and the weapons happened."

"Don't forget Bobby's accident and the ducklings."

"The ducklings." He rubbed his bottom lip. "They were hurt?"

"Yeah, sorta. Like, decapitated and torn into teeny tiny pieces." I pressed fingertips to my trembling lips. My eyes stung. I couldn't do this. I simply could not go through this again.

"Killed," he said, "like your friend, Mr. Stubbs."

"Yes," I choked, "like Mr. Stubbs. Are you, or are you not, determined to destroy this hotel and Mama and me with it?"

"I'm trying to leave this earth," he said. "To be set free."

"But you really don't know."

"I don't understand what's happening," he said. "I don't understand how you can see me, but I ain't flesh and blood. I don't understand how you strike me with all the force you can muster and I feel nothing but a rush of wind. I don't understand how I'm neither hot nor cold, but itch infernally."

That explained the scratching. If I wasn't so furious, I might've joked about lice after death.

"I don't understand why you're the only human who can see or hear me," he said. "I don't know why I deserve to be trapped. Or why I've only been able to appear around nightfall, and now well past it."

I chewed on a thumbnail and tasted dirt. I spit it out and wiped my mouth against my shoulder.

"I ain't ornery by nature," he said. "Bad things happened to me, too. But I've forgiven Horace."

I stared at the moon and thought of Daddy. He'd coached me on the moon's cycles from our backyard on Ivy Lane. This moon appeared full, but not quite.

"You, however, Cat Turner, are powerful angry."

It took a few seconds for that to sink in since I was musing about my daddy and wondering where he might be under the same moon. I turned slowly and stared at Culver.

"Are you saying," I paused to gather myself and square my shoulders, "I'm the one causing these accidents?"

He stared at me, his hands loose at his sides.

My heart pounded so hard I thought it might explode. Erupt from my chest, blasting poisoned barbs in every direction like the weapons from their display cases, dripping blood like wine from the ceiling of the wine cellar. How dare he, after everything I'd been through?

"Are you –" I couldn't form the words. I couldn't shape the thought. I closed my mouth and stared at him. I backed away. I might be in hell, but eventually I'd wake up and there'd be no ghosts and no evil Hamiltons and I'd have at least one friend in the world and my mother wouldn't cry herself to sleep every night and...

I stumbled away from Culver. "Don't speak to me," I said. "Ever again. I won't be back. I don't care what you do. Burn the hotel to the ground. With me in it. I don't care. Just don't. Ever. Speak. Again."

And then I ran blindly along the lane, passing the guard shack without stopping. I heard nothing. There were no shouts, no one called out. I wouldn't have stopped if they had.

I let myself in the employee entrance with my key. I bit hard on my lower lip as I raced up the stairs, two at a time and didn't stop until I reached my room. I sucked in every emotion, every tear, all my breath as my card beeped green to let me in. I stumbled to the bathroom, eased the door shut, splashed cold water on my face, scrubbed soap under my nails.

It wasn't until I kicked off my high tops and crawled into bed that I realized I'd forgotten Daddy's jacket at the cemetery. With the smell of him still on it.

I planted my face into my pillow and sobbed quietly, chokingly, until I could sob no longer, and the sky outside my window pinkened with the rising sun.

CHAPTER 47

It had been over a year since I'd stepped inside a church. And I wasn't quite sure what I expected, except I needed some peace and quiet I couldn't find at the hotel or now the cemetery. It was late in the day and I waited for the church secretary to climb into her Ford Escort and the minister to cross the lawn to his modest brick rectory before slipping inside the sanctuary.

I eased along the center aisle toward the pulpit and stopped at the steps. I stared at the face of Jesus as he rested, tired as a weary traveler on his cross. Arms stretched wide over the wood, his legs were bent, his bare feet nailed one atop the other. A white cloth draped his narrow hips.

Why was his expression so calm, so smooth? He was in agony, wasn't he? Those nails went through actual flesh, didn't they? People spit on him, called him names, mocked him, tortured him. And here, he appeared to be taking a nap. Or maybe he was already dead.

I knelt on the first step, the stone cold and hard beneath my knees. I imagined Jesus opening his eyes and gazing down at me. But he didn't. I pretended he was listening anyway.

"I'm sorry," I said. "I'm sorry for being selfish." I fingered the mangled flesh beneath my scarf. "I'm sorry for all the trouble I've caused. You know what I'm talking about." I bowed my head. "I'm sorry for the bad thoughts I've had about Mary Grace. And my school. And Mr. Stubbs." My breath caught in my chest, nearly too heavy to bear.

"I'm sorry about Mama and Daddy and causing so many problems for them. I'm sorry about my pride and stubbornness and not being able to make new friends. I'm sorry about the bad stuff happening at the hotel and lying and not being able to move on. I'm sorry about hanging onto bitterness." I stopped and opened my eyes and stared at the cross.

"I'm sorry about not being a better person and saying mean things to people and not liking Bobby Hamilton and not being able to help Culver Washington. But," I said softly in the stillness of the sanctuary, "if you could find your way to help me, I'd be eternally grateful."

The doors banged open, reverberating along the pews until the sound crashed into me. For one ridiculous moment, I thought my prayer had been answered. I glanced over my shoulder. Bobby Hamilton strode down the aisle, his hair tousled and darkened with sweat. His polo shirt was untucked. His topsiders slapped the floor.

"What're you doing here?" he said with a curl of his lip.

I got to my feet. "It's a church. I'm talking to God."

He stopped within reach. "You know," he said, "maybe I was wrong about you."

Hallelujah. I breathed a sigh of relief. In the back of the church, like a halo above his head, the last bit of sun streamed through the round stained-glass window with jeweled bits of iris and azure and gold glinting.

"Yeah," he said, "I take it all back. You're probably not a devil worshipper after all."

Finally.

"No," he said, "you're a witch."

I rolled my eyes heavenward.

"You're not worshipping the devil," he said. "You're conjuring spirits."

"How do you figure?"

"I followed you."

"Yeah?"

"I watched you scoop up duck soup over at the hotel. I watched you hide the box blubbering like a baby. I checked after you left to make sure what was in it. Pretty gruesome business."

My chest constricted. "So?"

"I followed you the next night to the cemetery. Pretty creeped out, I must say."

"So what? I buried the ducklings."

"And then you talked to somebody. Somebody who wasn't

there."

I thought back to my conversation with Culver. I was pretty angry. "I was talking to myself."

"I don't think so," he said. "You were pretty pissed at some-body who wasn't cooperating. Would that be Satan? Your master?"

"Well, which is it?" I sighed. "Satan worshipper or witch?"

"Maybe both."

"You realize how ridiculous you sound, don't you?"

"I've got it on camera."

"Really?" A fingernail of fear scraped the back of my neck. The clicking noise. The silver wrappers. The smell of mint. "Show me."

"So you can erase it? Not a chance."

I raised my hands in surrender. "You hold the camera."

"Phone."

"I thought your phone was destroyed."

"I got a new one, genius."

Of course he did. "Let me see."

He held the screen out of reach.

"It's awfully dark," I said. "You can't even tell what I'm doing."

"You can see you're in the cemetery. There's the angel marker."

"So what? I'm burying dead ducks in a cemetery. Hardly a crime."

"Wait, here, you're talking."

And sure enough, I rose to my feet and walked toward Culver.

"So, I'm talking to myself. Practicing a soliloquy. Who cares? I was a good actress at my school."

"I bet you were."

"I didn't mean it like that."

"See, I can twist things, too."

"But why would you? I haven't done anything to you."

"Tate says you're researching our family to take us down, de-stroy our reputation."

That big-mouthed brat. I knew I couldn't trust him.

"Like you're determined to destroy mine?" I said. "Look, I'm simply trying to solve a hundred-and-fifty-year-old mystery. If your family gets entangled in it, I can't help it."

"So, he's right."

"If you're not guilty of anything, you don't have anything to worry about."

"That's laughable," he said. "Facebook? Twitter? Instagram? You don't have to be right. You simply put it out there and the trolls and freaks and losers drool all over themselves to destroy you."

Lord knows, that was the truth.

"I'm not on social media," I said, "and I'm not putting anything out there but the truth."

"You're not going to put anything out there at all, little miss nobody. I'll take you down or my uncle will. But rest assured, you'll be run out of Fairly if you keep at it. Just like you were run out of Atlanta."

"I'm not from Atlanta." My voice echoed off the empty pews.

"If Uncle Stone can't make you stop, and that's a huge if, Uncle Bedford sure as heck will."

"The truth has to come out," I said, "before this whole celebration thing. Lies aren't good for the town, or your family. Ultimately, they'll destroy you."

"Oh, you think you've got the market on truth?" he said. "That's rich."

"What have I lied about?" I said, and immediately wanted to retract the question.

"Stop messing with my family," Bobby threatened. "Or you're gonna rain hellfire and all kinds of crap on your stupid little head."

"You be careful, too, Bobby Hamilton," I said. "Watch out for flying tree limbs and exploding debris. I'm not exactly in control of the spirit that's unleashed himself on this town."

"So, you're admitting you've conjured some spirit," he said. He fumbled for the record button on his phone.

"I didn't conjure him. He just appeared because of something Horace Hamilton did a long time ago. I'm working to get rid of him. But you go ahead and keep interfering. See who gets hurt."

"Are you threatening me?" He stuck his phone in my face. A beep indicated he was recording. His hand trembled as he glowered at me.

I stared back at him, ignoring the phone. He finally lowered it and turned it off.

"You leave my cousin alone," he said, "and maybe I won't show this to anybody."

"I'm not bothering your cousin. He finds me."

"He feels sorry for you, you little freak."

"Whatever. Nobody's got a leash on him."

"You're going to make yourself unavailable or else."

I snorted. "Or else what?"

"You get run out of this town same as you got run out of your school. How'd your mama handle that? My mom says she heard your daddy left you, and your mom's getting on in years. Not a lot of job opportunities for middle-aged women."

"Your mom would know, I guess."

"You shut your mouth. My mom doesn't have to work. We've got plenty of money. But maybe your mom doesn't mind working night shifts at the Days Inn, huh?"

"You're a jerk." I bumped him as I headed up the aisle. He shoved me so hard I sprawled on the floor, banging my shoulder on the wooden pew.

"Nice." I brushed the dirt from my palms and resisted the urge to rub away the sting. "You enjoy beating up girls? Makes you feel like a tough guy?"

He tossed the curls out of his eyes. "You started it." He hovered over me, his phone gripped in his fist. "You continue to mess with me, freak," he said, "and you're gonna end up as splattered roadkill."

CHAPTER 48

The afternoon of the Durbin-Cummings wedding, I descended the stairs to the lobby to find Tate Channing loitering near a towering bouquet of lilies on the table in front of the gift shop.

At the thumping behind me, I turned to find a young girl in a frilly pink dress with a garland of rosebuds perched on her blonde curls. She tripped down the steps, dribbling pale pink rose petals from a white wicker basket. She landed next to me, wide-eyed, and I pointed toward the bar. "Through there," I said, and she took off running.

I opened my mouth to warn her to slow down, but the elevator dinged open and a woman in pink chiffon strode past me, her dyed-to-match pumps in one hand, her long gown hitched in the other. She followed the girl through the bar.

Tate strolled toward me. "You've been scarce," he said. "I thought we were supposed to be working on this Culver thing." Had he seen Bobby's latest evidence? "Thought we might break into that storage room. But it appears you're busy."

I tucked my hair behind my ear. "It's the Durbin wedding."

"You in it?" He nodded at my pale-yellow dress, my favorite as dresses go, because it made me look older.

"Just helping out." I resisted the urge to fiddle with the spaghetti straps biting into my shoulders. "Mama makes me dress up for them." I swished my thumb against the itchy netting beneath the poufy skirt and pretended not to scratch.

"You look good," he said. "Nice scarf."

"Thanks." I fingered the chiffon a few shades darker than the dress as his compliment sent me floating. And then I stared past him and tumbled to earth.

"Holy Mother Mary," I said.

"What?" Tate turned and then whirled back to me. "What is it?"

I glanced out the window. Tiny fairy lights twinkled in the trees. Flickering torches lined the beach. Twilight had fallen and the wedding was about to begin.

And in the lobby, beyond the towering lilies, stood Culver Calhoun Washington.

"What is it?" Tate hissed.

"It's Culver." I pushed past him.

Culver moved toward me.

"You've got to leave," I said and stopped beside the table. From the front desk, Benito stared at us.

"Huh?" Tate said behind me.

Culver stopped on the other side of the table. "You said you'd help me." He pressed his fingertips into the gleaming wood.

"Then you decided to destroy my life."

"What are you talking about?" Tate said.

"Why would I hurt somebody sworn to help me?" Culver said.

"I did not swear."

"You gave your word." Culver's chin lifted. "Don't it mean anything?"

Tate's voice was low beside me. "Cat, you're scaring me."

I shrugged him off. "You can't expect me to help somebody hell-bent on destroying what little family I have left," I said.

"I'm not trying to do anything."

"It doesn't matter if you're doing it on purpose or not. You've got to get out of here before something worse happens."

"I got no idea how I got here."

"I'm gonna call a big fat bull on that."

Culver glanced toward the bar. "What's that?"

A violin hummed high and sweet. A cello joined in. Pachelbel's "Canon in D" drifted toward us.

"Cat," Tate hissed in my ear, "tell me what's going on." Before I could stop him, Culver skirted the table and headed toward the bar. I was right behind him and Willie glanced up from drying a glass.

"Willie," I said and stabbed a finger at Culver's back, "he's here."

I didn't have to explain. "Laws, sister," he said. "What're we gonna do?"

I shook my head helplessly. "Try to find Mama," I said and banged out the door. Tate caught up quickly and said, "What the heck are we doing?"

"Chasing after Culver." I gasped and halted.

The wedding guests gathered at the edge of the pier. The bride would walk the length of it to exchange vows with her fiancé out over the bay. Culver stood next to the crowd of guests. I strained on my tiptoes, searching for Mama.

Two six-foot torches flanked the pier walkway, flaming against the rosy sky. White satin ribbon swagged the pier railing. Full blown white roses and hydrangeas cascaded from gleaming gold candelabras. Candles flickered in the slight breeze.

The minister, groom, and best man waited at the covered end of the pier, jutting two hundred feet from shore. I couldn't find Mama among the guests, so I eased toward the reception area. My gaze swept the section of the lawn where the wait staff waited among the tables. They'd finished touching up the spread, adjusting the white net bows, tucking in drooping flowers, icing drinks, straightening napkins.

"Where're you going?" Tate said.

"To find Mama." I shaded my eyes. "And warn her."

"Does she even know about Culver?"

"Not yet. And this is not the place I want them to meet."

Culver ignored everything around him except the trio of violinists and the cellist seated to the left of the guests. He moved toward them as four groomsmen in black tuxedos crossed the lawn in single file and strolled onto the pier.

One by one, they took their places beside the groom. The music slowed and bridesmaids appeared, their pink gowns fluttering around their ankles, bouquets of pink roses and lavender peonies clutched in their fists.

"For heaven's sake," Tate hissed, "what's he doing?"

I shook my head.

Culver raised his arms, took a step, then another as he turned in a slow, stilted waltz. A woman glanced his way, frowning as she rubbed her bare arm.

As the last bridesmaid strolled onto the pier, Willie appeared in the doorway of the bar holding his dishrag, and wearing a scowl. The flower girl tottered over the lawn, scattering pink petals from her basket.

Tate grabbed my arm. "Can you see him? What's he doing?"

Culver turned slowly, elegantly, eyes closed.

"He's dancing," I said.

"He's what?"

The music ended and Culver stuttered to a stop. The wedding march began. The bride appeared around the corner of the building, clinging to her father, her curves barely contained in her strapless lace gown. She was less than half the age of her groom.

On her bleached blonde locks, Marcy Durbin wore a Cartier diamond tiara. Locked in the hotel safe for the last three weeks, it was Bill Cumming's great-grandmother's and survived the Titanic. It was reportedly worth half a million dollars.

The future Mrs. Cummings floated over the grass, her lace chapel train dragging through the trail of rose petals, her silk veil floating behind her. The guests sighed as she passed them and glided onto the pier. She reached the groom as the wedding march ended. Guests filed onto the pier after her and Tate and I moved to the edge to see.

The sun sank into the bay as the minister recited his litany of verses. Culver stood alone in the grass.

"Does he appear angry?" Tate whispered.

"No."

"Well, that's good."

"He looks...incredibly sad."

Culver turned to me and something inside me loosened, then broke, a crumbling, a falling apart. Then he shimmered silver and disappeared.

"Cat," Tate nudged me, "are you all right?"

Pressing a palm to my cheek, I nodded and searched the crowd for Mama. Willie disappeared back into the bar.

The ceremony wouldn't be long as tiny white lights lining the pier twinkled against the darkening sky. Please, I begged, let there be no accidents tonight. No mishaps, no fires, no tragedies. Just let something go right for Mama this once. It might be her last chance.

Then the minister finished. He pronounced them husband and wife and announced the kiss. They were entwined for so long the guests laughed and cheered.

I sighed with relief and with a glance skyward, said a quick "thank you".

The violins played the recessional and the crowd parted and lined the railings to allow the couple to pass. Above the music, I heard the first crack of splintering wood.

As the newlyweds marched toward us, guests laughed and hugged one other.

"Tate." I grabbed his arm.

"Is he gone?" he said. "Everything seems okay."

Another board creaked. "No," I said. "It's not. Do you hear

that?" A beam groaned. A column snapped, then another, and the dock tilted.

There were a few screams, but mostly startled cries as the right side of the pier collapsed and dumped everyone who didn't grab hold of the railing into the bay.

Tate and I stood frozen in shock, until the first high-pitched scream. Tate ran toward the beach and struggled to kick off his shoes before launching himself into the water. The guests closest to shore scrambled onto the sand. But many were deeper out, including the bride and groom.

I raced after Tate, but stopped to help two stunned elderly women onto the sand. Groomsmen struggled through the water with their bedraggled bridesmaids. The minister swam, then limped onto shore. He dropped onto the beach and dumped water out of one of his newly shined shoes, his other shoe missing.

I shucked my sandals in the sand, and stood shin deep in water, the sand sucking at my toes as I guided guests and the wedding party to shore. I searched the darkening horizon for Tate.

There was another scream from the darkened water. Tate tunneled through it toward the flower girl who floundered, arms flailing. He reached her and her arms strangled his neck. One-armed, he made his way back to shore. A few feet beyond them, a dark lump floated in the water.

"Tate!" I yelled, but he continued to plow toward shore. "Tate!" I screamed and jumped and stabbed at the water behind him. But he was already struggling with the little girl's arms around his throat.

"Hey," I glanced around, but everyone was either collapsed in the sand or staggering toward the hotel. I thought I heard sirens in the distance. I glanced back at the bay. The shape hadn't moved.

With a groan, I dove into the water. The coldness snatched at my breath and swiped wet hair out of my eyes and struck out in my best breaststroke.

I'd never been a strong swimmer and within a few seconds lost any semblance of form and dogpaddled for my life. The body floated a few feet from the listing pier and I passed Tate as I veered toward it.

"Cat!" he called, but I focused on the shape in front of me. I reached it and tugged at the dark wool of the tuxedo until I rolled the man onto his back. It was the groom.

"Mr. Cummings," I said. "Mr. Cummings." Without any idea what to do, I slapped a pale cheek. His head rolled and his eyelids fluttered. Even buoyed by the water he was heavy. "Help!" I yelled as

I tread water. "Somebody help me!"

But chaos ruled. I gathered the man's back against my chest, gripping the fabric under his armpits and kicked toward shore. We'd gone only a few feet when he came to life and thrashed the water. "Stop," I cried. "It's me, Cat Turner. I've got you."

But he fought and splashed and clawed until he'd entangled his arm in my scarf. Panicked, he flailed so violently his elbow connected with my nose and everything blackened for a second before my vision cleared.

I let go and kicked free, tasting blood. I fought to stay above water as Tate's head bobbed toward me. He struck out in a hard breaststroke as I tread water and struggled to untangle myself from my scarf.

Above me, boards creaked and groaned. I glanced up as the roof of the pier slid toward me. I lunged away from it as it crashed and wooden planks rained from the sky. The last thing I saw was Tate's look of horror, before something cracked the back of my skull and everything went black.

CHAPTER 49

The murky water pressed against me, filled my eyes, nose, ears. My hair floated past my face. This was it, then. The second death of a short, unaccomplished life. Culver would have to find his way home without me. Tate would have to find someone new to harass. Daddy would have to find somebody else to forget. But what about Mama?

I envisioned the headline. *Hotel Manager's Daughter Dies Again, Mom's to Blame.* What kind of manager, no, what kind of mother, would it make her? They'd crucify her.

But what was our big crime? Sure, we ran away with our tails tucked between our legs, determined to lay low and not draw attention to ourselves. Well, screw that.

Why was I running? I didn't die on purpose. I didn't want to have my throat mangled. I didn't ask for some portal to another realm be opened so I'd be inundated with glimpses of angels and demons at incredibly inopportune moments.

I might've called Mary Grace a bad name when she stopped speaking to me and wouldn't say why. I might've experienced some unkind thoughts, okay, maybe downright evil thoughts. But I didn't act on them. I asked for forgiveness.

I came here, wanting to put it behind me. I met Culver. And everything I worked so hard to forget seemed to start again. So, yeah, I'd be lying if I said it wouldn't be easier to just let go.

To stop striving. Stop explaining. Stop crying. Stop caving in.

Emmie did. Why couldn't I? I was so tired of being betrayed. But in the cold, dark void, it wasn't my best friend's face shimmering like a mirage before me.

"But Mrs. Chappell," I begged. "Why won't Mary Grace speak to me? What did I do to make her so mad? Let me apologize and make things right."

"Cat," Mrs. Chappell stared down her smug nose at me from her front porch, "we are good Christian people. Her father and I can no longer have Mary Grace consorting with the wrong kind."

"Wrong kind? I didn't create the Facebook page. It's a fake. Some guys from school designed it to make me look bad. Even Lizzie Lee was involved."

The palm she raised stopped me. Her eyes closed as if she couldn't bear the sight of me any longer. "Her father and I feel Mary Grace needs to move in a new direction, as you've so obviously done." Her eyes opened. "You're, well, you're too negative, Cat. Mary Grace could use a more positive influence right now."

"But I didn't do anything. Since my accident –"

"Cat," she cut me off, "Ford and I are quite firm on this. We can't keep her from seeing you at school, obviously. But we'd appreciate it if you stopped calling, stopped coming over, quit trying to regain something that's simply over and done."

"But we've been friends since kindergarten."

"People grow apart, Cat. Kids move on. You understand. Mary Grace simply needs to embrace a closer relationship with the Lord."

"I go to church," I said.

She backed into her doorway. "Run along now. You'll find new friends who share your," she hesitated, "new interests, I'm sure." She gave me a tight smile. "Why don't you gear your efforts toward that?"

She peered along the street and then ducked inside and slammed the door. The curtain in the bay window moved and I knew Mary Grace stood watching. She didn't even have the guts to face me.

I stood there stupidly, on the Chappell's front porch, the scarf Mary Grace gave me choking my neck. Everything I'd known, everything I thought I knew was thrown off kilter, stumbling, stuttering like a warped record, or Daddy's drunken stagger.

How I wish I didn't care. How I begged to be angry enough, mean enough to say, 'Screw you!' And I did, a few times in my head. Then I just curled up inside myself. And the wall went up, brick by brick, until I insulated myself from the whispers, the sly looks, the doors slammed in my face, the nasty things written on my notebook.

I understood. Finally. I was on the outside looking in. And

no one in that homogenous school would join me there. Not even Mary Grace.

As Mrs. Chappell's smirk shimmered away from me into the dark nothingness of the bay, I realized I was tired of being cold. I was sick to death of cowering in the dark. I wanted light and warmth and a breeze on my cheeks and the scent of jasmine in my hair. Crickets chirping and fireflies sparking against a velvet, starry sky.

"You want the truth you're so fond of shoving down everybody's throat?" Mary Grace said. "Okay, here's the truth, Cat Turner. You're simply not worth the drama."

The drama? The drama of dying and coming back to life? Of having headaches so bad they made me want to puke? Of having these images in my head, all the time, out of the corner of my eye and over my shoulder? The drama of flinching when somebody called me Frankenstein or warded me off with their fingers in the sign of the cross, or having my hand slammed in a locker when I attempted to snatch one of my discarded drawings out of it?

The drama of having my family's Easter cross set on fire in our own front yard and Brant Hollings and Eddie Willis strangling the sweetest cat who ever meowed with my scarf and being blamed for it? The drama of having a Facebook page created in my name showing sordid demon rituals and mutilations and heavens, I can't even describe what else.

Mary Grace and Mrs. Chappell may've turned their high and mighty backs on me, but they would not ruin my summer. They would not ruin my life. I would hide my scars. I would fit in. And they would not be given another thought. Not another nanosecond of my existence.

New town. New friends. Better than them. Loyal. True friends who speak up for others, who step outside their circle of comfort, who're interested in more than appearances. I wanted a friend willing to look past the flaws to the heart and dig a little deeper than the pancake surface of Cover Girl makeup.

Would I find such a friendship out there? I had no idea. I simply knew I wasn't settling anymore. I wasn't faking it for anybody. And I wasn't sinking to the depths of despair while my mother's future was on the line.

I'd keep fighting. I wouldn't stay down. I was done with other people making decisions for me. Telling me who they thought I should be. I'm Cat Turner. And I don't answer to Mary Grace. Or Mary Grace's mother, or Lizzie Lee, or Bobby Hamilton. I'm me. And I had a hotel to save and a ghost to free. And tethers I created in my own mind that I needed to sever.

"What's binding you, Cat Turner?" Culver said. Well, it's vanity. It's shame. It's fear so thick sometimes I can scarcely breathe. But I couldn't drown, couldn't die again. I had to rise. To kick and scream and fight with every stitch of resistance within me. That was the only way to move forward. The only way I could live.

I kicked hard, and silver wings fluttered beside me. The water stirred and I pushed harder and the water parted. The roar of beating wings filled my ears. I rose, lifting my face toward the surface. I punched hard against the darkness and fluttered my arms through the airless water.

A shimmer of silver flashed over my shoulder. A gasp of air seized my lungs. I kicked and pushed against the weight. I was lifted from behind. Silver sparked the corner of my eye as wings whirred and beat like a huge flock of geese.

I kicked and rose, my arms propelling me. The pressure eased. The water gave way. And I grinned in the darkness at my meteoric rise.

CHAPTER 50

I choked and gasped and rolled onto my side.

"She's alive!" someone shouted.

With a violent shudder, I wretched into the sand before collapsing onto my back. The sand was cool beneath me. I stared at the denim sky and tried to remember what happened.

Tate settled on his heels beside me, swiping his mouth with the back of his hand. A crowd of people hovered over us. Mama kneeled across from Tate, her cheeks streaked with tears. Thanks to me and the waterproof mascara I convinced her to wear, she appeared elegantly distraught.

Tate ran his tongue over his lips and mine tingled in response. I pressed trembling fingers against them as my teeth chattered. Before I could ask, Mama collapsed onto me and I struggled beneath the weight of her. "Baby, are you okay?" I could only mumble, so she finally pulled back and said, "Can you talk?"

I nodded and stared at Tate. "Did you –"

Someone barked, "Clear the area. Everyone, step back."

Mama was pulled away from me and Tate was shoved aside. I moved to follow him, but two men in white uniforms blocked him from view and pushed me back into the sand. One grabbed my arm and slapped a blood pressure cuff on it. Another flashed a pen light in my eyes.

They asked me a lot of questions and I don't remember if I answered correctly or not. When they finally allowed me to sit, I noticed my yellow rag of a scarf lying in the sand beside me. My hand flew to my neck as someone wrapped a blanket around my shoulders. The paramedics took Mama aside and asked her a bunch of questions. She answered them, dry-eyed. And struggled to find Tate in the crowd.

After the paramedics released me, I stumbled through the sand among the guests, women huddled in towels and blankets, hair straggling against pale cheeks, mascara running. Apparently, they didn't get the memo: *wedding ceremony, dip in the bay to follow, waterproof mascara a must.*

I turned as Sheriff Hamilton thundered across the beach toward Mama. I struggled through the sand to intervene.

He stopped to tower over her. "I've got a good mind to arrest you," he said.

"On what charge?" Her green eyes flashed sparks.

"I don't know," he whipped out his pad of paper. "Willful negligence or something."

"Sheriff Stone," Irene Fischer stomped toward us, an elegant walking cane kicking up puffs of sand as she advanced. "You have badgered this poor woman quite enough."

"I haven't even started," he said. "Who the heck are you?"

She drew back her shoulders and stood to her full height of five foot five. "Irene Fischer of the New Orleans Fischers," she said.

"I don't know you."

"Well, I know you, sir." Her cane bore her slight weight as she leaned toward him. "I've been coming to this hotel longer than you've been alive and I was here when these fool people elected you sheriff. And I'm warning you to back off, young man. This is none of Eva's doing, I can assure you of that."

"Exactly who is responsible?" he said. His gaze fell on us one by one. At the edge of the beach, the flower girl sniffled in her mother's arms. A fish splashed in the water. Shouts echoed in the distance.

Mama's spine stiffened. "If we knew that, Sheriff," she said, "we would've stopped them by now."

The sheriff squinted at her for a few seconds, then turned to me. "What about you, missy? You know anything about what's going on here? Another prank maybe to get your Mama to move back to Atlanta?"

Before I could speak, Irene Fischer said, "Are you quite daft, Sheriff?" His unruly brows shot up. "Catalina Turner is one of the finest young people I've ever had the pleasure to meet. And she nearly died tonight saving the groom. You have heard of Mr. William E.

Cummings, haven't you? Of Cummings Aviation?"

Sheriff Hamilton made a strangled noise.

"I thought you might recognize the name. So, before you go besmirching this good, hard-working family," she stabbed her cane dangerously close to his foot and he jumped backward, "you might want to actually make some notes on that pitifully blank notepad of yours." She cocked her head. "Why don't you harass some of the other guests? And then come back when you've got a few more details, hmmm?"

"Mrs. Fischer," the sheriff tapped his pen against his pad, "My job is to get the facts here. There's no need to get your dander up."

"Sheriff," Mrs. Fischer fixed her steel blue gaze on him, "my dander wouldn't be up if you'd confine yourself to the facts and not stagger off in wild accusations and innuendos. I can assure you," she jabbed her cane again, "we all want the truth."

"Sheriff," Deputy Pike stepped in to rescue his boss. "Your nephew Bobby's, looking for you. And I got some people over here who want to make a statement."

"Well, alrighty, then." The sheriff hitched his slacks and glared at us. "Finally, we got some people willing to cooperate." He sauntered away.

"Poof, be gone." Mrs. Fischer flicked her bejeweled fingers at him.

I smothered a laugh and said, "Where's Mr. Fischer?"

"Catalina, dear," she waved my question away like an annoying insect. "I left him napping in the room. Everyone knows I do my best work alone."

I glanced around and lowered my voice. "I need to ask you about Culver."

"Yes, dear?"

I paused to formulate my thoughts. "He says he doesn't have any idea why these accidents are happening. He's not even angry at Horace. And he…he blames me. He says I have something to do with them. My anger. Over my past. What's been done to me. Is it…is that even possible? I would never –"

"Of course not, dear." Mrs. Fischer leaned on her cane and stared out at the gently lapping water. "He could be lying," she said. "But he doesn't seem the type."

I followed her gaze out to sea.

"I suppose," she said eventually, "your negative energy combined with his desperation to leave could be manifesting itself in strange and violent ways."

"So, it is my fault."

"Oh, Catalina, dear, of course not. Sometimes poltergeist phenomena can attach itself to youthful energy. There may even be darker entities drawn to perpetuating mischief when the atmosphere is so. You can't help the bad things that've happened to you anymore than Culver can. But eventually," she fixed her piercing blue gaze on me, "for the sake of everyone involved, you must both figure out a way to make peace with your past and move on."

CHAPTER 51

Wedding guests continued to talk to paramedics and deputies. Divers searched the water for Mrs. Cummings' diamond tiara. A few guests sat at white-draped tables dotting the reception area and sipped chilled champagne, staring numbly at the bay.

I wondered where Culver was, struggling between feeling sorry for him and wanting to kick him from here to kingdom come. I refused to dwell on the fact that I died ever so briefly for the second time in my short life. I especially didn't want to obsess about Tate's lips on mine, even if it was just to save my life. But my lips betrayed me, still tingling as I searched for him.

I was cold despite the warm night and the blanket wrapped around me. I finally found him, sitting on a low rock wall jutting out into the water, separating the pier from the beach.

"Hey," I said. His wet shirt clung to his chest and his tennis shoes lay beside his bare toes buried in the sand.

"Hey."

"You saved my life." I dropped beside him and hugged the blanket around my shoulders, a fistful of it pressed to my neck.

He stared at the reflection of the moon on the water.

"I guess this must be pretty traumatic for you after what happened to Emmie," I said.

He studied me, from the top of my wet curling hair to my bare feet. I lost my shoes somewhere on the beach and could only imagine how I looked.

"I don't want to talk about it," he said.

"Well, thanks, anyway."

His gaze rested on my lips and I wondered if he was remembering, or regretting. "No problem."

We sat on the rocks, two dark blurs between the pier and beach, listening to the murmur of voices, the lap of water against the shore, the first strains of music coming from the reception.

I twisted around. "Looks like the reception's going on after all." Tate followed my gaze before turning back and staring at his feet.

We could've been anybody. There were so many people milling around probably nobody would notice if I simply leaned into him. Was it wrong to want to experience a kiss while I was actually conscious, to feel the warmth of his lips again, pressed to mine, his breath warm and faintly lemony?

My body was exhausted, but my nerves sparked electric as I shifted closer. He stiffened. I hesitated, but if not now, when? I had no idea what got into me except that I nearly died again and I was too exhausted to understand what I was doing. I rested my head on his shoulder, which was as unyielding as Elijah's marble angel. But as I froze and was about to pull away, he relaxed. His head tilted toward mine, his jaw resting against the top of my head.

He smelled of soap and sweat and a little like Ruby after splashing in Nana's pond. All I had to do was tilt my head back and my lips would be inches from his. If he pulled away, I might still have time to recover. I battled my desire to stay as we were, and wanting more. And while I knew he was hardly the safest option, he might be worth the risk.

He shifted and I glanced at him, clutching the blanket to my throat. His lips hovered over mine for a second before he closed his eyes. I closed mine and waited for the soft press of his lips. His breath tickled and I sighed and let him fall into me.

"There you are!"

His warmth left me and I opened my eyes to find two women huddled in blankets slogging through the sand toward us. It was Marcy Durbin Cummings and one of her bridesmaids.

Marcy's hair was fluffed dry, but her water-logged dress dragged through the sand behind her. She stopped in front of us and waved her bridesmaid on.

"Heroes of the day," she said and the blanket loosened around her shoulders. Her block of a diamond wedding ring winked in the moonlight.

"Well, Tate is," I said, "he saved my life."

"And you saved Bill's." Marcy glanced past us to where her husband stood with one of the sheriff's deputies, pressing a towel to the side of his head. She waved. He winked at her.

"I didn't do anything," I said, "except get fished out of the water."

Tate turned to me. "You swam out to bring him back."
"He must've hit his head when the dock collapsed," Marcy said. "He said you helped him regain consciousness."

"I didn't know what to do," I said, "so I slapped him. I'm sorry."

She laughed. "Well, it's not like the man's never been slapped by a girl before."

"You appear to be taking this pretty well," Tate said, "considering your wedding's been ruined."

"Oh, I don't know," she eyed her husband, "everyone's safe and accounted for and there's a lovely reception waiting on us." She smiled at us. "You don't get to be wife number four without knowing how to maneuver through some land mines." She let the blanket fall from her shoulders and dropped it alongside me as a breeze lifted a strand of blonde hair and curled it away from her cheek.

"You kids have fun," she said. She hefted her sodden train and draped it regally over her arm. "I believe that man owes me a dance." And she strolled toward him as he broke away from the deputy to meet her.

Tate scooped a handful of sand and sifted it through his fingers. He frowned and it was obvious our intimate moment had passed. The wedding couple approached the reception and the band broke into a Dave Matthews' song about crashing into things.

"So," Tate stared out at the water, "those are some wicked scars on your throat. That's why you wear the scarves?"

I didn't want to explain it to him. But leaving it to his imagination was worse. It took me a few seconds to screw up the courage. "I was in a restaurant one night over a year ago with my parents. You know, the kind of place that serves popcorn while you wait? Daddy said no, it would ruin my dinner, but I kept insisting, pitching a hissy fit. I can be pretty relentless sometimes."

"No," Tate said dryly, "not you."

I frowned at him. "Anyway, I wouldn't shut up about it and Mama finally gave in. So, I was cramming popcorn in as fast as I could and started choking. Daddy attempted to perform the Heimlich but couldn't dislodge the kernel. The paramedics were called, but I guess

I was already turning blue. Mama screamed for a doctor, but there wasn't one. Shelby's a small town. But there was a guy home from college training to be a vet. He started out in medical school and said he knew how to do a trach. The paramedics were still on the way when I stopped breathing.

"When I awoke in the hospital two days later, I was covered in bandages. It was a few more days before they let me see how bad it was. Our insurance wouldn't pay for what they considered cosmetic surgery. So, we've been saving for it ever since. Anyway, when I returned to school, I was called all sorts of names, Frankenstein being the most unoriginal."

"I thought you went to a Christian school."

"I did."

His gaze dropped to my neck, then skittered away.

"Yep," I said, "just like that. All day long."

"What?" He gave me a sideways glance.

"The look you gave me. You don't see it. But it's been a pretty common reaction."

"I'm not that shallow," he said without looking at me again. "We've all got scars."

I studied him as he stared out at the water. If he had any, I sure couldn't see them.

"So," he broke the silence, "I'm not sure the hotel can take much more of this."

"Neither can Mama," I said. "Your uncle wants to throw her in jail."

He jiggled his fistful of sand.

"You don't think that's crazy?" I said. "You don't think he's simply searching for a scapegoat?"

Tate shrugged. "What's he supposed to think? He has no idea about Culver. People are getting hurt. He has to do his job."

"Well, his job shouldn't involve harassing my mother."

"Why're you getting sore at me? I can't control my uncle."

"He's your family."

"He's the sheriff. He doesn't listen to me."

"He sure listens to Bobby."

"That's different." Tate tossed the sand and stood and brushed his palm against his thigh. He moved to stare out at the water.

"Bobby's more like your Uncle Bedford, isn't he?" I said. "He spies on people. He uses their weaknesses against them. He stops at nothing to get his own way. That's why his uncles like him better, right? He's more of a Hamilton and you're, you're a Channing."

"Stop making trouble where there is none."

"I'm not making trouble. I simply want to understand. Bobby was here tonight, you know."

Tate squatted and fisted another handful of sand. "So, Uncle Stone took Bobby under his wing. What am I supposed to say to him? Stop making trouble for this girl I just met and her mama 'cause all this crazy stuff started happening once they got here, but they're not in any way involved?"

I stood on trembling legs. "After everything I've told you, you still think Mama and I are to blame?"

"You're the one running around seeing ghosts," he said. "And hiding behind those silly scarves. Emmie would've never cared what people thought. She would've faced everything head on."

"Would she?" I cocked my head at him. "Or maybe she'd drown herself in pain pills and a bottle of booze."

He tossed the sand and stood. "That's low, even for you."

"Cat." Mama hurried toward us, her ruffled dress fluttering against her thighs. She'd gone out on a limb with that one because I'd talked her into it. But in a matter of minutes, she'd gone from elegantly distraught to ridiculously unprofessional.

"Honey, I've been looking everywhere for you." She tried to pull me into a hug, but I pulled away. "How's your head?" She ran a hand through my hair, but I brushed her off. "Is it still bleeding? Hurting?"

"I'm fine," I snapped.

Her eyelashes stuttered against her pale cheeks.

"Really," I said, "I'm fine. You remember Tate."

"Of course." She threw her arms around him and hugged him as he stood stiffly and stared over her shoulder at me. "You saved my baby." She pulled back to look him in the eye. "How can I thank you?"

"It's no big deal," he said and pulled away.

"It's a huge deal." She shook him by the arms. "I couldn't bear it if she..." She glanced at me and my mutinous face and then back to him. "Seriously, what can I do? Free lunch in the restaurant? A gift card to the gift shop?"

"There's no need, ma'am," he said, and she let his arms drop.

"Okay." She couldn't hide her disappointment. "If you ever need anything."

"Yes, ma'am," he said. "I'll be sure to ask. I've got to go. Cat," he barely glanced at me, "see you around."

He snatched his shoes and headed across the lawn. He skirted the hotel without a backward glance.

Mama turned to me. "Cat?"

"I'm going to bed," I said. "I have a headache." I followed Tate along the path.

"You want to talk to a paramedic?" she called.

"No." I kept walking. "I want to go to bed." By the time I reached my room I was swiping angrily at my tear-streaked cheeks just trying to get my key through the lock.

CHAPTER 52

The Cummings may have taken their baptism in the bay lightly, but as I expected, the *Fairly Standard* crucified us.

"Fairly Dangerous" was the headline splashing the front page and the hack reporter called for a myriad of investigations. Mama wanted to keep me home, but I was determined to get some real answers from Bragg Hamilton about what exactly was in Horace's ledger.

The shuttle dropped me in front of the toy store with a handful of guests who hadn't checked out after our latest disaster. The fact that Raquel Vega hadn't checked out was of some benefit. But she hadn't left her room, either, in three days. Two empty bottles of champagne and a half-eaten fruit tray awaited housekeeping every morning and there was much speculation that perhaps Miss Vega was on more of a bender than scouting out a location.

I rounded the corner past the hardware store and was deep in thought when the golf cart puttered past me. Footsteps pounded the sidewalk and Tate joined me, slightly breathless.

"Where you headed?" he said.

I kept walking.

"Seriously, where you going?"

I stepped out of the path of a barrel-chested woman and kept walking.

"Why're you not talking to me?"

I stared past him into the record shop. I should buy a record player. Collect albums. I remember Daddy playing Neil Diamond from the eighties. I should try it. I kept going.

"Hey," he grabbed my arm, but I shook him off. "You mad at me?" he said.

I clenched my jaw as the fringed ends of my scarf fluttered behind me. He caught up.

"You're mad, aren't you? What'd I do?"

I stopped past the record store. If he hadn't been hounding me, I might've gone in and browsed around, putting off my mission a few more minutes. But I didn't want to spend any more time with him than I had to. I pushed on.

"Why're you mad?" he said. He stuffed his fists in his pockets. I slowed as I grew closer to my destination.

"You're mad 'cause I left the other night?"

My feet dragged.

"Because it's not like we had plans. It's not like we had a date or anything."

"Shut up," I said.

"What?"

I stopped and glared at him. "Shut. Up."

"What the –" he stalked away and then stomped back to me. He ruffled his scruff of hair. "Who do you think you are, telling me to shut up?"

"I didn't ask you here." Something inside me bubbled to the surface, something dark and stinging, like acid. "I didn't ask you to hop out of your cousin's little golf cart and follow me. In fact," his head snapped back, "I didn't even ask you to come to the hotel on Saturday. So leave. Go." I shooed him away. "Don't look back."

"You asked me to help you."

"Forget it. It was a mistake. Be gone."

His eyes narrowed. "Fine," he said. "I felt sorry for you with your sad little drama of scars and schools and whatever. But do it by yourself. You think you can do it alone? Knock yourself out. See how far you get." He backed away. "But don't come crying to me," he stabbed a finger at me, "when everything blows up in your pointed little face."

"Go away!" I yelled and he threw up his hands and stomped off in the direction of his cousin waiting in his golf cart on the corner. I turned, eyes stinging, and took a deep breath. Hands trembling, I pushed open the door to Genesis.

Bragg Hamilton glanced from the magazine he was reading. I stalked toward him and stopped and before I could say anything, he said, "How's your mom?"

I opened my mouth to answer and realized I would commence to bawling if I said a word. So, I shut it and choked on the wad of tears clogging my throat.

He stared unrelentingly and said, "You want a co-cola? I got some in the back."

The dam burst and I bawled like a scalded baby. He straightened away from his magazine and stared at me as I shook and choked and gasped and wiped the snot from my nose with the back of my hand.

He fumbled behind the counter and produced a stack of Dairy Queen napkins. He handed them to me and backed away as I swiped at my cheeks, then my nose.

He waited until I was reduced to a rash of hiccupping and then said dryly, "To what do I owe the pleasure?"

The bell on the door jangled and with horror I turned to find Tate blocking the sunlight. The look I gave Bragg was one of pure wild-eyed panic. He took barely a second to tip his head toward the stairs. I didn't wait but jumped the chain and took the stairs two at a time before Tate could say a word.

"Whoa, there, T-Man," Bragg said as I hovered near the top of the stairs. "Let's give little Cat time to sheath her claws, eh? How's your mother?"

Tate grunted. "She's fine, Uncle Bragg." After a beat or two he said, "Why don't you call her sometime? Take her to lunch?"

"Work, boy, got to earn some bread."

"Nobody calls it bread anymore, Uncle."

"I know," he said, "I just enjoy annoying you."

"And you do an awesome job of it."

"Don't I?"

I couldn't tell if the banter was playful or not. I swiped at my face with the wad of napkins, hoping my little bit of mascara hadn't bled into raccoon eyes. The room was organized chaos with a worktable at one end covered in skulls, and – I squinted – chunks of fur? Boxes were stacked on top of boxes. A skulless skeleton sat propped in a corner. Beside it, a round table held a collection of wooden boxes of different shapes and sizes.

Some sported intricate carvings. Some were smooth and shiny. One was scarred with cuts and gashes deep in the blonde wood. I tiptoed over and opened it. It was full of keys. I poked a finger around them.

"Son, why don't you run to the hardware store and get us some co-colas," Bragg said.

I pulled out the oldest looking key, an iron skeleton key, and studied it in the pale light. It looked like it just might fit a rusty old dungeon of a lock.

"Co-colas? Uncle, you kill me," Tate said. "Don't you have a stash of drinks in the back?"

"I'm out," he lied. Money jingled. "Here's some quarters."

"But Bragg."

"Hurry up, kid," Bragg said. "You're not gonna miss anything."

"Stop calling me kid," Tate said. The doorbell jangled and fell silent.

I clutched the key in my fist, closed the lid to the box, and descended the stairs with it tucked under my arm. Bragg Hamilton sat on his stool, arms crossed, staring at the door.

"Why did you send him for more drinks?"

"I like to keep him busy," he said. "He's got too much energy to be cooped up in this store."

"You heard about what happened at the hotel Saturday night?"

He turned to me and his gaze dropped to the box in my hand. He stared at it for a second and then back at me. "I read the paper. Heard you were hurt."

"Just a bump on the head."

He pressed his lips like he wanted to keep from saying more and glanced toward the door. "Your mom okay?" He buried his hands deep into his armpits.

"Yeah, she wasn't on the pier when it happened."

"Good." He nodded. "That's good."

"But Sheriff Hamilton thinks she's somehow responsible." Bragg's face tightened as he studied the door. "He accused her of sabotaging the hotel."

"Good ole Stone," he said. "Never one to let facts or common sense get in his way."

"I need to figure out how to stop these disasters," I said.

"And you think you're going to find the answers here?" His gaze swung to me.

"I think you know the truth about Culver," I said. "I think you've known since Sam Perkins called you to the hotel eleven years ago."

Bragg hunched his shoulders and studied the rubber toes of his tennis shoes. "There've never been any problems at the hotel before," he said. "Red Maggie sightings, maybe. But no real mischief."

"I seemed to have triggered him."

He glanced at me. "Why you?"

I sighed. "It's a long story. Please don't make me tell it."

"You want to rummage around, spill my family secrets, but you won't do the same?"

"You're going to think I'm crazy."

"Listen, kitten," he said, "we're all half crazy." He stared at the door. "You think I don't know what people say about me?"

I set the box on the counter. "Show me the key that opens the door to the basement of the Fairly Grand and I'll tell you my story."

His gaze swung to the box. He stared at it for a long time. Then he reached for it and opened it. With a finger he pushed the keys around. "It's not here," he said.

I held out my fist and unfurled my fingers.

He peered at my palm. "That's it."

Tate banged through the door, carrying three sodas. "I had to go all the way to the drugstore," he said. There was a slick sheen of sweat across his forehead and the hair over his ears was darkened with it. "The hardware store was out."

"Oh yeah, I forgot," Bragg said. "Put 'em there."

Tate banged the cans onto the counter and said, "Don't you want one?"

"Maybe later." Bragg plucked the key from my palm.

"Later?" Tate huffed. "What's that?"

"The key to the storage room at the hotel," I said.

"Cat was about to tell me why she's responsible for the accidents at the hotel," Bragg said.

Tate glanced at me, but I moved away from him. "I didn't say I was responsible." I folded my arms and then unfolded them. I settled for rolling the fringe of my scarf between my fingers. "I said I may have triggered them."

"How?" Bragg folded his arms, the key clutched in his fist.

Tate leaned a hip against the glass counter, picked up a soft drink and fiddled with the pop top, making clicking noises without opening it.

"At the risk of boring you with my sad little dramas," I glared at Tate and he made a face and I turned away, "somehow, I've conjured a ghost." I bumped into the wall and rattled the set of beetle displays. Bragg frowned and I forced myself to stand still.

"Conjured a ghost?" he said. "Sounds ridiculous."

"Yep, I'm sure it does," I said. And then I told him the story of my first encounter with Culver, and then the next, and the next.

"Could've been a trick of the light," he said.

"I talked to him. He talks to me."

"Could be somebody messing with you."

"You think I want to believe this? I'm pretty full up with crazy already. I sure don't need more. And how would anybody else know his story?"

Bragg sighed and shook his head. "I've seen things I couldn't explain, too. Once on a dig in Argentina...never mind. So, he only appears at twilight?"

"Well, once past midnight."

Tate whipped around to stare at me.

I shrugged.

Bragg scratched behind his ear. "And something bad always happens? Like the golf cart accident?"

"The fire at the bicycle hut," Tate said. "The Civil War weapons in the furniture."

"The exploding wine," I said. I still couldn't talk about the ducklings.

"And then the pier collapsing," Bragg said.

"Each disaster worse than the one before," I said. "So, I thought if I didn't go back to the cemetery, the accidents would stop."

"But they didn't."

"He appeared at the hotel right before the wedding."

"You promised to help him," Bragg said.

"I don't have to see him to help him."

"Maybe he thought you were reneging."

A twinge of guilt pricked me. "I thought with the storage room being locked and nobody at the hotel having a key except Ed Winer, and that being the place Horace's ledger was originally found, maybe there'd be more evidence there. Where's Sam Perkins, anyway? Maybe he knows if there's more."

Bragg swiped his stubbled jaw. "He died in a car accident right after he showed me the book. Stone brought me his last effects, wallet, class ring. The key." The room fell silent except for the metallic clicking of the tab against the can in Tate's hand.

"Will you pull that thing already?" Bragg snapped. Tate dropped the can onto the counter.

"The Celebration of the Dead ceremony is a few weeks away," I said. "If Horace is trotted out like some hero with a statue and everything, and he truly did these awful things to Culver, I'm afraid of what might happen."

The room fell quiet. Then the wooden stool scraped the floor as Bragg got to his feet. "I guess it's time you kids found out just how much worse it could get."

CHAPTER 53

Tate and I arrived at the hotel to an empty lobby with only Benito milling behind the front desk.

"Where's your mom?" Tate said.

"Probably outside with the engineers. They arrived first thing this morning to check out the pier."

"They won't find anything."

"I hope not. I'd hate to think I really am crazy."

While Tate waited in the lobby, I ran to my room and emptied out my piggy bank of cash and stuffed it in my shorts' pockets. We were making progress and I wanted to entice Tate to keep it going. I exited the elevator and we slipped down the basement stairs. The key fit neatly into the lock, but it took some jiggling to get it to turn.

The door creaked open and we stood for a few seconds, blinking in the gloom. The room smelled of wet newspaper and mold. I fumbled along the wall for a light switch. Fluorescent light flickered overhead.

A bookshelf lined one wall. Cardboard boxes were stacked waist high and pushed to the center of the room. An office chair lay on its side with its black seat split and vomiting foam. I eased between the boxes. Grainy black and white photographs were propped against the opposite wall. I ran a finger along the top of one and wiped the dust on the seat of my denim shorts.

"How are we going to find anything in all this junk?" I said and jumped as a leggy brown spider skittered over the top of a box. "Is that a brown recluse?"

"We don't even know what 'it' is," Tate said. "Bragg said he thought there might be something more than Horace's ledger."

"Culver said Doctor Perkins kept meticulous records. If Sam Perkins never came back, there might still be something here."

Tate strolled to the stack of framed photographs, squatted, and thumbed through them. "Look at this." He pulled one from the stacks.

A handful of young men in 1940s uniforms crowded around a young woman on the beach in front of a thatched hut. Could the woman be Red Maggie?

Tate slid the picture into the stack and kept going. He flipped past girls on the beach in bathing costumes, girls in the lounge in long white gloves, men in top hats and tails in the ballroom. "What about this?" The last one appeared to be taken much earlier. It was faded and blurry, but clear enough to see men lying on pallets on the front lawn of the hotel, a few nurses in long skirts scattered among them. A soldier leaned on a pair of crutches off to the side.

"Closer, but it doesn't tell us anything," I said. "We already knew the hotel was used as a hospital. We need something specific about Culver or Horace."

"Well, that's all of them." He let the frames clatter together and stood and wiped his palms on the seat of his basketball shorts. We dug though boxes of mildewed invoices and receipts. We flipped through yellowed ledgers and old guest registrations.

I was hot and tired and dusty when I finally found a box of old ledgers and letters apparently rescued from the flood. The ledgers appeared to be notes the hotel manager made dating back to the opening of the hotel in 1832.

I found entries for every year from 1832 until June 1863. The next entry was dated January 1864, which left a half a year missing. Wasn't 1864 the summer Culver died? I pulled out a stack of letters wrapped in tattered, faded ribbon. They were also dated. And one year was missing, the same as the ledgers.

"What do you think?" I asked Tate. He fought a cobweb strung over a stack of old books.

"It's mighty suspicious," he said and flung the silky thread off his hand. It clung to his fingers. He struggled to peel it off with his free hand. It stuck. He finally swiped it on the back of his shorts with the rest of the dust. "Who else knows this junk is here?"

"Should I ask Mama?" I let a stack of yellowed letters fall into the box.

"She's got enough to worry about now," Tate said. "Most likely it's Uncle Bragg who has the answers."

"And yet, he won't challenge your Uncle Bedford," I said.

Tate shook his head and shrugged.

It took another hour of shuffling through boxes and digging through old newspapers and paperwork and photographs, crinkled and warped from the flooding, for me to finally find what I was searching for. Having tunneled our way through most of the boxes, I was stretching and rolling my head around my shoulders when I spied a small wooden box on the top shelf of the bookshelf and said, "What's that?"

Tate glanced from the cardboard box he was rummaging through. "What?"

"There." I pointed. The bookshelf was sturdy and I tested my weight on the lowest shelf before hauling myself to the next one.

"You're going to fall," Tate said behind me.

I found a toehold among the old books on the next shelf.

"Seriously," he said. I froze at the press of his palms on the seat of my shorts, fingertips brushing skin just below the frayed edges. My breath caught in my throat.

"Hurry up," he said. "I'm strong, but I can't hold you forever."

Sucking in my breath, I climbed the next shelf and his hands cupped the backs of my thighs, his thumbs dipping beneath the hem of my shorts. I tried to ignore the tingling as his breath tickled the backs of my legs. *Focus, Cat.* One more shelf and my fingertips touched the box. I sidestepped to get a better grip.

"Would you hurry?" He splayed his fingers wider across the backs of my thighs. "Grab it already."

I clutched the box to my chest. As I eased downward, my foot fumbled for a solid surface and missed. My knee banged the shelf and toppled books onto the floor.

"Oh, for crying out loud." Tate grabbed me around the waist, his palm sliding beneath my shirt, pressing against my ribs, and swung me off the shelf and to the ground. Stunned, I froze as he grabbed the box from me. He dropped to sit cross-legged on the dusty floor and opened it.

I lowered myself to a safe distance from him and counted one, counted two, steadying my breath, before I felt safe enough to peer inside. The missing ledger entries lay atop a few letters wrapped in faded red ribbon, and a few other items. I picked up a snippet of a newspaper article, yellowed and brittle, dated July 1863.

It reported that a sixteen-year-old woman was found floating face down in Mobile Bay. The article identified her as Lucille Ella Hazlet, daughter of Holcomb and Virginia Hazlet, from Jonesboro, Alabama.

It was unclear if Miss Hazlet was visiting friends in the area when she met her untimely demise. It was rumored she was searching for a young soldier she'd previously met, but it couldn't be confirmed. The cause of death was still under investigation. Mr. and Mrs. Hazlet were most sorrowful about the loss of their eldest daughter, Lucie.

Tate pulled out the ledger and flipped through it.

"Holy crappola," he said and I glanced from the scrap of newspaper. He stared at me in wonder. "There's an entry here. About Culver."

"You're lying."

He held the book for me to see. It took a few seconds for me to find the notation at the bottom of the page.

I have no choice but to come to the conclusion that my patient, Culver Washington, did not die of gunshot wounds as previously thought, but rather asphyxiation, as per the – the next part was smeared. And then – the skin beneath Culver's left eye had been split open since the last time I examined him. A smear of blood was found on the neatly folded blanket beneath his head. Based on the matching evidence, It is my conclusion that Culver was struck in the face, then suffocated with the blanket before it was returned neatly beneath his head. The only witness to the event was a patient, a colored man by the name of Roby, who suffered an eye injury and was temporarily blinded by the bandaging covering his head. During an interview with Mr. Roby, it was brought to our attention that he heard two men talking, or rather arguing. The patient, Culver Washington, whom he had come to know, and another man by the name of Horace, whom he did not know. Mr. Roby stated that after the man Horace left, Culver Washington spoke no other word. Hours later, he was discovered to be dead. I dare not put into writing where these conclusions lead me.

"Even the doctor won't say it," I said. "We need more proof. We can't stop the celebration on this little bit."

Tate frowned. "What are you talking about? We're not stopping the celebration. I'm not doing that to my family, to this community."

"What did you think was going to come of this?" I said. "What did you imagine would stop Culver? The fact that you and I know? We have to reveal Horace for the person he was."

Tate said, "This town wouldn't be here if it wasn't for Horace. My family's done a lot of good things. The library. Roads. The park on the bay. Harrie Ann's spent her entire life –"

"But your family's not being celebrated," I interrupted. "Horace is. It's wrong. He did horrible things."

"So, my family has to pay for his mistakes?"

"Of course not. Or they shouldn't. Why can't we celebrate the Hamilton legacy without honoring Horace?"

"Are you kidding? Are you completely immune to social media?"

"It hasn't exactly been my friend."

"They'll destroy us," he said. "Even a whiff of a racist comment and you're eviscerated. This? Framing an innocent black man for rape and then murdering him? You think there's been rioting in the past, you might as well run us out of town now. I don't care so much about myself. I'm not that tied to Fairly. But Harrie Ann is."

"I think you're tied a lot tighter than you think," I said. "Perhaps you care a whole lot more about your reputation than you're letting on."

"Who are you to judge?"

"I'm not judging. You accused me a few nights ago of being too concerned about what people thought of me. You're just as concerned for yourself. But, I've been through this already. There's not much left of my reputation. Not just in Shelby, but it's happening all over again here. My family was torn apart. I assure you, I know exactly what's at stake."

"So, your reputation's been a little tarnished. Got kicked out of some fancy private school most people couldn't afford. And you want the same thing to happen to me? Boohoo, feel sorry for yourself much?"

I scrambled to my feet. "You're a jerk," I said. He stood and towered over me. "You know nothing about me. Nothing but the lies your cousin and uncle have dredged up and spread. Here." I dug deep into the pocket of my shorts and pulled out a wad of bills, mostly tens and twenties. It looked like a lot of money. I rammed it into his perfectly chiseled abs.

He stared at my fist.

"Take it," I said. "It's the money I owe you."

"But we haven't finished."

"Deal's a deal. I don't have time to argue with you. It's obvious you don't want to be involved with this. And I don't have a choice. So, take your money and go."

"But I haven't earned it."

"You're not going to do what has to be done. I got it. Sorry I got you involved. Just go."

He refused to take the money. So I let it fall from my fingers and snatched the faded newspaper and ran out of the room and up the stairs. There was only one thing left to be done. And I'd do it alone.

CHAPTER 54

Bedford Hamilton's office building loomed tall and intimidating in its antique brick façade. One of the original buildings in Fairly, the town had grown from a few stores along Fairly Avenue to an orderly grid of antique stores and boutiques and restaurants under the Hamilton Building's watchful eye. It hovered over me, as dark and foreboding as Bedford Hamilton on the church steps.

With my back pressed to the brick wall, I surveyed the street. As usual, it was empty by 10:30 on a Sunday evening. I slipped inside the front door and eased it closed behind me. Moonlight revealed a wall of old-fashioned mailboxes labeled with numbers, not names.

Tate told me his uncle's office occupied half the second floor and his residence the other half. According to his secretary, he was in Mobile for the weekend at a conference on real estate law and wouldn't be returning until Monday afternoon. Still, the sooner I was in and out, the better I'd feel.

I tiptoed up the heavy wooden steps and winced at each creak beneath my Chuck Taylors. I stopped to listen for any sound of movement. The air was heavy, sweltering, and I dabbed at the sweat above my lip with the hem of my scarf.

It was a simple one, a smoky graduation from gray to black. I'm not even sure why I felt the need to wear one, except out of habit. Maybe it would help me blend into the shadows. I tucked the loose ends into my t-shirt, anyway, so they wouldn't get in the way.

Clicking on my flashlight, I found Room 204 and just for fun, tried the doorknob. It was locked. The stairs creaked below me. I killed the light, pressed myself against the wall, and held my breath.

Now was the time to bail. If I was caught, I could still pretend I was lost and looking for someone. But once inside, there'd be no explaining it.

Seconds ticked in the silence. Maybe it was my imagination, but I waited for a ridiculously long time before clicking on the light and training it on the keyhole.

I fumbled in my pocket for one of the bobby pins I'd brought along, straightened it, and inserted it into the lock. I fumbled for a release, a catch, something. The pin popped out and fell to the floor.

With a huff, I bent to retrieve it. As I straightened, a rough hand clamped against my mouth and jerked me backward. My cry was muffled and the flashlight clattered to the floor.

"Quiet," the voice hissed. I was ready to chomp on a finger when he said, "It's me."

I whirled around. "What're you doing here?"

"Keeping your butt safe."

"I don't need you."

Tate's whistle was low. "Breaking and entering? You've done that before?"

"Just go." I snatched the flashlight, off the floor and jammed the pin back into the hole.

"You'll never get it open that way."

"Go away."

"Stop being such a weenie."

"Weenie?"

"And keep your voice down."

"Why should I listen to you?" I hissed. "You're the jerk who made me cry."

"Awwwww," he laid a hand on my shoulder, "You cried? But that would require you to have a heart."

I shoved him hard and his shoulder rattled the glass.

"Easy, princess. You'll set off the alarm."

"What alarm?"

"The one I forget to tell you about."

"You," I sputtered, "you forgot to tell me about the alarm?"

"Yeah, goes straight to Uncle Stone's office."

"You set me up?"

"Don't be stupid. I'm here, aren't I?"

"I don't believe you, you jerk, you incompetent –"

"Easy, sunshine," he said, "you're testing my good nature."

"Good nature my –"

He bumped me out of the way and squatted to peer into the hole. He pulled a silver nail file from his pocket, inserted the point, and jiggled it. I huffed and shifted my weight. He jiggled some more.

"Oh, please." I rolled my eyes. "You have no idea what you're doing. What're you going to do when the alarm goes off?"

"Quiet."

With a huff, I folded my arms and leaned against the door as he continued to jiggle the file.

"Just admit you don't know what you're doing," I said. "You're going to get us caught." The door swung open and I stumbled into the room. A beeping sounded from inside.

"Sixty seconds," he said and crossed the room, banging his shin on wood. He cursed and whipped his phone out of his pocket and aimed the light low. He circled the massive desk in front of a wall of bookshelves. The beeping was insistent. A pinpoint of red light flashed at the windows, the door leading to the reception area, a framed medal on the wall, an oil painting of hunting dogs above the mantle.

Tate fumbled at the desk and cursed again. Hadn't it been sixty seconds already? I braced myself for an alarm, a siren, sheriff cars screeching to a halt outside the window, Sheriff Hamilton busting through the...and then the beeping stopped.

Tate leaned over the desk, propped on his outstretched arms, and swiped his mouth against the sleeve of his shirt. "A little closer than I wanted," he said.

"That's it?" I clutched my flashlight to my chest.

"We'll know in a few minutes. If Uncle Stone doesn't come busting through the door."

I glanced at the door, then hurried to close it.

"Until then," he said, "I suggest we get to work."

I joined him at the desk. "Where might it be?"

He surveyed the desk, the room, the bookshelf, the fireplace cut through the middle of it, the painting over it.

"Knowing Uncle Bedford," his gaze landed back on the desk, "his favorite saying is 'keep your friends close and your enemies closer.'" He jerked a drawer open. "I'll start here. You tackle the bookshelf."

I stood at the far left near the windows and stared at the shelves stuffed with rows of leather law books big enough to squash small woodland animals. Beneath the shelves of books was a row of paneled cabinets with scarred brass knobs. I knelt, jerked the first door open and swept the interior with my flashlight.

"Aaaaaah!" I cried and fell backward on my rear as a glowing white skull grinned back at me.

Tate peered into the hole. "Bragg," he said. "A gift, I suppose. Or a joke." He returned to rifle though the desk drawers.

With a hand calming my stuttering heart, I pilfered through the files beneath the skull, real estate deals and housing forms and copies of deeds and incredibly boring paperwork. I moved on to the next cabinet and the next.

As I crossed to the other side of the fireplace Tate said, "Bingo."

"What?" In my rush to see, I bumped into him and nearly knocked him off his feet.

"Hey," he dropped the book.

"Sorry," I reached out and grabbed him to keep from falling. My head banged his chin and rocked him backward.

"Dang, girl," he rubbed his jaw, "if you wanted me thataway, why didn't you say so?"

"Don't be an idiot," I hissed and put some distance between us. "We don't have time for this."

"Apparently." He bent to pluck the book from the floor and straightened. He cracked his neck to the left, then right, causing me to wince at the sound.

"What is it?" I said.

He slammed the book onto the desk and paused dramatically. "I found the ledger."

I trained my flashlight onto it a book the size of a legal pad bound in scuffed brown leather. Tate flipped it open. The first page read, *Life Record of Bedford Hamilton, 2000-2015.*

"This isn't Horace's ledger," I said. "It's your uncle's journal."

Tate flipped through the pages and stopped midway through the month of January 2008. He stabbed a finger at the page.

"So?" I said.

He snatched the flashlight and flashed it onto the entry. "This was the day Bragg told Bedford about the ledger, the meeting between Bragg and Dad."

"So?"

Skimming over the part about what a dumbass Bragg was, and how weak Stuart was, I read the words, *but redemption can be found at the foot of the cross.*

"What does that mean?" I glanced at Tate. His face had taken on an eerie glow above the circle of light. "I know your uncle goes to church, but he doesn't strike me as particularly religious."

"He's not. For him, church is business. Actually, to him,

everything's business."

"Then what's this?"

"A clue would be my guess."

I turned and slowly studied the room. "Is there a cross here somewhere?" I searched the bookshelves, the mantle, the walls, the windows. A car's headlights flashed bright and I ducked and peered over the windowsill. The car turned and disappeared down the street.

Tate slammed his way through drawers, cabinets.

"What about the reception area?" I said. "His residence?"

Tate propped his arms on the desk. "The reception area would be too public and his apartment too personal. He wouldn't want to see it every day."

"Well, there's only one cross I can think of anywhere around here," I said. "And it was in church. That day with Bobby."

Tate turned to stare at me.

"You know, the big one at the front of the sanctuary with Jesus hanging on it?"

"At First Baptist?"

"Yeah."

"Of course," he said and straightened from the desk. "So little Robbie could watch over it."

"Excuse me?"

"Uncle Robert. It's so like Bedford to put the burden on somebody else."

"I thought you said he'd keep it close."

Headlights flashed against the window and lit the room. They did not move on. Tate sidled over to the window and peered out. He swore.

"Uncle Bedford."

"What?"

"And I think he's seen us."

"He's supposed to be out of town," I said. "We've got to get out of here." I lunged toward the door.

Tate grabbed my arm. "Go to the church. The side door's never locked. There's wood paneling beneath the cross. Maybe there's a loose panel. Look for a crack or a seam."

"You have got to come with me."

"I've got to get this place back the way it was."

"You're going to get caught."

"It won't be as bad as getting caught with you. Now go." And he shoved me toward the door.

"I can't leave and let you take the blame."

"Go," he growled, "and maybe I won't have to. I'll be right behind you." The car lights shut off. Tate glanced out the window. "He's parked. Go. Now."

"Okay."

"Out the front," he hissed. "He's bound to come up the back."

I descended the stairs on tiptoe and was out the front door and running fast along Indigo Avenue without looking back.

The church was a straight shot, at the intersection of Indigo and Scarlet Lake Lane. I ran the entire four blocks to reach it. Plunging into the shadows, I found the side door off of a circular, covered driveway. It was locked. I groaned.

Skirting a low brick wall surrounding a playground with swings and a climbing fort, I found another door just past it and stumbled back as I tugged it open. Inside, darkness enveloped me. Having no idea where I was, I had to feel my way along a cold, concrete wall. I stopped and listened for sounds. Not a rustle of paper, nor a padding of feet, nor even a ticking clock disturbed the silence.

A click of my flashlight revealed an intersection of two hallways with doors running the length of them. The finger-painted artwork hanging outside each door indicated the children's Sunday school area. A bulletin board featured fluffy, cotton ball sheep and a paper shepherd leading with a popsicle stick staff.

Turning left, I passed double doors that appeared important and eased them open. It was a larger hallway, three times as wide as the one I was in. It led to an entryway with potted plants and groupings of chairs and the sound of gurgling water.

I followed the hall to the right until I came to another door and opened it. It was a narrow, single-file hallway. I followed it and it dumped me into the sanctuary, right behind the million-dollar organ.

The meager light of my flashlight bounced around the sanctuary as I circled the organ and climbed the marble steps. I stopped, eye level with Jesus' bare feet. Just as Tate said, the wall below the cross consisted of wood panels about three to four feet in size.

I knelt at the feet of Jesus and flashed the light over the panels. They looked perfectly identical. My fingers skipped along the creases, in and out of the grooves, tracing each one. I pressed and fumbled and thumped and tugged.

Sitting back on my heels, I realized this was crazy. There was no secret panel beneath Jesus' feet. I stood and flashed the light around the sanctuary again. This was definitely the only cross in the room. With my light, I illuminated the center aisle, up the steps, to my feet.

Was a cross patterned into the stones beneath me? I stepped

back. No, but it would've been if a stone hadn't been broken. It was a half cross and ended with the last stone intersecting the paneled wall.

Kneeling, I fingered the edges of the stone and it wobbled. My fingernail was too delicate to budge it. I huffed and glanced around. There had to be something to pry it up with. The pulpits were both bare. If I had a pen or a key or a...

Fishing inside my pockets, I found the bobby pin and slipped it inside the crack and tugged. The stone moved and I lifted it a little more. Then the bobby pin popped out and the stone slid back into place.

I swiped at the sweat above my lip with the back of my wrist. Tate should've joined me by now. Surely, he, of all people, could wriggle out of trouble with his uncle.

I slid the bobby pin back into the crack and with sterner concentration eased the stone until I could slip a finger against it and tilt it up, up, and out. My light flashed inside the hole. It was dark except for a glint of gold against the light. I eased my hand into it, praying there were no spiders or other creepy crawlies. Another inch downward and my fingers touched something. I found the edge of it and lifted carefully.

It hung on the small opening, but by twisting and turning it, I eased it out and laid it gently on the stone floor. Horace's ledger of accounts.

Where the leather was once black, mold and age grayed it in splotches. But the word *Accounts* was still stamped in gold on the front. Between the front cover and first page, a few faded ribbons were pressed flat. Strips of pink and green and blue. A crumble of what might've been a camellia or wild rose fluttered to the ground. The pages crackled, brittle and yellowed, as I flipped through it.

I stopped to skim over an accounting of the purchasing and selling of slaves. Ned Lacey was purchased in Atlanta for eight hundred dollars. Aurelia, a female child was thrown in for another hundred. Louie was traded to Murdoch Walker for fifteen acres along the western boundary. Tibbs, a twenty-year-old field hand was lost in a knife fight, incurring a loss of fifteen hundred dollars.

The last page was Horace's written confession in a feeble, scrawling script. I skimmed to the end of it:

I have done my best to right the wrong done to poor Culver Washington these sixty some years. If he'd had any kin, I would've made restitution with them. As it is, I can simply depend on the honorable character and good nature of my closest friend, Dr. Latimore Perkins, to set this matter aright. I would that another day durst expire with this great, evil guilt hanging over

*my name and the name of my family. I go to meet my Maker with a clear con-
science and sound mind.*

> *This is my last testament.*
> *Faithfully,*
> *Horace Tidewater Hamilton*

"This is it," I whispered. "It's real." I ran my fingers along the sprawling, fading words. And then light flooded the sanctuary.

I sat, shocked, as a voice thundered through the silence, "What in the good Lord's name are you doing?"

CHAPTER 55

Clutching the ledger, I stood as the last bit of nerve drained out my feet. Guilt gripped the back of my neck. The Reverend Robert Edward Lee Hamilton bounded down the middle aisle toward me, his penny loafers slapping the stone floor.

"What are you doing here, young lady, at this hour? What've you got there?" He glanced from the floor back to me, knowing exactly what I held.

"I'm sorry," I said. "But I need it. I'll return it as soon as –"

"Oh, no you don't." His double chin quivered. "I can't imagine what mischief you're up to, missy, but that's private property right there."

He stopped at the foot of the steps, a shorter, rounder, younger version of Bedford Hamilton. He pressed his thinning dark hair into his pink scalp with his palm. Apparently, Bobby got his looks from his mother. A simple gold band flashed on his dimpled hand.

"You see," I hesitated. How to explain it? "You see," I started again, "I know the story. The real story about Culver Washington."

Robert Hamilton paused with one foot on the bottom step. "You couldn't possibly."

"I do. And this book, Horace's ledger, proves it."

"I know all about you," he said. "Bobby's filled me in on your shenanigans." He clutched his hands over his quivering belly and twisted his ring.

"Apparently, Bobby's told everybody," I said, "but it's not true. It's a lie. I didn't do any of the things those people at school said I did."

"Look," Robert Hamilton climbed the stairs, "our family's been through too much tragedy already. We're barely recovering from the death of my daughter."

"I'm sorry for your loss."

"I don't want to talk about Emmeline. We've been through enough. Now we've got this ceremony bearing down on us and we will not allow our good name to be besmirched by some rabble-rouser." The ring circled and circled. "Lookie here, Cat. It is Cat, isn't it? Whatever's gone on in the past, this is a different place than Atlanta."

"I'm not from Atlanta, sir."

"We take the Lord seriously here. We take Christianity seriously. You can't come here and cause all kinds of ruckus."

"I'm not causing a ruckus, sir. Culver is. And what Horace did was wrong. It was murder."

"You got no proof."

"This book is proof." I tilted it toward him. "Horace's own confession."

"We can't even be sure he wrote it."

"Bragg said he did."

"Bragg." He snorted.

"Why are you so determined to conceal the truth?" I said. "Doesn't the Bible say 'the truth shall set you free?'"

"Don't you quote scripture to me, missy." He hovered over me.

"This," I raised the book, "is going to set Culver free. And freeing Culver will free the hotel and this town from more disasters."

"What on God's green earth are you talking about, setting Culver free? You're talking nonsense."

"He's bound to this earth," I said. "Horace bound him when he murdered him because he wouldn't take the blame for Lucie's rape."

"Girl," he peered into my face, "have you been drinking? Are you on drugs?"

I stomped my foot. "Of course not."

"I heard you've been hitting the drugstore awful hard."

I resisted rolling my eyes. "It's my mom," I said. "She has panic attacks. And Culver destroying the hotel is not helping."

"I heard you got kicked out of school for drawing nasty pictures."

"Like Emmie's pictures?"

"Don't you dare. She was a good Christian girl."

"Unlike me."

"Are you saying everybody's lying but you?"

"I don't believe Culver's lying," I said. "And Tate doesn't either."

"Bobby said you got that boy all tangled in knots. Turned him against his own family so he doesn't know if he's coming or going. Maybe you aren't a sure enough devil worshipper, but we've got a strong sense of family here. And my family's done more for this town than anybody ever thought of doing. Horace founded Fairly. There's a statue of him sculpted for the Celebration of the Dead ceremony. We cannot, on nothing more than the whim of some mixed-up teenager, destroy the fabric, the very foundation of this community."

A dribble of spit appeared on his lower lip. He licked it away.

"My family's important too," I said. "And Culver deserves his freedom and Horace wanted his story told." I tapped the book. "It says so. The very last page."

"You still can't prove Horace wrote it."

"Then why hide it?"

"And if he did, he most definitely was not of sound mind."

"He says he was. And Dr. Perkins agreed."

"Enough." He whipped a cell phone out of the pocket of his khakis. "This is a matter for Bedford."

"Living a lie doesn't sound very Christian to me," I said.

"Don't you preach to me." He punched in a series of numbers.

A door banged open and swayed the iron chandelier overhead. Sheriff Stonewall Hamilton strode toward us.

"Got a call from Bedford," he said and hitched up his khakis. "Appears we need to have ourselves a family pow wow."

The reverend stuffed his phone back in his pocket. "She's got the book."

"So, I see." The sheriff stopped beside his brother and held out his palm. "I believe I'll be taking that, Miss Turner."

I turned and stared at the face of Jesus. With his eyes closed and his face half turned, he appeared to want no part in the proceedings. And I wondered where my angels were when I needed them.

I turned back to the sheriff, who stood with one hand on his service revolver, his brows raised. "The ledger," he said.

And I laid it in his fleshy palm.

CHAPTER 56

I didn't feel so much like a criminal as I did an idiot riding in the back of Sheriff Hamilton's patrol car. Reverend Hamilton sat next to his brother in the front seat with a Plexiglas window between us. They were talking so low I couldn't understand much of what they said.

The back seat was an unyielding bench of plastic my sweaty legs kept sticking to. The ceiling was low, even for me, and I huddled there, panicking that there was no way to unlock the doors from inside.

We could've walked the four blocks. But perhaps the sheriff wanted me to experience how it felt to be treated like a criminal. And I guess I was.

Sheriff Hamilton led us up the stairs to Bedford's office with the reverend behind me cutting off any escape. As we reached the top of the stairs, the office door swung open and Bedford Hamilton hovered above us, as daunting as an avenging angel. He took the ledger the sheriff handed him and barked, "Get in," and slammed the door behind us, rattling the frosted glass.

Hamiltons crowded the room, lit with only Bedford's desk lamp and a floor lamp in the back corner. Bedford moved behind his desk, opened the top drawer, and shoved the book inside. He slammed it shut and stood protecting it, as tenacious as a pit bull.

The sheriff planted himself in front of the door. The reverend moved to stand beside Tate's parents, who Bedford apparently called. Belle Channing stood beside her husband, studying her long, scarlet nails.

Bragg stood in the back corner, away from the light, arms crossed, a shoulder leaning against the window frame. I was surprised to see him. Stuart Channing must have called him.

Tate stood near the window in front of his uncle, hands shoved in his pockets. And on the other side of the room, in a high-backed leather chair sat Bobby, an ankle resting on his thigh, clad in plaid Bermuda shorts and sockless deck shoes. Who called him?

"Looks like the gang's all here," I murmured and Bedford Hamilton narrowed his black eyes on me.

"Except your mother," he said. "Shall we call her, too?"

"She doesn't have anything to do with this," I said.

"Doesn't she? I thought she was the reason you broke into my office. Some convoluted idea that you might be able to help cover her incompetence at the hotel and save her job."

"She's not incompetent."

"Isn't that why you got Bragg involved? With some promise of her affection?" He snorted at the idea. "The hermit and the bumbling housekeeper."

"She's not bumbling," I said and flexed my fingers against sweaty palms.

"Is this why you brought us here?" Stuart Channing said. "To harass some poor kid about her mother?"

His wife stretched her fingers to study the tips of her nails.

"I brought you here to discuss Horace's ledger."

"You mean confession," Bragg said.

"I don't understand." Stuart glanced from Bragg to Bedford. "What's done is done. The girl knows. If she wants to go public, we can't keep her quiet."

"I can," Bedford leveled his gaze on me, "and I will."

"How're you planning to do that?" Bragg said. "Dispose of her?"

There was total silence in the room. The sheriff and Bedford exchanged glances. The sheriff's eyes narrowed.

"Of course not," Bedford said with a laugh. "That would be illegal."

"Not to mention immoral," Bragg said dryly.

Bedford glared at him. "That, too."

"So how do you propose to keep Miss Turner quiet?" Stuart folded his arms.

"Should I be here for this?" I said and sidled toward the door. "Wouldn't you rather discuss my imminent demise without my presence? Surprise me. I don't mind." I was a few feet from freedom.

Sheriff Hamilton's hand dropped to his revolver and I stopped moving. He cocked his head back toward the center of the room. With hunched shoulders, I edged away from the door.

"She has a right to speak out," Stuart said. "You can't muzzle her. Free speech, you know."

"I can damn well make it go badly for her mother if she does."

My stomach took a tumble and I swallowed hard.

"You can't threaten her," Stuart said. "She's a kid."

"She's a menace to this community!" Bedford shouted. "She's been nothing but trouble since she got here!"

There was a snort behind me and I turned. Bobby gloated over his steepled fingers.

"Well, she hasn't raped anybody," Stuart said. "And she hasn't murdered anybody, either."

"Oh, you've been waiting to throw Horace's sins at me since Bragg brought you the ledger," Bedford said. "Poor little Stuart, always feeling inferior to the big bad Hamiltons."

"I've never felt inferior to you," Stuart shot back. "You simply treat me as if I am."

"Can we get back on track?" Stone Hamilton said.

"If you'd taken care of her like I told you to," Bedford turned on his brother, "we wouldn't be in this mess."

"I am not breaking the law," Sheriff Hamilton said, "even for you."

"You didn't have to break any laws if you'd done what I told you. I'm a lawyer, for crying out loud. Nobody knows the law better than me."

"A lawyer who thinks he's God," Stuart said.

The door slammed open and knocked the sheriff out of his stance. He stumbled toward me. I scooted out of his way and bumped into Belle Channing. She frowned and insinuated herself between her husband and son.

The overhead light flicked on and we flinched and blinked at the brightness. It set the antique ceiling fan rotating in lazy circles overhead.

"What in tarnation is going on here?" Harrie Ann appeared behind the bulk of her son. "I heard shouting all the way to the street." She shut the door behind her as her gaze swept the room. "A family meeting without me?" She stared at her eldest son. "Bedford, what's this about?"

"Mama," he said, "it's nothing for you to worry about. It's been taken care of. Now run along home. Stone, drive her home."

"Don't you patronize me, son." Her eyes flashed. "I'm not one of your doddering old clients you're used to bamboozling."

Bedford drew to his full height. "I beg your pardon."

"Don't," she waved away his indignation, "begging doesn't become you. Now will somebody please tell me what in the Sam Hill is going on? You," her gaze landed on me, "what are you doing here?"

I glanced at Tate. He turned to stare out the window.

When there was no explanation forthcoming, Bedford stepped in. "Apparently, she broke into my office."

"And dragged poor Tate in here with her," Belle Channing chimed in.

I gave Tate a look, begging him to speak, but he shoved his fists further into his pockets and stared out the window.

"You have evidence?" Harrie Ann asked Bedford.

He nodded.

"Well, what'd she take?"

"Nothing, apparently." He tapped a finger lightly on his desk.

She turned to me. "This is very serious business, young lady. Why did you break into this office?"

"I was looking for something." Bedford's tapping grew louder. I glanced at Bragg. He turned to stare out the window with Tate.

"Bragg's involved too?" Harrie Ann said. She studied her youngest son's profile for a few seconds before focusing on me. "What were you looking for?" The tapping became a pounding in my head.

"A ledger," I said. "Horace's ledger."

"Horace Hamilton?"

"Okay, that's enough." Bedford thumped the desk with his knuckles. "We're going to forget this whole nasty business. She didn't take anything. I won't press charges. All said and done, there's been no real harm. Stone, take Mama home. She's bound to be dead on her feet."

I glanced from Bedford to Stone to Stuart to Bragg and then back to Harrie Ann, who waited expectantly. And it dawned on me. Harrie Ann didn't know about Horace's ledger, which meant she didn't know about his confession, or his sins. Tate's look of confusion confirmed it. He stared at his uncle behind the desk.

Whatever evil plan Bedford Hamilton had for Mama and me after this meeting, my only hope was to appeal to Harrie Ann's mercy and sense of justice. I had absolutely nothing to lose. Or so I thought.

"Mayor," I said, "I need Horace Hamilton's ledger and his confession –"

"Cat, don't," Tate said.

I turned to him. "I don't have any choice. You know why I

have to do this."

"You have no idea what you're doing."

"That's right," Bedford chimed in. "You're confused. Tired. We all are. It's been a long night." He glanced at his watch. "It's nearly midnight. I'll give Miss Turner a ride to the hotel. Stone can take Mama home. We'll all get a good night's sleep –"

"Stop." Harrie Ann's voice was deadly quiet. She turned to me. "Miss Turner seems to have something she wants to tell me. Something the rest of you appear desperate to keep from me. And quite frankly, I'd appreciate knowing what it is. Miss Turner?"

Bragg swiped his brow and refused to meet my gaze. Tate shook his head. Stuart clenched his fists as his wife clung to his arm. Bobby smirked from his chair. The reverend frowned and twisted his ring.

Sheriff Hamilton moved to stand behind his brother, his back against the bookshelves, arms folded, expression blank. Bedford leaned forward and pressed his knuckles into the desk as if he could keep the book safe and my mouth shut by sheer force of will.

"Cat," Harrie Ann said, "what in blue blazes is going on here?"

I told her everything. About Culver, his murder, the accidents at the hotel, my possible complicity and Horace's confession. All of it.

"You're flat out crazy," Bedford said into the silence after I finished. "Bobby's right. You belong in the loony bin. Ghosts and cemeteries and headless ducks and late-night confessions. You're nothing but a silly girl whose imagination has run amok. I've been patient and I've been kind and now you need to leave. Somebody take her home. I don't have the stomach for it, after all." He half turned and sucked in a deep breath.

"Where's the ledger?" Harrie Ann said.

"Are you serious?" Bedford said to her. "You believe this cockamamie story?"

"Where's the book, son?" She frowned and tilted her head toward her right shoulder to stretch her neck. She massaged her left shoulder.

"Mom," Stuart said, pulling away from his wife, "are you okay?"

"Give me the ledger," she said to Bedford through clenched teeth. Her hand dropped from her shoulder to her chest, which she pressed with the heel of her hand.

All eyes swung to him. "I'll show it to you later," he said, "but you're looking pale. Sit down. Robert, get her some water." The minister, wide-eyed, didn't move.

"Nathan Bedford Forrest," his mother said, "give me that book right now or so help me God, I'll have you investigated by the Alabama Bar Association."

"Mother!" Belle Channing gasped.

"Keep quiet, missy." Harrie Ann barely glanced in her daughter's direction. She held out her palm.

With a heavy sigh, Bedford opened the top drawer of his desk, pulled out the ledger and handed it to her.

She took a few seconds to run fingertips over the faded cover before flipping through the crackling pages. She turned to the last page and read silently, her lips moving with the words. She lingered for a few seconds, staring at the page. She pressed the back of her hand to her cheek. A sheen of sweat glistened her upper lip.

"I'm sorry," I said.

"You sure as hell are," Bobby said.

Harrie Ann gasped and stared at a spot on the wall behind Bedford's head, her left hand fisting and unfisting.

"Mom?" Stuart said.

She pressed the fist into her heart as the book tumbled from her fingers. She swayed on her feet.

"Mother!" Belle cried.

Stuart caught the mayor before she fell and lowered her gently to the rug.

"Call 911," Bedford ordered Stone as he skirted his desk.

My horrified look found Tate.

The disgust on his face said, *I told you so.*

The room quickly spun into motion as someone found a pillow and someone loosened the mayor's belt and someone talked hurriedly into their cell phone and someone began to cry and a siren wailed in the distance.

I slipped from the room, unnoticed. And as usual, unwanted.

CHAPTER 57

"You want to leave?" Mama said. "We'll leave. Ed Winer's fired me, so there's no reason to stay."

We sat in the hotel bar, eating burgers and chips. The room was empty at three o'clock in the afternoon, except for Wet Willie. He stood hunched over the counter reading the newspaper in between flooding me with Shirley Temples on the house.

Mama sipped a glass of wine. There were dark circles under her eyes and the skin was puffy as if she'd been crying. But she dug into her burger with a gusto I hadn't seen since my choking accident.

"Did he even give you a reason?"

She tilted her head at me with half the burger left in her hands. She dabbed at a bit of ketchup with her thumb and wiped it on her napkin. "Besides the fact that the bicycle hut went up in flames, supernatural forces dispatched weaponry into the lobby, the dock collapsed during the most prestigious wedding of the season, and the Fischers skipped out on thousands of dollars' worth of bills? No, he really didn't." She bit into the burger.

"You could probably keep your job," I said, "if you revealed what happened with Rosalie."

She chewed and chewed and swallowed. "It wouldn't be worth it in the long run. And I wouldn't do that to Rosalie. It's her secret to tell."

I mulled over my own depressing experience with exposing

the truth. "Where will we go?" I pushed my plate away. She plucked a chip off of it and studied it.

"No idea, kiddo. Maybe hang out with Nana and Ruby for awhile until I find another job." She popped the chip in her mouth and crunched.

"Can you get another job after this disaster?" I glanced around the bar and out into the lobby, where Gloria and Benito stood whispering and staring at us.

Ed Winer appeared beside them, waving his arms like a maniac. Benito scurried back to the front desk and Gloria sank into her chair and picked up the phone and pretended to make a call. Ed Winer stomped back to his office and Gloria replaced the receiver and stared at me. I turned away.

"I'll have to," Mama said and sipped her wine. She covered a tiny hiccup with her hand and set her glass on the table.

"Maybe I could get a job, too, to help out."

"Sure." She smiled. "But schoolwork comes first."

School. The thought of it made me want to toss up what little burger I'd eaten. I thought I'd be going to school with Tate in the fall. Tate, my new friend, my only friend in the past year. Tate, who could no longer stand the sight of me. Tate, whose grandmother I nearly killed. I frowned as Mama finished her burger.

"Yeah, we should go," I said. "There's probably nothing for us here."

"Yeah," she agreed. "It's a shame. "I truly thought we'd like it here. A new beginning." She pointed to my burger, "You gonna eat that?" I shook my head and slid the plate closer to her. She picked it up, bit into it, and chewed thoughtfully. "We started over once," she said. "We can do it again. So, where do you want to go?"

"Someplace far from here." I stared out the window toward the bay. "With beaches and a place for Ruby to roam."

"Catalina?" Mama said.

"What?" My gaze swung back to her and I pointed to the left corner of her mouth. "You've got more ketchup." She swiped at it with her napkin.

"No," she said, "I mean, Catalina."

I shook my head.

"California. It's an island. With beaches. And hotels, right? Your father and I wanted to go there on our honeymoon, but we only got as far as Gulf Shores. But we always loved the name."

"So, I'd be Catalina from Catalina?"

"It could be worse."

"No disrespect, but after nearly destroying a hotel and a town and the most prominent family in it," I said, "I'm not sure how it could get worse."

"It wasn't your fault, Cat. None of it."

"Well, some of it was." I stirred the melting ice in my glass with the straw.

"I should've paid more attention," she said. "I should've been there for you. I keep failing you, don't I?"

"No." I flicked the straw away. "Your hands were full. You asked me to lay low and I didn't. I thought I had this grand, noble thing I had to do. And it ended in a big mess."

"What could you have done differently?"

"I could've not given the mayor a heart attack."

"Honey," she laid a hand on mine, "her family kept the secret from her all those years. It's not your fault. And Culver appearing? There's nothing you could've done to stop that, either."

I flopped back in my seat. "Why me?" I said. "Why did I have to be the one to see him? Why couldn't somebody else save him?"

She leaned back and wiped her palms on her napkin. "Who knows," she said, "but that you were created for a time such as this."

"You're saying this was predestined?"

She shrugged. "I have no idea. I just don't believe there are that many true coincidences anymore."

"Then God must have an amazingly wicked sense of humor."

We sat silently for a bit with no sounds but the clinking of her glass and the crunching of chips. I watched her finish my burger.

"Do you ever wonder if I hadn't been such a brat, so determined to eat popcorn that night," I fingered the soft chiffon of the scarf she'd given me for my birthday, a light, airy robin's egg blue, "how different our lives would've been?"

"No." Her glass banged the table causing Willie to glance up from his newspaper. "I never do. I can't afford to, and neither can you."

"But Daddy would still be with us, and you'd still be working in Atlanta, and I'd still have friends –"

"Stop it," she said. "Right now. I won't live with 'what ifs'. This is where we are now. We can't go back. We can't redo. We simply keep moving on. One step at a time. Here," she pushed my plate toward me. "Finish your chips."

I shook my head at the forlorn plate with its sad, wilted lettuce and mush of tomato pushed to one side. I plucked a chip and tapped it against the edge. They were homemade. I sighed and popped it in my mouth and crunched as I gazed out at the croquet lawn.

"Who's that?" Mama said, staring over my shoulder. I turned to find a bald young man in a dark suit bent over Gloria's desk. After a few seconds of conversation, she peered around him and pointed at me. He turned and as his eye caught mine, I hunkered in my seat.

"Who is it?" Mama said, as I peeked over my shoulder.

I gripped the edge of the table as the man strolled toward the bar. There was no time to run. No time to hide. He opened the door and Willie straightened from his paper.

"Cat?" the man said, his gaze direct and forbidding. "Cat Turner? Can you please come with me?"

CHAPTER 58

"Come on in here, little lady," Mayor Hamilton called from her hospital bed. "I won't bite. Barely got any strength left, anyway."

She sat propped against a mound of pillows, hair fluffed, red lipstick on, reading glasses perched on the tip of her nose. A stack of papers lay in her lap. A disconnected IV pole and pump was pushed to the wall behind her. A bandage covered the back of her hand.

Roses lined the windowsill, the bedside table, even a small chest in the corner. Red roses, pink roses, yellow roses, and even a dozen dyed blue. Vases of carnations, tulips, lilies, and daisies were scattered around the room. Ruffle-headed hydrangeas in pink and blue, as well as waxy peace plants lined the floor. It appeared as if the florist had relocated to Room 312.

My escort moved to the corner of the room near the window and propped a shiny black wingtip on the seat of a slick green chair. Balancing his laptop on his knee, he typed into it.

"You know," the mayor said, "I don't even care for roses. Give me a good pot of English ivy and I'll have the thing climbing the wall in no time." She peered at me over her glasses, then took them off and folded them on top of the papers. "Thank you for coming to see me, Cat," she said. "I hope it didn't feel like you were being summoned to the principal's office."

"No, ma'am," I lied.

"Good, good. We've had a bit of a rough patch, haven't we,

Cat Turner?"

"Yes, ma'am," I said. "I'm sorry about giving you a heart attack."

"Oh, pshhhh." She waved the idea away. "Doc says it's all the fried catfish and cherry cheesecake I've been eating. Didn't have anything to do with you at all."

"I'm glad to hear it. I mean I'm glad it's not my fault. I mean, I'm glad you're okay."

She chuckled. "I must say you've kept this summer pretty lively for Fairly."

"Mama and I've been talking about moving away before school starts."

She pursed her lips. "Well, you got to do what you got to do." She studied the ceiling for a few seconds before dropping her gaze back to me. "I'm not sure one measly summer is enough time for Fairly to put her best foot forward, though. You haven't even seen the art festival in May. It's something I'm mighty proud of."

"Yes, ma'am."

"And I sure do hate for Tate to lose a good friend."

"Well, ma'am," I picked at my thumb, "I'm not sure Tate and I are exactly friends. He isn't even speaking to me now."

Harrie Ann continued as if I hadn't interrupted her. "You know," she said, "I didn't grow up in Fairly."

"No?"

"I'm from up north. Minnesota. Small town. My parents owned a fishing camp on Lake Wedowegee. Soon as I was big enough to carry a stack of towels, I assisted the guests who'd come and stay with us. Sort of like your mama. It was a tough job, trying to make all those people happy."

"Yes, ma'am."

"It was hard, but good training for being a mayor. Helped me develop and hone my problem-solving skills."

"Yes, ma'am."

"One thing I learned, and it's terribly cliché, but you simply can't make everybody happy all the time." She picked up her glasses and cleaned them on the edge of the thin blanket covering her knees. "And some people you can't make happy no matter what you do. Know what I mean?" She peered at me.

"I guess so." Bobby and his relentless persecution came to mind.

"My late husband, God rest his soul, was one of the guests at our fishing camp one summer. We took a shine to each other and after a brief courtship, we married, and moved back here. His mother, Maylene Hamilton, hounded me relentlessly. She considered me something of a carpetbagger's daughter. I talked too uppity. Too much and too loud. I never could figure out which fork to use. I never learned my place. Silly stuff, really, but it hurt, nonetheless."

"Yes, ma'am," I said. "Did she ever come around? To accept you, I mean?"

"Yes, she did," Harrie Ann said. "About a month before she died at the ripe old age of ninety-two."

"That's a long time to try to make somebody happy," I said.

"Yes." She rubbed her brow. "Yes, it is."

"Mayor?" The man glanced from his computer. "You okay?"

She waved away his concern. "Just a little tired."

"I should go," I said, "and let you rest."

She raised a hand to stop me. "What I'm trying to say, Cat, is this community is family. And what families do is accept and love each other, despite our flaws, heinous though they may be sometimes. Horace did horrible, despicable things. There's no sugar coating or whitewashing it. But then, he did some good things, too. And he repented and wanted to make things right in the end. People can do and say what they want. Can't nobody stop them. But I can't help but let God be the judge."

"Yes, ma'am."

"It takes a lot of courage to tell the truth, Cat, especially such an unpopular one. I don't mind telling you, I'm a little nervous about this celebration bearing down on us. I'm going to be delivering a vastly different speech than the one I planned. Culver Washington's story has to be told, whether it saves us or not."

"I'm sorry it's going to be so hard on your family, Mayor. I wish I'd never gotten involved."

"Well, I'm not sure you had much choice in the matter. And I guess what I'm struggling to say is, I admire your courage and tenacity. You've got some grit, girl."

She stabbed her glasses at me. "And I'd be proud to serve as your mayor if you and your mama change your mind and decide to stay." She sighed and stared out the window. Then turned back to me. "I don't want to keep you." She slipped her glasses back on. "It's a beautiful summer day and I'm sure you have better things to do than hang around some old fogey in the hospital."

"Yes, ma'am," I said. "I mean no, ma'am."

She chuckled and studied the sheet of paper in her lap. "Go on, Cat Turner. Go see what kind of trouble you can rustle up."

CHAPTER 59

In the glow of the dying sun, the cemetery seemed more magical than I'd known it all summer. The breeze teased the bearded moss. The scent of the last bit of magnolia floated in the air. The trees blurred into the shadows of another world, somewhere between here and there.

In the twinkling twilight, the summer seemed a dream. Was it real? Any of it? It was easy to imagine, on a night like this, it was all in my head. The memories floating, drifting through time to a place I couldn't follow.

And then Culver appeared. And he seemed to be the most real thing I knew.

"They're going to tell your story," I said. "The truth."

"They are?"

"Well, the mayor is. Harrie Ann. Horace's great-great-grand-daughter-in-law."

"Do you think it'll work," he said, "after all this time?"

"I hope so."

"How long will it take, do you reckon? For me to fade from this place?"

I shrugged. "Possibly in a blink of an eye. Or it may be a gradual thing."

"Or it might not happen at all." He scratched his elbow. "Do you reckon anybody's gonna care if I'm gone?"

"Does it matter as long as you're free?"

"Would it matter to you," he said, "if you left the earth and no one cared?"

"I suppose so." I turned from the sadness worn into his face. "If it makes any difference, I care."

"But Horace's family, the Hamiltons," he said, "do they reckon I'm just an evil haunt to be gotten rid of?"

"No one thinks you're evil," I said. "You were murdered, for heaven's sake. But it's going to be hard on them. They're the ones left to take responsibility. And it'll be harder on some than others."

"What do you think's gonna happen to me?"

"What'd you mean?"

"Where will I end up, do you think?"

"In heaven? Don't you think?"

"I'm a little scared. I wasn't scared when that bullet tore through my side. And I wasn't scared when Horace pressed the blanket to my face. But I've been here so long..."

I stepped to him and placed a hand on his forearm. His skin was rough beneath my fingertips and the hairs prickling his arm were more substantial, more real than the last time I touched him. But barely for a second, and then it shimmered away.

"Do you believe we get what we deserve?" he said. "I mean, after our death?"

"Lord, I hope not." I studied the angels surrounding Elijah Pickens' grave. "I hope we get a lot better than we deserve."

And then softly, a strain of music drifted toward us, Mozart maybe, or Strauss, a violin, or a cello, from the direction of the country club. Perhaps it was a party, or a dance.

"I never got to dance," Culver said, "not with a girl. You reckon there'll be dancing in heaven?"

"I can't imagine why not."

He gazed in the direction of the country club.

Time ticked on and I wasn't sure how much time we had left together. It could be any minute. It could be forever.

I cleared my throat and said, "I danced a little." I scuffed the toe of my Converse in the dirt. "Mama signed me up for this cotillion thing. We learned to waltz and foxtrot and everything. Which was crazy, because who's ever going to waltz anymore, right? It's all dabbing and nae naeing these days."

"The waltz," he said, "my favorite."

"I'm not sure if I can remember." I shrugged. "But we could give it a whirl."

I held out a hand and he hesitated before taking it. It was

smoother than I expected, his fingers, long and strong. With his palm barely a wisp of a touch at my waist, we moved haltingly, awkwardly, in time to the music. As we let the music flow through us, we became more confident.

I closed my eyes as the breeze lifted a curl from my cheek and I breathed in the last bit of magnolia. I smiled at Culver and moved in time with his lithe body. We twirled slowly among the tombstones without knowing someone watched from behind the pines.

Tate stood with a palm pressed to ruffled wood, as Culver and I moved with the music, swirling and twirling, a faint smile on my lips, appearing to embrace nothing more than a soft, southern breeze.

CHAPTER 60

I had no idea if I'd ever see Culver again. I suspected not, since I'd visited the cemetery three twilights in a row with the excuse of sketching something besides angels. Maybe the tilt of tombstones, or the grandfather oak, or maybe even little white plastic Easter bunnies. Culver never appeared, even though the celebration was a few days away. So maybe Mayor Hamilton's word was enough.

I avoided town. I heard from Martina the street vendors were setting up throughout the week to sell incense, decorated crosses, skull masks, and folk-art skeletons. The bakery was busy making marigold-shaped cookies, candied pumpkins, and sugar skulls.

Musicians and street performers fine-tuned their acts and jockeyed for the most high-traffic locations. Air-filled bouncy things were already blocking off major streets.

The florist ordered orange and yellow marigolds by the case, flor de meurto, flower of the dead. Several arrangements were designed for the hotel to join in the celebration. Rosalie said marigolds were used to attract the souls of the dead. Which led me to worry. If we'd barely gotten rid of one ghost, did we truly want to attract more?

Private altars were built and tissue paper flowers strung from store awnings. Cardboard skeletons hung from shop windows. The more prominent cemetery at the edge of town was cleaned and awaited the decoration of the townspeople after they paraded in colorful costumes from the library along Fairly Avenue to the gravesite.

Harrie Ann's speech would kick off the parade. It was rumored Horace Hamilton's statue was already privately unveiled and placed in an unobtrusive spot in the cemetery to watch over the Hamilton family plot.

At twilight, a more solemn candlelight procession would end once again at the decorated gravesites and prayers would be offered, led by the honorable Reverend Robert E. Lee Hamilton.

I must admit, I felt a little out of the loop, but kept busy at the hotel until our departure. It was our last day and I was in my room, finishing packing. I folded my blue jean shorts into my suitcase as Mama burst through the door, her cheeks pink, eyes bright. "You are not going to believe this," she said, "come quickly."

"What? I'm packing my stuff." Which was sort of a lie because I'd never truly unpacked it.

"Drop it." She made a flurried motion with her hand. "You've got to see this."

"What?" I whined. But she disappeared.

By the time I hit the bottom of the lobby stairs, Sheriff Hamilton stood beside a deputy with Ed Winer gesturing wildly at him. Irene Fischer handed the sheriff a flutter of papers and Mr. Fischer stood to the side, picking his teeth with a blue plastic cocktail sword.

Mama stood slightly apart, hugging her elbows, glancing among the three parties. I passed Benito and Giselle, with their mouths dropped open, and a few guests who turned to stare.

"This is outrageous," Ed Winer blustered. "It's a scam. No one's kicking me out of my own hotel."

"It's not your hotel any longer," Mrs. Fischer said. "Nor the Algenons." She tapped a long, tapered fingernail against the papers in Sheriff Hamilton's grip. "The Fairly Grand has been purchased by I to I Enterprises. It's clear from this document here."

Sheriff Hamilton scanned the page, then the next, then the next. He glanced up.

"Looks official to me," he said to his friend. "Sorry, Ed. Apparently the Fischers are the new owners. Sure you don't want to discuss this in your office?" He nodded to a couple who passed him with a curious stare.

"No, I do not," Ed Winer said. "There's got to be something you can do. They skipped out on thousands of dollars' worth of bills. Arrest them."

"Ed, they own the hotel," Sheriff Hamilton said. "They don't have to pay any debt. It's theirs."

"I'm going to sue," Ed said. "That's what I'm going to do. Sue your butts from here to kingdom come. And you," he stabbed a finger at Mama, "this is your doing. Your threatening and blackmailing me into hiring you. If I hadn't already fired you, I'd fire you again."

Mama stepped forward, her chin raised a notch. "It was actually Rosalie," she said. "You might want to take it up with her. Perhaps she'll be glad to tell her story after all. The community, and even the sheriff, might be interested in hearing what she has to say."

"What's she talking about, Ed?" the sheriff said.

"What? Nothing. Never mind. But I'm going to talk to my lawyers. You can count on it."

"You do that." Irene Fischer fluttered her ringed fingers at him. "File your little lawsuit or run along like a good boy. But I'd be careful about complaining to the Algenons. They've been alerted to your behavior and might not be so inclined to keep you on as manager of their other properties. I'd tread lightly there."

She stalked forward until they were nearly nose to nose. "Until then, please vacate the premises. It's my hotel now, and Eva Turner is my new general manager, if she'll have the position. And you, Ed Winer," she poked his chest with a sharp talon, "are officially fired."

Mama and I exchanged shocked expressions as Ed Winer stormed off. I sidled next to the new owner of the Fairly Grand.

"Mrs. Fischer," I said, "do you have any idea about owning a hotel?"

"Catalina, darling," she smiled at me, "like everything else, I make it up as I go."

CHAPTER 61

The valet on duty came to get me. It was Saturday and I was in the bar, helping Willie fold napkins for the dinner crowd. Someone was waiting for me outside, the valet said. I glanced at Willie. He shrugged and folded the linen in half, then quarters.

"Go on, then," he said.

I stepped outside to the valet parking to find Tate Channing leaning against his new relic of a Mustang convertible. Dark as dull spinach, it appeared to have barely survived the Vietnam War.

"What do you want?" I said.

"Thought you might want a ride to the celebration."

"And you couldn't bother to come inside and get me?"

"I could if this was a date, which it most definitely is not."

"And why would I go anywhere with you?"

"Because I didn't dump you when you attempted to take my family down."

"Actually, you kind of did."

He flashed a palm to stop me. "We can discuss it on the way. Just get in. We're going to be late."

I shouldn't go. He'd been a jerk. And totally unreliable. And a bit of a baby. "If I go, I should definitely tell Mama."

"We'll call her on the way," he said. "Now get in. I don't want to miss Hurricane Harrie's spin on this one."

"You sure this isn't a date?"

"Don't be stupid. You're practically a baby."

"I'm fifteen. And if I'm such a baby, why do you insist on hanging out with me?"

He cocked his head, an arm propped on the dented door. "I enjoy babysitting. Now get in or get left behind." He opened the door, slid behind the wheel and rumbled the engine to life.

I hesitated for one long, drawn-out second, mustering as much self-control as I possessed. And then I blew out my breath, thought *what the heck*, and climbed in. The front seat was an old-fashioned bench seat of cream leather. The only thing separating me from Tate Hot Shot Channing was a dozen stalks of ruffled orange marigolds.

"Are those for Emmie?"

"And Culver," he said. "I thought you might want to honor him, too."

I glanced over my shoulder for the seatbelt. Nada.

Tate grinned. "Sometimes you gotta give death a chance."

The car coughed and wheezed and sputtered as we rumbled out of the parking lot and I grabbed the windowsill as we veered toward town. As we increased speed, the wind pushed my hair off my face and fluttered the ends of my scarf behind me.

"This was the best my money could buy?"

I tugged at my scarf. I'd dug the one Mary Grace had given me out of the bottom of my suitcase. The turquoise leopard print. It was a new day. Time to move on. It was just a scarf, after all. Nothing special. But once again, I'd tied it too tight and it was stifling.

"The money you left on the ground," he shot me a glance before focusing on the road, "wasn't even a drop in the bucket. But it needed to go to some good use. Heck, I might as well have helped you for free."

I fiddled with the fluttering scarf, working to loosen it. "You should've helped me for free."

"Help you destroy my family?"

I glanced at him. He stared at the ribbon of road before us. We passed his church on the left.

"If I could've done it any other way, I would've," I said. "You know that."

He gazed toward the bay, his hair ruffled by the breeze, and I tilted my head back and let the end of summer wash over me. School would be starting in two weeks. My freshman year at Fairly High. Tate would be a junior, there. Bobby would not. He'd enrolled in the Christian academy across the bay so he could work on his modeling career.

I closed my eyes against the breeze and tugged at the scarf.

Why was it so dang suffocating? Me and my stupid vanity. I'd have to completely untie it.

I opened my eyes and worked on undoing the loose knot at my neck. As we passed Mel's Quick Stop, a squirrel darted onto the road and Tate swerved to miss it. My finger jerked the scarf loose. And I was free.

Before I could stop it, the wind caught the silk and hurled it behind me. I whirled in my seat as it fluttered to the ground and rested in the middle of the road. My hand flew to my neck with the horror of being exposed in broad daylight. With wonder boy Tate Channing.

He slowed the car and glanced backward. "Do we need to go back and get it?"

"Yes," I said, "please."

We pulled onto the side of the road and turned in time to see a truck pull out of Mel's and flatten the scarf with its muddy tires. I stared at my newfound courage as it lay splattered in the middle of the road.

A Pontiac Firebird roared over it, then a black F150 pickup. Tate struggled not to laugh, but finally gave in. His laugh was deep, and rumbly, sending a chill to the base of my skull.

I thought back to the beginning of summer, getting run over by a souped-up golf cart, meeting my first ghost, and everything that'd happened since.

And I couldn't help but laugh with him.

Tate grinned at me and it hit me just how much like the bay his eyes truly were.

"You still want it?" he said.

I gave the muddied, tattered silk one last glance. "Maybe not," I said and settled into my seat. He gunned the car back onto the road in a roar of burned rubber.

As we hurtled toward town, I turned my face to the heavens in time to catch a flash of silver wings in the sunlight.

A huge shout of gratitude goes to my amazing readers for their invaluable insights, Millie Thomas Gardner, Dr. Bonner Engelhardt, Melissa Gambill, and Kaylen Hamilton. Also, no words can truly convey my appreciation for my brilliant editor, Teresa Kennedy, and book designer Andrew Earley.

I also owe a bottomless debt of gratitude to Boo Cole Archer, the official giver of wings. And to the most patient human being on the planet, Tucker Mattox, I am eternally grateful and forever yours. You always give me a reason to believe. And last, but by no means, least, a heartfelt thank you goes to the two most awesome kiddos a mother ever had the privilege to raise – the incredibly encouraging Ty Mattox, and the fearlessly creative Carly Mattox. I can't help but say, "Told you."